THE BOOK OF FIRES

THE BOOK OF FIRES

Paul Doherty

CRÈME de la CRIME

This first world edition published 2014
in Great Britain and in the USA by
Crème de la Crime, an imprint of
SEVERN HOUSE PUBLISHERS LTD of
19 Cedar Road, Sutton, Surrey, England, SM2 5DA.
Trade paperback edition first published 2015 in Great
Britain and the USA by SEVERN HOUSE PUBLISHERS LTD.

Doherty, P. C. author.
  The Book of Fires.
  1. Athelstan, Brother (Fictitious character)–Fiction.
  2. John, of Gaunt, Duke of Lancaster, 1340-1399–Fiction.
  3. London (England)–Fiction. 4. Tyler's Insurrection,
  1381–Fiction. 5. Great Britain–History–Richard II,
  1377-1399–Fiction. 6. Detective and mystery stories.
  I. Title
  823.9'2-dc23

ISBN-13: 978-1-78029-066-9 (cased)
ISBN-13: 978-1-78029-549-7 (trade paper)
ISBN-13: 978-1-78010-588-8 (e-book)

All Severn House titles are printed on acid-free paper.

Severn House Publishers support the Forest Stewardship Council™ [FSC™],
the leading international forest certification organisation. All our titles that
are printed on FSC certified paper carry the FSC logo.

MIX
Paper from
responsible sources
FSC® C013056

Typeset by Palimpsest Book Production Ltd.,
Falkirk, Stirlingshire, Scotland.
Printed and bound in Great Britain by
TJ International, Padstow, Cornwall.

To our second beloved granddaughter, Edie Grace Doherty,
with all our love.

PROLOGUE

'Another kind of fire for the burning of enemies where ever they are . . .'

Mark the Greek's 'The Book of Fires'

Richard Sutler, serjeant-at-law, and Crown Prosecutor in the King's Bench at Westminster, empowered to plead before the King's justices of oyer and terminer, was a proud, some would even say arrogant man. He was self-made, the child of marsh people from Poplar, close to the muddy waters of the Thames. Serjeant Sutler had, in his words, pulled himself up by his own bootstraps. He was, in the opinion of a Westminster wit, the sort of fellow who would cheerfully give you the shirt off your back. Another tartly claimed that Sutler knew the gamut of human emotions from A to B. Tall and commanding with a sharp, shaven face, popping-eyed with the mouth and jaw of a hungry lurcher, Sutler was in his heyday, especially on the morning of the feast of Saints Perpetua and Felicity, women of Carthage martyred by the cruel Emperor Severus in the amphitheatre of that city. Full of his own worth, Richard Sutler did not realize that on that cold, dark February morning he was about to be brutally murdered; in the words of scripture, a fate sprung on him 'like a trap'. Death would strike like a thief in the night and Master Sutler certainly did not know the day nor the hour.

As usual, the serjeant had risen early in his comfortable chambers in Casket Lane within bowshot of the great abbey of Westminster. He had washed, shaved, oiled his skin and donned his best robes, pulling on his high-heeled Spanish boots before swinging round his shoulders a pure woollen cloak edged with the costliest ermine. Sutler collected his chancery satchel bulging with documents which, within the day, would despatch a cartload of felons to the gallows at

Smithfield, Tyburn stream or even outside the towering fortified gatehouse of the abbey. Sutler was full of his day as he
made himself comfortable in the whispering recess of the Gates
of Purgatory, a handsome tavern which stood on the corner of
Casket Lane, close to his own comfortable wainscoted
chamber with its fine silver-inlaid furniture, woollen Turkey
rugs, coffers, chests and aumbries, not to mention that lux-
urious four-poster bed Sutler had been so reluctant to leave
after the previous night's drinking here in his favourite tavern.
The taproom now lay empty. People had flocked to the Jesus
Mass. Once this was finished, they would come here to break
their fast on strips of roasted pork and capon, dusted slightly
with a savoury peppered sauce and served on the softest
manchet coated with crushed spiced herbs. Sutler, however,
had decided to leave matters spiritual for the moment. He
wanted to prepare for the day's business. Above all, he wanted
to revel in his most recent triumph: the searching out, arrest,
conviction and execution of Lady Isolda Beaumont, widow
of Sir Walter, merchant, former soldier, adventurer and close
friend of the Regent, John of Gaunt. Lady Isolda was a self-
made widow. Sutler had proved that. The serjeant squirmed
on the thick cushioned seat. He stretched out his hands towards
the two capped braziers which had been wheeled into the
comfortable corner enclave beneath one of the taproom's
beautifully painted stained-glass windows. Sutler had proved
how Lady Isolda had helped her failing husband through the
Gates of Eternity with a goblet of rich posset generously
laced with the most deadly poison. At first she had protested
her innocence. An easy enough task for a beautiful young
woman like Isolda with her corn-coloured hair, sloe-blue eyes
and lips full and generous as the rose. She could dress in
gowns of damask and samite, wear gauze veils as demurely
as any nun, but she still remained an assassin. Sutler had
proved that well enough, his only regret was that her accomplice, the clerk Reginald Vanner, had fled, mysteriously disappeared. Sutler comforted himself that it was only a matter of
time before Vanner was seized and thrown into Newgate.
Reginald Vanner, formerly clerk to Sir Walter Beaumont, had
been put to the horn, proclaimed as a murderer with a bounty

on his head, thirty pounds sterling if he was brought in alive, fifteen for the head only. Vanner had been proclaimed '*utlegatum*', beyond the law, a wolfshead who could be slain on sight. Sutler sipped at the silver tankard, his own, which the taverner kept specially for him. He reminisced on his recent great triumph. He had received the personal thanks of the Regent as well as those of Gaunt's nephew, the young King Richard II. Such royal gratitude had been expressed with the grant of land in Middlesex. A small manor but one with fertile fields, a well-stocked carp pond and a thick rich copse of trees.

Sutler cradled the tankard between his hands. Lady Isolda and her accomplice, Vanner, had considered themselves very subtle: their crime had been perpetrated in a matter of seconds, a few heartbeats, but serjeant Sutler had been more cunning than either . . .

'A relic, sir, a true relic from the Holy Blood of Hailes.'

The serjeant glared at the tinker dressed in a motley collection of rags, a felt cap on his tattered grey hair, his scratched leather jerkin festooned with miniature cockle shells, amulets and brooches which boasted, at least in theory, that he had visited all the great shrines of the kingdom and beyond. Sutler leaned forward aggressively and the relic-seller scuttled away. Sutler returned to his reflections. Gaunt had commissioned him to investigate Sir Walter's death and he had done so thoroughly, detecting Lady Isolda's very clever sleight of hand. He had closed in swiftly like any good lurcher in pursuit of a deer. He had trapped her and brought her down. Oh, the lady had tried to seduce her way out of the trap, pressing herself close, whispering all forms of sweet inducements. Sutler smirked to himself; little did she or anyone know the truth. The serjeant-at-law peered over his tankard at the svelte round buttocks of the tapboy as he leaned over a table to clear away some pots. Sutler licked his lips. No one knew where his true predilections lay. Indeed, Lady Isolda had been greatly surprised by his reaction. Sutler placed his tankard down. Isolda had been convicted: all her parry and thrust, as well as that of her lawyer Nicholas Falke, had proven futile. She had been found guilty. Justices Tressilian,

Gavelkind and Danyel had imposed the ultimate horrid penalty for the murder of a husband by his wife: Lady Isolda had been sentenced to be burnt alive at Smithfield. The punishment was imposed '*sine misericordia*' – 'without mercy'. No opiate was to be offered, nor could the Carnifex, the executioner, slip through the surging smoke to garrotte her. Sutler, despite his arrogance, flinched at the memory of the burning: Lady Isolda standing on a stool, lashed to that soaring execution stake! He closed his eyes. The memories were still strong: the smoke billowing, the flames licking greedily around their victim. Sutler opened his eyes. He wondered why Lady Isolda hadn't bargained for her life. Surely she must have known the whereabouts of that secret codex, Mark the Greek's 'Book of Fires'? A manuscript which described the devastating liquid fire that could devour an entire ship, or so they said . . . A crackling from the hearth carved in the shape of a gaping dragon's mouth caught Sutler's attention. He watched the turnspit press the creaking iron on which half a piglet was spitted. The leaping flames, the sweating boy, the way the fire scorched the white, fleshy pork brought back memories of that macabre execution. Sutler quickly finished his ale, despatched the tankard back to Mine Host, grabbed his chancery satchel and staggered out of the main door into the narrow alleyway. Sutler stood taking deep breaths. He glanced to his left. The runnel snaked before him, the muck and filth, frozen hard by a hoar frost, glittered in the grey dawn-light. Sutler glimpsed a hooded figure holding a bucket shuffle out of an enclave, one of those recesses used as a laystall where rubbish could be heaped. He peered at the shambling, awkward figure.

'Some beggar trying to sell water as the purest from the spring,' he muttered, and strode purposely forward. As he walked through the thinning mist, Sutler realized the waterman beggar was carrying a pail in one hand and a lantern in the other, the flame of the tallow candle glowing fiercely against the frosted horn covering. Sutler bit his lip in anger. The beggar looked as if he was reluctant to give way. The serjeant-at-law was almost upon on him when the beggar, head and face hidden by a deep capuchon, stepped aside. Sutler sniffed and swept by. His high-heeled boot caught a piece of frozen rubbish. He paused to regain his balance and felt a sticky substance splash the right side of his face. He turned abruptly and glared. The beggar stood, his bucket now empty as its contents, tossed over the back of Sutler's costly cloak, dripped on to his hose and boots. The serjeant-at-law glanced down then back up in anger. The beggar stepped closer. He snatched the candle from the lanthorn and tossed it ever so leisurely towards Sutler, who could only stare in open-mouthed amazement. The flaring candle caught his cloak and the fire seemed to erupt all around him. He tried to take his cloak off but the fiery tongues darted about him. Sutler struggled, mouth opening in a hideous scream as the flames swiftly engulfed him . . .

Sir Francis Tressilian, Royal Justiciar and Judge in the King's Bench, was also preparing for what he did not know was his last day on earth. Tressilian loved the law and all the pomp and ceremony surrounding it: the herald, the criers, the proclamations and processions, the blaring trumpets, the costly woollen robes, white-furred red hats, the glittering badges and insignia of office and, above all, the obsequiousness which accompanied him everywhere. Tressilian smirked to himself as he sat on the jakes stool in the Golden Cresset tavern close to Westminster Hall. All the pomp and ceremony of a judge were certainly missing here, though Tressilian prided himself on hiding his weak stomach and watery bowels. Like Richard Sutler earlier in the day, Tressilian had risen, dressed and hastened to break his fast. He'd eaten a little too swiftly and now sat in the garderobe in the tavern stableyard. Justice Tressilian tried to compose himself as he listened to the sounds from outside. A knocking on the door annoyed him. He was supposed to sit here and take his ease, not be disturbed! He shouted at the would-be intruder to withdraw and got to his feet. Only then did he notice the liquid seeping beneath the door. Tressilian could only gape as the pool splashed about him. He abruptly broke from his surprise, but it was too late. One, two and then a third lit taper were tossed over the door to fall into that widening pool of mysterious liquid, now lapping

over his soft leather boots and woollen leggings. Tressilian's
hands went out to the latch even as the ground around him
erupted into fire, the flames roaring up turning the King's
Justiciar into a living, screaming torch.

PART ONE

'This fire, once started, will burn increasingly for a year.'
Mark the Greek's 'The Book of Fires'

Brother Athelstan, Dominican priest of St Erconwald's in Southwark, pulled his thick serge cloak about him. He scrutinized the sky, watching the night fade and the first streaks of dawn lighten the dark. He was fascinated by the way stars faded and disappeared. Did they simply diminish, he wondered, beneath the growing power of the sun even though it was still winter? The friar chewed the corner of his lip and wondered what the authorities such as Friar Bacon and Bartholomew the Englishman wrote about the phenomenon of dawn and dusk. Athelstan crouched and scratched the scarred head of his constant companion, the great battle-worn one-eyed cat Bonaventure.

'You will get your warm milk soon enough, brother cat. Until then we will watch the first red streaks of dawn streaming like Christ's blood through the firmament.' Athelstan once more looked up at the sky and sighed. He grasped the rusting bar which stretched between the moss-eaten crenellations of his ancient church tower and pulled himself up. Once steady, he looked over the side, turning his head slightly against the brisk, freezing breeze. He murmured a prayer as he looked down, for the church tower soared to a dizzying height. He brushed aside his unease as he glimpsed the pinpoints of moving lights, the torches held by his parish council: these were supervising the arrival of the sick, the lame and the cripples eagerly wending their way into St Erconwald's for the last stage of the night-time vigil which would end with the Jesus Mass at dawn. He squatted down with his back to the stone wall, absentmindedly stroking Bonaventure, who slid on to his lap. In a week's time Athelstan and his parish would celebrate the great feast of St Erconwald with a solemn High

Mass, ale tasting, cake savouring, dancing and carols ending with a special masque staged by Judith, Mistress of the Parish Mummers.

'God bless you, Judith,' Athelstan whispered. 'You will need all the patience our great and saintly patron can bestow.' In the nine days preceding the feast the nave would be open all night so the infirm and crippled could shelter close to the chantry chapel.

'The chapel contains a tomb, Bonaventure,' Athelstan murmured. 'But the tomb does not contain St Erconwald. He lies buried in St Paul's. No, our tomb houses powerful relics of that famous and saintly bishop.' Athelstan screwed his eyes up as he tried to recall the list. 'Ah, yes, that's it! Part of his cloak, a rod from his horse litter, the belt around his hair shirt and,' Athelstan smiled, 'a piece of the handbell used to summon his parishioners.' Athelstan returned to his thoughts. St Erconwald's vigil was an ancient custom which, according to the bell clerk and parish archivist Mauger, dated from the murky, misty past long before William the Norman crushed the Saxons at Senlac Hill. According to both tradition and legend, miraculous cures had occurred here during the novena night vigil. 'But none since I have been parish priest, Bonaventure.' Athelstan sighed, getting to his feet. 'I just thank God for the constant miracle of sunrise and,' he crossed and pulled back the trapdoor, 'a peaceful vigil.'

Athelstan, followed by a very hungry cat, made his way carefully down the winding spiral staircase and into the church. Watkin the dung collector and Pike the ditcher, leading henchmen of the parish council, had organized things well. The nave was lighted by flaring torches placed in their sconces on each rounded drum-like pillar along either transept. Charcoal braziers crackled merrily supervised by the pretty, dark-eyed widow woman Benedicta, whilst Cecily the courtesan, assisted by Crispin the carpenter, ensured that the straw palliasses for the pilgrims remained clean and soft. The smoky cinder-centred warmth of the nave was a welcome relief to the friar's own icy vigil on top of the church tower. Athelstan had meant to take a chafing dish of burning coal to keep his mittened fingers warm, but he had forgotten this. He went across to a brazier to warm his hands and stared around at the pilgrims shrouded in their blankets on palliasses arranged as close as possible to St Erconwald's chantry chapel where Athelstan would celebrate the Jesus Mass. In the transept, Imelda, Pike's wife, and Joscelyn, the one-armed former river pirate and owner of the Piebald tavern, gathered with Merrylegs the pie-man and his brood of little Merrylegs to organize bread, cheese, dishes of dried vegetables, strips of pork and tankards of light ale for the pilgrims. Athelstan was touched by the kindness and compassion of his parishioners, who, though certainly not wealthy, were prepared to share their food with strangers. He smiled to himself. Of course, there was profit to be made. Many parishioners had set up stalls and booths along the enclosure outside. They offered a range of petty goods and geegaws. Athelstan never asked for their origin, whilst Beadle Bladdersmith just looked the other way.

Athelstan peeled off his mittens and walked up the nave. The Hangman of Rochester had left his anker-hold in the transept and already unlocked the door to the rood screen. Athelstan went through this and stared around the sanctuary – all was in order. Athelstan genuflected towards the pyx, a roundel of sparkling gold hanging from a thin silver-filigreed chain next to the fluttering sanctuary lamp in its red alabaster jar.

'Father?' Athelstan turned. The Hangman of Rochester, garbed in his usual night-black jerkin, hose and cloak, stood rather nervously, Athelstan thought, shuffling from foot to foot.

'Giles of Sempringham.' Athelstan used the hangman's proper name, which he had set aside after outlaws had murdered his wife and child. A talented fresco painter, Giles had given up his chosen calling to assume the name and repu-tation of London's most skilled hangman, his first victims being the wolfsheads who had slaughtered his family. Athelstan walked closer. The hangman's long snow-white face, his hair matted and yellow as a tangle of straw, appeared tragic. Nevertheless, Athelstan recognized that the hangman had found peace here in St Erconwald's. A disused chantry chapel had been converted into a comfortable anker-hold. Occasionally the hangman would leave the cell to carry out his duties as an executioner, but his real task was a series of brilliantly executed frescoes on the walls of the church which stirred the envy of other parish priests. 'Giles,' Athelstan repeated. 'You seem lost in thought.' He felt a mild panic. Were his parishioners plotting something? 'Giles, what is it?'

'Father, I wonder if we have the purveyance to feed all these?' The hangman spread his hands. 'Some of the infirm are very weak and a good few are filthy. They need to be washed.'

'I thought the Fraternity of Free Love . . .' Athelstan referred to an eccentric group of parishioners who openly espoused the idea that love could solve all problems. Athelstan allowed the brotherhood or fraternity to meet here on the strict understanding that their philosophy did not include sexual licence. They had assured him it did not, though Athelstan entertained his own deep suspicions.

'The Brotherhood,' Athelstan repeated, 'remember, Giles, they promised to set up a great *lavarium* in God's Acre next to the old death house. Godbless the keeper said he would assist.'

'People are frightened of Thaddeus,' the hangman grumbled. 'Despite Godbless' efforts, that goat will devour everything, including a wash cloth. Perhaps we can use the new death house? Praise the Lord we have no corpses.'

Athelstan agreed and walked across the sanctuary. He knelt before the pyx, trying to cleanse his mind and heart of all sin, asking for God's guidance to celebrate the Mass and Eucharist in a worthy fashion. He rose and entered the sacristy. He took off his cloak, washed his hands and face at the *lavarium* then vested swiftly assisted by Crim the altar boy, who scampered in and out as busy as a squirrel along a branch. Candles were lit in the chantry chapel. Cruets set out along with the wine and sacring bread. Athelstan unlocked the parish chest and took out the missal, the Book of the Gospels and a small pyx for the viaticum as he hoped to take the Eucharist to Merrylegs' father, who lay mortally ill in a narrow chamber above his son's pie shop. Mauger tolled the bell. Crim rang the Sanctus chimes in the chapel then returned to the sacristy. He grasped the candleholder and, at a nod from Athelstan, led the friar out across the sanctuary and down through the rood screen into the chantry chapel. Athelstan began his Mass, consecrating the bread and wine, exchanging the kiss of peace and distributing the Eucharist, moving amongst the dark shapes of the infirm as well as his own flock of parishioners. The friar was aware of flitting shadows, the smell of incense and candle grease mingling with the smoky odours of the braziers and the stale, heavy stench of unwashed bodies. Eyes glittered out of rugged faces, tongues jutted out between decaying teeth to receive Christ's body under the appearance of bread. Athelstan became acutely aware of the human flesh in all its frailties; the dumb, deaf and blind. Hobbling cripples and wound-scarred former soldiers. He returned to the altar built against the wall, St Erconwald's statue to his left. The press of bodies warmed the chapel and the constant ejaculatory prayers were an unending refrain. Athelstan kissed the altar stone and turned to deliver the '*Ita, Missa est*' – the Mass has finished, the final blessing, when a voice called out.

'Praise to the Lord Jesus, a miracle! I am cured! Brothers and sisters, I am cured. I am cured. A miracle! God be praised! St Erconwald be thanked. I am cured . . .'

The statement caused uproar in the church. Figures shoved and pushed. Candles and torches were moved, flames streaking in the draught as doors were flung open. Athelstan finished the Mass and shouted for silence as Watkin, Pike and others of the parish council tried to subdue the outburst. Athelstan returned to the sacristy where he divested swiftly, telling Ranulf the rat-catcher to bring the entire parish council into the sanctuary, whilst Beadle Bladdersmith imposed order. Athelstan needed to see this miracle, whatever it was. He went back into the sanctuary and sat down on the priest's chair. The hubbub beyond the rood screen was growing, with shouts of 'Alleluia!' and 'Glory to Christ!' ringing through the cavernous nave. Athelstan ignored this. Watkin, Pike and Crispin brought cresset torches close about the sanctuary chair and a tall, dark figure stepped into the light. He pulled back his deep hood, loosened the heavy ragged cloak and let it fall to the ground. He undid his belt and handed it to Ranulf. Athelstan leaned forward and stared in utter disbelief at the smooth unshaven face, the deep-set eyes, snub nose and firm mouth and chin of the man before him. He continued to scrutinize the stranger, ignoring the whispers around him, his black tangled hair streaked with iron grey, the now un-mittened hands, their skin and flesh unmarked.

'Fulchard of Richmond!' Athelstan gasped. 'I met you when you first arrived here. Pike introduced you. I gazed at the left side of your face and body, but your right side . . .' Athelstan shook his head. 'You were a cripple leaning on a crutch. I remember the right side of your face, down the length of your body, horrifying burns . . .'

The man unclasped his dirt-stained chemise and drew it off, followed by a grimy linen undershirt. Athelstan repressed a shiver. He rose to his feet and walked slowly forward. Fulchard stood, hands hanging down. Ranulf crept near and touched the man's shoulder.

'I saw them too,' Ranulf rasped, 'your horrible burns.'

'Twenty years I have suffered.' Fulchard's broad Yorkshire voice carried around the sanctuary. 'Twenty years of scalding burns inflicted when I was a mere stripling in Outremer.' He touched the side of his face, his fingers turning down. 'From head to toe, the entire right side, the flesh erupted, corrupted, an open, weeping sore.' Fulchard had everyone's attention now. Athelstan walked slowly around the man, studying him intently. The friar was certain this was the same Fulchard that he'd met the previous day. He had seen that horrible open wound, the way the man hobbled, his looks, his gestures. Athelstan was certain this was no counterfeit or crank. Fulchard had hobbled in and out on his crutch, his scarred burns open for everyone to see: now, the flesh was white and unmarked. Athelstan could detect nothing amiss. He recalled the man's voice – it was the same although a little stronger. He stepped close so his face was only inches from Fulchard's. He recognized the mole, high on the left cheek, the shape of the good eye. Athelstan crossed himself, took off his own cloak and wrapped it around Fulchard.

'What happened?' he whispered close to Fulchard's ear and, as he did, Athelstan smelt a lovely fragrance like that of some exquisite perfume. Athelstan was agitated. At the same time he mentally beat his breast. He preached about a Risen Christ. How all things were possible with God including a miracle. So why did he have these doubts?

'What happened?' he repeated, gesturing at Watkin to bring a sanctuary stool for Fulchard to sit on whilst he returned to the celebrant's chair. Silence now reigned, even the turbulent noise from the nave had subsided. 'You are in the presence of God,' Athelstan intoned. 'Master Fulchard of Richmond, tell me what truly happened, from the beginning.'

'I was born in Knaresborough in the shire of York, the son of Ralph and Elizabeth Spicer. My father was a leech, and I became his apprentice. Of course, in the wild years of youth, the blood runs hot and the heart is a merciless hunter for things fresh and new. I was placed in the care of the Benedictines at Rievaulx Abbey but I tired of the brothers. I journeyed abroad, serving in a cog out of Whitby. I then began my travels. I have seen the icy-massed forests of the north where huge white bears prowl and where Leviathan plays in the sea close by. I have visited Outremer. I have kissed the Sacred Stones in the Holy Sepulchre and stood on the demon-swept shores of the Dead Sea. I have wandered here and I have wandered there. Eventually I journeyed to Athens to earn more coin. I worked in the kitchen of a tavern. I was put in charge of the turnspit. One night, the eve of the feast of St George, the tavern master was preparing a sumptuous feast. Oilskins were brought down into the great kitchen, I carried one here.' Fulchard tapped his right shoulder. 'God knows what happened. I admit, I had been drinking heavily and I staggered. The bulging oilskin abruptly split, drenching the right side of my body. At that very moment, I was passing the great hearth where a fire danced as merrily as the tongues of Hell, and so it proved to be. The flames seemed to leap out at me as if drawn by the oil.'

'I have seen that happen,' Merrylegs spoke up. 'I am always wary of my oven. I keep oil well away from it.'

'True,' Joscelyn the taverner added, 'if you are drenched in oil the fire races to embrace you as eager as any lover for his sweetheart. Oh, sorry, Father,' Joscelyn coughed, 'I shouldn't have said that, should I?'

'But it's true.' Athelstan smiled. 'In my youth I served in the king's array in France.'

'Did you, Father?' Watkin and the rest chorused. They were as greedy as a host of hungry sparrows for any tittle-tattle about their priest's former life.

'I served in France,' Athelstan repeated, 'at a siege where the defenders poured down oil followed by fiery brands. Some of them missed but the oil had a life of its own. I saw fire move as swiftly as the wind. Master Fulchard, continue.'

'I was burnt, roasted from my head down the entire length of the right side of my body. I was only saved by an old soldier. He knew what to do. He wrapped me in a cloak soaked in vinegar. He saved my life, an English mercenary but one with a good heart. He later took what money I had and used some of his own to help me. I was shipped to the Hospitallers in Rhodes. From there I travelled back to England. My life was saved but I was scarred, a hard, open wound, the pain a dull constant ache. I moved to Richmond in Yorkshire and from there journeyed around the northern shires.' Fulchard pointed to the heavy, thick wallet on his belt still held by the rat-catcher. 'Read the letters I hold from the Hospital in Rhodes, licences from the Mayor of York and others. Indeed, I have a more recent one. When I journeyed to Southwark for the vigil, I suffered great pain. I attended the House of Mercy in the hospital at the Priory of St Bartholomew, Smithfield. I was seen by Philippe the physician.'

'Philippe,' Athelstan intervened, 'I know him well. A most skilled doctor, merciful but thorough.'

'He examined me,' Fulchard continued. 'He gave me a tincture to dull the pain. I was to sprinkle it on anything I drank or ate.'

'Who accompanied you here?' Athelstan asked. 'You must have had help?'

'I did.' A voice came from behind the clustered parish council. A man pushed his way through and came to genuflect beside Athelstan. The stranger had a square, thick-set face slightly yellowing in the poor light, though his eyes were sharp and bright. He looked harsh and forbidding with unshaven skin and balding head yet his voice was low and cultured.

'And you are?'

'Fitzosbert. Former priest, former soldier, former clerk, former this and former that.' He answered Athelstan's smile with his own and held up the stump of his left hand. 'Once a priest, Father, until I became involved in this and that. Hazard was my downfall. The roll of the dice, be it cogged or not. Defrocked by Despenser Bishop of Norwich, the sheriff of the same county eventually took my left hand. I met Fulchard in Richmond on my tour of the shire. He told me a curious tale.'

Athelstan glanced at Fulchard.

'I told Fitzosbert, Father, how I was sheltering in a hospice near Richmond, also dedicated to St Erconwald. I had a vision, a dream: a man in a long robe appeared to me. He had long hair, a beard and carried a crozier. He said he was Erconwald, formerly Bishop of London and now a Lord of Heaven. He told me to go to St Erconwald's in Southwark and experience God's mercy. So I did. The journey was hard and difficult but, unlike Fitzosbert here, I have full licence to beg. In return for a little payment, Fitzosbert helped me. I arrived here at the beginning of the vigil . . .'

'And what actually happened during the night?' Athelstan blessed Fitzosbert and indicated he should stand with the rest.

'I fell asleep close to the door of the chantry chapel. I was warm and comfortable. You began your Mass. I did not know if I was dreaming or not. I glanced at the chantry chapel door, my eye drawn by the glow of candlelight. This began to grow stronger and move like a mist across the floor. I could not tell if I was asleep or awake but, as the light crept closer, it ran like liquid gold, snaking across the floor, curling past other pilgrims until it reached me. I felt as if I was back in that tavern so many years ago in Athens. I was kneeling, my whole body was swept by a sweetness I could never imagine. Then it left. I wondered what had happened and realized there was no pain. I roused myself and stared down. I thought it was a sham, some trickery. My body was healed. I didn't know what to say or do. I wanted to wake up and yet at the same time stay in that most pleasant dream. But then as the Mass ended, I fully realized what had happened, that I wasn't dreaming.' His voice faltered.

'And you did not leave the church during the night-time vigil?'

'No, Father, ask those around me. When I was crippled, I needed help to get up, grasp my crutch. I have to clear people out of my way. Father, I will leave my crutch here . . .'

Athelstan held up a hand.

'Mauger,' he ordered, 'Watkin and you, Benedicta, go back into the nave. Bring all those who were close to Master Fulchard. Do so now.'

'I was, Father,' Fitzosbert spoke up with a lopsided grin. 'But I suppose you need stronger witnesses?'

'I suppose I do,' Athelstan retorted. 'Now, let's wait a while.' He heard the raised voices of members of his parish council calling for witnesses. A short while later six pilgrims stumbled and staggered into the great pool of light, gnarled, twisted and suffering. All clad in rags, they displayed hideous wounds, raw scars and fearful injuries. Athelstan rose, blessed them and walked forward to exchange the kiss of peace. As he did so, he opened his purse on the cord around his waist and pushed a coin into each of their hands feeling their cold skin, their coarse, twisted fingers.

'Watkin,' Athelstan murmured, going back to his chair, 'make sure these six eat well this morning. Now,' he raised his voice, 'what did you see?'

The friar listened as the witnesses, some thick with accent, describe how Master Fulchard of Richmond had hobbled into the church the previous evening. They had been close around him as they prayed and slept. Two of the pilgrims said they would go on solemn oath how, in the early hours, Fulchard began to stir and chatter, talking in his sleep. They all agreed he had not left the church, nor had anyone approached him. They witnessed no disturbance whatsoever apart from a certain restlessness just before he woke. Once the pilgrims were finished, Watkin, Pike and others from the parish council chorused how they had witnessed the same. Athelstan could only sit dumbfounded by what he had seen and heard.

'Look,' he stammered, 'I need to think and pray. Master Fulchard will join me in the priest's house. Afterwards, Joscelyn, he will lodge at the Piebald, yes?'

The taverner swiftly agreed. The watchful silence was now broken as Athelstan's obvious acceptance of what had happened dawned on the rest. The friar instructed Mauger and Benedicta to look after the sacristy and sanctuary. He rose, nodded at Fulchard and left through the rood-screen door. The nave was packed with people all agog with news at what had happened. The story of the 'Great Miracle' had spread wide and fast. Athelstan had to shoulder his way across the nave, through the Devil's Door and into God's Acre. Even Godbless, the beggar man who had turned the old death house into a comfortable cottage for himself, and the omnivorous Thaddeus were waiting for news amongst the decaying tombstones and battered crosses.

'I have seen angels flying!' Godbless shouted.

'In which case,' Athelstan retorted, 'you have certainly seen more than I have. Now look, Godbless, keep a vigilant eye on God's Acre, because the angels you see are causing all this excitement.' Athelstan strode on, Godbless' praises ringing in his ears. He reached his house, unlocked the door and entered the warm, well-scrubbed flagstone kitchen which served as his chancery, store room and, as he joked, solar and dining hall. Everything was in place. The fire banked. The charcoal braziers glowing. The air sweet with the oatmeal mixed with honey and spice bubbling in the black pot-bellied cauldron on its tripod above the fire. Athelstan quickly scrutinized every-thing, his communion chest, the lectern, his chancery coffer and well-ordered bed-loft. He opened the door in response to Bonaventure's constant scratching and served the tomcat his morning drink of warm milk. Once Bonaventure was satisfied, Athelstan prepared the table ladling out the oatmeal and filling two blackjacks with light ale. Fulchard arrived escorted by members of the parish council. Athelstan thanked them but insisted that he and Fulchard would eat alone. Once he was at table, Athelstan closely inspected the miracle as Fulchard hungrily ate the oatmeal. The friar recalled meeting the pilgrim the previous day and marvelled at the change. He could detect no physical scars and yet, in the better light of his house, would go on oath that this was the same man: the voice, the mannerisms and certain marks he'd noticed on the good side of the pilgrim's face. Once Fulchard had finished, Athelstan demanded to see the letters and licences he carried. The pilgrim opened his wallet, spilling its contents out on to the table. Athelstan sifted through them, studying each very carefully. Fulchard, by his own admission, possessed a host of letters and licences allowing him to beg in a wide variety of places, as well as describing his disabilities. Athelstan scrupulously examined both the writing and the appropriate seal on each document. After all, the consummate skill of cunning men who forged licences and could change appearances as deftly as any conjuror was well known. Athelstan studied both Fulchard and his documents. He was sure this was not the case here. The friar sighed and rose to his feet.

'Master Fulchard, I insist you remain in my parish as I, according to canon law, must pass all this on to the curia, the council of the Bishop of London.' Athelstan grasped his chancery satchel, laid out his writing implements and hastily drafted a letter to Master Henry Tuddenham, clerk to the Bishop of London's council, detailing what had happened in his parish. He re-read this and, satisfied, swiftly sealed it, telling Fulchard to eat more oatmeal and drink another blackjack of ale. Athelstan left the priest's house and re-entered the church. St Erconwald's had been transformed. Usually at this hour the nave lay silent but now it was busy and frenetic as a Smithfield fair. Athelstan drew up his hood and pushed his way through the throng. His parishioners, true to form, were self-appointed keepers of the shrine and first-hand witnesses to what Watkin claimed to be 'Southwark's one and only Great Miracle'. All the sharp-witted denizens of the ward had swarmed in: the foists, the nips, the cunning men, conjurors, strumpets, pimps and their prostitutes along with tinkers, traders and relic-sellers. They rubbed shoulders and, in some cases, felt the pockets and purses of the ordinary gaping visitors. The noise was constant. The stench of packed, sweaty bodies in dirty clothes wafted everywhere. Someone intoned a hymn to St Erconwald only to be drowned by a coster shouting, 'Mussels, fresh mussels blessed by St Erconwald himself!' The trader bawled even louder over the laughter his remark provoked. Further down the nave, a travelling puppet show, a box with an opening at the top perched on a barrow, told the story of St Erconwald as Athelstan had never heard it before. The friar tried to remain tolerant but when he glimpsed an itinerant cook with heavily salted pork chops slung on a dirty cord around his neck, his good humour faded. He told the cook he could not fire his stove in church and strode off angrily towards the sanctuary. The Hangman of Rochester, on guard at the rood screen, took one look at Athelstan's face and hastily opened the door. Athelstan swept into the sanctuary, beckoning the hangman to follow.

'Giles, I want the entire parish council here, and I mean now before I finish reciting ten Aves or there will be no fair.'

The hangman hurried off and, one by one, the parish council trooped into where their priest stood on the top step of the high altar.

'Right, my beloveds, my little flock.'

'The nave belongs to the people,' Pike protested, 'the sanctuary to the priest, if we . . .' Pike swallowed the rest of his sentence as Benedicta brought the heel of her boot down on his toes whilst Athelstan took a step down, face white with anger.

'Whatever you say, Father,' Pike stammered.

'Good, Pike. This is our parish, not the council of the Upright Men, and I am your priest. Mauger, I have a letter for you to take to Master Tuddenham. Joscelyn, collect Fulchard from my house and lodge him at the Piebald. Benedicta and Crim,' he winked at the altar boy, 'you and Giles will scour the sanctuary and sacristy to ensure all is well. The rest of my beloveds, including Pike, will clear the church. Pilgrims are most welcome – the rest can use the enclosure outside. Merrylegs,' he beckoned at the pie-man, 'I am going to take the Sacrament to your sick elderly father.'

'The Ancient One of Days will be most pleased,' Merrylegs lugubriously replied.

'Which is more than I am,' Athelstan snapped. 'So, let us begin . . .'

oOoOo

Sir John Cranston, Lord High Coroner of London, rose from his judgement chair and walked over to the horn-filled window of his courtroom at the Guildhall. He opened the window and stared moodily down at the broad, cobbled bailey which stretched to the soaring, battlemented gatehouse leading into Cheapside. He had just finished reading the indictment against Ralph Tailor of Cripplegate: 'That he did feloniously rape Alice Beggar of Queenhithe, and did carnally lie with her in her own house from day to day and night to night. The same said Ralph continued to indulge publicly in the shameful and abominable sin of debauchery . . .'

'Satan's tits!' Cranston growled. 'From one stew pot of wickedness to the next.' He gazed round the judgement chamber; everything had been removed from the walls: crucifixes, triptychs, painted cloths, tapestries and other ornaments. All these, together with court rolls and other manuscripts, had been taken down to the steel-bound arca, the massive security chest in the Guildhall cellars.

'Everything which can be stored away has been,' Cranston murmured to himself. This included his own buxom wife, the Lady Maude, his poppets Stephen and Francis the twins, his wolfhounds Gog and Magog, together with his household retainers. Cranston had sent them deep into the countryside and the protection of a moated, fortified manor house. He'd also arranged for the families of Oswald and Simon, his scrivener and clerk, to join them. Brother Athelstan, however, was a different matter. The little Dominican priest was obdurate. He would not flee when the Great Revolt broke out, even though he conceded that London would be sacked. Cranston certainly agreed with that. He had clashed openly with the Regent, John of Gaunt, and others of the Royal Council who believed the mailed might of royal troops would prevail. How they would fortify the Tower and crush all dissent from there . . .

'Nonsense,' Cranston whispered to himself. 'The Tower will fall. The Upright Men have their own agents deep in that gloomy fortress.' He stared down at the bailey, watching people slither and slide on the frost-encrusted cobbles. A sumpter pony skittered, provoking the destrier of a knight banneret guarding the Guildhall to rear, whinnying noisily, its sharpened metal hooves slicing the air. Oh, yes, Cranston reflected, when the Day of the Great Slaughter occurred, the citadels would certainly fall and it would take more than mounted knights to crush the bloody eruption. Cranston knew the city underworld, the mummers' halls and castles which housed the London mob, that demon with ten thousand heads. They were waiting, and when the sign was given they would rise. The masters of misrule, the captains of the canting crews, the rulers of the rifflers would sound their horns and unfurl their ragged banners. Their followers would swarm like rats from a burning hayrick, stream from their damp, mildewed, rotting tenements to feast on the fat of the city. Hordes of other rebels would pour in from the north, south and west. They would certainly seize London Bridge and cut the city into two. Cranston narrowed his eyes and chewed the corner of his lip. Gaunt would not compromise. The hated poll tax continued to be levied and the Commons sitting at Westminster provided very little relief for the poor. Not only London was threatened but the surrounding shires and, more importantly, even further north in the eastern counties. The Upright Men were busy fortifying the Fens in Lincolnshire, drawing in the dispossessed, the runaways and rebels as well as the outlaws, sharp as any hawk's beak at the prospect of plunder. At least Gaunt recognized the real threat the Fens posed, with their marshes, morasses and narrow-snaking shallows hidden by reeds that sprouted in thick clusters. The Fens were fast becoming a fortress, a mustering place for all those ready to wage war against the Crown. Gaunt had ordered the construction of a vast flotilla of punts – flat-bottomed, easily assembled barges which could thread the needle-thin waterways of the Fens. The barges were being built on the Southwark side and would soon be transported by land and sea in time for a great *chevauchée* once spring broke.

Meanwhile, the harsh mills of justice had to grind on. Gaunt had asked the coroner to investigate the bloody, tangled mystery surrounding the execution of the city beauty, Lady Isolda Beaumont. Cranston had met her on a number of occasions and he knew something about the woman's hideous death and its equally horrific aftermath. The coroner glanced at the hour candle on its copper stand. The flame was approaching the

ninth ring – time for him to be gone! Cranston hurriedly
strapped on his warbelt and seized his cloak and beaver hat
before bellowing instructions and farewells to Simon and
Oswald, who were crouched over their chancery desks in the
adjoining chamber. The coroner stamped down the stairs and
out into the freezing cold of the grey day. The business of the
Guildhall had now begun, its dungeons and cells being swiftly
emptied. A long line of city bailiffs garbed in the red and
murrey livery of the city led by Flaxwith, Cranston's chief
bailiff, with his constant companion, the ugly-faced mastiff
Samson, were herding out a gaggle of prisoners for punishment. The felons would be taken down to the different stocks,
pillories and thews to be exhibited and mocked until their
sentences were complete. The prisoners, manacled and dazed,
staggered about. To drown their cries, a few of the bailiffs
carried drums, trumpets, cymbals and three sets of bagpipes.
Cranston walked down the line of hapless miscreants, reading
the placards slung around their necks which proclaimed their
offences. A woman had created a vile nuisance by constructing
a pipe from her own privy chamber to her neighbour's garden
and ignored a court writ to remove it. The justices had ruled
that she was to carry part of that pipe for a half a day in the
thews of Poultry. A counterfeit physician had fed a patient a
nostrum so noxious the poor man had found it almost impossible to urinate for a week. The counterfeit physician was
being mounted on the back of a bony street nag. He would
face the rear with the horse's tail in his hand for a bridle.
Around his neck hung two dirty urine flasks and a pisspot.
Behind him a vintner would be compelled to drink, wry-
mouthed, the corrupt wines he had attempted to palm off on
others. There was a fisherman who had freshened a stale catch
with blood; a milk-seller found guilty of mixing chalk with
his drink; four strumpets caught drunk and soliciting beyond
Cock Lane; and finally two wrestlers who had decided to
engage naked in a raucous fight on the steps of a London
church. Cranston walked down the line. He had a swift word
with Flaxwith and strode off to the gateway just as the bagpipes
began to screech and the punishment procession moved off.

Once in Cheapside, Cranston walked purposefully, one hand

on the hilt of his sword, the other close to the purse beneath his cloak. Cheapside was busying for another day's frenetic trading. War might come. Revolt might threaten but trade was London's blood. Shop shutters rattled up and sheets were removed from the great broad stalls that ranged in long lines down the mercantile thoroughfare. Church bells chimed the hour of divine office as market horns brayed to commence business. Apprentices scurried as swift and nimble as monkeys to set out wares, all quick-eyed, searching out passers-by for any potential customer. A songster had already set up his pitch on a broken barrow and trilled loudly about a maiden with 'skin white as snow on ice'. Shop signs, a bush for the vintner, three gilded quills for the apothecary, a unicorn for the goldsmith and a horse's head for the saddler, creaked noisily in the brisk breeze. The food purveyors were out, offering fat capons and plump rabbits. Geese tied to the stalls honked. Chickens and ducks, trussed tightly by the legs, floundered in a welter of feathery wings. Pastry shops offered sweet wafers and even sweeter wines. Milk-sellers, with pails slopping either end of their yolks, bawled a price which would gradually decrease as the day progressed and the milk staled. Market beadles were arguing with a cheese-seller who allegedly had made his product richer by soaking it in broth. The discussion had provoked a quarrel upturning a spice stall so the spilled powder of sage, fennel, basil and coriander was being crushed under foot to sweeten the air now turning rather rancid from the pack of unwashed bodies. Odour from a nearby soap-maker, busy mixing soda and wood and animal fat, thickened the stench. Cranston surveyed the crowds in all its varying colours and glimpses of city life: the priest, garbed only in his shirt, walking barefoot, a white wand in one hand, an incense bowl in the other, public punishment for his sin of lechery. A black-smith, his open-fronted shed next to a tavern, supervised sweaty-faced apprentices serving a table-high furnace. A tanner collected warm dog dung to soften scraped hides. A wine crier, standing in the entrance to an alehouse, readied himself for a proclamation. Itinerant coal-sellers, hay merchants, barbers and dish-menders touted noisily for business. A market beadle proclaimed what must be: bead makers must use perfectly

round beads; butchers should not mix tallow with their lard
or sell the flesh of dog, cat or horse. Makers of bone handles
must not trim their products with silver to make them look
like ivory. Candles must be what they are, pure beeswax or
tallow and not adulterated with cooking fat or any other base
substances. Schoolboys, their hair cropped close, horn-books
under their arms, stopped to listen to these market heralds
before hurrying on to the aisle schools of St Paul's and elsewhere. Funeral processions wound their way through the
crowd, the thuribles of the altar-servers fragrancing the air.
Wedding parties, cymbals clashing and flower petals fluttering,
processed to the place of festivity. Gong cart gangs tried to
clear the filthy refuse heaped in laystalls and elsewhere. A
wonder-worker, or so he called himself, 'From Nicaea and
other cities of the east', offered in a ringing voice a marvel-
lous cure for impotence, namely the head of a ram which had
never meddled with a ewe, its horns knocked off and boiled
in holy water from the Jordan.

Cranston grinned at the sheer effrontery of such a claim as
he continued to inspect the crowd he pushed through. The
legion of pickpockets and petty thieves had already seen
the coroner and slunk away. Cranston had a habit of recog-
nizing the likes of Fairy Fingers, Robber Red Breast and Peter
the Pilferer and bellowing a warning about them to all and
sundry. Cranston was equally vigilant over a more sinister
enemy, the Upright Men, whose assassins were known to seek
out Crown officials and strike with sword or dagger. Cranston
drew comfort that his friendship with Brother Athelstan
tempered resentment against him. Nevertheless, the coroner
was wary. The Upright Men were plotting furiously, though
Cranston was growing mystified as he sensed an unexpected
abeyance in the dread creeping through the city. The
Earthworms, the fantastically garbed horsemen despatched by
the Upright Men into Cheapside or elsewhere to cause chaos
and mock the power of the Regent, had abruptly ceased their
attacks. Cranston's spies had also reported a lack of activity
by the Upright Men in those bastions of the city underworld
around Whitefriars and elsewhere.

Cranston wondered why as he turned into Parsnip Lane,

where Justice Gavelkind had his town house squeezed between a tavern, the Hoop in Splendour, and the St Mary Magdalene, the workshop of one of London's leading perfumers. Cranston had agreed to meet Gavelkind outside the latter and strode down the long, narrow lane. He glimpsed the justice leave his house then the coroner stopped in astonishment. A figure, shrouded in black like a Benedictine monk, stepped out of an alley mouth holding a bucket. Gavelkind paused and turned as if greeted by this mysterious figure, who then hurled the contents of the bucket over him. Gavelkind staggered back. The black-garbed figure followed; dropping the bucket, he opened a lanthorn hanging on a door post, took out the flaming tallow candle and hurled it at the justice. For a few heartbeats nothing happened. Gavelkind was beating at the mess covering him until blue-gold sparks appeared. These flickered momentarily before erupting into tongues of flame which overwhelmed him. Cranston raced forward but it was too late. The lane was deserted. Gavelkind, engulfed in the raging fire, staggered to the right and left blocking the path. The fire-thrower had disappeared. Cranston could only stare in disbelief as Gavelkind, no more than a mass of flame, stumbled screaming towards him. Customers from the tavern hurried out to view the horror as Cranston took off his cloak and tried to douse the blazing inferno . . .

oOoOo

The market horn was sounding the end of trading and the bells of the city churches clanged for vespers when Athelstan, summoned by Cranston's messenger, the green-garbed Tiptoft, slipped into the Holy Lamb of God in Cheapside. This was, in the coroner's own words, Cranston's 'private chantry chapel'. Sir John was determined to bring Athelstan into the gruesome mysteries confronting him. The coroner had already seen off the two beggars lurking as usual near the door: Leif the one-legged and Leif's constant companion, Rawbum. Now he rose to exchange the kiss of peace with Athelstan before asking the buxom Mine Hostess to serve fresh pots of ale and a dish of cold meat for both himself and, as he joked, 'his

Father Confessor'. For a while, Athelstan and Cranston ate and drank in silence. Once finished, the coroner sat back, polishing his horn-spoon on a snow-white napkin.

'Thank you for coming, Brother.' He turned to face the friar, who had become such an important part of his life.

'Sir John, you have a tale for me; I certainly have one for you.'

'Fire!' Cranston replied. 'A tangled tale about fire and how it can be used. First let me regale you with what you will define as the facts.' He took a sip from his tankard and made himself more comfortable in the deep window seat of the tavern. 'Listen, Brother, and listen well. Walter Beaumont was born in York, the son of a mercer. He left the family home and served as a soldier beyond the Narrow Seas. He travelled to Florence, ostensibly involved in the wool trade; secretly he wanted to become a *peritus*, an expert in the use of cannon and culverins. More importantly, he strove to learn the secrets of the different powders which fire these machines of war. He became a captain of one of those mercenary companies, they called themselves the "Luciferi", or the "Light Bearers". Beaumont's free company was different from the rest, they brought cannon fire to the battlefield.'

'I saw the same in France,' Athelstan murmured, 'such machines are becoming more numerous . . .'

'And more deadly, Brother. Three years ago, at the siege of St Malo, Gaunt mustered more than four hundred cannon; some, weighing over a hundredweight, could cast heavy stone balls, quarrels or even lead bullets. The old king and the Black Prince,' Cranston sniffed, 'loved these machines of war. They held a dreadful fascination for our royal princes.'

'They were used at the battle of Crecy?' Athelstan asked.

'Yes, yes they were. Now, from a very early age, Walter Beaumont recognized the value of such terrible machines and steeped himself in their use. He acquired the name of "Black Beaumont" for his love, knowledge and skill of gunpowder. On his return to England, he imported great supplies of saltpetre, sulphur, colophony, amber powder and turpentine. He established foundries to manufacture cannon and create the powder and missiles they would need. Beaumont became Master of the King's Cannon, Master of the Royal Ordnance at the Tower and elsewhere. He served with great distinction in the royal array. The Black Prince himself knighted Beaumont outside Calais.' Cranston waved a hand. 'You can guess how such a life story unfolds. Beaumont married, his wife died in childbirth. A childless widower, Sir Walter married again, a great beauty, the Lady Isolda. I suppose Sir Walter thought he lived in some romance; wealthy, well patronized with a beautiful wife. Sir Walter, as you may know, owned an extensive and well-endowed manor – a veritable mansion.'

'Ah, yes,' Athelstan intervened. 'Firecrest Manor, lying between the city and Westminster. It possesses spacious meadows, gardens and orchards which front the river. I have seen its majestic water gate with its own wharf and quay.'

'The same,' Cranston agreed. 'A veritable Eden, a seeming paradise.'

'And the serpent?'

'Sir Walter fell ill. He was a goodly age. Nothing serious. A flux in the bowels, bile in the stomach. He had no children: his brother, Sir Henry, also a merchant, together with Henry's young wife, Rohesia, live with him.'

'And there are others?'

'Thomas Buckholt, Sir Walter's steward, a man devoted to his master. Reginald Vanner, mark that name, Sir Walter's chancery clerk, of the same age, or thereabouts, as Lady Isolda. Oh, yes, and Rosamund Clifford, Lady Isolda's waiting maid. Now, suspicion began to hint, whisper, even gossip that Sir Walter was being poisoned.' Cranston paused, staring round the warm taproom savouring the mouth-watering odours seeping out of the kitchens where Mine Hostess was preparing strips of ham glazed with mustard. 'Lovely place.' Cranston smacked his lips just as a cohort of corpse-bearers bustled in, doffing their dark worsted cloaks and peeling off white face masks decorated with small black crosses.

'Sir John?'

'Ah, yes. On the twenty-first of February past, the eve of the feast of the Chair of St Peter, Sir Walter was in his bedchamber. He slept alone in a very comfortable room with its own hearth and garderobe. Buckholt the steward believed

Sir Walter was resting for the night and brought up the usual goblet of highly spiced hot posset. He reached the top of the stairs leading to the gallery where Sir Walter's chamber stood. Lady Isolda swept out of her room. At the same time the clerk, Vanner, came pounding up the stairs saying he needed to talk to Buckholt urgently. Lady Isolda offered to take the goblet in to her husband. Flustered, Buckholt agreed. He handed the goblet over and went downstairs with Vanner. Now let me hasten to add that Buckholt, by his own admission, was deeply suspicious of both Isolda and Vanner.'

'Why?'

'Lady Isolda had been married for five years. Sir Walter had fallen ill. According to Buckholt, she and Vanner were playing the two-backed beast, enjoying a deeply adulterous relationship. Buckholt believed, and still does, that Lady Isolda was a demon incarnate, a succubus who fastened on any man she wished to use.'

'And the posset?'

'Well, Buckholt went downstairs with Vanner but found that the issue about certain indentures waiting to be sealed and signed by Sir Walter could have easily waited for the following day. Alarmed, Buckholt hurried back up to his master's chamber, where he found Lady Isolda feeding her husband the posset from the goblet but also taking sips herself. Buckholt did not like the way she was looking at him. Embarrassed and confused by his own suspicions, Buckholt waited until his master was asleep. He then insisted on taking the goblet back to the buttery.'

'Where he also sipped what remained of the spiced wine?'

'Yes, Brother, and suffered no ill effect. He drained the goblet completely and examined the goblet but could find nothing untoward.' Cranston paused to glare across at the noisy corpse-bearers. Matters took a different turn when Mine Hostess swept in from the kitchen yard, screaming at them. Apparently they had not finished their task but had left the cadaver destined for St Michael and All Angels in an outhouse in the tavern. The mort cloth had slipped from the cadaver's face and terrified the wits out of one of the maids. Cranston chuckled as the corpse-bearers hastily drained their tankards, grabbed their possessions and fled the taproom.

'The next morning,' Cranston continued, 'Sir Walter was found dead in his bed. A local physician, Milemete, was summoned. He concluded that Sir Walter's weak heart had given out. He could not say whether Sir Walter's death was malignant. Buckholt was not convinced and neither was Sir Henry. They sent to St Bartholomew's for the family physician, Brother Philippe. He also examined the corpse. He could detect possible malignancy though he could not determine what noxious herbs might have been in the posset. He certainly alerted suspicion that death was sudden, swift and unexpected. Naturally the finger of suspicion pointed at Lady Isolda, who had fed Sir Walter his last drink. She, of course, angrily denied it. She might have won the day. However,' Cranston sipped from his tankard, 'the finger of God intervened. The buttery clerk maintains the goblet Buckholt brought down from Sir Walter's chamber – he was going to wash it and store it away with the rest—'

'Was not the same cup?'

'Yes. The buttery clerk had both prepared the posset, a veritable rich mixture, and poured it into a goblet. He then placed it on a silver tray with a napkin when he noticed a chip on the goblet stand. He decided not to change the cups but to deal with that later. However, the goblet Buckholt brought down did not have that mark.'

'In other words, Lady Isolda changed cups?'

'Yes. The buttery clerk informed Buckholt, who scoured his master's chamber, indeed the entire house, especially the bushes and plants below the window of his master's chamber.'

'Nothing was found?'

'Nothing. But Buckholt was persistent. He petitioned the Regent, John of Gaunt.'

'Who was a close friend of Sir Walter's?'

'If Gaunt could be close to anyone, it was Sir Walter, a bosom friend of the House of Lancaster.'

'And the supplier of powerful culverins and cannon to it?'

'Of course, my dear friar.' Cranston sniffed. 'Gaunt would have turned to thee and me but we had just finished the business at the Candle-Flame and I was out of the city. So Gaunt summoned a Crown prosecutor, Richard Sutler, serjeant-at-law,

a graduate, a very brilliant one from the Inns of Court, a
most wily and seasoned prosecutor. Sutler swept into
Firecrest Manor and began his investigation. He examined
the pewter goblets, a set of twelve with a matching jug.
Sutler took them out into the sunlight. He scrupulously
studied each one. Firstly, he could not discover any splinter,
crack or mark on any of the twelve goblets. Secondly, he
noticed each goblet had a shiny finish but one of these looked
more recent than the others. According to Mortice the buttery
clerk, the goblets had been bought decades ago. Eleven of
them would justify their age but one seemed much more
recent. All the goblets bore the same potter's mark but one
of them was finely etched. Sutler consulted the Guild and
they declared that the goblets were the work of one of their
members, the Ramyer family. Sutler searched them out. The
father had died but the son recognized the mark and, more
importantly . . .'

'Maintained one of them was a more recent product?'

'True, learned friar. Even better for Sutler, Ramyer declared
how his family only made these goblets in batches of twelve.
More damning, Ramyer described a recent sale of twelve such
goblets to a man whom Ramyer later identified as the clerk,
Reginald Vanner. Sutler returned to the hunt. He failed to
discover any extra new goblets nor could he discover the
whereabouts of the alleged goblet Mortice the buttery clerk
had identified. All he really had were Buckholt's allegations
that a goblet was substituted whilst he was distracted and that
the poisoned goblet his master must have drunk from had
disappeared.'

'The garderobe,' Athelstan spoke up. 'The murderer had
secreted a second goblet. When Buckholt went down stairs to
deal with Vanner, a second goblet was produced. Some of the
posset was poured into it and put aside. The original goblet
was sprinkled with poison and administered to Sir Walter.
Once the old knight had drunk what was needed, the original
goblet was hurled down the privy sinking into the filthy cesspit
beneath that part of the house.'

'Excellent, my little friar. Sutler reasoned the same. He
brought out dung-collectors from Cheapside, the clearers of the

laystalls and dung hills. He also employed masons to open the garderobe and the cesspit beneath.'

'And they found the goblet?'

'They certainly did.'

Cranston was about to continue when Mine Hostess, still flustered and red-faced from her affray with the corpse-bearers, served the piping hot platter of ham, dishes of vegetables, bread and a pot of butter. Cranston ordered two cups of the best Bordeaux. Once the friar had blessed the meal Cranston fell on his food, determined to satisfy a hunger which, according to him, 'still raged like a wolf inside his belly'. They ate in silence. Athelstan could only clear so much of his platter and the coroner devoured the rest. Once he had finished, Cranston leaned back, a cup in one hand and a piece of bread in the other.

'So you can imagine the case, Brother?'

'Yes, I certainly can.' Athelstan used his fingers to emphasize the points. 'Firstly, there is the altercation at the top of the stairs. Buckholt is distracted. Lady Isolda takes the cup. Buckholt finds the diversion was deliberately of no consequence. Secondly, by his testimony, Lady Isolda was the last person to give her husband any drink or food. Thirdly, why was the goblet thrown down the garderobe? The only explanation must be that Isolda wished to get rid of certain evidence and to create a pretence that all was well, hence her drinking from the same cup. Fourthly, the testimony of the buttery clerk that the cups were changed – the only person who could have done that was Lady Isolda. Fifthly, Sutler's discovery that Vanner had bought a new set of goblets. Why did he do that? Why did he only keep one and why was that disguised as part of the old batch? Yes, yes,' Athelstan nodded, 'the case against Lady Isolda was most compelling.'

'Sutler argued the same. Lady Isolda, because of her status, was committed to trial before the King's Bench and a jury of citizens from Westminster hastily assembled. Sutler prosecuted the case before justices Tressilian, Gavelkind and Danyel. Believe me, Brother, three of the harshest and most grim judges, an unholy Trinity who have little love for their fellow men, and women in particular, high-born ladies especially.

They regarded Isolda Beaumont as hawks would a coney. Little mercy was to be expected. The case against her was compelling. She was the last to hold the goblet, the last to feed her husband. Then there was the disappearance of the goblet, the purchase of a new one and the discovery of the old one in the cesspit. On these five issues, Sutler built his case then developed it with further evidence.'

'And Lady Isolda's motive?'

'Freedom, liberty and the opportunity to seize her husband's great wealth, not to mention her involvement with Vanner.'

'Was he indicted?'

'Certainly. Lady Isolda was arrested on a Friday but Vanner abruptly disappeared on the Thursday beforehand. He has been put to the horn with a price on his head, dead or alive. Every skull-cap, outlaw-hunter to you, Brother, in London is searching for him.'

'And Lady Isolda's defence?'

'She was advised by one of the best attorneys this side of Hell, Nicholas Falke. If rumour be true, Master Falke was deeply taken, as most men were, by Lady Isolda, but to no effect. He could protest and argue but both judge and jury thought different.'

'And her maid?'

'Rosamund Clifford, although very loyal to her mistress, appears to have no dealings with her in this matter. I understand she was grievously sick, confined to her bed when Sir Walter was poisoned. She was not called to give evidence by either party.' Cranston sighed noisily. 'In the end Lady Isolda was found guilty by a jury of her peers. I suspect those three justices delighted in passing harsh sentence on her.'

'And the ancient punishment for a wife murdering her husband,' Athelstan murmured, 'is death by burning.'

'*Sine misericordia*,' Cranston agreed, 'without mercy. All three justices insisted no gunpowder pouch be hung around her neck to hasten death. Nor could the Carnifex, the Smithfield executioner, go through the smoke to strangle her or slit her throat.'

'There is more?'

'Oh, yes, my good friend, much more, a veritable maze of

mystery. Lady Isolda was lodged in Newgate for almost a month before her execution. She met death bravely enough. I learnt this from Lady Anne Lesures. Lady Anne is the widow of a former comrade I stood shoulder to shoulder with in France. He used the ransoms gathered there to amass wealth as an apothecary and a spicer. Adam Lesures also served with the Luciferi and returned here with Sir Walter. He died some time ago. Since then Lady Anne has devoted herself to noble causes. She is Abbess of the Order of St Dismas, a secular order which visits the city prisons and ministers to those condemned to die – she and her mute servant, Turgot, who follows her everywhere like Samson does Flaxwith. Anyway, she visited Isolda virtually every day to give her comfort.'

'Did she believe Isolda was innocent?'

'No.' Cranston paused. 'Not really. Lady Anne is shrewd – she keeps her own counsel. I do respect her. Others, however, believe Lady Isolda to be a true innocent, such as Edward Garman, who also served in the Luciferi, a former Hospitaller and now prison chaplain, appointed to Newgate by the Bishop of London. Garman may have shriven Isolda. He certainly accompanied her to execution and always believed she was innocent. Like her lawyer, Falke, he worked desperately to obtain a pardon or some form of commutation but he was crying into the dark. Gaunt was obdurate. No pardon, no mercy.' Cranston turned in his seat and lowered his voice, 'Brother, have you ever heard of "The Book of Fires", or to be more precise, "The Book of Fires attributed to Mark the Greek"?'

'Yes,' Athelstan replied slowly. 'Our library at Blackfriars possesses a few extracts, though not very clear ones. A greatly prized manuscript?'

'It certainly is! That book, together with the writings of the Franciscan Roger Bacon, provides a treasury of information about gunpowder and other such combustibles. Mark the Greek in particular describes what is known as Greek, sea or water fire, supposedly invented centuries ago by Kallinikos of Heliopolis.'

'Sir John,' Athelstan exclaimed, 'you have been very busy!'

'Yes, and I will tell you why. I visited the great library in

Westminster Abbey. Dominus Matthew the archivist was a treasure of information about secret manuscripts.'

'Sir John, what were you pursuing?'

'Beaumont had a copy of "The Book of Fires", which went missing from his chamber either just before or after his death. He had promised to allow Gaunt's chancery clerks to copy it for our noble Regent. We all know why Gaunt would want such information.'

'As would others?'

'Yes, Brother, so we come to Lady Isolda's defence. She maintained she knew nothing about Vanner buying new cups. She could not understand why a goblet was found in the privy and believed it was placed there. She maintained that if her husband was poisoned it could have been administered by Vanner earlier in the day without her knowledge. More significantly, she maintained that her brother-in-law, Sir Henry, or Buckholt, or both, allegedly stole "The Book of Fires", as they were secret adherents of the Great Community of the Realm and its leaders the Upright Men. She depicted Buckholt as a fervent adherent of the rebels, and Sir Henry as a rich merchant eager to appease them.'

'A shrewd move.' Athelstan nodded. 'Gaunt and his henchman, Thibault, Master of Secrets, would be horrified at that.'

'Sutler, however, openly ridiculed such an idea, as well as Lady Isolda's attempt to argue that others, even Vanner, with whom she denied any tryst, could have been involved in her husband's death. He dismissed her allegation that the story of the goblets was merely a pretence to entrap her.'

'She actually argued that?'

'Yes, as she did, time and time again, that Vanner might be the guilty party.'

'Was any explanation offered about Vanner's disappearance or flight? Sir John, Vanner has gone into hiding. That is proof of guilt. But of course,' Athelstan scratched the side of his face, 'Vanner might be guilty but that doesn't prove that Lady Isolda was innocent and, I suppose, Sutler argued the same?' He sipped from his cup. 'Yes, I can see why Sutler's prosecution held firm. He could prove everything: the goblet being handed over; Isolda making her husband drink; the goblets being exchanged; Vanner buying new ones. Did Sutler touch on the relationship between Sir Walter and his lovely young wife?'

'Oh, there were hints but nothing serious. Questions were raised about Sir Walter's stomach ailments. Of course, that's a dangerous path to go down, isn't it, Brother? Sutler could not prove Sir Walter's belly sickness was caused by poison, whilst the intimate relationship between husband and wife is very difficult to judge. Sutler was very careful as Falke argued how there was great tenderness, friendship and cordiality between Sir Walter and his wife. Sutler replied there was no real proof for that. He let the facts speak for themselves. Lady Isolda had a great deal to gain by becoming a very rich widow, whilst the balance of proof that she murdered her husband indicates a deep malevolence, at least on her part, towards Sir Walter. If Vanner was seized and questioned, perhaps he could have helped Isolda's case. But let's say he has fled, Brother, and is deep in hiding; surely a trained clerk such as he would have done something to help his former lover – a letter to the justices or the sheriff?'

'And "The Book of Fires", Sir John?'

'Cannot be found, and Gaunt wants us to find it. I can understand why. Greek fire is highly dangerous – even when thrown on water it will still ignite. Dominus Matthew at Westminster cites authorities such as Leo the Isaurian on its power. Now the classic use of Greek fire is to hurl small pots against an enemy followed by a flame. Swift and sudden destruction ensues. Sometimes Greek fire can be shot from long tubes like a stone from a cannon. Water only makes it worse. They recommend the use of sand, vinegar or human urine to extinguish it. Now,' Cranston sipped from his goblet, 'Isolda Beaumont died in the flames at Smithfield. About three weeks later, on the Feast of Saints Perpetua and Felicitas, Richard Sutler was making his way down to his chambers at Westminster. Halfway along an alleyway, according to not the best of witnesses, he was attacked. A pot of liquid was thrown over him, followed by a candle flame. He was soaked and the fire seemed to shoot up from the very ground. He was turned into a living firebrand. All that was left was a blackened, twisted monstrosity. Later the same morning, Justice Tressilian was easing himself in a cubiculum in the latrines of a tavern close to Westminster Hall. Perched on the close stool, his hose about his ankles, he too was attacked. Fire-bearing liquid was poured under the door, soaking his boots and hose. A candle flame was thrown in. Tressilian did what we would all do. He leapt to his feet, beating at the flames and, of course, soaking himself even further in that dangerous liquid. He was burnt to death. This morning, I was supposed to meet Justice Gavelkind in Parsnip Lane. The justice left his house. A cowled figure swiftly approached. What looked like the contents of a small pot were thrown over the justice, a flame was hurled and, within a few heartbeats, Gavelkind became a tongue of fire.'

'And his assailant?'

'Shielded by the inferno he created, he fled whilst Gavelkind was reduced to blackened flesh.'

'So Gaunt has turned to you?'

'And to you, Brother, I am afraid.'

'It would seem,' Athelstan declared, 'as if someone, perhaps Vanner the fugitive, is punishing by fire all those who destroyed Lady Isolda in a similar way. Acts of cold, horrid revenge. I would also suggest they are using information which might originate from that rare manuscript, Mark the Greek's "The Book of Fires". Sir John, from what you know, how difficult would it be to collect all the elements for this fire?'

'Oh, very easy, Brother. Greek fire, or something similar to it, has been used for centuries. I could go out tomorrow and buy sulphur, pitch, resin, bitumen, saltpetre and quicklime. The secret probably lies in the actual composition. What are the best quantities to use, perhaps there is one element that is special? Once the liquid is ready, very similar to a potion mixed by a physician or apothecary, it's poured into a small capped pot and can be carried in a sack, bag or satchel. The pot is dropped, mix it with flame and you have a raging inferno difficult to control or extinguish.'

'So, Sir John, when and where do we begin?'

'Soon,' the coroner smiled enigmatically, 'and we will begin here, Brother. But let's leave that for a while. Whilst hurrying about the city I received your stark message about a miracle at St Erconwald's. What's happened? Is Pike now a devoted man of prayer? Has Watkin vowed never to touch ale?'

'Seriously, Sir John, listen now.' And the friar described in short, pithy sentences all the details of the Great Miracle. Once he'd finished, Cranston whistled under his breath.

'I heard the rumours, Brother. Muckworm and Tiptoft met me in Cheapside. They are this city's best source for all news and scandal. They were full of it. Do you believe it, Brother?' Cranston gestured at the tavern door. 'This city swarms with cranks, conjurors, counterfeit men, the whole canting crew of priggers, prancers and poncers. Certain magicians in Whitefriars are masters of the art of changing and transformation. They could turn both of us into lepers to confuse and confound the most skilled physician. However,' Cranston paused, 'it's another matter to hide gruesome wounds, burns which have stripped the skin and marbled the flesh.' The coroner blew his cheeks out. 'I would say it's nigh impossible.'

'Fulchard of Richmond appears to be genuine, Sir John. I recognize him as the same man I met when the vigil commenced. I have inspected his warrants, letters and licences. I have talked to those around him in the nave. I have established that he did not leave the church during the night.'

'And now, little friar?'

'In such cases the Bishop's curia takes over. Master Tuddenham, the Archdeacon's court together with a cohort of scribes, clerks and even physician Philippe have assembled in my house. I issued strict instructions to the parish council. Tuddenham and his retinue will stay in St Erconwald's until the day after tomorrow. The Piebald is packed to overflowing, especially as Master Fulchard is staying there. So, Sir John, I will be looking for fresh lodgings tonight.'

Cranston sat smiling to himself.

'Sir John?'

'I think I might be able to help.' Cranston paused as the tavern door opened and a youngish man, slim and well proportioned, approached the window seat, pulling back his hood to reveal a rubicund, cheerful face under thinning sandy hair.

Athelstan noticed how the well-spaced eyes were expressive even as his lips moved soundlessly. He shook Cranston's outstretched hand and turned smilingly to clasp Athelstan's. He then stepped back, indicating with signs that they follow him.

'Good evening, Master Turgot. Brother Athelstan, may I introduce Lady Anne Lesures' faithful henchman, who since birth has been a mute but has probably uttered more wisdom than a host of well-tongued scholars. We are to follow him. Lady Anne and the rest have assembled, so it's time to settle our bill and be gone . . .'

PART TWO

*'If you smear it then let it dry, it burns as soon as a
spark falls on it and cannot be doused.'*
Mark the Greek's 'The Book of Fires'

On the south side of the Thames, though well beyond
London Bridge, stretched a wasteland, marshy and
treacherous. Even in the full light of day this moor-
land of coarse grass, wild straggling bushes and twisted, stunted
trees did not lose its air of dank threatening menace. A haunt
of ghosts, the dwelling place of earthbound malevolent spirits,
or so the local peasants gossiped. Its sense of dread was deepened by those who prowled the heathland: smugglers, outlaws,
river pirates, as well as the warlocks and wizards who sheltered
in the grass-filled dells to perform their own macabre rites.
Successive sheriffs had vainly tried to exorcize the evil aura
of such a place by sweeping it with mounted archers and
erecting soaring gallows against the sky, four-branched scaf-
folds, each decorated by a rotting corpse, all to no avail. One
outlaw gang led by a defrocked priest who rejoiced in the
name of Friar Foxtail now ruled the heathland, though only
with the permission of the Upright Men, whose Earthworms
also patrolled that sombre place. On that particular evening,
long after the bells had marked the last verses of the 'Salve
Regina', the curfew being tolled and beacon-fires lit in steeples,
Friar Foxtail had been given strict instructions about what to
do. He was to clear the heath of all trespassers and build a
fire close to the Devil's Stump, a massive, ancient oak split
by lightning during a fearsome storm. He was to leave, close
to the fire, a freshly skinned coney basted with oil and herbs,
as well as a wineskin and a few drinking cups. On no account,
Friar Foxtail was warned, should he or anyone else approach
the solitary stranger who entered the wasteland. This stranger
would come hooded, masked and carrying a lanthorn. Friar

Foxtail accepted that he had no choice in the matter; instead, he and his coven had decided to leave the heathland and plunder newly built warehouses further along the riverside. As the Upright Men had predicted, the stranger appeared, drawn on by the flare of the campfire. At one point he paused, crouched and only rose at three piercing whistle calls from the Upright Men grouped around the fire. Eventually he walked forward. The Upright Men, faces hidden behind masks carved in the form of different birds, just sat staring at the stranger who squatted down opposite.

'Welcome.' The Raven, Captain of the Upright Men, leaned forward. 'Welcome, Brother. You have heard the news from the city? Well,' he laughed throatily, 'of course you have. The assassin, now called the "Ignifer", the Fire Bringer, has appeared. Three royal officials burnt to death. Whatever the killer's reason we welcome such slaughter. Sutler has seen to the hanging of some of our comrades, whilst the justices relish their harsh and cruel sentences against the Sons of the Soil.' He paused. 'Eat, drink! Please do. You are our honoured guest.' Another Upright Man scurried forward, knife flashing in the firelight. He cut strips from the coney and put these on an earthenware platter along with a deep bowled cup of rich red wine. The stranger ate swiftly, as did the Upright Men. Once they were finished, the Raven, wiping his fingers on his jerkin, leaned forward again.

'Please accept our condolences on your sad loss.' His guest nodded. 'You received,' the Raven continued, 'the same information we did?'

'Yes. Where did you get it?' the stranger asked. 'That was always regarded as a great secret.'

'It still is.' The Raven laughed. 'But not to us. More importantly, did you understand it?'

'Yes.'

'And did you make it?'

'I have brought some. I will show you.' The stranger rose. 'You must come with me,' he insisted. 'Stand well away from the fire and bring everything you have.' The Upright Men obeyed. Rising to their feet, they followed the stranger into the dark. He leaned down and picked up an earthenware pot where he had left it on his approach. The pot was no bigger than the palm of his hand. The stranger unstoppered the lid then, like a child playing skittles, weighed the pot in his hand as if it was a ball, gauging the distance between himself and the now dying fire. The Earthworms watched intently. Satisfied, the stranger hurled the pot. It shattered against the smouldering embers and the campfire surged up with a roar as fierce as any furnace. The Upright Men clapped their hands exclaiming in surprise.

'We have our fire!' the Raven exclaimed. 'Fire from heaven or, as Gaunt will experience, fire from Hell . . .'

oOoOo

Cranston and Athelstan, huddled in their cloaks, followed Turgot, his face and head hidden by a deep capuchin, out of the Holy Lamb and along Cheapside turning into Poultry, the richest trading area of the city. Its name was ancient but its purpose had changed. No longer were ducks and capons up for sale; Poultry had become the heart of London's wealth. The day's trading was finished. Merchants were now clearing stalls and boarding up shop fronts. Bailiffs and hired mercenaries, drawn blades glittering in the dancing torchlight, patrolled the streets vigilant for any felon lurking in the shadows. Such a close guard was necessary. The goods being stored away were costly cloths from Douai, Bruges, Ypres and elsewhere. There were silks from Lucca, linen and flax from Flanders and wool from the Midlands. Even in the fading light the red, vermilion, rose and scarlet cloths shimmered invitingly. The air was rich with the smell of pepper, saffron and salt, sugar from Syria and the purest wax from Morocco. Barrels of cinnamon were being sealed, a precious spice imported from beyond Outremer, whilst the fragrance of cassia reminded Athelstan how the trees which carried it were allegedly guarded by ferocious winged animals. The friar could only marvel at the wealth being taken out, heaped and checked before being moved to the great arca, or strong boxes, deep in the cellars of the palatial houses either side of Poultry. These were gilded mansions boasting highly decorated and embossed gables,

gleaming plaster and, in many cases, windows of the purest
glass. Athelstan glimpsed a pile of rubies, lapis lazuli,
diamonds, pearls and ivory rings all gathered in the dish of a
set of scales guarded by two mercenaries with weapons
bristling. Cranston and Athelstan were inspected but never
troubled. They turned into Old Jewry, dominated by the dark
mass of St Olave's Church. The houses here were truly magnifi-
cent, four storeys high and divided from each other by an alley
either side. Turgot stopped at a door and knocked. A servant
opened it, introduced himself as Picquart the steward and
beckoned them into a stone-paved entrance hall.

The house was comfortably warm. Candles glowed in
spigots fastened above linen panelling, whilst soft rope-matting
washed in herbs and spices covered the floor. On the left, a
half-open door revealed a rich furnished chamber, an arras
hanging on the wall and finely polished oak furniture, tables,
chairs, chests and cushioned stools. They passed a great open
kitchen where servants scurried about. A yawning hearth built
into the wall dividing it from the hall gave off gusts of sweet
warmth. Picquart led them into the solar, where others were
waiting seated around an oval table which glittered in the light
of a myriad candles placed along the rims of three lowered
Catherine wheels. The hall was furnished with gleaming dark
oak panelling but the lights, the candelabra and the flames
from the roaring fire in the bell-like hearth made it a place of
merry cheer and relaxing comfort. A woman rose from the
top of the table and walked gracefully towards them. She was
dressed like a Cistercian nun in a light-grey gown and veil:
her patrician face, framed by a starched white wimple, emphasized the authority of her commanding dark eyes, and her nose
was sharp above a firm mouth and chin. Athelstan reckoned
she was a woman past her fortieth summer.

'Good evening,' she murmured. 'Welcome to my house. I
am Lady Anne Lesures.' She smiled at Athelstan and winked
quickly at Cranston. She then clasped the friar's hand and
bowed her head for his blessing. Athelstan delivered this
and was almost knocked aside by Sir John as he scooped Lady
Anne up in his arms, half raising her to kiss her lips and
forehead before lowering her gently down.

'Oh, if I was a bachelor!' Cranston breathed. 'Lady Anne, it is so good to see you. Come.' They exchanged the full kiss of peace followed by Cranston's spate of questions which Lady Anne, her face beaming with pleasure, said she would answer some other time as they had to meet the others. She led the coroner and friar around the table. Each of her guests rose, scraping back their chairs to clasp hands and receive Athelstan's hasty blessing. The first was Sir Henry Beaumont, the late Sir Walter's brother: he was fat-faced and rather corpulent, his thinning hair combed forward to cover a balding pate. Sir Henry was dressed in a costly blood-red jerkin with hose to match; his cambric shirt was snow-white, the collar open. Athelstan glimpsed the precious bejewelled crucifix on its silver chain. Sir Henry struck the friar as most eager to please, highly nervous and rather apprehensive. Rohesia, Sir Henry's wife, was pretty in a severe sort of way: auburn haired, eyes constantly narrowed, head slightly tilted back, lower lip jutting out as if judging all who came under her scrutiny. She was dressed rather soberly in a brown veil and an old-fashioned gown of the same hue with white bands at the cuff and neck. Edward Garman, prison chaplain of Newgate, was of medium stature; bald, his clean-shaven, oval face burnt a deep brown by the sun of Outremer. He was light and swift in movement; his large eyes looked troubled, his fleshy lower lip slightly quivering as if he was preparing to protest. Garman was dressed simply in a mud-coloured robe, stout sandals on his feet, a set of small Ave beads circling his left wrist, a white-rolled cincture around his waist. Nicholas Falke the lawyer was blond-haired and earnest-faced; his small eyes screwed up against the light, a snub nose above rather pretty, womanish lips which constantly twitched. Falke was dressed in a dark-blue jerkin and hose, the high stiffened collar of his undershirt jutting up just under his chin. Buckholt, Sir Walter's steward, looked what he was: the stolid, stout, reliable house retainer who let nothing pass him by. He was square-faced with a strong mouth and jaw of a stubborn man, an impression heightened by deep-set, guarded eyes. He dressed demurely in a long old-fashioned *houppelande* which fell beneath the knees of his dark woollen hose. Rosamund Clifford, now apparently

Lady Rohesia's personal maid, was garbed in a Lincoln-green gown, her dark hair hidden by a tightly clamped veil. She was petite and pretty with ever-darting eyes and puckered lips. Athelstan could not decide whether she was fey-witted or just acting the part.

Once the introductions were finished, chilled white wine and small bowls of marzipan were served to each guest. Cranston sat at the head of the table with Lady Anne on his right and Athelstan on his left. The friar immediately laid out his writing implements as the coroner, who had eaten all his sweetmeats, now turned on the friar's. Athelstan leaned closer and whispered on the whereabouts of the miraculous wineskin.

'Left it at the Guildhall,' Cranston murmured, 'silly fool, but I know my precious is waiting for me there.'

'Sir John,' Falke intoned as if ready to plead, 'we have come, we have waited and we still wait.'

'Was she innocent?' Cranston barked, his voice ringing through the solar. 'I repeat, was Lady Isolda innocent of murder? Let me assure you, someone certainly believes that. You must have heard about an assassin, the common tongue now calls him the Ignifer – the Fire Bringer. He has thrown what I suppose is Greek fire over two judges as well as the prosecutor who sent Lady Isolda to the stake. They died as horribly as she did. In my view, the Ignifer believes he is carrying out well-plotted vengeance for the gruesome death of an innocent victim.' Cranston jabbed a finger at Falke. 'That is why we are here. I asked Lady Anne to be our hostess, to gather all those who were involved in the prosecution of Lady Isolda to this meeting.'

'Are we all in danger?' Lady Rohesia snapped. 'Are we all to be turned into living tongues of flame? Surely this Ignifer can be caught?'

'You may not be marked down.' Buckholt's voice carried sombrely. 'But I certainly am. You asked a question, Sir John. Was Lady Isolda innocent? She was not. I know what I saw. She was the last to feed her husband that tainted posset. The goblet she used was discarded. She hid it and replaced it with another.' Buckholt stared around. 'In God's name, what more can I say but what I have sworn on oath?'

'Yet we don't really know,' Falke cried, 'that Sir Walter was poisoned. We have nothing but the opinion of a physician.'

'We also have further evidence,' Cranston retorted. 'Firstly, there is the goblet that Reginald Vanner specially bought. Secondly, Vanner diverted Buckholt, who is so distracted he hands the posset to Lady Isolda, who takes it to her husband and makes him drink. Thirdly, she apparently gave Buckholt a different goblet in return. Fourthly, the goblet Buckholt first brought from the buttery ended up in the cesspit, and apparently such a change took place in a very short time. Sutler simply argued how the posset was poured into a second goblet, which was poisoned, fed to Sir Walter and later discarded.'

'There, Master Falke,' Athelstan declared softly, 'Sir John describes a grim logic of events with a life of their own and what can be said in reply?'

'Vanner,' Falke retorted, 'he has fled or has he not, Sir Henry?'

'Yes, yes.' The merchant knight couldn't disguise the slur in his voice. 'So it would appear.'

'Lady Isolda,' Falke declared, lips twitching, 'swore how Sir Walter told her Vanner had fed him a strange-tasting wine earlier in the day. Some poisons take time for their malignancy to become apparent. That's possible, isn't it?' He turned and gestured at Buckholt.

'Of course,' the steward replied, 'anything is possible, but Sir Walter suffered no ill effects.'

'Parson Garman also visited him early in the morning and brought the usual figs in almond sauce,' Falke declared. 'My point is others offered Sir Walter food and drink.'

'Is that true?' Athelstan asked. 'Parson Garman, you knew Beaumont of old? You served in his free company of the Luciferi? Yes?'

Garman nodded.

'These figs in their almond sauce?' Cranston asked.

'A true delicacy.' Garman replied quietly. 'Sir Walter, when he served in Outremer, could not resist them. I bought them as a reminder, a comfort.'

'Did he eat them?' Athelstan interjected. 'Sir Walter, I understand, had a delicate stomach?'

'I brought them.' Garman shrugged. 'I left them. What happened to them afterwards I cannot say.'

'Sir Henry?' Cranston turned to the merchant knight. He pulled a face and gestured at Buckholt.

'They disappeared,' the steward declared. 'I never saw them. Sir Walter may have eaten them. He certainly was particular to that delicacy. He may have given them away. Or,' he smiled thinly, 'they too may have been thrown down the garderobe.'

'Apart from the past and his love for figs in an almond sauce,' Athelstan nodded at Garman, 'was there any other reason for your visit to Sir Walter?'

'Of course there was, Brother,' Lady Anne retorted, 'I visited Sir Walter to beg for alms for my good causes. Parson Garman did the same.'

'I seek aid from many people,' the prison chaplain declared.

'And was Sir Walter generous?'

'Sometimes, like all wealthy men, shrewdness was more important than charity.' Garman half smiled at the hiss from Sir Henry.

'And the pewter goblets,' Athelstan asked Falke, 'the one Vanner bought and the other found at the bottom of the garderobe? What was Isolda's response?'

'She had no knowledge about any of that,' Falke replied. 'She only used the one brought by Buckholt. She maintained that the goblet found in the garderobe might have been accidently dropped there by Sir Walter himself.' Falke ignored Buckholt's sharp laugh. 'Sir Walter did like his posset. It wasn't unknown for him to carry a goblet into the garderobe to sip as he eased himself.'

'And the goblet Vanner bought?'

'Lady Isolda maintained he probably did it on Sir Walter's order,' Falke answered. 'That would be logical. A goblet was lost and its owner asked his clerk to replace it.'

'Nonsense!' Buckholt sneered. 'Firstly, why did Vanner buy twelve and get rid of the other eleven? I wager they lie somewhere in the gardens of Firecrest Manor, probably at the bottom of the mere. Sutler made the same point in court.'

'And secondly?' Athelstan asked.

'Again,' Buckholt retorted, 'I pointed out in court that the purchase of cups, goblets and platters was not Vanner's responsibility but either mine or the buttery clerk, Mortice.'

Falke shrugged and lapsed into silence.

'And what else can be said in Lady Isolda's defence?' Athelstan asked.

'She was innocent.' Garman, hands down on the tabletop, head bowed as if praying, abruptly sat up. 'I shrived her. I cannot say what Isolda actually confessed but she loved her husband, yes?' No one gainsaid him. 'No acrimony or argument before his mysterious death, yes? Sir Henry, you were his brother. I speak the truth?'

'Yes, yes, you do.' Sir Henry blinked. 'Sir John, Brother Athelstan, we were not truly part of this. The Lady Isolda was gracious enough. True.' He half smiled. 'There appeared to be no hostility between herself and my late brother. Yet I sensed an unhappiness, perhaps a disappointment.' He shrugged. 'But that's common enough in a May–December marriage.'

'You talk of unhappiness?'

'Brother, that is just suspicion. I don't have a shred of proof.'

'And now you are Sir Walter's heir?'

'Yes, I am. My brother died without begetting a child and,' Sir Henry waved a hand, 'Lady Isolda has gone to God.'

'I believe they were happy enough.' Garman was determined in his defence. 'Lady Isolda declared herself innocent. I prayed with her, as did you, Lady Anne. She was particularly devoted to St Joachim, the father of the Virgin Mary.'

'Yes, yes, she was.' Lady Anne sighed. 'I visited her very day. Well, at least until just before the end. Sir Jack, Brother Athelstan,' she beat her fingers against the tabletop, 'I am a widow, childless.' She glanced over her shoulder at Turgot standing like a shadow close behind her. 'Except for Turgot here, an orphan, a foundling, the son I never had,' she turned back, smiling, 'a graduate of the chapel school at Westminster no less, a true scholar, Brother Athelstan. Now,' her smile faded, 'my husband died a most wealthy man.' Again she glanced over her shoulder at Turgot. 'I have my household and my work. I am the Abbess of St Dismas, a lay organization,

men and women like myself, who visit our filthy prisons,'
her voice turned harsh, 'at the Fleet, Marshalsea and
Newgate, even that pit of Hell, the Bocardo in Southwark.
Now, as regards this matter. I felt a double duty towards
Lady Isolda.'

'Why?' Athelstan asked.

'First, she was a noble woman . . .'

'Of noble birth?' Cranston asked.

'I am coming to that, Jack.' She smiled faintly. 'Isolda
was a noble woman, condemned to a gruesome death.
Execution by burning is truly horrific. However, let me return
to the beginning. As some of you know, I was instrumental
in Isolda meeting Sir Walter.' She sipped delicately at her
wine and pinched Cranston's hand playfully. 'Jack, don't go
to sleep on me! Now,' she continued, 'the abbey of St Mary
and St Francis just south of St Botolph's houses Franciscan
nuns commonly called the Minoresses. One of their great
services is that they take in foundlings, baby girls either
abandoned by their mothers, Lord save them, or handed over
to the good sisters,' she shrugged, 'to avoid scandal. God's
work.' She paused. 'Many a girl child is saved from a miscar-
riage, planned or otherwise. Isolda was one of these, a mere
babe in arms, or so I understand, when she was left in the
manger before the statue of the Virgin just outside the nunnery.
The Minoresses provide an excellent school. Isolda attended
it, following the rule of a novice. As for me, I am also a
member of the Guild of St Martha. I and other ladies of
noble birth take these young women under our wing. Isolda
was one such: a maiden learned, schooled, of courtly manner
and good repute.' She smiled sadly. 'Isolda, as many of you
know, was truly beautiful. Now, the Guild would invite these
young novices, suitably attired, to attend *convivial* – festivities and banquets, particularly at Westminster. Our set purpose
was to introduce these young ladies to bachelors of good
name and standing. In such company, supervised by the
Guild, only men with honest intentions and of the proper
status can approach our young ladies. Sir Walter was taken
with Isolda and, to cut a long story short, love ran its course.
They became betrothed, hand-fast at the door of St Michael

and All Angels. That was five years ago. I thought all things were well until her arrest, and I walked into that cell at Newgate.'

'You talked to her?' Athelstan asked.

'We talked, we prayed. Sometimes I would take needlecraft with me and encourage her to help.'

'Did she talk about her crime?'

'No, Brother, we are very strict on that. We are there to pray, comfort and offer spiritual guidance,' Lady Anne fluttered her long, white bejewelled fingers, 'and, to be honest, to distract. I brought her news from the city, of the fighting in the Narrow Seas. Understandably,' Lady Anne sighed, 'our rules were broken. Isolda hotly protested her innocence. I tried to lead her back to some other matter, then,' she nodded at Garman, 'it happened.'

'Father?' Cranston asked.

'Two days before her execution,' the chaplain declared, 'I came to visit Lady Isolda. Due to her wealth and status she was able to rent a prison chamber.' He paused, wrinkling his nose. Athelstan sensed the chaplain was trying to hide his contempt for the rich; just the tone of his voice, the flick of his eyes, that slight thrill to his face and voice. He was a secretive man, Athelstan concluded, who hid his feelings well. The friar recalled gossip he had heard in his own parish – how Garman had close ties with the Upright Men and the Great Community of the Realm.

'Anyway,' the chaplain ran a finger around the rim of his goblet, 'I heard Isolda screaming. When the turnkey admitted me, I found Lady Anne huddled close to the door.'

'Very frightened, I admit.'

'And the cause of this quarrel?' Athelstan asked.

'Once again, Isolda tried to protest her innocence. She realized there would be no pardon, that she faced a horrid death. I made the mistake of telling her that I understood but of course I didn't. Isolda grew very angry, screaming that I understood nothing. That I was to blame for her meeting Sir Walter. That she would not have married him if were not for me.' Lady Anne dabbed at her eyes. Behind her Turgot grew restless and moved forward but she glanced over her shoulder and he stepped back. 'I left her a set of Ave beads. I understand she threw them away.'

'That reminds me.' Garman pushed back his chair, opened his wallet and handed Lady Anne an Ave ring, but the chain was snapped and most of the beads missing. 'I picked this up from the floor after you left.' He handed it over.

'That was the last time I saw Isolda,' Lady Anne whispered. 'I didn't attend her death. I couldn't.'

'Who visited her in the condemned cell?' Cranston asked.

'I'm afraid only three people,' Garman replied, 'Master Falke, Lady Anne and me.'

'We did not think it was appropriate,' Lord Henry spoke up. 'None of the household wanted to. Rosamund was still ill.'

'And who attended her execution?' Athelstan asked.

Garman slightly raised his hand. 'It is my duty,' he murmured, 'one of the most hateful parts. I sat in the execution cart opposite her reciting the Dirige psalms.'

'And Isolda?'

'Brother, it was if all life had been crushed in her. She just sat listless.'

'Had she received any potion?'

'No.' Garman shook his head. 'Keeper Tweng was under strict orders from the Regent on the day before her execution – anything she ate or drank had to be tested. I recall doing so myself on more than one occasion. Isolda, understandably, had little appetite for food or drink.'

'And at Smithfield?' Athelstan asked, aware of the silence. Everyone in this chamber recognized the sheer blasphemy of a public burning: the screams, the stench, the noise of the crowd and all the gruesome paraphernalia which festooned such a death.

'Isolda was carried in dead-faint to the execution stake.' Garman's voice was hardly above a whisper. 'She was bound to the pillar. The Carnifex fired the straw and the smoke plumed up.'

'And the Carnifex showed her no mercy?'

'None,' Garman agreed. 'He was forbidden to go through the smoke to deliver a swift death.' Garman crossed himself.

'Isolda was very beautiful. Such a soul could not be capable of murder. She confessed her innocence to me and I believed her.'

'And your mistress?' Athelstan smiled at Rosamund, who turned in her chair, doe eyes blinking furiously.

She gestured at Lady Rohesia. 'On the same day that Lady Isolda allegedly murdered her husband, I was discommoded, confined to my chamber with a severe bout of the sweating sickness. Ask anyone . . .'

'That's true,' Buckholt declared kindly. 'The poor girl became as wet as anything, the sweat fair shimmering on her.'

'Did you believe in your mistress' innocence?' Athelstan persisted.

'Father, I . . .' she stammered, 'I was surprised, shocked. I was ill. I couldn't visit her in prison.'

'Poor girl,' Lady Anne intervened. 'It was I who visited her. She was only strong enough for a walk in the garden.'

'Continue.' Athelstan turned back to Rosamund.

'Brother, what happened to my master and mistress was tragic. All I could recall were the warnings.'

'What warnings!' Athelstan and Cranston spoke together.

'About a year ago,' Sir Henry replied, 'yes, Buckholt?'

The steward nodded.

'Sir Walter received messages, scraps of parchment thrust into the hands of servants entering the manor or left outside the porter's lodge.'

'How many?'

'At least six.'

'And the message?'

'"As I and ours did burn,"' Sir Henry replied, '"so shall ye and yours." The writing was scrawled, the parchment dirty and wrinkled.'

'Who would threaten Sir Walter like that and why?' Cranston asked.

'Sir John, my brother, did not know, and neither did I. The messages stopped as abruptly as they began.'

'And "The Book of Fires" by Mark the Greek?' Athelstan stared across at Lady Anne, now lost in her own sad thoughts.

'"The Book of Fires,"' Sir Henry's voice fell to a whisper,

'is a great secret. They say it is passed on from one Emperor of Constantinople to another . . .'

'I know its history,' Athelstan interjected, 'as I know your brother owned a copy. It's now gone, so where was it kept?'

'In a bound leather casket in his bedchamber, the key always around his neck, or so we were led to believe.' Sir Henry rubbed his face. 'On the morning Walter was found dead, the key was still there and the casket locked. However, when I opened it, the book was gone. Who stole it, how and when?' Sir Henry shook his head. 'No one knows.'

'What did it look like?'

'I saw it many years ago, just after my brother returned from Outremer. Small yet thick, tightly bound in an embossed calf-skin cover. Only my brother knew its contents.'

Athelstan stared around the chamber. This is a desert of emotions, he thought. Lady Isolda is gone and everyone seems to want to bury her memory deep. It was understandable: Sir Henry and his wife were prosperous merchants. Falke had lost his case and could do nothing. Buckholt had been vindicated. Parson Garman and Lady Anne had performed their duties as diligently as they could. Rosamund seemed lost in her own world. Nevertheless, Isolda's execution had left a devastating legacy.

'The Ignifer!' Athelstan exclaimed. 'The assassin who has murdered three people and who could kill and kill again.'

The assembled guests moved in their seats, hands going out to their goblets or the sweetmeats, anything to distract their nervousness.

'Sir John, Brother Athelstan,' Falke declared, 'we sit here and talk about Lady Isolda but Reginald Vanner should be your real quarry.' The lawyer, face all determined, leaned forward, ticking the points off on his fingers. 'Firstly, Vanner could have been involved in Sir Walter's murder. Secondly, Vanner was Sir Walter's clerk. He had access to "The Book of Fires". Thirdly, he must know something about Greek fire. Fourthly, he has disappeared. Fifthly, he has a motive. He is now a proclaimed outlaw, a wolfshead to be killed on sight. Consequently he has nothing to lose in waging war against those who were responsible for the death of a woman who might have been his lover.'

'I would agree,' Sir Henry murmured. 'Vanner could be the Ignifer.'

'Sir Henry,' Athelstan asked, 'how easy is it to make Greek fire?'

'Not too difficult,' Sir Henry declared. 'There are different types, ranging from,' he spread his hands, 'simple kitchen oil to a substance which is quite unique. "The Book of Fires", I suppose, would describe all these categories and list the correct proportions and right elements for each.'

'Sir John,' Lady Anne spoke up, 'Jack, my friend, I am tired. Surely you have finished here?'

Cranston looked at Athelstan and nodded.

'In which case, Sir Henry,' the coroner stretched, 'I would ask you a great favour: lodgings for Brother Athelstan and me at Firecrest Manor. At the moment St Erconwald's is rather busy.'

'I heard,' Lady Anne exclaimed. 'Some story about a miracle? I must visit your parish.'

'The Bishop of London's people are there,' Athelstan answered, staring down at the tabletop. Cranston's request had taken him by surprise, though he swiftly conceded the wisdom of it. Tuddenham and the parish council would keep the miracle-seekers at bay, whilst a visit to Firecrest Manor might prove useful.

'As for myself, of course,' Cranston pushed back his chair, 'at the moment I am living like a bachelor, so fresh lodgings . . .'

'Of course,' Sir Henry declared, getting to his feet. 'Sir John, Brother Athelstan, we shall be pleased to escort you there.'

'I will do that,' Lady Anne intervened, grasping Cranston's arm. 'I need to have a few words with my old friend Jack and discover more about the miracle at St Erconwald's.'

The meeting broke up. Sir Henry assured Cranston and Athelstan that two comfortable chambers would be ready and both of them would be his honoured guests. Chaplain Garman wandered over to invite Athelstan into his chapel at Newgate. Rosamund Clifford sat lost in her own thoughts until Lady Rohesia called her away. Cranston became deep in conversation with Lady Anne, so Athelstan crossed to study the paintings hanging on the walls above the linen panelling. He found them fascinating. The paintings, from the new schools in northern Italy, were held in gold-scrolled frames and glowed brilliantly both in colour and depiction. Athelstan noticed how Lady Anne had a special devotion to her holy namesake St Anne, mother of the Virgin Mary. At least four of the paintings celebrated this holy relationship, with others describing events from the Virgin Mary's youth. Now and again the artist had scrolled the tribute in the corner of the painting, '*Sicut mater, sicut filia*' – 'As the mother, so the daughter.'

'My patron saint.'

Athelstan turned. Lady Anne stood smiling at him, behind her the ever faithful Turgot.

'I think Sir John wishes to go,' she added.

Cloaks were collected and, with a hired torch-bearer going ahead of them, Lady Anne led Cranston and Athelstan out into the cold, bleak street. All trading was now done. The call of the bellman could be clearly heard. Lanthorns glowed from the doorposts of the houses casting pools of light around which the shadows danced. Rats squeaked – black darting shapes followed by the blurred outline of hunting cats. Dogs howled up at the full winter moon. Here and there from some cranny or corner a beggar, licensed to plead in that part of the city, shook his clacking bowl for alms. Cranston drew his sword as Lady Anne led them briskly on.

'Don't worry,' she called over her shoulder, 'Turgot will be our guard.' Athelstan turned and glimpsed a cowled figure with a drawn blade of a sword glinting like a flame of warning. A soothsayer shuffled out of the dark, asking if they wished their fortune described, only to scuttle away as Cranston bawled at him to 'Go back to the Halls of Hell!' Once they had cleared the street Lady Anne stopped. Further back their escort also paused whilst Lady Anne shooed the torch-bearer out of earshot. She beckoned Athelstan and Cranston closer and pulled down her muffler. 'I did not wish to appear vindictive, harsh of tongue or hard of heart, but Lady Isolda was a veritable virago, beautiful with blonde hair and lustrous blue eyes. She was a most attractive lady: in her soul, however, she was selfish, spoilt and arrogant.'

'And capable of murder?' Athelstan asked.

'Yes,' Lady Anne nodded, 'yes, Isolda was capable of murder. I believe she killed her husband for no other reason than she had grown tired of him. She would have used Vanner for her own evil, selfish purposes.' Lady Anne crossed herself. 'She would have escaped justice if not for that sharp-eyed buttery clerk Buckholt's suspicions and Sutler's logic and persistence. Lady Isolda was a murderess and one who could – and did – dupe the likes of Falke, Garman and Sir Henry.'

'Why do you tell us this now?' Athelstan asked.

'Because it is the truth and because I believe Vanner was just as wicked. He may well be the Ignifer – but come, Sir Henry will be waiting.'

They entered an area well known to Athelstan as it lay close to his mother house at Blackfriars. Athelstan, lost in his own thoughts about what he had seen and heard, was faintly aware of the noises of the night. He heard a sound and glanced up. A cloaked figure had stepped out of an alleyway. At first, Athelstan thought he was dreaming. The figure seemed to swoop towards them then hurled something which smashed at the feet of the torch-bearer. For a few breaths nothing happened until the flame of the lowered torch dipped towards the liquid lapping around its holder's boots and the ground erupted, a fierce fire which sped up the torch-bearer's body, leaping to devour him. The torch-bearer, screaming in agony, fell to his knees, which only made matters worse. The raging fire also screened their attacker, who disappeared as Cranston took off his cloak and tried to beat out the flames. Athelstan hastened to help. Lady Anne raised the hue and cry with screams of 'Harrow! Harrow!' Doors and shutters flew open. People in their nightshirts hurried out. The silence of the night was brutally shattered with screams and shouts. People bustled out then crept back at the horror blazing in their street. Turgot came running up waving his hands at his mistress to keep away. Cranston was trying to beat the flames but the fiery pool of liquid was trickling closer. Athelstan leapt forward and dragged the coroner away.

'Stay back, Sir John, for God's sake,' he exclaimed, 'there is nothing to be done!'

Athelstan could only stand terror-stricken at this heinous murder of a truly innocent man. The fire was now dying, its victim a twisted, blackened corpse over which the flames ran like deadly caresses, as if seeking any part not yet burnt. Bailiffs and wardsmen arrived. An enterprising merchant brought out a canvas sheet soaked in bitter, pungent vinegar, as well as a tun of sand. Both were used to douse the flames and cover the puddle which had caused it. Athelstan knelt on the ground. He felt his knee scrape something sharp. He moved back, picked up a shard of the broken pot and sniffed at the glistening, odourless oil. He rubbed it between his fingers and felt how thick the substance was. He dropped it, then closed his eyes and intoned the prayers for the dead. A deep revulsion at such a sickening death gave way to a violent rage which cut across the psalms he was murmuring. He paused and in his heart uttered a powerful curse against the assassin, a passionate prayer demanding justice and punishment for this most atrocious sin. The torch-bearer had died in agony, an innocent working man, one of the poorest, earning paltry pennies and for what? To die like this?

'Come.' Athelstan crossed himself and rose. He took a deep breath.

'Lady Anne.' His hostess, face all pale and juddering in the torchlight, now rested on Turgot's arm. 'Mistress, go back home. Sir John and I will find our own way. And be careful, for this truly is a place of deadly sin . . .'

oOoOo

Athelstan knelt on the prie-dieu before the altar in the small but delicately furnished chapel of Firecrest Manor. The chapel was a perfect jewel, a beautifully decorated chamber of prayer which, like the rest of the house, exuded an air of exquisite opulence. Sir Walter, Athelstan reflected, had amassed a great deal of wealth from war and his other business activities. Athelstan had risen before dawn, shaved and washed before donning his robes and sandals. Afterwards he'd walked the gleaming, oak-panelled galleries of the manor, visited the butteries, kitchens and refectory where servants were already kindling fires, laying out chafing dishes and moving sealed, sweet-smelling braziers to crackle and glow. Tapestries of many hues decorated shiny plaster walls, the oaken staircases were polished to a gleam. Thick Turkey rugs and soft white rope matting covered most of the floors. Cabinets, side cupboards and open aumbries displayed precious gold and silver plates. The manor boasted a long hall with an elaborately carved minstrel gallery; a cavernous hearth, leather-back chairs and a long polished elmwood table with a gorgeous golden nef, a model of a war cog in all its splendour at the centre.

Athelstan crossed himself and sighed. Such wealth and comfort were a stark contrast to the smoky tenements of his own parishioners. The friar stared up at the figure on the crucifix. Despite his surroundings, he could not forget the abomination he had witnessed the previous night. Cranston had solemnly promised the torch-bearer's family would be given the most generous assistance. Athelstan had celebrated his daily Mass here in this jewel of a chapel, offering it up for the repose of the soul of that poor, hapless man. The friar had prayed, even as he beat his breast, that God would judge and punish such evil. Athelstan rose genuflecting towards the pyx and left the chapel. The manor had now come to life. Servants and maids hurried about. Savoury odours drifted from the kitchen. Outside echoed the sounds of the stableyard. Athelstan stopped a servant and asked her to bring Buckholt to the bottom of the main staircase. The steward arrived, a brown leather apron about him, and explained how he had been surveying stores of powder, resin, saltpetre and other combustible commodities in the manor's great warehouse.

'Will the loss of "The Book of Fires" injure your trade?' Athelstan asked, grasping the newel post.

'No.' Buckholt shook his head. 'The different powders and their strengths are fairly well known in the trade be it here or across the Narrow Seas. Our most serious rivals are the merchants of the Hanse. "The Book of Fires",' he lowered his voice, 'lists, describes and analyses the different types of fire as well as how it can be strengthened, varied, safely transported and stored. Sir Walter had a phrase for it: "Everything in nature expresses itself in a hierarchy." Greek fire, the real Greek fire, truly is the Emperor of Flames, a fire which seems to feed on itself and, in some cases, is totally impervious to water.' He paused. 'I heard what happened last night. The attack on you and Lady Anne. From what Sir John has said,' he indicated with his head, 'he is in the buttery breaking his fast. Believe me, our Lord Coroner is very fortunate to be doing that.'

'You mean the fire that was thrown at us last night was the finest and the most deadly?'

'Yes, Brother. Only a small bowl was tossed but, as Sir John describes, it is like the heaviest glue and clings to its victim as close as his own skin.' Buckholt peered at Athelstan. 'But why? Why should the Ignifer attack you?'

'Why indeed?' Athelstan stared past the steward at a tapestry hanging on the wall depicting St George in combat with a fire-breathing dragon. The previous night's attack truly puzzled him. The murder of the torch-bearer was a dire act, but what had been the real object of the assault? Himself and Sir John? Or Lady Anne? Bearing in mind what she had told him about her quarrel with Isolda in Newgate, it was probably her. The meeting called last night at her house must have been known and attracted the Ignifer, whoever that was. Perhaps the assassin just waited and watched, seizing any opportunity.

'Brother?'

Athelstan shook his head. 'I am sorry. I was just thinking.'

'Brother, I took the liberty of bringing someone you may wish to talk to.' Buckholt walked away and returned with Mortice, a fussy little man, the clerk of the buttery who had noticed Sir Walter's goblet had been exchanged. He simply repeated what Athelstan had already learnt and waddled away to resume, as he put it, 'A whole list of very important duties.'

'Very well.' Athelstan tapped Buckholt on the shoulder. 'I want to repeat what happened on the night Lady Isolda took the posset into her husband, yes?'

Buckholt pulled a face but agreed. He climbed the staircase and turned right into the gallery. Athelstan followed him up to the top.

Buckholt indicated where he had met Lady Isolda. 'She

took the goblet from me; I went downstairs and she came in here.' He led Athelstan into a spacious, elaborately furnished bedchamber with a wide window in an enclosure above a cushioned seat. There were chests and coffers, tables, chairs and stools. A great four-poster bed shrouded in deep blue damask curtains dominated the room. At its foot, Athelstan glimpsed a richly polished cedarwood coffer, its lid thrown back. Buckholt confirmed it once contained 'The Book of Fires'. Athelstan scrutinized it and went across to the garderobe built into the corner of the wall. He opened the door, its exterior covered in stiffened, painted leather. The chamber inside was quite spacious. The hole in the lid of the jakes box was large enough to easily drop a goblet – it would have fallen down the chute sinking deep into the messy underground cesspit below.

Athelstan took Buckholt to the top of the stairs and asked him to go down and stay as long as he remembered being distracted by Vanner. The steward agreed. Once he'd left, Athelstan strode back to Sir Walter's bedchamber. He carefully rehearsed what he'd been told about Isolda. He pretended to take a goblet from his gown; half fill it, sprinkle in powder and pour in some of the posset then feed this to his make-believe victim. Once satisfied, Athelstan hurried across to the garderobe, sustaining the pretence of throwing down the goblet before returning to sit on the edge of the bed, sharing the goblet he'd left as Lady Isolda must have done. Athelstan concluded he had more than enough time to do all this before Buckholt returned. However, one fact puzzled him: he certainly did not have enough time, according to his reckoning, to persuade her husband to hand over the key around his neck, open the casket, take out 'The Book of Fires', hide it on her person and return to the bed.

'Isolda did not have enough time,' Athelstan murmured to himself. 'And that's only the start. Why should Sir Walter surrender so quickly and easily a manuscript he had kept hidden for decades? If Lady Isolda forced him, surely there would be the ugliest confrontation?' Puzzled by this, Athelstan sat on a stool. Buckholt, who had returned, stirred restlessly, pleading that he should return to his duties.

'Master Buckholt,' Athelstan glanced up, 'I will take you into my confidence and ask you a question. I could not express it yesterday but it troubles me.'

'Brother?'

'Why should Lady Isolda go through this ritual of waiting for you to bring up a posset? Surely at any time during the day she could have brought her husband a goblet of wine, milk, water or whatever?'

'Falke mentioned this during her trial. He also pointed out Parson Garman had brought an almond sweetmeat which had disappeared.'

'Yes, I remember that.' Athelstan smiled as Buckholt slightly coloured. 'Master Buckholt, are you partial to almonds?'

The steward nodded. 'Brother, I am. Now and again Parson Garman brought such a delicacy. At first Sir Walter used to eat them but then, as he sickened, he gave them away to his servants. Brother, ailments of the belly are common enough here at Firecrest Manor but Sir Walter was most subject to them. In fact, that answers your original question. During the trial, Master Sutler rightly pointed out that Sir Walter's stomach was very sensitive. He had grown very fussy about what he ate and drank, especially uncut wine. Ask any of the servants or indeed Physician Philippe. However, one thing Sir Walter did like, and looked forward to, was his evening cup of posset.' He shrugged. 'It was a daily ritual, well known to the household.'

'And?'

'Sutler argued most convincingly that if Lady Isolda, or indeed had anyone else, had tried to coax her husband to drink something tainted during the day, it would be more than obvious. For a start, Sir Walter would protest. Other people would discover it, and if Sir Walter died soon afterwards . . .'

'True,' Athelstan conceded. 'The Lady Isolda had little choice but to exploit this ritual. Moreover, posset, dark wine laced with herbs, would provide a most effective disguise. If Lady Isolda had brought such a drink out of time that too would have been noticed. So,' Athelstan sighed, getting to his feet, 'this brings us to a further point which Master Sutler must have emphasized. Lady Isolda wanted to create an opportunity to poison her husband but do it in such a way that no suspicion could ever fall on her. She must be seen sitting, sipping from the same goblet. She must return that goblet to the buttery where someone else might decide to drain the dregs. Yes, that's what happens in great households. You have just proved it. Garman brings some sweetmeats, Sir Walter doesn't want them so he gives them away.'

'I would agree, Brother,' Buckholt murmured.

'So we have it.' Athelstan moved across to the window, running his finger around the heraldic design on the mullioned glass. 'Lady Isolda wanted to show that the goblet she held was untainted. According to Sutler, however, she served her husband a poisoned chalice and, if it had not been for the sharp-eyed buttery clerk and your own keen suspicions, Lady Isolda would now be the sole owner of these great riches. She gambled, she should have won but by God's grace she lost. However, Master Buckholt . . .' Athelstan turned, crossing his arms and staring down at the floor.

'Brother?'

'My apologies. I have established that Lady Isolda had more than enough time to do what she was accused of, except,' Athelstan gestured towards the coffer, 'remove "The Book of Fires". Would Sir Walter allow her to hold it, to read it?'

'No,' Buckholt retorted, 'never! I never saw "The Book of Fires". Sir Walter did make reference to it being kept in a very safe place which would be a revelation to everyone. He once muttered about it being held on the island of Patmos.'

'What did he mean by that?'

'It made little sense to me. You know, Brother, sometimes I wonder whether "The Book of Fires" really existed.'

'And yet Sir Walter must have used it to create different combustibles?'

'True, Brother. Sir Walter once said he could raise the fires of Hell here on earth yet he seemed frightened, cautious of doing that.'

'Why?'

'I don't know.'

'Where did he get the manuscript from?' Athelstan asked.

Buckholt just shook his head. Athelstan went over and stared down at the coffer at the foot of the bed.

'Mark the Greek's "The Book of Fires".' He spoke half to himself. 'A rare manuscript. Nobody would sell such a great secret. Therefore I deduce that Walter Beaumont stole it from someone. When would he do that? During his journeys in the east? Now,' Athelstan wagged a finger, 'if he had stolen such a precious manuscript, those who owned it would be very angry and pursue him as a thief. I wonder if Sir Walter could not exploit the full secrets of that book lest he attract the attention of its original owners? Was he wary of revealing all its secrets lest he incurred the vengeance of those who still might pursue him, and who would that be? Well, I would wager the Greeks from their great city of Constantinople. After all, Sir Walter was threatened, wasn't he?'

'Yes, Brother but, if Sir Walter had stolen the book, why didn't his pursuers just kill him?'

'Oh, for a number of reasons; this is London not Constantinople. Sir Walter was a close friend of the Regent. More importantly, they didn't want Sir Walter's death, they just wanted their book back. Indeed, if they'd killed him that might never happen. No, they would try bribes. I just wonder if Sir Walter was busy raising the price?'

'He never mentioned that to me.'

'No, no, he wouldn't. As you and others have informed me, "The Book of Fires" was something Sir Walter kept to himself.'

'Brother Athelstan, is there anything else?'

The friar raised his hand in blessing. 'I am sure there is, Master Buckholt, but you will only answer what I ask and that will take time.'

The steward left and Athelstan walked around the chamber, pausing before a gilt-edged painting. The scrolled sign beneath proclaimed 'Lady Isolda Beaumont' followed by the name of the artist. Athelstan peered closer. Like many a wealthy burgess, Sir Walter had hired one of those many Italian painters now flocking to London to seek a patron amongst the rich and powerful. Such craftsmen brought not only a fresh array of colours and settings, but a keenness for accurate depiction. If this was so, Lady Isolda had been a truly beautiful woman. She had an oval face and perfectly formed features, arching brows over the lightest blue eyes, a laughing, full mouth and, beneath the white gauze veil, the richest golden hair braided with bejewelled silver twine. She conveyed a deep certainty, a serenity about herself, though there was something mocking in that look of pure innocence. Athelstan marvelled at her beauty, yet he recalled the old proverb of someone being too sweet to be wholesome.

'You can see why Sir Walter and others were smitten, Brother Athelstan.'

Athelstan whirled around. Lady Anne, with Turgot beside her, stood in the doorway to the bedchamber.

'Good morning, Brother.' She came forward, clasped his hand and kissed him on each cheek. 'I had to come and see how you were. What happened last night,' she let go of his hands, 'was truly dreadful. I have sent money to the torch-bearer's family. I have also arranged his requiem and provided payment for a chantry priest at St Nicholas in the Shambles to sing Masses for him until the Octave of Pentecost. Truly murderous!' she exclaimed. 'I asked Turgot here what he saw.' She raised her hands. 'Turgot and I have mastered the sign language of the Cistercians. Now, he was trailing about ten yards behind us. His task was to make sure no one followed. Everything, however, remained serene until that figure emerged. At first, Turgot thought it was a beggar. Only when the flames caught did he realize what was happening.' She paused. 'I believe I was the intended victim. In future, if I make such a journey again, I will have an armed guard. Brother, I urge you to be equally prudent.' She pointed at the painting. 'Such a tragedy! At first everybody admired her. Now, this Great Miracle?'

Athelstan grasped her proffered hand and they left the bedchamber, going down to the buttery, where Sir John was in deep conversation with Sir Henry and Lady Rohesia. They welcomed Athelstan and Lady Anne, who joined them around the well-polished oval table. Morning ale, cuts of chicken and pancakes were served. The conversation was desultory after expressions of shock at the attack the previous evening. Lady Anne pointed out, and they all agreed, how this part of the city was ideal for such an assault with its twisting runnels and narrow lanes. The discussion then moved to the growing crisis in the city: the plotting of the Great Community of the Realm. On this, Sir Henry proved obdurate, denouncing the rebels, insisting that Gaunt would ruthlessly crush all insurgents in the city and the surrounding shires. Athelstan gently guided the conversation on to the threats Sir Walter had received a year ago and asked to see the actual messages. Sir Henry hurried off to his chancery chamber and brought back a clutch of parchments. They were dark and ragged, the ink rather faded but the letters were well formed. The message was the same time and again. The specific warning clear and stark: 'As I and ours did burn, so shall ye and yours.'

'Do you think that's the Upright Men?' Sir Henry asked plaintively.

'I don't know,' Athelstan replied, handing them back. 'They certainly have the ring of a proclamation about them. Of course, you supply Gaunt with powder for his culverins and cannon. The Upright Men would resent that.'

'So when the great revolt comes,' Sir Cranston asked, 'have you, Sir Henry, like other merchants, contributed secretly to the coffers of the Upright Men, a sort of tribute so that when the Day of Slaughter dawns you and yours will be safe?'

'Never!' Sir Henry's reply was almost a shout. 'Oh, I know about the Great Community of the Realm, their leaders and their chants. God knows what my brother truly thought! He was, in all things, secretive, but you are correct – few mansions will be safe.' Sir Henry rose and closed the buttery door. 'Buckholt,' he continued, returning to his seat, 'is a most loyal steward – well, he was to Sir Walter. I am not sure whether I will retain him, and one of my reasons for that is Buckholt's support for the Great Community of the Realm, his open admiration for the Upright Men. I know that from the chatter of the servants, who,' he took a deep breath, 'sing his doggerel chants. So, to answer your question, Sir John, when and if such a treasonous revolt occurs, I shall hire mercenaries – the very best – to defend Firecrest Manor.'

'As shall I,' Lady Anne declared sharply.

'Nonsense!' Sir Henry blustered. 'My brother always maintained, and he had his informers, that you, Lady Anne, your house and your retainers would be regarded as sacrosanct by the rebel leaders, Jack Straw and Wat Tyler. You do such good work in the prisons. You have helped the families of those whom Gaunt has arrested and executed. Sir Walter believed that when the revolt breaks out your house will be safer than the Tower or Westminster Abbey.'

Lady Anne blushed and lowered her head.

'Our situation is different,' Sir Henry continued. 'I find it difficult to sift friend from foe. Last night,' he glanced quickly at the closed door, 'Edward Garman, prison chaplain at Newgate during Lady Isolda's imprisonment there? We have heard rumours that Garman is very close to the Upright Men. Tongues wag and gossips chatter how Garman may have even been involved in the escape of rebels from Newgate.'

'True.' Sir John, who had been strangely quiet, broke from his own reverie. 'Very true,' he repeated. 'I studied Garman last night – he certainly stirred memories. Garman has acquired a certain reputation delivering sermons and homilies very similar to those of the hedge priest John Ball. Garman talks of a Commonwealth, of a *"Bonum Commune"* – a "Common Good". He has shown great partiality to any Upright Men seized and imprisoned by Gaunt's agents.' Cranston grinned at Athelstan. 'But I've heard other priests preach the same and, in the end, is that so wrong? To want to live in peace and justice?' Sir John blinked, staring down the table. 'Remember that quotation from the Book of Micah, how does it go? "Three things I have asked of thee, says the Lord: to love tenderly, to act justly and to walk humbly with your God."' Cranston's words created an uncomfortable silence.

'It's one thing to preach Christ,' Lady Anne murmured, 'but,' she gestured at Turgot standing behind her, 'when we visit Newgate we also hear rumours. Garman just doesn't preach, he plots and, Sir John, the revolt is coming. Newgate will be stormed. I am sure the royal council realize that. The prison will be seized and all its malefactors allowed to join the gangs. Priests like Garman should be warned.'

'And he has been,' Cranston replied. 'But Garman is a cleric, subject to Church law, and we must have proof of conspiracy to treason.' He spread his hands. 'The worst we can do is remove him, but on what grounds? He has proven to be a devoted pastor. The Bishop of London could replace him but not many priests, if any, would want such a benefice, whilst a replacement could be worse in every way . . .'

Lord Henry began to question Cranston about city politics. Athelstan sat silent. He knew the coroner was correct. Many village priests, as well as those who worked amongst the poor, were openly espousing the Upright Men as the only possible cure for the kingdom's ills, yet that wasn't relevant now.

'Vanner!' Athelstan's exclamation silenced the discussion. 'Vanner has apparently fled, for whatever reason. If he is alive, he is a fugitive, a man sliding through the shadows fearful of capture. Let us say Vanner is the Ignifer – could he fashion and prepare Greek fire?'

'He may have stolen "The Book of Fires",' Sir Henry countered, 'but . . .'

'I wager Vanner was not involved in the manufacture of cannon, culverins and powder?' Athelstan asked.

Sir Henry nodded in agreement.

'Even if he had "The Book of Fires",' Athelstan continued, 'how can he, a clerk, slip through the streets of London dealing out death whenever, wherever he wishes? Sir Henry, I understand there is a hierarchy of strengths when it comes to Greek fire?'

'Yes, Brother. It's like any other weapon with a range of power and force. You can have a small hand-held crossbow or the powerful Brabantine, which can bring down a mailed knight.'

'Very good.' Athelstan rubbed his hands together. 'So, if Vanner was the Ignifer he would need to buy certain commodities, but how could he do that as a fugitive? Where would he get the money from? He is a soft-handed clerk fleeing for his life. He will need a place to shelter, to sleep and feed. More importantly, as I have said, he has to buy certain items, deal with merchants who could well recognize him. Then there is the problem of storage, of manufacture, and all this brings me to one logical conclusion.' Athelstan paused as he reflected on what he just said. 'Impossible,' he breathed.

'Brother?' Lady Anne asked. 'What is impossible?'

'I suspect, indeed I am sure that Vanner is not the Ignifer. In fact, he is dead, and has been for many days, even before Lady Isolda was executed.'

'Dead?' Sir Henry queried.

'To be more precise murdered but where, how and by whom I cannot say. Sir Henry, where are Vanner's papers, his manuscripts?'

'Like Lady Isolda's, they were destroyed. Sutler never established who did that.'

'But he suspected Lady Isolda?'

'I think so.'

'And I will need to examine Sir Walter's papers.'

'Of course, Brother. Do you want to do that now?'

'No,' Athelstan shook his head, 'only when I am ready.'

'I will arrange that,' Sir Henry declared. 'Now, Sir John, Brother Athelstan, you would like to see the gardens?'

Both agreed and got to their feet. Lady Anne sidled up beside Athelstan with a spate of questions about the 'Great Miracle'. Thankfully she fell silent as Sir Henry led them out through a postern door into the spacious gardens which ran down to the curtain wall and the majestic Watergate fronting the Thames. Athelstan could only marvel at their extent, which was as great as any demesne around a shire manor. There were orchards of apple, pear and other fruit trees, and an impressive falcon fountain, the great bird of prey cast in bronze, perpetually hovering over a broad, lead-lined pool. There were grassy areas, herb plots, flower beds and tunnelled arbours fashioned out of coppiced poles lashed together with willow cords. Over these grew vines and climbing roses, a tangle of greenery awaiting the sun. Athelstan was particularly taken by the arbours, trellised pentices furnished with turf seats and benches of Purbeck limestone positioned to provide the best view over the gardens. Sir Henry, full of pride, showed them the carp pond, broad, reed-ringed and well stocked, before leading them into an ancient copse of oak and beech which provided a dark woodland aspect. At its centre stretched a broad glade around a deep green-covered stagnant pool. Athelstan walked through it all and smiled as he recalled his own small garden often savaged by Thaddeus the goat or Ursula the pig-woman's gigantic sow.

He wondered if Hubert, their resident hedgehog, was sheltering in the hermitage, a small wooden dwelling fashioned especially for their garden-dweller by Crispin the carpenter. Lady Anne returned to question him about the miracle. Athelstan finally excused himself and went back to Sir John, who stood on the edge of the mere staring sadly down at the thick green slime lacing the water.

'This garden is very beautiful, Brother, but I wish spring would come. On my father's farm I used to go out and worship the first daisies of the year. I would sit and listen to a thrush sing its first sweet song of spring. I'd study the apples growing fat, the hazelnuts branching fresh and green. I would walk and watch the brown gorse move under the breeze or glimpse a fox, a trail of red, sloping through ripening corn. I'd lean against old garden posts covered in holes where a host of hot-eyed sparrows would peck for grains. I love spring.' Sir John glanced up, tears in his eyes. 'But not this year, Brother! This year will be different! I know that! No maypole dancing but murder and mayhem.' He waved around and beat his breast. 'Brother, I think these murders are linked to the coming revolt.' Cranston ground his teeth. 'Nothing, my good friar, is what it appears to be. There is something very wrong here. I feel it in my water, in the beating of my heart and the flowing of my humours.'

Athelstan stepped closer. 'Sir John, you are poetical, even mystical.'

Cranston grabbed him by the shoulders. 'Little monk.'

'Friar, Sir John.'

'What's the difference? Listen.' Cranston drew him even closer. 'I have been lost in thought about what has been happening here but also about your great miracle. I have sent our green-garbed Tiptoft throughout the city, alerting all the weird and wonderful in our underworld to be vigilant about a man burnt down the entire right side of his body. Believe me, Brother, if any change was made it would be discovered. I did the same for Vanner. I've posted proclamations on the Standard at Cheapside, St Paul's and the great gibbets at Tyburn and Smithfield, but there's nothing.' He withdrew his hands. 'I suspect you are correct. Vanner is dead. He wasn't responsible for last night when that poor bastard died. The Ignifer passionately believes Lady Isolda was innocent and so he, or she, is intent on dealing out a grisly death to all who connived in Isolda's condemnation. Yet who could that be? Sir Henry and Lady Rohesia wax prosperous on Sir Walter's death? Buckholt is glad to see her gone. Rosamund the maid is a noddle-pate, surely? Lady Anne Lesures doesn't have the means – I cannot see her scuttling through the streets. More importantly, Lady Anne believes Lady Isolda was as guilty as the Lord Satan himself. Finally, she and Turgot were with us last night. So we come to other possibilities. Falke, who passionately believed in her innocence? Parson Garman or,' Cranston shrugged, 'is it someone else with their own motivation?'

'Sir John,' Athelstan replied, 'I accept what you say but I would add that these are not murders of the heart but the will. They are, I suspect, rooted firmly in the past. So much is.' He breathed. 'Look at me, Sir John, a farmer's boy, a son who broke his parents' hearts by running away to join the royal array, coaxing my younger brother to accompany me only for him to die outside Moyaux.' Athelstan lapsed into silence; he did not wish to go down that well-trodden path. 'That experience,' he whispered, 'shaped me. So, what dark forces from the past breathe life into all this murderous hate?' He felt Cranston's hand on his shoulder.

'Miracles, Brother?'

'We certainly need one here, Sir John.'

'No, the charade at St Erconwald's?'

'You suspect it is trickery?'

'I know it is. I accept what you say, Brother. We believe a crucified Jew rose from the dead, that during the Mass bread and wine become his glorified body and blood. But St Erconwald's? Let's be honest, Brother, that little parish entertains more mischief than a hedgerow of sparrows. All my couriers and searchers, Tiptoft, Muckworm and the Sanctus man, are on the alert. They are not only hunting Vanner but also a cripple, not a Londoner but a Yorkshireman burnt down the entire right-hand side of his body.' Cranston paused. 'I believe there is mischief afoot, Brother, but, so far, I can't detect a thing. I have spies all over this city, yet nobody has reported anything.'

'Sir John, Brother Athelstan.' They turned as Buckholt hurried towards them. 'Master Falke is here and wishes to have words with you.' The steward led them to where Falke was waiting in the small buttery. The lawyer was pacing up and down, his blond hair wet with sweat, his face all flushed. Athelstan could smell the wine even before the lawyer stopped his restless pacing, his face only a few inches from the friar's.

'Master Falke, you have been drinking?'

'Most of the night,' the lawyer slurred. 'I heard what was said last night.' Froth bubbled from his lips. 'Now, you listen,' he hissed, 'to what I know. Sir Henry and Lady Rohesia are no more than scavengers. They were eager, desperate for Sir Walter to die without an heir. They quietly rejoiced at Isolda's arrest. Sir Henry was his brother's henchman. I don't care what he says, I am sure he pays more than lip service to the Upright Men.'

'Master Falke, what are you implying?' Cranston asked. 'That "The Book of Fires" might have been stolen by Sir Henry as a bargaining counter with the Upright Men? Do you have proof?'

'No,' Falke dabbed at his mouth, 'nor do I have proof that Buckholt is secretly a rebel. Did you know his father served with Sir Walter when our noble merchant was a mercenary? I tell you this,' Falke swayed on his feet, 'Buckholt never liked Isolda, nor did Sir Henry. Lady Anne Lesures may act the grand lady, be all compassionate and caring, but she upset Lady Isolda by refusing to listen or accept her plea of innocence. Maybe Lady Anne has forgotten that she was responsible for Isolda's marriage. I could tell you more. Parson Garman liked to visit Sir Walter and I suspect their relationship lies tangled in the past. He too served in the Luciferi. Oh, yes!' Falke spread his hands, moving to the left then right. 'You have seen the splendour of this house. Like the paint on a whore's face it hides all forms of filth and lewdness.' Falke put a finger to his lips. 'Sir Walter was hot, not for Lady Isolda, his God-given wife, but her maid Rosamund, Rosa

Mundi,' he spat out, 'Rosa of the World. Yes? More like Rosa Munda – Soiled Rose.'

'Master Falke,' Cranston retorted, 'Sir Walter was not fit for turbulent bed sport.'

'No, he wasn't. He just wanted to entice that young lady into his bedchamber to administer to him slowly with her hands and mouth.'

'And did she?' Athelstan snapped. 'For heaven's sake man, make your point!'

'The fair Isolda was a foundling raised by the Minoresses, but so was Rosamund. The venerable Lady Anne introduced her to this household as Lady Isolda's maid.'

'And?'

'According to household gossip and rumour, Buckholt himself was very sweet on Rosamund. Some people claimed she may have been his daughter. Others maintained he wanted to be betrothed to her.'

'Proof,' Athelstan insisted. 'You are a lawyer, Master Falke. You deal with evidence, not scandalous gossip.'

'Well, he visited the Minoresses when Sir Walter was courting Lady Isolda, and Buckholt never missed the opportunity to accompany him.'

'So,' Cranston poked Falke in the chest, 'you are insinuating that our noble steward Buckholt nursed deep grievances against Sir Walter? Amongst these, Buckholt's support for the Upright Men and his tender feelings for Rosamund Clifford? If the latter was true, I agree, he would not have been happy at Rosamund's rather strange duties in the Beaumont bedroom. Are you implying that Buckholt was the murderer, desperate to cast his guilt on Lady Isolda?'

'It is possible.'

'But if Lady Isolda knew about her husband's lust for her maid, surely she objected?'

'She did. Sir Walter dismissed her protests. He claimed Rosamund was given to fey fancies.'

'Why,' Athelstan asked, 'was this not argued at the trial?' He forced a smile. 'Of course, gossip and tittle-tattle are not evidence, are they, Master Falke? You can gossip away to us in the buttery but repeat this in a court? Moreover, I am sure that Richard Sutler, a veritable lurcher of a man, would have twisted such tittle-tattle back on Lady Isolda, accuse her of lying, of fabricating – but,' he plucked at Cranston's sleeve, 'we shall bear in mind what you have said, Master Falke, now our stay here is done. Sir John and I have other matters to attend to . . .'

PART THREE

'The second kind of flying fire is created this way . . .'
Mark the Greek's 'The Book of Fires'

The 'other matters' Athelstan referred to preoccupied him long after the compline bell had tolled. He sat in the well-scrubbed kitchen of his little priest house and stared down at the elegantly written memorandum drawn up by Master Tuddenham. The Bishop's envoy had been most thorough. He had questioned Fulchard and Richmond, his companion Fitzosbert and all relevant witnesses. He had summoned others he needed to question, whilst one of his clerks, skilled in detecting forged seals and letters, had scrutinized all the documents Fulchard carried with him. Tuddenham had carefully sifted the evidence and reached stark conclusions.

Item: Fulchard the cripple and Fulchard the healed man are one and the same person. Philippe the physician journeyed across the Thames in order to inspect the patient. He recognized the same man, albeit cured, who had visited the House of Mercy at St Bartholomew's Hospital only a few days earlier. Philippe had noted the same height, looks, hair, eyes and distinguishing marks. The physician had added two codicils. Firstly, the man he had originally inspected was not only grievously injured and scarred but, because of his hideous wounds and the exertions of his journey south, also very weak. Secondly, if there were any differences noted, these could be explained by the cure itself.

Item: on the night of the Great Miracle, witnesses had seen Fulchard, cowled and cloaked, hobble on his crutch into St Erconwald's and lie down in the nave close to the saint's chantry chapel. He had lain there all night: those close by noticed him twitching and moaning but nothing remarkable. On one occasion Fulchard had sat up to drink from a waterskin

then lain down again. He did not leave his place until the end
of the Mass and the cure was proclaimed.

Item: Master Tuddenham and his clerks had scrutinized
Fulchard's letters, licences and warrants: they listened to
Philippe the physician's account and closely interrogated rele-
vant witnesses. Tuddenham emphasized that, apart from
Fitzosbert, these were strangers from different shires.
Consequently, the only logical conclusion was that a miracle
had, thanks be to God, occurred. Tuddenham added how
the Bishop of London's searchers, as well as those of the
Archdeacon's court, had made careful scrutiny throughout
Southwark and the city to ensure there was 'no other', as
Tuddenham tactfully put it, 'Fulchard of Richmond'. Nothing
had been discovered. The same searchers had questioned the
boatmen along Southwark quay as well as Master Robert
Burdon, keeper of the gates on London Bridge. They too had
nothing to report.

'And,' Athelstan picked up a parchment from the table,
'neither have Sir John's searchers and he hires the very best
– greyhounds in human form.' Athelstan leaned back in his
chair and stared around. All was in order here. Master
Tuddenham had used this small house to conduct his inves-
tigations and left with his entourage. Benedicta, with the help
of some of the parish council, had then swept through the
house, cleaning, scrubbing, changing and preparing for his
return. A pie and a bowl of pottage stood in the oven next to
the hearth, and there was fresh ale, bread and milk in the
buttery. Athelstan had checked his three-locked chancery chest
and personal coffer. Woda the washer woman had cleaned his
two robes and changed the blankets on his bed. Crim the altar
boy had ensured that Bonaventure had feasted like a prince
so the great tomcat now lay sprawled by the hearth lost to
the world. 'Yet everything is not in order,' Athelstan whispered. He peered down the table. Merrylegs senior had slipped
into death tended by a Crutched Friar who was visiting the
church because of the Great Miracle. The friar had administered the last rites and Athelstan intended to celebrate the
requiem Mass the following morning and commit the body
to the grave. The family plot in God's Acre had been dug and

prepared. 'Which brings me to that other small mystery,' Athelstan murmured. Apparently, the night before, Godbless the beggar, keeper of God's Acre, had been visited in his cottage, the old parish death house, by some pilgrims eager for news. They had shared a tun of ale with him and celebrated until both Godbless and his nefarious goat Thaddeus had become hopelessly drunk. According to Benedicta, long after the chimes of midnight, Godbless was found riding a staggering Thaddeus around the tombstones singing at the top of his voice how he had been visited by his kinsman, Oberon, Prince of the Fairies. Pike and Watkin eventually put both man and beast to bed. Athelstan had paid a visit but Godbless was still 'full of the drink', as he put it, whilst Athelstan had never seen Thaddeus so quiet. He had left them to sleep it off and returned to his home to have supper and study Tuddenham's report.

Athelstan rose to his feet and began to pace the kitchen. He crossed himself and intoned the '*Veni Creator Spiritus*' for guidance. The Great Miracle could pose serious problems. The Bishop of London had made his decision and the case would be referred to synod of English bishops and then on to the Pope. If Rome agreed, St Erconwald's would become an official place of pilgrimage, but what then? Athelstan tried to control his disquiet: his faith was a faith of miracles, yet he felt deeply uneasy about what was happening. If Sir John was suspicious, he was even more so. The same unease disturbed his mind about the grisly murders carried out after the execution of Lady Isolda. Why had they happened? Was the Ignifer someone who passionately believed the dead woman was innocent? Yet the burden of proof, Athelstan conceded, lay heavily against Lady Isolda. She was certainly no innocent lamb despatched to the slaughter. Of course, there was the mysterious Vanner, but Athelstan was almost convinced the clerk was dead and not in hiding. Undoubtedly, the Ignifer knew about Greek fire and might even possess 'The Book of Fires'. From the little Athelstan had learnt, once the secret formulas were known it was easy to manufacture that liquid death. Nevertheless, murders of Sutler, Gavelkind and Tressilian were beyond him, brief moments in time leaving

very little, if any, evidence to study. But the attack on Lady
Anne? He and Cranston had been with her and Turgot when
that shadowy assassin had slipped out of the darkness. Who
could move so swiftly? Athelstan pulled a face. Virtually
everyone he'd questioned. Some of these regarded Lady Isolda
as guilty but two men passionately believed in her innocence,
Garman and Falke. One of these, or both, could be the Ignifer.
And what about others, were they telling the truth? Sir Henry,
Buckholt, even that pretty-faced maid, Rosamund? Athelstan
crouched next to his great tomcat. 'It's possible, Bonaventure,
that any one of these might be a murderer. As for why, it's
in the past,' he murmured. 'Somewhere deep in this tangle
of human souls sprouted a root which has waxed strong and
poisonous. I am the gardener, Bonaventure, me and Sir John,
heaven help us. This tangle is thick and thorny – it will take
time to uproot and that means more deaths.' Athelstan straight-
ened up. 'Ah, well, it's time to see what is happening in my
church.'

Athelstan fastened his sandals, donned his cloak, pulled up
its deep hood and slipped out into the night. The cemetery
and the great enclosure before the church were busy. Cresset
torches glowed on the end of poles or were stuck into wall
crevices. Makeshift braziers crackled their heat. Bonfires fed
with rubbish flamed the darkness. The pilgrims and visitors
gathered close to these to warm themselves or to cook scraps
of meat pushed on to ready-made skillets, pans or prongs.
The air bubbled with the stench of sweaty bodies, roasting
meat and wood smoke. The noise was constant. A babble of
voices broken by the occasional hymn, shouted psalms as
well as noisy salutations, laugher, curses and oaths. People
swarmed in and out of the church under the watchful eye of
Bladdersmith and his *comitatus* of bailiffs. Benedicta and
other women of the parish assisted. Imelda, Pike's wife, a
true virago, stood on the top step of the church directing
people as well as collecting pennies in a sealed wooden box
with a slit on top. All the denizens of Southwark and beyond
had crawled out of their rookeries and mumpers' castles, or
what Cranston called 'the Dungeons of Darkness and the Halls
of Hell'. They'd all assembled to make a profit: apple-women,

watercress-sellers, onion pickers with their produce slung on ropes around their necks; vendors of sheep and pig's trotters pushed and shoved by milk and water men. Poachers from the fields around, garbed in hare and rabbit skins, offered the pink, glistening flesh of their quarry hanging from poles over their shoulders. Boners and grubbers who scoured the midden heaps and simplers who foraged for herbs, mushrooms, snails and grubs offered their potions along with chunks of cat meat. Despite the late hour, this ragged, motley garbed mob surged backwards and forwards, desperate to sell to the pilgrims pushing their way up and down the church steps. Jongleurs, troubadours, firedrakes, puppet masters along with street musicians tried to entertain the crowd. Men-at-arms from the Tower and the gatehouse at the Bridge swaggered around trying to catch the eye of the orange-wigged whores who, under the pretence of prayer and pilgrimage, solicited ever so quietly for custom.

Athelstan walked through God's Acre. He stopped to check on Godbless and Thaddeus. Both were fast asleep, so he made his way carefully out into the enclosure, past bothies and tents set up by the pilgrims. He entered the church. More people thronged there, going up and down the transepts or queuing for entrance to St Erconwald's chapel. Everyone paused to admire Fulchard's crutch, now discarded but given pride of place, hanging above the saintly bishop's tomb. Fulchard, flanked by an ever-so-demure Cecily the courtesan on one side, her sister Clarissa on the other, sat in a throne-like chair before the rood screen so pilgrims could touch and talk to him in return for an offering placed in a sealed box at his feet. Athelstan sketched a blessing in the air and passed quietly on, praying for guidance as he wondered how long this feast of miracles would last. He left the church and took a vantage point on the top step, staring over the concourse and the people milling there. The friar studied the crowd carefully and felt a chill of apprehension as he noted the large number of young, able-bodied men who moved amongst it. Intrigued, he went back into the church and stared around. Crim and the ladies of the parish were busy arguing, assisting and organizing, but Athelstan couldn't glimpse Watkin, Pike, Ranulf and the rest

of that coven of mischief. He left the church, pushing his way
through the crowd. He strode swiftly down the lane, past
Merrylegs' darkened pie shop and stopped beneath the garish
sign of the Piebald. He was about to knock on the door when
a man stepped out of the darkness; the meagre light from a
lanthorn hanging on its hook glittered in the blade of a half-
drawn dagger.

'Who are you and what do you want?' The guard slid
between Athelstan and the door.

'The Archangel Gabriel,' Athelstan snapped. He pushed the
man aside and rapped on the obviously locked door. The guard
came back just as the door swung open and Watkin stepped
into the pool of light.

'Why, Father?'

'Why, Watkin?' Athelstan mimicked back. 'Please tell this
gentleman to leave your priest alone.' The guard hastily withdrew. Athelstan stepped into the warm mustiness of the
taproom. The chamber lay in darkness except for the ghostly
pool of light cast around the great common table on which
Merrylegs senior, garbed in his funeral clothes, lay stretched
out, his bare feet sticking up, his grizzled head and thin-lined
face almost hidden by the corpse wimple wound tightly about.
The corpse's closed eyes were sealed by two coins, whilst a
small wafer of bread rested between his bloodless lips. Votive
candles, about sixty in number, ringed the corpse. Along each
side of the table sat the men of the parish with Watkin at the
top and Pike seated at the other end. They all clutched tankards of Joscelyn's choice ale and used the blackjacks to hide
their faces as Athelstan walked across to greet them with a
blessing.

'Father,' Pike started to rise and the others followed suit,
'we are having a funeral vigil.'

'I am sure you are.' Athelstan smiled. He glanced around.
They were all there, even the hangman, along with a number
of hard-faced, solemn-eyed strangers. Athelstan decided not
to stay. He realized this was no funeral vigil. This was a
meeting of the Upright Men from this ward and probably every
other in Southwark. He talked quickly about the arrangements
for the requiem Mass tomorrow, blessed the gathering and

left. Once outside, Athelstan walked halfway along the lane and stared up at the slit of starry sky.

'I wonder, Lord,' he whispered, 'do forgive me yet I truly do, if this Great Miracle has anything to do with the mischief being plotted back there . . .'

oOoOo

Thomas Pynchon, linen draper par excellence, or so he styled himself, spent his last night alive feeding and rewarding those fleshy appetites so roundly condemned by the preachers whom Pynchon half-listened to during Sunday Mass as he leaned against the wall of St Mildred's in Bread Street. The church stood close to his three-storey town house: a fair dwelling of pink and cream plaster, gleaming black timbers and glazed windows though the top ones were covered in oil-thickened linen. On that particular night, his last one on earth, Thomas Pynchon had been trying to stifle the terrors which dogged his soul during previous evenings. He waked sweat-soaked, fearful that some boneless wraith might be rising like a plume of black smoke in the corner of his bedchamber. He sat in terror wondering if the wraith had a gripping hunger, a feverish thirst for his immortal soul. During the day, busy amongst his apprentices, Pynchon would glimpse some blonde-haired, bright-eyed girl and all his fears would blossom afresh. Once again he'd wonder if some demon, some life-thief, was stalking him. Pynchon stopped on the corner of Bread Street and gazed back at the three stout mercenaries hired to guard him. He glimpsed the tavern door under which a glow of light beckoned invitingly.

'I will take a stoup of ale,' he called out, 'then I will return.' The mercenaries grunted their agreement. Pynchon slipped into the comfortable sweet-smelling taproom and made his way over to a window seat. A slattern fetched his order, a tankard of the strongest frothy ale. Pynchon took a deep sip, leaned back and sighed. Despite his terrors this had been a most enjoyable evening. He had dined sumptuously at the Full Delight, a discreet tavern for the well-to-do bachelor about town, and Pynchon was indeed a very wealthy bachelor.

He had feasted on minced chicken in almond and rosemary sauce, venison steaks broiled in vinegar, red wine, ginger and a little cinnamon, followed by quiche of fish with a green topping. Delicious sweet wafers in a hippocras sauce had finished the meal before Pynchon had climbed the tavern stairs to sample the pleasures of a generously endowed, buxom chambermaid with olive skin and hair as dark as the night. Pynchon had insisted on that. He wanted no golden-haired woman with fair skin and ice-blue eyes. Such a sight would only thresh his soul with a flail of fresh terrors. It would remind him of Isolda Beaumont standing erect and proud at the bar before the King's Bench, glaring furiously as Thomas Pynchon, foreman of the jury, solemnly pronounced the guilty verdict. Looking back, that proud face, those arrogant eyes had invoked a curse through which all the ghastly horsemen of the Apocalypse had stormed – at least in Pynchon's mind. At the time he had been proud of what he had done. He had boasted how he'd argued with others of the jury that a unanimous guilty verdict was the only one they could reach. Afterwards he had regaled colleagues in the Guild as well as his many customers about what he had achieved. How he had been resolute as an iron gate against any plea for mercy. Indeed, as foreman of the jury, Pynchon had attended Isolda's execution, determined that the Carnifex show no mercy and that the crowd did not hurl blocks of wood or stone to render the victim senseless. Justice had been done and that should have been the end of the matter, but not now. The mysterious Ignifer had appeared in the city dealing out terror and death to all involved in Isolda's execution. Two of the judges and prosecutor Sutler had perished by fire, burnt to death as easily as some rubbish heap on a sweltering hot day. More recently a similar murderous attack had been mounted against Lady Anne Lesures, with whom Isolda Beaumont had publicly quarrelled. The terror was spreading. Justice Danyel and six other members of the jury had fled to the fastness of the Tower. Three others had taken sanctuary at St Paul's. Pynchon, however, could not leave his trade nor, after his recent pronouncements, did he want to be a laughing stock dismissed as a coward. Consequently he had hired those three stout fellows and taken careful precautions in the cellar of his town house. He had proclaimed as much, openly mocking the Ignifer.

Pynchon's eyes grew heavy. He was sleepy from all he'd eaten and drunk, not to mention his recent bed-wrestling with that spirited wench. Pynchon drained his tankard, lurched to his feet and staggered out of the tavern, helped by his retainers, as he called them.

The linen draper made his way down Bread Street past the grim huddled figures crouching there rattling clacking dishes and whining for alms. Pynchon, as always, ignored them. He found the key to his house, opened the door and stumbled in. His swaggering bullies swept through the building. They reported all was well and retreated into the warm kitchen. Pynchon opened the door to the cellar. One of the guards came up behind him and made sure his master went carefully down the steps into the passageway. Sconce torches were lit. Pynchon reached the strong room, unlocked the door and took the lanthorn the guard had hastily prepared. Pynchon slurred his goodnights then locked and bolted the door from inside. He stood and ensured the heavy lock was turned and all four bolts were pulled firmly across. He staggered across to the table, put the lantern down and sat on a stool. He wrinkled his nose at the slight smell but gazed proudly at the comfortable cot bed, its mattress and bolster stuffed with the softest flock and covered with a gold, red-spangled counterpane. He leaned across and patted the arca, the heavy iron strongbox with its three locks. All was secure here. The cellar was of good brick and hard stone; even the timbers in the ceiling had been hidden under a thick coat of cement. A grille high in the wall let in air. He sniffed and shook his head. Perhaps he should air the room better and get rid of that strange smell. Then the draper rose and undressed, staggered on to the bed and drifted off to sleep. He awoke abruptly at what sounded like a footfall in the far corner, a sound of dripping as if there was a leak. He gazed into the darkness, mouth gaping at what looked like fireflies, one after the other, falling through the darkness. He staggered from the bed, his legs becoming tangled with the blankets. There was a sound like a rushing

wind and Pynchon stared in horror at the flames which seemed
to leap up from the floor. He grabbed a blanket and rushed
to smother the fire. He slipped on the grease-covered floor
and struggled wildly to get up even as the first searing flame
licked his body. Screaming, Pynchon clambered to his feet.
He stumbled towards the door but he had taken the key out
and the bolts were drawn fully across. Screeching in pain,
Pynchon collapsed to his knees as a sheet of fire engulfed
him.

oOoOo

Athelstan joined Cranston in Bread Street as the angelus bell
rang its message. The friar had risen early to clear St
Erconwald's and ensure Merrylegs senior was laid to rest
according to the rites of the Holy Mother Church. The corpse
had been removed to the parish death house suitably draped
with black serge. Just after dawn, the women of the family
gathered to wash the cadaver with perfumed water. Afterwards
they anointed it with a little balsam, placed it in a linen shroud,
sheathed it in a fresh deerskin and carefully stowed it in the
parish coffin draped in a black pall with a silver cross sewn
in the centre. The coffin was solemnly conveyed to rest on
trestles in the sanctuary. The requiem Mass was celebrated.
The coffin was blessed before being carried out in solemn
procession to the far corner of God's Acre. Athelstan
committed the corpse of Merrylegs senior to the ground. 'Dust
to dust, ashes to ashes, in joyful hope of the Resurrection.'
Athelstan performed the rites amidst gusts of incense. He was
surprised at how many attended, including Fulchard of
Richmond, as well as how serenely matters proceeded. Parish
funerals were usually a time of chaos, the wrong grave being
dug or, as the last time, Watkin had become so drunk he'd
followed the coffin into the ground and had to be hauled out
with ropes.

Cranston's messenger, Tiptoft, had arrived just as they were
leaving the cemetery, begging the friar to join Sir John in
Bread Street, where 'Another horrid murder has occurred.'
Athelstan now waited outside Thomas Pynchon's house as

bailiffs cleared the cellar strong room as well as purging the pungent smoke fumes. Athelstan, threading Ave beads through his fingers, stared down this prosperous street. He was always fascinated at the contrasts in human life. Two houses away maids and slatterns were waging their ceaseless war against fleas and bedbugs. On windowsills, tranchers of stale bread, covered with turpentine and birdlime with a lighted tallow candle in the middle, were being laid out to attract and kill such irritants. Chamber pots and jakes jugs were being emptied into the sewer. The different smells of houses, being opened to the day, mingled with those more savoury odours from nearby pie shops and pastry stalls. Athelstan sighed – such commonplace things, yet in Pynchon's house gruesome murder had been perpetrated.

'Brother, we can go in now.' Cranston pulled down the muffler of his cloak and they followed Flaxwith into the house. The place reeked of fire and smoke. Athelstan and Cranston used rags soaked in vinegar to cover nose and mouth as they made their way carefully down to the cellar strong room.

'Look at it!' Athelstan gasped. 'Apart from the furniture, everything is fashioned out of stone. Wooden beams and pillars are hidden under thick layers of cement, yet it would prove no defence for Pynchon. In fact, it became a trap where he was burnt to death.' Athelstan looked around. The chamber was like a spent furnace. All the contents, except for the great iron arca, had been reduced to crumbling shards or feathery ash which floated through the air, carried by the still-curling tendrils of smoke. The whitewashed walls were blackened as was the crumbling cement over the roof beams. The friar walked back to the door, badly damaged by the fire. He noted the stout lock and heavy bolts. The stench was still intense. Cranston and Flaxwith were coughing so Athelstan insisted they leave, going up into the kitchen where the pathetic remains of the draper were laid out on a canvas sheet. The fire had been merciless. Pynchon was nothing but a blackened, twisted lump of charred flesh and bone. The face was unrecognizable; the bone grey with hardening nodules of fat. Athelstan swiftly recited the last rites, overcoming his feeling of nausea. He anointed what remained of the head, hands and feet with holy oil. He then pulled back the heavy horse blanket to cover the remains and followed Cranston and Flaxwith into the comfortable well-furnished solar.

'What and how?' Athelstan abruptly asked, accepting Sir John's offer of the miraculous wineskin. He took a deep gulp, swilling the rich wine around his mouth to get rid of the taste of smoke and burning.

'Pynchon,' Cranston replied, taking back the wineskin, 'was foreman of the jury which convicted Lady Isolda. He was very proud of what he had done and made no attempt to hide his glee at the verdict he and the others brought in. Once the murders started, he hired guards and moved to this strong room.'

'They are now very common,' Flaxwith declared, glancing down to where Samson crouched, tethered to a table leg. The mastiff held a piece of parchment between his jaws, something he always did. 'All along Cheapside, Poultry and the rest,' Flaxwith declared, 'they are buying swords, hiring dogs and, when the revolt comes, they will hide in their strong rooms.'

'And Pynchon died in his,' Athelstan declared. 'So what actually happened?'

'He returned home last night deep in his cups,' Flaxwith replied. 'His guards saw him safely down to the cellar. They heard him lock the door, withdraw the key and pull across the four heavy bolts.'

'And the grille high in the wall?' Athelstan asked.

'Fashioned by a master mason out of a hard rock, or so I am informed. It has square gaps for the air to seep through.'

'Let's examine that.'

Flaxwith led them out into the garden ringed by a red curtain wall. The garden lay frozen and bleak in the vice-like grip of a winter's morning. Herb plots, flower beds and the patches of grass were all crusted white. The smell of burning hung heavy here. Flaxwith took them over to the grille just above the level of the hard, packed soil. Athelstan crouched down to examine it. The air holes were small, no more than an inch square. Satisfied, Athelstan returned to the strong room. Flaxwith fetched a ladder and Athelstan climbed up to inspect the grille from the inside. He came down shaking his head.

'How did it all occur?' Cranston asked. 'Surely the Ignifer would create noise, I mean, the entire chamber set alight?'

Athelstan stood, fingers to his lips, staring up at the grille before making his way into the darkened far corner beneath it. He closed his eyes and thought of the grille. How could a liquid be poured through it? He opened his eyes and smiled as he recalled a tapster draining a cask of wine by inserting a tube and sucking on the end to draw up the dregs. Or a boy with a set of bellows, and the games he and the other urchins used to play with each other. They would fill the bellows with water then squeeze out a hard spurt through the metal tube on the end.

'That's what happened here,' he declared.

'What did, Brother?'

'Oh, there's only one way the Greek fire entered this room, and that's through the grille. Think of a set of bellows, Sir John, with a tip which could fit through one of those gaps, its bags full of oil. The Ignifer simply stuck the metal end into a hole in the grille and gently squeezed the oil so it ran down the wall on to the floor. Pynchon made a most grievous mistake. I am sure he boasted about his strong room and so drew attention to it. The Ignifer would climb the garden wall, observe the grille and plan accordingly. He would keep Pynchon under strict observation and await his opportunity. Our linen-draper left his house last night deserted and returned deep in his cups.' Athelstan indicated with his head. 'The Ignifer gained entrance to the garden under the cover of night and squeezed in the oil. Pynchon returns, he is tired, drunk, and the far corner of this chamber is shrouded in darkness. He is unaware of what is happening. Perhaps he smells the oil or, if it was odourless, the reek from its container, but that does not alert him. Outside the assassin waits, quietly watching that grille. He sees the glow of lantern-light, hears the lock being turned, the bolts pulled, all the sounds of his drunken victim preparing for the night. The Ignifer then returns to his task: more Greek fire is poured through the grille. Pynchon may have heard it but it's too late, he is trapped. One or more slender, lighted tapers, small glowing pieces of wax, are pushed through the gaps. Think of a needle with a fire on the end. Pynchon is alerted but the sparks fall. The oil is ignited. Greek fire blazes swiftly and greedily up. Remember the recent attack on us, Sir John, how speedily those flames leapt as if they had a life of their own?'

'But the smell?'

'Sir John, this is true Greek fire. I suspect it is both colourless and odourless. Again, after the attack on us, I knelt down to pray for that poor man. I also picked up a shard of the pot the killer had used which was not caught up in the fire. I smelt it. I could detect virtually nothing. As I've said, the only odour might come from the container it was kept in. Anyway, Sir John, I suspect that's what happened to poor Pynchon.'

'Rumour flies faster than a sparrow,' Cranston observed. 'The gossips maintain the fire comes from Hell. God's judgement on those responsible for sending an innocent woman to her death. Already there are grumblings in the Commons about the justice of this, how the entire case should be reviewed.'

'No, no, Sir John. This was not the work of an angel or demon.' Athelstan led the coroner out of the cellar. 'Trust me, all of this is down to sheer human wickedness.' He paused. 'We'll resolve this as we always do, by careful examination, logic and evidence. To do that we have to talk. We are in the city, so I think it's time we visited the Minoresses in their convent.'

They left Bread Street, making their way towards the Tower. A freezing cold day though the sun was welcoming enough. They tramped through the icy sludge, keeping a wary eye on what was underfoot as well as the low-hanging signs and the upper casement windows from which chambermaids threw all kinds of filth. A relic-seller, garbed completely in horse skin, his antlered head covered by a scarlet cloth, offered the teeth of Goliath from his tomb in a miraculous cave overlooking the Dead Sea. Cranston told him to shove off, but the macabre sight made Athelstan reflect on the miracle at St Erconwald's. He ruefully conceded that neither he nor Master Tuddenham had found anything to create even a reasonable doubt. The Ignifer was a different matter, bereft of any proof or evidence. So far that assassin had struck at least four times with deadly effect. Three of his victims were simply caught out in the street, an easy enough task. Athelstan glimpsed a maid carrying a bucket towards him, on a nearby doorpost a lantern still glowed. How swift would it be, the friar asked himself, for the maid to throw the contents of her bucket over someone, grasp the candle from the lantern and hurl it at her victim? Trudging slightly behind the wine-swigging coroner, Athelstan estimated it would take no more time than to recite an Ave or a paternoster. The Ignifer's first three attacks had counted on surprise but the assault on Pynchon had been more cleverly planned. Apparently the draper had confidently proclaimed how he was securely protected; that had now been exposed as an empty boast. Pynchon lay dead, one further horror following the execution of the Lady Isolda. The Ignifer was proving to be very cunning. He might not strike at all of those involved in Isolda's condemnation and execution, nevertheless he had created a world of deep dread for anyone who had anything to fear. Athelstan thumbed his Ave beads. He could not enter the soul of the killer. He suspected that like some hungry wolf sloping through the undergrowth, the Ignifer would lie low for a while, let peace descend and strike again. Lifting his head, Athelstan glimpsed a courier hastening through the streets carrying his white wand of office, garbed in the splendid tabard of the House of Lancaster. John of Gaunt, Athelstan reflected, was also deeply involved in Isolda's burning. Would the Ignifer strike at him? But how and when? In the meantime, the assassin would spread his miasma of fear, a veritable mist provoking all forms of dire threats and menaces.

Athelstan broke from his reverie. Cranston was bellowing at two apprentices from a nearby smithy who were hurling pieces of charcoal at each other. His shouts and the ugly muttering of others drove the sooty-faced imps back into the smithy. They walked on. Athelstan's attention was caught by an itinerant preacher garbed like St Christopher, or so he proclaimed, as he warned about the 'foul, bubbling stew of corruption of the city, rich with murderous misdeeds and all forms of wickedness'. Athelstan quietly agreed with the words. He felt uneasy, as if they were being watched and shadowed, though he could not detect anything amiss. They reached St Andrew's Cornhill, a veritable haven for felons, a dark den of thieves, apple squires, nips and foists. Cranston was immediately recognized. Insults were hurled, followed by clods of icy filth. Cranston drew both sword and dagger and the danger receded. They went up Aldgate towards the imposing entrance to the Minoresses. Just before the great double-barred gate, Cranston plucked at Athelstan's sleeve and pointed to a large life-like statue of the Virgin half-stooped over an empty cradle. Beside the statue hung a bell under its coping, a red tug rope dangled down to lie curled in the empty cradle.

'If a mother,' Cranston explained, 'does not want her baby, she places it in the cradle and pulls the rope.' He turned and pointed back down the street. 'The mother would probably hide there to watch and wait until one of the good sisters appeared.' He approached the gate and pounded on the wood. A hatch high up in the door opened and a face peered out.

'Jack Cranston,' the coroner declared, 'and Brother Athelstan, parish priest of St Erconwald's.'

'Oh, the miracle!' a voice exclaimed.

'Yes, we are.' Cranston laughed. 'Now come on, Sister, open up. Our legs are freezing and I do not want the cold to rise any further.' The portress giggled, the postern door swung open and both the coroner and friar stepped inside. They followed their blue-garbed guide across the cobbles, through the great cloisters and into the parlour of the guesthouse. A warm sweet-smelling chamber, its white walls were dominated by the cross of San Damiano and painted scenes from the lives of St Francis and St Clare. The rushes on the floor were green, supple and fragrant with powdered herbs. The portress ushered them to chairs placed around a square table and wheeled in two capped braziers to provide greater warmth. She explained that Mother Superior would be with them soon – in the meantime, would they like refreshment? Blackjacks of ale and dishes of soft herb cheese on strips of manchet bread were just being served when Mother Clare bustled into the guestroom. A cheery-faced woman, the Mother Superior gave a scream of delight at seeing 'Old Jack'. She then embraced both him and Athelstan in a warm, tight hug of welcome.

'Well,' she indicated that they retake their seats, 'eat and drink. Remember what St Francis said, and this even includes Dominicans.' She winked at Athelstan. 'The first rule of a Christian is to be hospitable. Good, you are eating. Now, why are you here? Oh, no,' her fat fingers flew to her chubby face, 'of course, Lady Anne Lesures is already here.' Her voice fell to a whisper. 'Poor Isolda Beaumont.'

'She was left here as a foundling?'

'Yes, Brother, we took Isolda. I was novice mistress at the time,' she shook her head, 'just over twenty years ago. We called her Isolda Fitzalan because she was left in the gate cradle, wrapped in a cloth boasting the arms of the Fitzalans . . .'

'Azure and Or, a branch of oak, vert and fructed or . . .'

'Precisely, Sir John – correct to the last detail.'

'The Fitzalans.' Athelstan glanced swiftly at Cranston. 'Surely Thomas Fitzalan, the present Earl of Arundel, is powerful? Feared even by Gaunt?'

'Don't let your imagination run away with you, Brother.' Mother Clare smiled. 'The Fitzalans are legion in number. I suspect that one of their young women from a minor branch of the family became pregnant out of wedlock and decided she must give the child away.' Mother Clare sighed and helped herself to a strip of toasted cheese. 'The swaddling blanket is no real indication of birth, it could be used by some maid or servant to show the child was noble born.'

'Why Isolda?' Athelstan asked. 'A rather unusual name?'

'Very simple, Brother. We found a scrap of parchment pushed into a fold of the blanket on which the name Isolda was written.'

'Are many such children left here?'

'A few, always girls, and remember, Brother, many mothers often change their mind and return for their child.'

'But not in Isolda's case?'

'Never.'

'What was she like?'

Mother Clare touched her starched white wimple. 'She was, even as a little girl, extraordinarily beautiful, graceful in all her ways.' Mother Clare put her face to her hands then took them away. 'God forgive me, Isolda was also avaricious, wilful, obdurate and selfish.' The nun crossed herself swiftly. 'There. I have said it, God forgive me but it's the truth. Isolda was greedy for wealth and power.'

'And did she get that through her marriage to Sir Walter?'

'No.' Mother Clare blew her cheeks out in a long sigh. 'Isolda often returned here after her marriage, ostensibly to help Lady Anne and others with our novices.'

'And?'

'Isolda always had a bitter litany of recriminations against her husband. He was wealthy, his purse bulged with coins, but the purse strings rested very firmly in his hands.'

'Are you sure?' Cranston asked.

'Jack, would I lie to you?' Mother Clare blew him a mock kiss.

'So,' Cranston shook his head, 'Isolda had little or no money for herself?'

Mother Clare nodded in agreement.

'Nicholas Falke, God bless him,' Cranston breathed, 'is a very experienced serjeant-at-law. He is also expensive.'

'So who paid him to represent Lady Isolda?' Athelstan asked. 'It could have been "pro bono" or, in this case, "pro amore" – love. Falke was, and still is, much smitten with Lady Isolda.' The friar turned to Mother Clare. 'Do you know?' She pulled a face and shook her head.

'So in your view, the marriage was a failure?'

'Brother,' she replied, 'after her marriage Isolda often came here. At first she acted the great lady, being feasted and feted. Time passed. She was married to Sir Walter for five years, but we noticed the change. She became deeply unhappy but, there again, I wasted little time on that. Isolda was rarely satisfied. I think she resented her husband for many reasons.'

'Did Vanner ever come with her?'

'Oh, yes, an obsequiously faithful shadow, a man of keen wit but few words. I suspect Isolda liked to see him dance attendance.'

'And Rosamund Clifford, her maid – she too was a foundling here?'

'Yes, she was.'

'Rumour claims her father was Buckholt, Sir Walter's steward?'

'Rumour, Brother, can go hang itself,' Mother Clare retorted. 'That is nonsense. All I can tell you is that after Sir Walter married Isolda, Lady Anne Lesures secured Rosamund a place in the Beaumont household.'

'And the relationship between the two women?'

'Rosamund was as different from Isolda as chalk is from cheese. Pretty, very demure, very much in awe of Isolda.' She paused, scratching her chin. 'Indeed, both came back here. I suppose they regarded this house as the only home they truly had.'

'Do you know if Isolda met anyone else in the city?'

'Brother, I am immured here. I cannot say where Lady Isolda went.'

'And the murder of Sir Walter came as a shock?'

'God save us, Brother. It chilled our souls. At first I couldn't believe what had happened. I thought it was a mistake. In the weeks before Sir Walter died, neither Isolda nor Rosamund came here. We only learnt what happened . . .' Her voice faltered, and Athelstan leaned over and squeezed her hand.

'Mother Clare,' he said softly, 'all we want is the truth.' He withdrew his hand.

'After Sir Walter died we had visitors enough: Lady Anne Lesures, Sir Henry, Buckholt, Garman and of course Master Nicholas Falke, the lawyer. The household of Firecrest Manor were always welcome here. The Beaumonts have always been generous patrons of this nunnery.' She blinked. 'Sometimes I wonder why. I mean, you men are so eager to make reparation for the sins of the flesh, especially those of hot-blooded youth.'

'I can't comment on that,' Cranston retorted. 'There is only one woman in my life, the Lady Maude, God bless her. Anyway, since the murder?'

'Sir Henry still visits us. He has made it very clear that the murder of his brother was Isolda's doing and hers alone, no reflection on the Minoresses or our good work here.'

'But Sir Walter came here after his marriage?'

'Yes, until he fell sick and weak. Sometimes he would send Buckholt, his steward.'

'And Parson Garman?'

'Edward Garman is a former Hospitaller, now a priest, chaplain at Newgate and,' her smile widened, 'my very distant kinsman. Oh, yes, like all men he was much smitten by Isolda and, as with Master Falke, came here after the murder to discover more about her past, her childhood, anything that could be used in her defence. Falke and Garman passionately believed in Isolda's total innocence. However,' she added flatly, 'Buckholt told me about me about the posset cup. God forgive her but that was damning evidence.'

'And Lady Anne Lesures?'

'Oh, Anne, like many a young woman, married a man much older than her, a powerful city merchant, a patron of this house. He introduced Lady Anne to us. Good Lord, I have known her for so many years. Adam Lesures was an apothecary, a spicer and a very good one despite his deep love for rich red wine. Lady Anne has inherited his place in the Guild. Adam was also, so I understand,' Mother Clare lowered her voice, 'a member of Sir Walter's free company, though after he returned, Adam ploughed his own furrow and left Sir Walter to his own devices. Adam became a patron of our house and, as I say, introduced us to Lady Anne – Anne Lasido as she was then known, the daughter of a London wool merchant.' Mother Clare touched the wooden tau cross hanging on a cord around her neck. 'Lady Anne proved to be of great assistance to us, introducing our novices to noble and genteel society according to a particular young woman's talents and inclinations. Lady Anne had a great admiration for Isolda but, like me, she was not fooled by Isolda's air of cloying sweetness. We thought marriage to Sir Walter would answer her needs and change her.'

'And Isolda continued to come back here, I mean before the murder?'

'Of course.'

'Did she,' Athelstan asked, 'ever refer to "The Book of Fires"?'

'I have heard of that,' Mother Clare replied. 'Of course, Sir Walter was the King's Master of Ordnance. Rumours abounded that the Beaumonts possessed secret formulas. Isolda sarcastically referred to how her husband's wealth came from fire.'

'And did she discuss her marriage to Sir Walter?'

'Not so much discuss as pronounce. As I have said, she resented his control. Isolda really wanted to be by herself and do what she wanted. You could see the marriage was not one made in heaven and on that,' Mother Clare rapped the tabletop with her fingers, 'let me explain. On a number of occasions, just weeks before the murder, Isolda visited our small library. She was as learned in her horn-book as any scholar at St Paul's, though her real interest, or so I thought, was the tales of Arthur and Avalon. You can imagine my surprise when I decided to follow her into the library. I hid in the shadows – you see, her visits had made me curious. Anyway, something happened and she had to leave quickly. Once she had gone, I crossed to the book she had placed on the lectern. To my surprise it was the *Codex Juris Canonici* – the Code of Canon Law. When I opened the book, the marker, a red ribbon, lay across the chapter on seeking an annulment to a marriage.'

'An annulment!' Athelstan exclaimed. 'Did she ever say anything about that?'

'Never, Brother. I don't know if she was seeking an annulment. Did she hate her marriage so much, resent her husband so deeply? I don't . . .' She broke off at a knock at the door. A young novice entered and whispered a message.

'Oh, bring her in,' Mother Clare trumpeted. She glanced around the novice. 'Come in, Lady Anne. I have no secrets from you.'

Lady Anne Lesures, garbed in robes very similar to the nun, swept in, smiled at Cranston and Athelstan then pecked Mother Clare on the cheek.

'Brother Athelstan,' she explained, 'I have been very busy. I wish I'd known you were coming here.'

'Why?'

'Oh, never mind, I shall explain before we leave.'

'Come,' Mother Clare beckoned, 'come in, Anne, and close the door. I was telling Sir John about Isolda reading the code about annulment.'

'Did she ever discuss it with you?' Athelstan asked.

'No.' Lady Anne's face sharpened. 'Never. Isolda was spoilt, wilful and greedy but she had a high opinion of herself and her marriage. I didn't give it a second thought. Indeed,' she rubbed the side of her face, 'I'd forgotten all about that.'

'And you were friendly with her husband, Sir Walter?'

'Brother Athelstan, as you can imagine, we walked the same meadow and rested in the same orchard: banquets, celebrations, guild days and festival occasions. I would pester Sir Walter for alms for a number of good causes. Sir Walter was very kind. He entrusted his *Novum Testamentum* – his New Testament – to me, a great family treasure. However, about a year before he died, Sir Walter grew sickly, tired, reserved and withdrawn, so I had fewer dealings with him.'

'During the trial,' Cranston observed, 'it was alleged that Sir Walter's sickness could have been due to a slow poisoning. Sutler seemed to believe that, as did Buckholt.'

'Sir John,' Lady Anne grasped Mother Clare's wrist, 'we know nothing of that.'

'And Reginald Vanner?'

'As I said,' Mother Clare declared, 'Isolda just used him like she used everyone else. Yes, Lady Anne?'

'Oh, I agree.'

'And "The Book of Fires", Lady Anne? Did Isolda ever discuss that with you?'

'Brother Athelstan, I know about "The Book of Fires". Adam, my late husband, fought with Sir Walter and the Luciferi in Outremer.' She held up a gloved hand. 'No, Brother, they certainly did not act as comrades in arms. Adam, like many mercenaries who often adopt a new name and identity during their fighting years, was most reluctant to speak about his time in the House of War.'

'I would agree with that,' Cranston murmured. 'But Adam and Sir Walter were enemies?'

'No,' Lady Anne retorted. 'Their relationship was cold, distant but professional. I gathered there was bad blood between them but Adam remained tight-lipped. I, on the other hand, had a most cordial relationship with Sir Walter.' She fluttered her eyelids flirtatiously. 'I think Sir Walter liked me.'

'And my original question about "The Book of Fires". Did Isolda ever discuss it with you?'

'Very rarely. When she was imprisoned I did ask her of its whereabouts – had she stolen it? But all she knew was that Sir Walter had said its hiding place would be a revelation to all. How few would even guess it was safe on the island of Patmos – and no, Brother, I don't know what he meant by that.'

'And Buckholt?'

'Forget the rumours, Brother Athelstan, about Buckholt being Rosamund Clifford's father – that's nonsense. After Sir Walter was introduced to Isolda he often visited this convent, and Buckholt would accompany him. In a word, Buckholt became very sweet on Rosamund.' Lady Anne licked her lips. 'I introduced Rosamund into the Beaumont household with Sir Walter's permission. We hoped Rosamund and Buckholt would become betrothed, but they certainly did not. Buckholt loved Rosamund but she would have none of it. Some people argued that was another reason for Buckholt's hatred. He believed Isolda had turned Rosamund against him.'

'Did Isolda,' Athelstan asked, 'have such power and influence over Rosamund?'

'Oh yes,' Lady Anne declared. 'That's why we introduced Rosamund into Sir Walter's household, I mean, Rosamund and Isolda being so close. They seemed to be born for their respective roles, Isolda the great lady and Rosamund the trusted maid.'

The conversation petered out. Athelstan rose and walked around the chamber. 'Garman, Lesures and Beaumont,' he spoke over his shoulder, 'served in the Luciferi. Apparently the company broke up and the soldiers went their separate ways. Beaumont held "The Book of Fires" and kept it to himself. Could the manuscript be the cause of the breakup of the Luciferi, Lady Anne? Mother Clare?'

'I'm not sure,' Lady Anne replied. 'Adam refused to talk about his service.'

'And the same is true of Parson Garman,' Mother Clare quickly added.

'I think you are correct, Brother,' Lady Anne continued. 'Sir Walter amassed a great deal of information about cannon, powder and, above all, Greek fire, but he refused to share these secrets with others. Knowing Sir Walter's greed for both money and power, I suspect he cheated them out of it and no man, especially a soldier, likes to proclaim how he was tricked and duped.'

Athelstan nodded and returned to his chair.

'One further matter,' Cranston asked, 'Parson Garman? He also visited you here, Mother Clare. He met Isolda and was much taken by her. What else?'

'Edward is a distant kinsman in more ways than one,' the nun replied. 'In his youth he too served with the Luciferi. Afterwards he lived for a while as a Hospitaller in Outremer. He returned to London to be ordained, was appointed as chaplain and became a spokesman for the poor, especially the wretched prisoners in Newgate. He didn't just come here to visit Isolda but also to see Lady Anne.'

'Oh, don't . . .' Lady Anne waved a hand playfully.

'What?' Athelstan asked.

'Lady Anne does good work for us but she also performs sterling service as the Abbess of the Order of St Dismas, which is dedicated to helping prisoners in Newgate. Now,' Mother Clare's voice fell to a whisper, 'Edward Garman, God bless him, knows about the Upright Men – he is passionate about their cause. They have assured him that when the Great Revolt occurs he will be amongst the saved not the damned. When the black and red banners are raised, Newgate will be stormed and any official, be he Crown or Church, will face summary trial and execution.'

'I understand,' Cranston murmured, 'many places will be marked down for destruction, whilst others will be protected, and the same goes for individuals.'

'We are the same here,' Mother Clare added. 'All we do is help the poor. Edward Garman came here to beg Lady Anne's help for certain prisoners. In return, Garman promised that Lady Anne's house, her person, possessions and retainers would be protected even if all London burns. Sir Walter, God rest him, always believed that because of Lady Anne's work amongst the prisoners of Newgate, her house would be the safest in London when the revolt breaks out.'

'I am sure,' Lady Anne tried to hide her blush, 'that Brother Athelstan will also be safe. You are highly regarded.'

'I'm not too sure,' Athelstan retorted. 'What the Upright

Men decree now and what will actually happen when the mud is stirred is another matter. But,' he sketched a blessing in the air, 'Sir John and I must leave you.' He paused. 'Oh, Lady Anne, I just remembered. You said you had something to say to me?'

'I did not know you were coming here,' she explained, 'so I sent Turgot with a letter to you at St Erconwald's. On the night we were attacked, Turgot returned to the corner of that alleyway. You recall it, a thin slit of blackness from where the Ignifer launched his murderous assault? Turgot knows those runnels, slender as arrow shafts which cut through the lanes and shops. He has formed relationships with the beggars and other outcasts who haunt such dark places. Men and women like himself, mutes and cripples.' Lady Anne drew in a breath. 'There is one in particular – Didymus.'

'Didymus,' Athelstan intervened. 'That's Greek for "twin"?'

'Ah, yes,' Lady Anne continued, 'that's the mystery. Didymus maintains he is a twin. He claims his brother is always with him, though nobody else can see him.'

'Not the most reliable witness,' Cranston joked.

'Sir John, Didymus sees and smells things we do not.'

'Smells?' Athelstan asked.

'As he did the night we were attacked,' she replied. 'Apparently Didymus was in his enclosure discussing matters with his twin brother. Didymus, like Turgot, was educated by the Cistercians. He is skilled in their sign language. On the night of the attack, Didymus saw our assailant creep up the runnel and pause. Didymus informed Turgot how this person was heavily cloaked like a priest,' she pulled a face, 'or a woman. He emphasized the latter because he claimed he caught the strong fragrance of a delicate perfume. Turgot questioned Didymus closely. The smell was like that of crushed lilies, very strong and pervasive. The figure did not notice Didymus and passed on. Didymus followed and actually glimpsed the attack taking place at the end of the alleyway. Well, not every-thing. He glimpsed the flare of flames and heard the hideous screams. Didymus, not the bravest of souls, fled to hide in his enclave. Now,' she leaned across the table, 'what is remarkable is Didymus' description of the perfume. Sir John, Brother

Athelstan, Mother Clare will be my witness – that is the same
fragrance Lady Isolda always wore.' She smiled thinly.
'Anyway, that is the information that Turgot has taken by letter
to St Erconwald's . . .'

oOoOo

Athelstan and Cranston stood outside the house of the
Minoresses and stared down Aldgate.

'Interesting,' Cranston murmured. 'I've just remembered
Didymus. Despite his apparent folly, he has reputation for
being sharp-eyed. On reflection I would say he is a reliable
witness. I just wonder who our assailant was, heavily robed
and reeking of a woman's perfume? Anyway, what now,
Brother?'

'I think we should return to Firecrest Manor, Sir John. I
have more questions for them all. And that's the problem,'
he added, 'many questions, few answers.' Athelstan stared
around. He felt uncomfortable, that chill of apprehension
when he suspected he was being watched had returned yet
he could not detect the cause, though that would be difficult
in this part of the city. The world and its wife processed
through here; the good and the great as well as that shifting,
constant swarm of London's underworld, those who lived,
lurked and prowled in its shadow. Athelstan stepped aside as
a troop of Poor Toms swung by bare-legged and bare-armed,
their hair gathered in elf-locks, hollow boots shuffling along
the ground. Nearby a line of lunatics, shaking their chains
and roaring some madcap song, distracted others making their
way to dine at the many cook shops. The colour, noise and
stench were intense after the hallowed serenity of the
Minoresses. Cranston led him off, Athelstan walking just
behind, remained ever-vigilant, searching the crowd for
anything suspicious. He was shoved and pushed by emaciated
beggars pleading with hands outstretched, waving their
clacking dishes under his nose. Gaunt faces glared out of
ragged hoods and tattered capuchons. Horses neighed, donkeys
brayed and dogs constantly barked. Athelstan glimpsed a
slow-moving, lumbering convoy of supply carts with its

military escort on its way to the Tower. Shouts, yells and screams pierced the air as two market bailiffs chased a cunning man they had unmasked. The miscreant, his crutch over his shoulder, now leapt like a hare through the crowd. A group of musicians took up residence near a horse trough, but they were so drunk, one of them, wailing on a set of bagpipes, tipped over and fell into the water, provoking raucous laughter from a group of traders bringing their mounts to drink. The toper kept playing his bagpipes provoking the wandering dogs to snarl and bark even more. Horsemen trotted by. Dust clouds swirled in the ice-cold air. Athelstan tried to shake off his unease. He conceded that the true cause might not be so much the noisy crowd but the mysteries they were facing. Truly tangled, probably more than any they had ever confronted. The friar felt many lies had been peddled . . .

'Brother, Brother?' Cranston had walked back. 'Athelstan, what is the matter? Why are you . . . ?'

The friar just shook his head.

'Look around, Sir John, we are in the company of rogues. Look at their crafty, gleaming eyes, fingers ready to pick purses. They slide out of their dirty dens like slugs after the rain.' Athelstan pointed to a cunning man offering the heart of a turtledove wrapped in the skin of a dog to passers-by as a sure remedy against unchaste thoughts.

'Oh, Brother,' Cranston followed his direction, 'and they all come my way. There are many here who'll be buried in the air at the end of a piece of hempen rope – that's how these rogues describe a hanging.'

'But not today,' Athelstan murmured. He stood, swaying slightly.

'Athelstan?' Cranston was now concerned. He knew this little friar sometimes experienced attacks of numbing panic.

'Sir John, are we in danger? I can feel . . .' Athelstan broke off. The convoy of carts to the Tower had now been blocked by a group of Flecti – the Kneelers. These men, their faces hidden behind white masks and garbed in bright yellow robes with a crude red star painted on their backs, were following their own high-backed cart, which displayed a soaring wooden cross in the centre. Such pilgrim groups were becoming increasingly common in London: public penitents doing reparation for their sins through processions, fasting and visiting city churches. Times were hard and fast changing. Plague and Pestilence walked hand in hand. The war in France was lost. Heresy and dissent flourished in the Church. The papacy was still weak, having just returned from its exile in Avignon. Prices were high. Food scarce. Taxes heavy. Trade disrupted. A deeply unwholesome broth was being cooked to bubbling and soon it would spill over. Groups like the Flecti were simply an expression of a deep underlying anxiety. Athelstan watched as the Flecti, about fifty in number, crept behind their cart. The leader would shout, '*Flectamus Genua*' – 'Let us bend the knee,' and all would crouch down, heads bowed.

'*Orate!*' Pray! the leader shouted.

'*Miserere Nobis Domine!*' his followers bellowed back. 'Lord have mercy on us!'

'*Levate!*' Arise, the leader cried, and the Flecti stood up and continued their rhythmic ritual. Yet something was amiss. The Flecti appeared very organized, moving in a military phalanx. Such groups were notorious for wandering about, breaking up in a crowd. Moreover, the Flecti were now spilling around the Tower carts, coming between them and the military escort. The officers in charge were also alarmed. Abruptly the Flecti surged forward, swords, daggers and clubs appearing from beneath their cloaks.

'Flecti be damned!' Cranston shouted, drawing both his weapons. 'Upright Men! And they are after those carts.' The ambuscade was now sprung. Some of the Upright Men knelt and released crossbow quarrels to empty the saddles of the military escort. Others attacked the line of foot and swarmed over the carts. A broad black banner was abruptly hoisted aloft to ripple ominously in the freezing breeze. The Upright Men were not only intent on seizing Gaunt's stores but on displaying their power. For a few heartbeats the crowd thronging about fell silent, watching the sharp change of events in shocked surprise. This soon gave way to noisy panic. Many fled the battle now raging around the carts. Women, shrieking with terror, grabbed their children and fled to the nearest church for sanctuary. Others sought shelter in alehouses and taverns yet, even as the crowd scattered, the legion of rogues and rifflers, roaring boys and ruffians surged towards the fierce bloody struggle in the hope of plunder. The fighting was now spreading. A convoy of knights appeared, drawn swords shimmering as they strove to clear the carts of attackers, but more Upright Men streamed out of the mouths of alleys and runnels. Sir John grasped Athelstan and pulled him away, only to be surrounded by a group of Upright Men garbed in white masks and yellow robes. They glimpsed the royal insignia and chain of office around the coroner's neck and swiftly closed in a clash of whirling steel. Cranston met them sharply. Athelstan picked up a fallen morning star and rushed to help his friend. Swinging the club, the friar beat back one attacker, whilst Sir John, surprisingly light and fast on his feet, closed with the other assailants. Athelstan forgot the freezing cold, only aware of scraping steel, the rasp of sharp breath and the litany of hissed curses. He struck and struck again but his opponent was swift, moving backwards and forwards eyes glittering behind the mask as he searched for an opening. Athelstan lunged, the attacker stepped back and the friar stumbled to one knee. He raised an arm against the expected blow but others had come between him and his assailant. Athelstan staggered to his feet and stumbled back. Sir John was also being protected. Four men, cloaked and hooded, armed with sword and dagger, were driving the Upright Men away in a glittering arc of steel. They were professional swordsmen more interested in forcing their assailants to flee than inflicting bloody wounds. Athelstan glimpsed dark, swarthy faces. He noticed the cloaks of these unexpected angels were of good quality. The same was true of their high-heeled boots, silver spurs clinking at every step. Sir John grabbed Athelstan's arm, dragging him away from the conflict. The assault on the carts faded, the Upright Men disappearing into the maze of alleyways with what plunder they had seized. More soldiers were streaming into the great enclosure stretching down to Aldgate: archers from the Tower and even a company of Spanish mercenaries camped out at

Moorfields. Athelstan stared around. Their mysterious rescuers had disappeared as swiftly and as silently as they had emerged. The friar felt the savage attack had purged his own anxiety as he followed Sir John across Aldgate and on to a thoroughfare leading down to the river. The coroner, having readjusted his warbelt, paused to take a generous slurp from the miraculous wineskin before offering it to Athelstan.

'We still go to Firecrest Manor, Brother?'

Athelstan took a full mouthful of the rich Bordeaux.

'Of course we do.' Athelstan handed the wineskin back. 'Sir John, I am truly sorry about earlier. I was daydreaming.'

'You were anxious, highly so?'

'Yes,' Athelstan conceded. 'This business at Firecrest, "The Book of Fires", the attacks, it's different from the other mysteries that have challenged us. I feel there is something important we have missed. And, of course, there is the business at St Erconwald's.' He smiled up at the coroner. 'Trust me, Sir John, I would love to experience a miracle.' Athelstan slumped down on a plinth of stone and stared up the lane. He wasn't speaking the full truth. He dare not tell Sir John how sometimes, as today, he wished to be free of all this. He would love to escape back to the calm serenity of the cloisters, some hall at Oxford or Cambridge or even a village parish deep in the countryside. He scrutinized the narrow thoroughfare, the filthy sewer choked with filth and sludge, the shuttered windows, lock-fast doors, the crumbling plaster and decaying beams of the houses three or four storeys high, some held up by crutches as they leaned over to block out the sky. The stench was offensive, the cold now tingling the sweat on his body. Athelstan closed his eyes, breathed a prayer and got up.

'Come, Sir John, enough of my morbid thoughts.' They walked further down the street. Athelstan saw dust trailing from the scaffolding holding up one of these tottering tenements. He heard a shout behind him and turned. Four men stood at the mouth of the alleyway, dark shapes against the poor light. Athelstan's heart sank – more grief and trouble!

'Sir John?' The coroner had also noticed the strangers and drawn both sword and dagger.

'Satan's tits,' Cranston whispered. 'Come, Athelstan, flight is better than fight.' They backed further up the thoroughfare. One of the four men stepped forward, shouting and gesturing at them to return, pointing up at the scaffolding. Cranston and Athelstan, however, continued to retreat. Again the stranger shouted, first in English then in Norman French.

'Be warned! Be warned! *Avisera! Avisera!'*

Athelstan recalled the dust falling from the tenements. He whirled around and glimpsed the figure high on the scaffolding, the pots arching like two balls through the air. He grabbed Cranston's cloak, dragging him back up the street. They collided, staggering and clinging to each other as if drunk. Athelstan heard the pot smash close by, followed by the whoosh of one fire arrow and then another. Both coroner and friar fled as the breadth of the entire alleyway behind them erupted into sheets of flame, the fire following the liquid snaking from the shattered pots as remorselessly and as swiftly as any predator its prey. The conflagration greedily seized and consumed everything in its path, racing over midden heaps, so swift Athelstan heard the rats screaming in alarm and agony. He and the coroner, however, were fortunate: they were now free of the racing fire. Athelstan stared up at the scaffolding but the black, bleak figure had vanished. He glanced over his shoulder; his rescuers had also disappeared. The alarm had been raised. Cries of 'Harrow! Harrow!' echoed. Doors and shutters were flung open. Householders spilled into the street. Cranston had the presence of mind to shout at them to bring sand, dirt and vinegar-soaked sheets. Luckily the flames had not spread to the wooden-beamed houses either side, though the occasional blue and orange flame flickered dangerously close here and there.

'Come, Friar.' Cranston plucked Athelstan's sleeve and they went back the way they had come. 'Shall we eat and drink our fill, Brother?' Cranston offered his constant remedy to any danger.

'I don't think so.' Athelstan's fear had given way to anger. 'I sensed we were being followed and that was true,' he laughed abruptly, 'by the Ignifer as well as our angel escort, who have rescued us twice in one morning. I wonder who they are and why they save us? Sir John, this mystery is deep, dangerous and tangled.' He paused. 'If I didn't know better, I would truly wonder whether Lady Isolda didn't escape the fires of Smithfield and, like some vengeful wraith, now pursues her persecutors.' Athelstan walked on, vigilant about the sights and sounds around them. 'And there's the rub,' he added. 'We were not party to her death, so why the attacks on us?'

'Do you think she was innocent, Brother?'

'Lady Isolda was spoilt and wilful,' Athelstan paused as a cripple scuttled across the street in front of him, his wooden hand rests clattering on the frozen ground. Somewhere in a chamber above them a boy's voice chanted the '*Kyrie*' from the 'Lamentations' of Good Friday. 'Aye, Lord, have mercy on us.' Athelstan translated the refrain. 'And Lord have mercy on Lady Isolda and Sir Walter – their marriage was certainly not made in heaven. I wonder who wanted that annulment? She, Sir Walter or both? Was she looking at that Codex of Canon Law because her husband was threatening her?' Athelstan scratched the side of his face. 'And if there was an annulment, I wonder on what grounds? No, Sir John, it's idle to speculate on that or her innocence. We must get to Firecrest Manor as soon as possible. I want answers to certain questions as well as establish who was absent this morning. Strange, isn't it, Sir John?'

'What is?'

'We are dealing with these mysteries, we suffer attacks by the Ignifer, yet we also face danger from the Upright Men. Violence seems to meet us at every turn.'

'Because?' Cranston gripped Athelstan's shoulder. 'That is the way of the world. The way things are. Such assaults are common and we have just been caught up in one. A similar ambuscade was sprung three days ago in Farringdon ward. A few days before that, a string of pack ponies were seized in Cripplegate. Clement of Chatham, one of Gaunt's tax collectors, was kidnapped outside St Michael's Cornhill. The revolt is imminent, Brother, what – two, three months at the very most? Like fruit come to fullness, it has to burst. All we can do is prepare. Look at the signs, Brother, as you would the weather; the clouds gather, the wind picks up and the storm is ready to burst upon us.'

'And in the meantime?' Athelstan gathered his cloak about him. 'Murder awaits, scuttling before us. We catch its shadow but never the substance. So, let us see what new things Firecrest Manor can tell us.'

PART FOUR

'It burns up all things on which it is thrown by bow or catapult.'

Mark the Greek's *'The Book of Fires'*

Cranston and Athelstan arrived at the manor only to be informed that no one was available. Sir Henry, Lady Rohesia and Buckholt had gone into the city to deal with certain matters; Rosamund the maid had accompanied them. Mortice the buttery clerk, all puffed up with self-importance, his eyes gleaming like those of an angry ferret, brusquely informed them they would either have to wait or go. He soon changed his attitude when Cranston grabbed him by the shoulder and shook him into a more humble and cooperative mood. They were shown into the well-furnished buttery adjoining the kitchen. Here Cranston set up, as he put it, his 'seat of judgement'. A cook hurriedly served bowls of a steaming hot, well-spiced pottage, dishes of cheese and dried fruit, freshly baked bread and two large blackjacks of ale. One of the turnspits was 'inducted into the service of the Crown': Cranston gave him a coin and ordered him to go as swift as a pigeon to the city Guildhall to fetch the coroner's official scurrier, the red-headed, green-garbed Tiptoft. Athelstan washed himself at a nearby *lavarium*, cleaning off the dirt of the city and the effects of the furious fight near Aldgate. He quickly ate the food, drank the ale, made himself comfortable in a corner and fell asleep. He awoke at least two hours later, according to the day candle on its spigot. Sir John, looking remarkably refreshed, informed him that Tiptoft had been and gone.

'Nothing,' the coroner declared, 'he had nothing to report. Fulchard of Richmond appears to be genuine enough. It would seem a miracle has occurred and he was cured. No lookalike had been seen by any of my searchers and the same is reported by the Harrower of the Dead and the Fisher of Men.'

Athelstan whistled in surprise. He had confided in Cranston that the only way the Great Miracle could be disproved was to demonstrate that someone, however they did it, had taken the place of Fulchard of Richmond, whilst the real cripple had, even though it was nigh impossible to prove, been spirited away. Such a theory, however, lacked any form of evidence. The Fisher of Men had searched the river, the Harrower of the Dead all the lanes, laystalls and alleyways of Southwark – nothing had been found.

'And the same goes for Reginald Vanner,' Cranston added. 'Brother, you are correct. Vanner is dead, but by whose hand, why and how or where his corpse is hidden: all are a mystery.'

'Then come, Sir John.' Athelstan undid his chancery satchel. 'The household have returned?'

'Aye, and have resigned themselves to further questioning.'

'Then let's begin. If it's to be done,' he smiled at the coroner, 'it's best done swiftly and ruthlessly. We shall take Sir Henry and Lady Rohesia first.'

Cranston asked Mortice, who'd been appointed usher, to fetch both of these. They arrived looking very ill at ease and sat down at the buttery table opposite the coroner and his *secretarius*.

'We have answered your questions,' Sir Henry bleated.

'Then answer them again,' Athelstan snapped. He had slept well but the memory of the violence earlier in the day still affected him.

'You are a merchant, Sir Henry. You deal in cannon, culverins, fire, missiles and gunpowder. You and your brother hold a commission for this from the Crown. You own foundries, warehouses and all the impedimenta of a great merchant. Yes?'

Sir Henry agreed.

'You also own "The Book of Fires" by Mark the Greek?'

'I don't, Brother. I never held it. Sir Walter kept it very close. Of course, he talked about it being in a coffer or casket in his own bedchamber. I don't think it was ever there. In all the years I worked with Sir Walter I swear I never opened it, let alone read it.'

'Yet Sir Walter dealt in fiery liquids, he distilled oils and ground powders which could inflict great damage?'

'Yes, but on certain special creations my brother insisted on working by himself. All our craftsmen and their apprentices would fetch things, go here and there or do this and that but, in these matters, Sir Walter acted by himself. Of course,' Sir Henry hurried on, 'this was when he was hale and hearty. As he sickened, he withdrew from the trade. Sometimes, perhaps he was preparing for death, he openly regretted what he had done, the wealth he had accumulated and the way he had done it. He declared that the whereabouts of "The Book of Fires" was a matter of revelation, safe on the island of Patmos. Of course, I didn't know what he was referring to. Patmos is a Greek island, perhaps he visited it as a young man or something happened to him there. I assure you, "The Book of Fires" was Sir Walter's great secret. He once informed me that the mysteries it held should be left hidden. Sir Walter believed we human beings have a hunger to discover new ways of destroying each other.'

'Of course,' Athelstan replied tartly, 'and that would include himself? As the scripture says, "What doth it profit a man if he gain the whole world but suffer the loss of his immortal soul?"'

'Perhaps.' Sir Henry refused to meet Athelstan's gaze.

'But "The Book of Fires" definitely exists?'

'Certainly, Brother, though I have no knowledge of its whereabouts.'

'Brother Athelstan,' Lady Rohesia leaned forward, 'we are not lying. We want that book, as others do. It holds secrets which could provide even greater wealth.'

'Where did it come from?' Cranston asked.

'Another mystery.' Sir Henry took a deep breath. 'In our youth Walter and I were apprentices, traders, craftsmen. I was content with that but my brother had a wanderlust, a deep curiosity which pricked and spurred him on. He left London and travelled abroad to Outremer, then on to Constantinople. There are rumours he even journeyed along the Great Silk Road to the fabulous kingdoms of the East, but in truth I know little about that.'

'How long was he absent?'

'Oh, about fifteen summers. He left a young man and returned a veteran soldier, a warrior and a most cunning and skilful trader and merchant. He was hardly home a year when I realized how much he had learnt. We began to produce fine powder, better culverins, bombards and cannon. We could manufacture a substance to be used in mining a wall, attacking a gate or defending a castle against besiegers: a fire with horrendous effect, easy to ignite, devastating once lit and most difficult to douse. Only then did we discover that Sir Walter nursed great secrets and had a copy of "The Book of Fires".'

'And its origins?' Athelstan repeated Cranston's original question.

'Brother, I do not really know. Search Sir Walter's manuscripts – everything about his years abroad still remains a mystery. I learnt only a few facts; he was here, there, everywhere. He learnt different languages and used these to disguise and hide even more cleverly all he knew about fire and its use in war. Sometimes in his cups he'd betray a few facts. He apparently led a troop of mercenaries, like the famous White Company in France or Hawkmoor's in Italy. He called them the "*Luciferi*" – the "Light Bearers", his own private army. Walter became a *peritus*, highly skilled in cannon, powder and fire, all the impedimenta of war. He led a *comitatus* similarly trained.'

'Did any of his present household serve with him?'

'No. Buckholt, Mortice and the rest were hired on his return, I believe Buckholt's father was a member of his company but he died abroad.'

'Did your brother's past,' Athelstan asked, 'ever surface to confront and threaten him?'

'The warnings just over a year ago. I did wonder . . .'

'Yes, yes,' Athelstan replied, 'how did they go, "As I and ours burnt, so shall ye and yours"? Yet these abruptly ended. Anything else?'

'Occasionally,' Sir Henry declared, 'we would have visitors – Greeks: men muffled, cowled and cloaked. They came here to meet my brother but what their business was he wouldn't tell me. Occasionally my brother would go into the city and elsewhere; he would insist on being by himself. Again, I cannot help.'

Athelstan stared at this plump merchant prince, the sweat glistening on his thinning pate and rubicund cheeks, the constant shifting eyes, the stubby fingers never still, whilst beside him Lady Rohesia sat as if carved out of stone. You are not telling the full truth, Athelstan thought, but, there again, you are a weak man. Your brother ignored you. Athelstan glanced at Lady Rohesia, who probably was the source of any strength her husband showed. Athelstan drummed his fingers on the tabletop, aware of Sir John moving restlessly beside him.

'Did you approve of your brother's marriage to Isolda?' the coroner asked.

'I neither approved nor disapproved. It was none of my business.'

'Oh, yes it was,' Athelstan accused. 'Sir Walter was hale and hearty when he espoused Isolda. He was deeply in love with her, at least then. She could have conceived a son, and if that had happened you would no longer be Sir Walter's heir – but of course that didn't happen . . .' Athelstan pulled a face, 'Well, it's obvious. Walter and Isolda are dead – there is no other possible heir except you.'

'I could object to that.' Sir Henry quivered with indignation.

'Object as much as you like, it is still the truth.' Athelstan caught the smugness in these two worthies. They were cocksure, confident. He sensed their underlying attitude – they would cheerfully confess that they had done nothing wrong, though whether they had done anything right was another matter. 'Did you hear either Sir Walter or Lady Isolda mention the possible annulment of their marriage?'

'Never,' they chorused together, a little too quickly, Athelstan thought.

'And the fees paid to Master Falke to defend Isolda?'

'Again,' Lady Rohesia spoke up, 'we don't know. When she was committed to Newgate we sent her comforts, necessities. We thought she had money or that Falke defended her pro bono.'

'Before all this happened did Falke ever come to this house? Was he on speaking terms with Sir Walter or Lady Isolda?'

'Never, never,' Sir Henry repeated emphatically.

'Did Edmund Garman, Newgate chaplain, visit here?'

'Yes, yes, he did.'

'Why?'

'I suppose because my brother is a rich man and Garman wanted alms for the prisoners. I do know Sir Walter furnished a small chapel in Newgate. I have little to do with Garman. Rumour has it that he too served in the Luciferi before he left to become a Hospitaller.'

'Were you ever present at their meetings?'

'No, why should I be? My brother dealt with petitions and requests. I am a merchant.'

'And when did Sir Walter become ill?'

'Oh, about a year ago.'

'In the light of what actually happened,' Athelstan asked, 'do you now think that Sir Walter was being poisoned in the months before his death?'

'Perhaps, but hindsight makes us all very wise. My brother used to love his food. He had a terrible weakness for figs in almond sauce. I believe Parson Garman, who had learnt of this delicacy whilst abroad, would bring him some.'

'I repeat my question: did you suspect poison?'

'No. Nor did our physician, Brother Philippe. I believe you know him, Brother Athelstan?'

'I certainly do. I have a very high regard for him. I will be asking his opinion. By the way, did Brother Philippe attend young Rosamund?'

'Yes, he did, but he could detect nothing except the fever. Brother Philippe became very busy with this household. Rosamund fell ill on the very day that Lady Isolda took the goblet from Buckholt.'

'Tell me now,' Athelstan glanced quickly at Sir John, who now sat with his eyes half closed, 'your brother travelled abroad about . . . ?'

'Forty years ago.'

'And he was away for about fifteen years?'

'Yes.'

'He returned and married?'

'Yes, but his first wife, Matilde, died of a bloody flux only a few months after their wedding. By then my brother was winning a reputation as a great merchant. In fact, we both were. The House of Beaumont was respected, and still is, by Crown, court and Church.'

'Your brother was a widower. Did he seek consolation with other ladies? Please,' Athelstan smiled, 'I don't want to give offence but simply comment on what many men do.' He shrugged. 'And, I confess, some priests as well.'

'He certainly did.' Rohesia lost some of her stone-like demeanour.

'Could that be the reason,' Athelstan chose his words carefully, 'Sir Walter was so generous to the Minoresses in Aldgate, well known for their care of female foundlings?'

'Yes, yes.' Sir Henry coloured slightly and shifted in his chair. Athelstan wryly noticed how he edged away from his wife and the friar wondered if Sir Walter had made reparation through alms to the Minoresses for his brother's sins as well as his own.

'Before you ask,' Sir Henry measured his words, 'it is possible my brother may have sired a bastard child, a girl but,' he added hurriedly, 'I really can't say.'

'No, no, you can't,' Athelstan agreed sardonically. 'In fact, you can't say much about anything.'

'And your brother's murder?' Cranston, smacking his lips, pulled himself up from his chair. 'Did you notice anything amiss, out of place, in the weeks, days preceding his death?'

'Vanner!' Lady Rohesia exclaimed. 'We noticed he and Isolda grew much closer. Of course, at the same time, my brother-in-law was confined more and more to his bedchamber. Isolda, when she wasn't consulting with Vanner, and neither of us can tell you about what, also kept to herself. Oh,' Lady Rohesia waved a gloved hand, 'we sensed something was wrong but we had no proof and we were very busy. Sir Walter's death was a great shock, then the allegations were made and Sutler swept like a tempest into the house. Sir Walter was found dead on Tuesday morning. On the following Friday, just before compline, Sutler returned with a guard and a warrant for Isolda's arrest.'

'And Vanner?' Cranston asked. 'He was your brother's clerk. You must miss him?'

'Yes, I do,' Sir Henry tapped the table, 'but now he is gone. He was last seen on the Thursday before Isolda's arrest going out into the garden just after the angelus bell.'

'He must have fled?'

'Apparently so, Sir John, but he took none of his possessions with him, no money or valuables.'

'And his manuscripts?'

'I think he took most of them. Brother Athelstan, you may see what is left – nothing remarkable or noteworthy.'

'And your brother's chancery?'

'Of course, we have been through all his papers, Rohesia and I, assisted by Mortice and Buckholt. Do you know, Sir John, Brother Athelstan, that I searched, as did the others, but we discovered nothing from those years my brother spent abroad? No mention of "The Book of Fires". Oh, there are *billae*, memoranda, indentures and lists of this and that, but nothing really significant.'

'And "The Book of Fires" itself?'

'I've told you, Brother, Sir Walter hardly ever referred to it, and when he did he gave that sly smile, tapping the side of his nose and claiming its whereabouts would be a revelation to everyone but that it was safe on the island of Patmos, and no, I don't know what he meant.'

'And this morning?' Athelstan asked. 'You went into the city accompanied by Buckholt and Rosamund?'

'Yes.' Lady Rohesia raised her eyebrows. 'Why? Has something happened?'

'Did you stay together?'

'No, when we reached Cheapside we went our separate ways.' Lady Rohesia gestured. 'We all had different tasks, errands, items of business.'

'For how long?'

'Brother, at least two hours. Sir Henry said we should all meet at the Standard as the bells chimed for noon,' she glanced at her husband, 'and so we did.'

Athelstan sensed he would make little progress on this issue: it would be difficult, if not impossible, to prove one or more of them slipped away to launch that murderous attack so he just nodded, tapping his sandalled feet against the floor.

'Now, Sir John, are we finished here?' Sir Henry asked.

Cranston looked at Athelstan, who nodded. Once they'd left, Athelstan sat back in his chair.

'We never did anything wrong,' he whispered. 'But, there again, we never did anything right.'

'Friar?'

'An epitaph inscribed above Hell's door, Sir John. Believe me, that precious pair could tell us more but chose not to. Ah, well, you have summoned Falke and Garman?'

'Yes, and let's see if they have arrived.'

Nicholas Falke, blond hair all dishevelled, face flushed, blue popping eyes blinking with anger, was ushered into the buttery. Mortice served more ale.

'Sir John, Brother Athelstan,' Falke began, 'I am very busy.'

'Aren't we all?' Cranston replied. 'So let's be brusque and brisk. Tell the truth and you will have nothing to fear.'

'Sir John, are you threatening me?'

'Yes. I am Lord High Coroner of London and this session is as valid as any court. So first, before you defended Lady Isolda did you have any dealings with her?'

'No.'

'So why did you defend her? Come on,' Cranston snarled and banged on the table, 'I will have you put on oath and, if you lie, haul you off to Newgate on a charge of perjury.'

'For the love of God,' Athelstan whispered, 'Falke, you did your duty. You tried your best but Isolda has gone to God. We need to know why you, a complete stranger, a well-respected lawyer, defended her. Isolda, so we understand, had very little money of her own?'

Falke, raising his hand in a sign of peace, scraped back his chair and walked over to the window. He pulled back the shutters and stared through the thick mullion glass.

'I truly believed that Isolda was innocent. I accepted and still do that the story about the goblets was a mere fabrication. Isolda maintained Sir Walter must have been poisoned by others.'

'Like whom?'

'Oh,' Falke didn't turn round, 'Buckholt, even Vanner. But I saw these accusations as the outpourings of a tormented mind. All she could cite was household gossip.'

'And Vanner?'

'She admitted he was her ally here at Firecrest and, like the others, had grievances against his master. She pointed out that Sir Walter could have been poisoned before she gave him the drink or at some time during the night. People could have gone in or out of his chamber – after all, he wasn't found dead until after daybreak.'

'And "The Book of Fires"?' Cranston warned. 'You must answer our questions truthfully.'

'Ah, well.' Falke turned and walked back to his chair. 'I did not know Isolda Beaumont before her arrest or imprisonment. I was visited in my chamber by a Greek merchant, Nicephorus – he and his three companions, professional swordsmen. I later found out they were from the elite Imperial corps of the Varangian Guard at Constantinople. Nicephorus was most pleasant, calm and courteous. He wanted me to defend Isolda. I asked him why. He said that was his business. I told him to make it mine.' Falke sipped at the tankard. 'He was direct. He didn't care if Isolda was innocent or guilty, he simply wanted the whereabouts of the manuscript, or at least Sir Walter's copy, of Mark the Greek's "The Book of Fires".' Again Falke paused to drink. Athelstan watched him and recalled those mysterious rescuers earlier in the day.

'I pressed for more. Nicephorus said it was a long story and did not concern me. However, once I accepted his commission, he gave me details. As a young man Walter Beaumont travelled to Constantinople. He served in their mercenary corps of gunners, where he deepened his knowledge of gunpowder, cannon, projectiles, Greek fire and all the secrets of the Imperial army. It was a time of unrest. The Turks were redoubling their attacks. Matters were made worse by earthquakes, plagues and civil war. Eventually peace was restored when John Cantacuzene emerged as the victor, assuming the title of John VI. However, during the unrest, Walter Beaumont and his mercenary troop took part in the pillaging of the Imperial palace. According to Nicephorus, they were not after treasure; instead Beaumont, with a few of his companions, no more than six henchmen, invaded the secret chancery of the Emperor's library. There, in a locked arca which they forced, they found a copy of Mark the Greek's "The Book of Fires". Beaumont stole this and fled. Now Beaumont led a company.' Falke paused.

'Luciferi?' Athelstan gently prompted. 'The Light Bearers?'

'The Luciferi,' Falke agreed. 'Some of them were caught and executed. Beaumont and others escaped and returned to England. However, the Imperial court had to be careful. If they issued demands to the English Crown, our late King Edward III and his warriors would have become deeply intrigued. "The Book of Fires" is greatly valued, the knowledge it holds highly prized. The Imperial court did not wish to emphasize this too much. Moreover, Beaumont soon became a very powerful merchant directly patronized by the Crown. Finding Beaumont was easy enough but the Greeks dared not do anything against him lest the whereabouts of "The Book of Fires" died with him.'

'So Nicephorus asked you to defend Isolda and, by doing so, discover the whereabouts of "The Book of Fires"?'

'In a word, yes, Brother Athelstan. I was given a fee, a good gold coin, and promised much more if I located the precious manuscript. Sir John, Brother Athelstan, I am talking about a veritable fortune.'

Cranston whistled under his breath. 'In God's name,' the coroner whispered, 'why do they want it back so much? Surely the Greeks have copies? Of course,' he clapped his hands as he answered his own question, '"The Book of Fires" is a veritable treasure trove with all its formulas and secret mixtures. Others want it!'

'Precisely, Sir John. The Greeks use such fire, the Imperial navy carries it. It's the last line of defence against their enemies. The Turks are swallowing up one territory after another. One day the Greeks will have to confront their darkest nightmare, a Turkish army laying siege to Constantinople. Greek fire would be crucial to its defence, whilst the Turks would use it with devastating effect. Nicephorus was desperate to retrieve "The Book of Fires".' Falke shook his head. 'Sometimes Nicephorus changed his story.'

'In what way?'

'He talked of Sir Walter, or "Black Beaumont", pillaging the Imperial chancery and escaping with a close group of Luciferi. Nicephorus hinted that Imperial agents killed some of these but others of the company may have been murdered by Black Beaumont himself. And something else.' Falke paused to collect his thoughts and Athelstan sensed the man was telling the truth. 'There may have been two copies of "The Book of Fires". Beaumont gave one back but withheld the other.' He shook his head. 'I am not too sure. You must remember my sole task was to defend Lady Isolda. They paid my fee and provided me with extra money so Lady Isolda could have her own cell in Newgate, squalid though it was. If she'd been thrown in with the common herd, God knows what would have happened.'

'And Lady Isolda knew all this?' Athelstan asked.

'Naturally. She conceded that the Greeks had approached her very soon after her marriage to Sir Walter, offering a veritable fortune for the return of what she called "that damnable book". I begged her to tell me what she knew. All she could reply was that Sir Walter kept it secret.'

'Do you know,' Athelstan asked, 'if the Greeks approached other members of the Luciferi? You did say some survived and returned to England?'

'Yes, yes.' Falke nodded. 'I asked the same question. They said it had been easy to find Walter Beaumont but the rest were not so simple. Sir John, you must know this, men who travel abroad to be mercenaries often change their names and identities.'

'I agree,' the coroner grunted. 'On one occasion I did it myself.'

'Anyway, to return to Lady Isolda, I pressed her to tell me what she knew. She replied that Sir Walter was too cunning even to share such secrets with his brother.' Falke rubbed his face in his hands. 'Nicephorus was honourable; he paid for the cell and necessities as well as a generous fee. I continued to defend Isolda. I truly believed in her innocence. In the end she could not explain away the testimony of Mortice or Buckholt, whilst the disappearance of Vanner did not help her case. All she could maintain was that she was the victim of a cruel plot.'

'On the question of money,' Cranston asked, 'was Sir Walter a generous husband?'

'No. He kept a tight rein on what he called his "high-spirited filly" of a wife. He was not overly generous to her.'

'Did she blame Vanner?' Athelstan asked.

'She said it was possible that he was the killer, that he fed Sir Walter some potion before or after he drank that posset.'

'Interesting,' Athelstan murmured, 'how she accepted that her husband had been poisoned.'

'Oh, yes, but not by her.'

'Did she,' Athelstan asked, 'ever refer to a possible annulment of her marriage to Sir Walter?'

Falke gaped in astonishment. 'Never,' he spluttered. 'That was part of her defence, how her relationship with Sir Walter was cordial.'

'Of course, of course,' Athelstan murmured, 'she would, wouldn't she? Now, Vanner disappeared the day before her arrest. Did she ever enquire about his whereabouts?'

'No, not really. She said Vanner might have had a hand in Sir Walter's murder, but she was more concerned about herself than anyone else. You can understand why: she faced disgrace, humiliation and a savage death. She maintained her innocence. She claimed she was a victim of a clever plot by others in the household, Buckholt, Mortice, Sir Henry and Lady Rohesia. Sir John, you are a law officer, you can appreciate my situation in defending her. She hadn't a shred of evidence to support any counter-allegations and the case against her was so pressing it might well have been the outcome of a very clever plot. The question of the goblets, Sir Walter falling ill . . .' Falke let his words hang in the air.

'And the Greeks?' Cranston asked. 'Have they troubled you since?'

'No. I was paid my fee, Nicephorus was honest and honourable.' Falke wiped the sweat from his face. 'They have left me alone. Sir John, Brother Athelstan, I have told you what I can. I really must leave.'

'Were you busy this morning?' Athelstan asked.

'Yes, around the Inns of Court: I attended a session of the King's Bench in Westminster Hall. Why?' Falke leaned forward. 'Has something happened? It did, didn't it? I have witnesses. I can swear to where I was. I . . .' He paused as Athelstan lifted a hand.

'Master Falke, we are finished – you may leave.'

'Well, Brother?' Cranston asked as the door closed behind the lawyer.

'I don't know, Sir John, I truly don't. We have a number of strands here: the innocence or guilt of Isolda; the truth about a host of secrets at Firecrest Manor such as the whereabouts of Vanner; the role played by Sir Henry and his wife. There's the identity of the Ignifer, the annulment of Isolda's marriage, the business of "The Book of Fires" and the fact that some of its dreadful secrets are being used to murderous effect. We deal with the present, Sir John, but many of these mysteries trail back decades. Ah, well, has Parson Garman arrived?'

Cranston rose and went to the door. He talked to Mortice and returned, followed by the tall, lanky figure of Brother Philippe, Canon of the Order of St Augustine and principal physician in the House of Mercy at the Hospital of St Bartholomew, Smithfield.

'Garman is unable to come,' Cranston explained, 'he is attending executions over Tyburn stream.' He smiled. 'However, I believe you are acquainted with our next guest.'

'Indeed I am.' Athelstan stepped round the portly coroner to exchange the kiss of peace with Philippe Layburn, who, in Athelstan's opinion, was the most skilled physician in London. The Augustinian, his long, weather-beaten face smiling in pleasure, hugged Athelstan close.

'You're still too skinny, Dominican,' he whispered. 'You should eat better.'

'Sir John does that for me,' Athelstan replied, stepping back and studying the Augustinian from head to toe. 'Brother physician, you look well.' What always fascinated Athelstan was Philippe's sharpness; it seemed to express itself in almost claw-like fingers and eyes as keen as those of a hunting hawk.

'Brother Athelstan, I am well.' Philippe sat down, gratefully accepting the tankard of ale Cranston poured for him on the side-dresser and brought across.

'Thank you for coming, Philippe.' Athelstan gestured around. 'We live and work in very dangerous times. You've heard of the Ignifer?' Philippe nodded. 'He appears to have marked Sir John and me down for death and it's all connected to Firecrest Manor, where you are physician, yes?'

'One household amongst many.'

'And Sir Walter?'

'Brother, an enigmatic man. I fed him physic but I hardly knew him. To be honest, his household always seemed cloaked in secrets and mystery.'

'And Lady Isolda?'

'No better than her husband. She wore her beauty like a shield, fair of face and lovely of form. Isolda kept her distance and she made sure you kept yours.'

'And her health?'

'I never had to tend to either Isolda or Vanner the clerk, but Sir Walter was close to his sixty-sixth summer, a man whose body had certainly been battered by time and indulgence.'

'In the year before he died,' Cranston asked, 'Beaumont fell ill, greatly confined to his bed. Could that have been poison?'

'It's possible, Sir John. Look,' the physician sipped from his tankard, 'Brother Athelstan, we have discussed this before. It is very easy to disguise poisons. Too much foxglove and the heart can be seriously affected. Too much arsenic, and remember it can be used for stomach ailments, and the person dies. I would go on oath that some of my patients who died of so-called natural causes were truly poisoned, but it's one thing to allege, another to prove and convince a jury. Sir Walter is a fine example. He had served abroad. God knows what ills, miasmas, contagions or diseases he'd encountered. He returned to London and lived high on the hog; his belly, bowel, blood and humours must have been affected by all of this. Yes, I had my suspicions, but it was a question of much suspected and nothing really proved. I gave him potions to purge, cleanse and restore his humours. I urged caution in what he ate and drank. After a while, this wasn't necessary – Sir Walter ate and drank very little.'

'But on the morning you examined his corpse you concluded that he had been poisoned?'

'I disagreed with the local physician Milemete – though, there again,' Brother Philippe spread his hands, 'it's hard to link cause and effect. I examined Beaumont's corpse most carefully: his face was liverish, eyes slightly popping, a white sputum or froth coated his lips and chin. Here,' the physician patted his own stomach, 'purplish blotches. Now,' he supped from his tankard, 'there are physicians who would argue that such symptoms could be caused by malignant humours rather than a potion. You must also remember, as I told Sutler, that Sir Walter was known to take his own remedies – for example, the last cup of posset was thickly coated with herbs and spices. The wealthy ignore my advice and, as both of you know, many gardens contain more poisons than a sorcerer's cabinet. When I arrived in the house that morning, of course, there were whisperings and mutterings, so I was most scrupulous. I examined the inside of Sir Walter's mouth, which had turned singularly dry. I was able to establish that he had drunk a thick, rich posset. I removed some of the crushed herbs, little shreds caught between his teeth and gum. I noticed a blackness of his tongue, mouth and throat. I detected an offensive smell and I concluded that the posset had been used to disguise something. Sutler pressed me on this and I had to be careful. I did concede that I couldn't prove it beyond reasonable doubt. I used a less rigorous assessment, namely, that on the balance of probability Sir Walter appeared to be poisoned. Sutler seemed satisfied with that.'

'Of course, he would be,' Athelstan conceded.

'You must remember my conviction deepened when Sutler produced more proof. If that steward and buttery clerk had not given evidence, it would have been very difficult to prove anything against Isolda. According to Sutler, Isolda seized the posset to feed her husband, she changed the goblet and Vanner, who went into the city to buy an extra goblet, appears to have been her accomplice. Both judges and jury fastened on that and, Brother, what real defence did Isolda muster?'

'And the maid?' Cranston asked. 'Rosamund Clifford?'

'Very strange. I was summoned to attend Sir Walter's corpse. Buckholt told me that Rosamund was lying very ill. Of course, I examined her. She had been vomiting until her belly ached. She had a fever, a terrible thirst and looseness of the bowels, but she was also very young and vigorous.'

'Could she have been poisoned?' Athelstan asked. 'It's strange that she fell ill on the same day Sir Walter died.'

'Brother, coincidence is one thing, proof is another. Rosamund had an ailment of the belly but such a condition, though not as serious, was common in this household.'

'Was it?'

'Oh, yes, Brother, belly sickness, bowel disorders, ailments of the spleen and other conditions but nothing fatal. The same applied to Rosamund. She did not die. I did ask her if she could explain the cause of her illness. She was unable to. I told her to drink good clear water and not to consume anything else until her stomach became calm and the fever abated. I distilled her a potion, dried moss mixed with sour milk. She recovered but by then her poor mistress had been arrested, tried, condemned and executed.'

'And the Great Miracle at St Erconwald's?'

'Brother, I met Fulchard of Richmond on his arrival in the city. He came into the House of Mercy at the hospital because of his condition, badly burnt down his right side, weak and infirm after his journey south. Such terrible injuries are eye-catching. I also noted his left side, the colour of his hair and distinguishing marks. You might ask why. As a physician, I would reply that's a habit. If a man's hand is shrunken, you immediately look at the other to compare, to judge, to assess. He told me about his past life and the hideous injuries he'd received years ago in a Greek tavern. I gave him treatment and a letter of attestation which,' Philippe gestured at Cranston, 'he could use in London if stopped by the city bailiffs who wage constant war against counterfeits.'

'True,' Cranston grunted.

'Anyway,' the physician continued, 'Master Tuddenham summoned me to St Erconwald's and presented me with a Fulchard of Richmond who was all healed. Of course, I found him stronger, fit and able, intelligent and reflective, yet still the same man. I noted the mole high on his left cheek, I questioned him about his past experiences. Brother, I could find nothing to say he wasn't Fulchard of Richmond. Like you, I am a priest. Our faith teaches that due to God's grace miracles do happen. Master Tuddenham is a lawyer, a master of logic. I had to tell him the only conclusion I could reach. A miracle had occurred. That there was no other evidence to suggest trickery.' Philippe sighed and drained his tankard. 'Brother Athelstan, Sir John, what have I talked to you about? Signs and symptoms, and that is what we all deal with, particularly in physic where the rash on a man's chest or back can have a hundred and one causes. It can be symptomatic of a wide variety of contagions, a predictor of minor infirmity or some deadly disease. The same is true of Fulchard. I found him the same man with all his symptoms cured. I could produce no evidence to contradict such a story.'

The physician made his farewells and left. Buckholt then joined them. Athelstan questioned him closely about the events of that fateful day, but the steward would not concede anything he had not declared before.

'I hated Isolda,' he confessed. 'I despised her. She poisoned Sir Walter and I believe she weakened him in the months before his death. She used Vanner as she used anybody. She loved no one but herself. Master Sutler had the truth – she was an assassin.'

'You mention Vanner?'

'And I have answered you, Brother. She used him. I know what I saw that day. I believe both of them were involved in Sir Walter's murder.'

'Did you serve with Sir Walter abroad?'

'No.' Buckholt shook his head. 'My father did and died in Outremer. I think that's why Sir Walter gave me a post in his household. And before you ask, I have never seen "The Book of Fires". I don't know where Sir Walter kept it or what he meant by his riddles. I don't know where it is now. Perhaps Vanner knew more than I but he's probably dead.'

'What makes you say that?' Athelstan asked sharply.

'Vanner liked his comforts. He hasn't fled. He took none of his possessions except his chancery satchel. He's not been seen, he's just disappeared. I suspect Isolda killed him, though God knows how, when, where or why.'

Athelstan studied this stubborn, resolute steward who seethed with hatred for his former mistress. Did that hatred, he wondered, cause him to lie, and what was its source? Did he believe Isolda had frustrated his yearning for the fair Rosamund?

'Did you have any dealings with Falke, Lady Anne or Parson Garman?' Athelstan asked.

'Very little. Why should I?'

'Garman is parson at Newgate. They say he is close to the Upright Men. A supporter of the Great Community of the Realm.' Cranston jabbed a finger. 'They also say the same about you.'

'I don't know who "they" are,' Buckholt snapped. 'Most of London supports their cause. Gaunt is hardly popular, is he? Anyway, what has that got to do with Sir Walter's death?'

'Aren't you frightened?' Athelstan asked softly. 'The Ignifer is dealing out judgement.'

'You mean the ghost of Lady Isolda,' Buckholt jibed. 'Yes, that's what they say. Only a soul steeped in wickedness such as hers could wreak such horror.' He lifted his hand. Ave beads were wrapped around his fingers. 'I put my trust in God. I know what the Ignifer is doing.'

'What?'

'He is leaving me for last so I can drink and feed on all the terrors which are supposedly coming for me. I will deal with that when it happens. I do not regret what I did.'

'But you do regret some things, don't you?' Athelstan retorted. 'Rosamund Clifford? You used to visit the Minoresses with Sir Walter. You became acquainted with young Rosamund?'

'No, Brother, I didn't become acquainted; I fell in love with her. I truly did and I still am.'

'But she rejected you?'

'She's possessed by her mistress.'

'What do you mean?'

'Ask her yourself. It's quite simple. Rosamund only thought what Lady Isolda thought. Rosamund only did what Lady Isolda approved of. As I said, ask her yourself.'

'And this morning?' Athelstan queried.

'What about this morning?' Buckholt flinched as Cranston banged the table.

'Rosamund and I accompanied Sir Henry and Lady Rohesia into Cheapside. We went our separate ways on different tasks and met a few hours later at the Standard.' Buckholt refused to meet Athelstan's gaze.

'What tasks?' the friar demanded.

'Oh,' Buckholt flapped his hand, 'very few. I inveigled Rosamund into the Bishop's Mitre off Cheapside.'

'I know it well,' Cranston murmured.

'I tried to talk to her but she wouldn't listen. I . . .' he took a deep breath, '. . . let her go, drank too much and staggered out to complete my errands.' He looked at Athelstan. 'That's the truth.'

Athelstan could see Buckholt was growing more taciturn, so he dismissed him and summoned Rosamund Clifford into the buttery. The dark-haired, pretty-faced maid, garbed in a cloak draped over a russet dress with white edging at neck and cuffs, almost crept into the room. She sat down on a chair, hands in her lap, smiling demurely as if she was truly perplexed about why she had been summoned. Athelstan stared hard at this young woman, fighting to curb his own anger and resentment. He disliked her holier-than-thou attitude, that air of bewildered innocence, as if all the horrors happening around her were of no concern whatsoever.

'You were a foundling, and a novice at the Minoresses?'

'Yes, Brother.'

'You have no knowledge of your parents?'

'No, Brother.'

'And your mistress' relationship with Sir Walter?'

'In all things harmonious, Brother.'

'And the poisoning of Sir Walter?'

'Brother, I fell ill on the same day. I was gravely sick, confined to my chamber.'

'Did your mistress ever discuss the possible annulment of her marriage?'

'Brother, such matters were beyond me.' Rosamund blinked quickly. 'I was only her maid.'

You are a liar, Athelstan reflected. You know the truth about that. You are too good to be wholesome, too sweet by half. He stared at a point above Rosamund's head. He'd once heard a lecture on the human soul. How many believe the body houses the soul, whereas this theologian argued that the soul houses the body. Did souls brush each other and speak silently in their own spiritual language? Athelstan closed his eyes. He felt that now. Rosamund was a secretive, sly and subtle spirit hiding behind a mask of feigned innocence.

'Brother?'

Athelstan opened his eyes. He glanced at Sir John and winked quickly.

'Sir John, as coroner of this city, I want you to arrest Rosamund Clifford now.'

'On what charge?' Rosamund screeched, springing to her feet, her face twisted in resentment.

'Sit down, mistress,' Cranston roared, 'or I will have you in chains!'

Rosamund obeyed, bringing her clenched fists to her face and glaring at Athelstan, who leaned across the buttery table.

'Have you ever seen,' he asked, 'a human being burnt alive, mistress? Hideous! Even the bloodthirsty crowds who gather to watch at Smithfield become sickened by the sight. They throw stones to stun him or her to lessen the pain. A short while ago, I witnessed a poor torch-bearer, a totally innocent soul, burn to death for being in the wrong place at the wrong time with the wrong people. That was the first assault on me. This morning the Ignifer launched a fresh attempt. Others have also been murdered for doing nothing more than their duty. Sir John and I are desperately trying to resolve mysteries including the possible innocence of your executed mistress.' Athelstan's voice rose to a thunderous shout. 'We want your help but all we get are your honeyed lies pattering through your pretty mouth. Very well, Sir John. Flaxwith and your bailiffs are outside. I suggest we take mistress Rosamund to Newgate.'

'On what charge?' she screamed again.

'Oh, possibly murder, frustrating the Crown in its searches, lying, perjury.' Athelstan waved a hand. 'Sir John, I would be grateful if you could arrange it.'

Cranston, who now realized what Athelstan intended, hastily
complied. Flaxwith and his bully boys entered the buttery and
escorted them out into the hallway. The commotion had roused
the household. Sir Henry and Lady Rohesia, escorted by
Buckholt, hurried to protest, but Athelstan wasn't in a giving
mood and they were soon out into the freezing twilight. They
made their way swiftly up through the tangle of streets towards
the fleshing market which stood close to the iron-gated
prison. The butchers and slaughterers and had now finished
their grisly trade. Huge bonfires burnt the day's rubbish. Stalls
were being taken down by apprentices who moved amongst
the horde of beggars, fighting the half-wild dogs for giblets,
offal and other discarded globules of flesh. The air stank of
brine and blood. Salt and vinegar sharpened the breeze. Huge
high-sided carts were being prepared to take away the gutted
cadavers of cows, pigs and a host of slaughtered birds. The
cobbles gleamed red from the washing vats now being emptied.
Urchins danced in and out close to the bonfires to roast white
scraps of meat they had filched. Beadles, supping from blackjacks, wandered about, their iron-tipped canes whisking the
air. Flaxwith and his bailiffs forced their way through the
broad concourse which stretched in front of the sombre, soaring
mass of Newgate prison. Athelstan knew it well. A hall of
horror piled upon horror. A place of calamity. A dwelling from
the darkest Hell. A bottomless pit of violence where voices
screamed and howled unheard. Athelstan kept his cowled head
down as he entered that stygian kingdom of absolute despair.
Newgate was greatly feared even though its keeper, Matthew
Tweng, an old soldier friend of Sir John's, had been appointed
to implement reforms. Tweng certainly faced a herculean task.
The air was foul, riven by the most wretched cries, howls and
screams. The very walls sweated in a glistening mess. Huge
cobwebs spanned corners. The fleas and lice underfoot were
so thick and plentiful, every step crunched and crackled.
Vermin swarmed impudently. Smoke and cooking stenches
swept through mingling with the rank odour of cesspits, close-
stools and open garderobes. They crossed a maze of shuttered,
stinking wards where the screeching of lunatic prisoners
echoed constantly. They picked their way around the filth

which swilled ankle-high, kicking aside the prowling dogs and
pigs. Athelstan glanced over his shoulder. Rosamund Clifford
looked as if she was about to faint. Athelstan steeled himself.
He recalled that poor torch-bearer turned into a living flame. He
whispered what he wanted and both coroner and keeper
promised they would do a full and complete circuit of this
antechamber to Hell. They visited the underground dungeons,
known as the stone-hole, and they entered the 'Newgate
kitchen' where the quartered bodies of recently executed traitors were being hacked, boiled, soaked and tarred. The heads
of all three victims lay close by, waiting to be cauldron-cooked
in a broth of blood, bay-salt and cumin seeds. Once ready, the
severed tangled remains would be publicly exposed throughout
the city. Close to this were cells where gaunt-faced prisoners
loaded with chains shuffled like ghosts, mad eyes glared at
them through grilles high in the dungeon doors. They left the
building, passing across the great yard where a prisoner was
being pressed to plead under a heavy door loaded with chains
and stones. Tweng unlocked an inside gate, iron spikes along
its rim. They were now in a dry stone dwelling where, for a
high price, prisoners could be lodged more comfortably, though
it was still bleak and soulless. Athelstan was aware of iron-
gated windows, thick oaken doors festooned with bars, bolts
and spikes. Rosamund Clifford was almost prostrate when the
heavy door of the cell where the Lady Isolda had been housed
was unlocked. A square chamber with a black wooden floor
and whitewashed walls, the furniture was paltry: a cot bed,
table, stool, chair and jakes pot. Athelstan ordered Rosamund
to sit on the bed with a glowing lanthorn on the table beside
it.

'You can sit there and reflect,' Athelstan declared. 'Come,
Sir John.' They left the chamber, with the keeper locking the
door behind them.

'She may be a pretty young maid,' Athelstan murmured,
'but she is also a bare-faced liar who is prepared to lead us a
merry dance around the maypole of truth. Master Tweng,'
Athelstan shook the grim-faced keeper's hand, 'I am grateful.
Now, sir,' he plucked at the keeper's sleeve, 'may I impose
on you further? Sir John and I must wait a while before

revisiting our demure maid.' Tweng showed them to a small cubicle, no more than a recess with stone seats built in beneath the heavily barred lancet window. He asked if they needed anything else. Athelstan shook his head. Tweng left as they made themselves comfortable, pulling their cloaks tightly around them.

'A busy day,' Cranston yawned, 'and a dangerous one.' He gestured with his head. 'Do you really believe Rosamund is hiding the truth?'

'Yes, I do, Sir John. I sense what is happening with her. I reflect on Buckholt's words and he has studied the woman he loved. She is possessed by the soul of her mistress. Sir John, I have lived my life in male communities: the novitiate at Blackfriars, hall life in Oxford. In such communities men form intense relationships, sometimes as sexual, intimate and loving as any marriage. The same deep and even illicit friendships are formed in nunneries. I know that because I have heard many a confession. Now most of these friendships are truly innocent. They spring from a deep dependence but, occasionally, I have come across friendships, particularly between young women, which are deep and intensely passionate: it's almost as if the soul of one possesses the other. A domination emerges which is breathtaking. The tie between those women is stronger than any oath a warrior knight makes to his lord, a monk to his abbot or even a wife to her husband. I truly believe that's happened here.' Athelstan rose and paced the paved gallery running past the enclave. He paused, closed his eyes and listened to the soul of this dreadful building nick-named the Jug, the Stone, the very pit of Hell. Foul odours polluted the air whilst he could hear, though faintly, the constant, raucous noise of the prison: yells, curses, screams, shouted orders and cries of dreadful pain. Rosamund would also hear these. Athelstan prayed she would weaken; he was desperate to plan a way forward. He was tired of being deliberately frustrated, of not being able to grasp anything substantial. He was in a chamber of leaping, shifting shadows with no idea of the truth . . .

'Brother?'

'Come, Sir John.'

'Our guest awaits.'

Rosamund was still sitting on the edge of the bed, as close
as possible to the pool of light from the lanthorn. She glanced
up fearfully as they entered, shivered and returned to plucking
at the folds of her dress. Cranston took the stool brought by
the turnkey and sat down. Athelstan picked up the lanthorn
and walked over to the bleak whitewashed wall. Former
inmates had carved graffiti, usually prayers such as '*Jesu
Miserere*' – 'Jesus have mercy', or '*Kyrie Eleison*' – 'Lord
have pity'. He carefully studied the most recent scratchings
and glanced over his shoulder at the turnkey.

'Lady Isolda was the last person to be imprisoned here – I
mean, before Mistress Rosamund arrived?'

'Yes, Brother.'

'How was she as a prisoner?'

'Few visitors came. She kept to herself. There was that
outburst when she attacked Lady Anne. Towards the end –
well, she went to the execution cart like a dream-walker.'

Athelstan nodded and, holding up the lantern, used his finger
to trace the letters which looked as if they had been recently
carved there, 'LIB' – Lady Isolda Beaumont. The friar stared
in puzzlement at the scratches next to it, the letters 'SFSM'.

'Rosamund?' Athelstan repeated the letters. 'Do you understand what these mean?'

The maid rose and stumbled across to stand beside the friar.
'No!'

Athelstan turned swiftly and caught the slight cast in her
eyes. He recalled his studies on demonology and possession.
For a few heartbeats he wondered if Lady Isolda's ghost had
set up house in the soul of this young woman. Oh, she looked
frightened and cowed, yet there was something else, a secret,
stubborn resistance.

'Shall we begin?' And, taking her by the elbow, Athelstan
led her back to the bed. 'That scratching on the wall means
nothing to you?'

'I told you, Brother, nothing.'

'Sir Walter and Lady Isolda were married for five years.
How long were you her maid?'

'Four.'

'You knew each other at the Minoresses. You must have grown up together?'

'Yes.'

'You were close friends?'

'Yes.'

'Are you telling me the truth?' Athelstan persisted. 'We can leave you here to rot, not in a comfortable cell but deep in the bowels of this pestilential place.'

'I am telling you the truth, Brother.'

'Did your mistress murder Sir Walter?'

The dark eyes shifted and the pretty lips puckered, as if the death of her master was slightly amusing.

'I don't know. I truly don't.'

'I think you know more than you tell us, Rosamund. But let's come to your illness. You succumbed to the sweating sickness on the same day Lady Isolda gave the posset to Sir Walter?'

'Yes. Brother Philippe will attest to that. I lay ill. I only fully recovered after my mistress died.'

'And your relationship with Sir Walter?'

'I helped him.' She sniffed. 'When we were alone I put my hands under the coverlet. I played with him until he was satisfied.'

'Did you visit him the day he died?'

'Yes, very early in the day. He asked for my ministrations. I complied,' she shrugged, 'reluctantly, but I think he liked me to act all coy and shy.'

'Did you talk?'

'Only about what he wanted.'

'And his health?'

'Sir Walter was very much the same. He complained of his belly being delicate. I soothed him and I left. I noticed nothing untoward.'

Athelstan hid his surprise. Rosamund was very cunning. She must have realized that she would have to concede something, which is what she was doing now.

'And your mistress knew of such ministrations?'

'Oh, yes.' Rosamund leaned forward. 'Sir Walter could not bear her near him, so he asked me to comfort him.'

'What?' Cranston broke from his doze.

'My mistress,' Rosamund now perched on the edge of the bed like some conspirator with Athelstan and Cranston as her confederates, 'told me she had married for wealth but she found Sir Walter as mean as a miser with little passion in bed or the parlour. I think she frightened him. According to my mistress, he was impotent with her.' She sniffed, looking all petulant. Athelstan wondered if the young woman wasn't fey-witted. 'Sir Walter became angry with my mistress and that's when the lies emerged.'

'What lies?'

'That Isolda was really his daughter.'

'Why on earth should he think that?' Athelstan exclaimed.

'According to my mistress, in his bachelor days Sir Walter Beaumont had been a great one for the ladies. He had enjoyed many mistresses. He knew for certain, or so he claimed, that baby girls, his offspring, had been left in the care of the Minoresses. Isolda had immediately caught his eye. Only after the marriage did he begin to wonder whether the likeness between Isolda and one of his paramours was because they were mother and daughter.' Rosamund paused at a piercing scream which ran through the prison, a blood-chilling cry from the press yard.

'*Peine forte et dure*,' Athelstan whispered. 'Justice can crush. Remember that. So,' he continued, 'Isolda was bitterly estranged. What did she make of her husband's scruples?'

'Nothing but a pretence, a sham, a pretext to get rid of her. Isolda was convinced he was planning an annulment.' She chewed the corner of her lip. 'He was encouraged by that fat tub of lard his brother and his bitch-wife, Rohesia. Lady Isolda hated them and so do I. They planned that Sir Walter should die without an heir.'

'Lady Isolda had to accept all this?' Athelstan asked.

'Yes, but Sir Walter also made lewd references to me, to the possibility of me becoming his leman, his mistress. Lady Isolda agreed to this – she had to. Firstly, Sir Walter might become crueller. Secondly, she begged me to use my skill in making her husband confess to the whereabouts of "The Book of Fires".' Rosamund fell silent as if listening to the nightmare sounds of the prison. 'Before you ask, Brother, Lady Isolda believed she would be cast off. She told me that if we acquired that book we would both be very, very rich. Sir Walter welcomed my ministrations. He said I was very skilled. I asked him about "The Book of Fires". Sir Walter refused to even mention it, so I withheld my favours.'

'And?' Cranston asked.

'Sir Walter laughed. He mocked me. He became evasive. He then told me he had left the book on a Greek island called Patmos, and that its whereabouts would be a revelation to everyone. Later he changed his story, claiming that book was locked in that casket in his bedchamber. Other times he rambled and grew feverish. He claimed there were spies paid by the Greeks in his household.'

Athelstan held up a hand. 'Greeks?'

'Yes, from Sir Walter's past. He would then tell me about his early days. How he had served in Outremer. How he relished the intrigue. He described the different women he'd possessed and the fortune he'd accumulated.'

'But he never showed you "The Book of Fires"?'

'No, the closest he ever said "The Book of Fires" was . . .'

'In that casket in his bedchamber?'

'Yes. However, when it was opened after he died, the casket was empty.'

'And this alleged spy of the Greeks?' Athelstan asked.

'I don't know – possibly Vanner. I do believe they approached a number of the household at Firecrest Manor but Vanner knew no more than I did. Brother, I can assure you on oath, the whereabouts of that manuscript are a total mystery to me.'

'Was Vanner Isolda's lover?'

'I don't think so.'

'He wasn't, was he?' Athelstan retorted. 'Perhaps she promised favours she never gave. She used him as she used you?'

For a brief moment Athelstan saw the anger flare in Rosamund's eyes, a tightening of the lips and jaw, almost as if she had been struck, then she blinked.

'Isolda would never use me. I know the truth.'

'Oh, I am sure you do, but whether you are telling it now is another matter. Vanner? What happened to him?'

'He disappeared, fled whilst I lay ill.'

'And your mistress? Did she meet anyone else outside Firecrest Manor? Go into the city on some mysterious errand?'

'I was her maid,' Rosamund coolly replied. 'Where she went I was supposed to follow. Yes, there were occasions when she would not want me to accompany her.'

'Whom did she meet? The Greeks?'

'I suspect so. They wanted "The Book of Fires" – my mistress told me so. They promised her gold. But there were other occasions. I think you are correct, Brother – she met someone else apart from the Greeks.' Rosamund shrugged prettily and glanced away. 'I don't know who.'

Athelstan stared down at the ground. This woman was leading him up the devil's staircase away from the truth. She was telling him a mixture of fable and fact. She would not confess to her true relationship with Isolda nor betray her mistress in any way.

'Don't you think it was a coincidence,' Cranston asked, 'that you fell so seriously ill on the day Sir Walter was allegedly murdered by his wife?'

'Sir John, as you say, it was a coincidence. I cannot explain it.'

'Did lawyer Falke know your mistress before the death of Sir Walter?'

'No, no, certainly not.' Rosamund's relief at the change of direction in the questions was obvious.

'And Buckholt,' Athelstan asked, 'he was sweet on you, yes?'

'I could not tolerate him. I told him so.'

'He believes you rejected him because of Isolda?'

'Nonsense! Buckholt was lewd and greedy for me. I wanted nothing to do with him. He hated my mistress and she despised him.'

'So Buckholt's testimony about your mistress and the goblet of posset might have been a lie?'

'I think it was. The same goes for that little runt of a buttery clerk, Mortice. Lady Isolda truly disliked him. She thought he looked at her lecherously.'

'And Lady Anne Lesures?'

'I know very little of her. Kind, considerate, a fairly constant visitor to both the Minoresses and Firecrest Manor. She introduced me there as Lady Isolda's maid and companion. Lady Anne recognized how close we had been in the nunnery. She believed that after being placed in the Beaumont household I would make a good match.'

'But not as grand as Sir Walter, you mean, with Steward Buckholt?'

'Perhaps, but that was Lady Anne, not me. I was devoted to my mistress and made that very clear to Lady Anne. I told Buckholt the same this morning in a Cheapside tavern.' Athelstan nodded in agreement. He was correct: the only person who mattered to this young woman, whether living or dead, was Lady Isolda.

'And your origins?' Cranston asked.

'I don't know. I was a foundling and raised as one by the Minoresses.' Athelstan caught the steel in her reply. Both she and Isolda were of the same spiritual stock. They'd hardly been born when they were given away, whatever the reason, by their own kith and kin, who had rejected them as babies. No one had really cared for them, so why should they care for anyone else? Such an attitude would have bound them closely together. Cranston rose at a rapping at the door. He went, had a few words with someone in the passageway and came back.

'Parson Garman has returned from the execution ground. He awaits you in the chapel.' Athelstan turned back to Rosamund. 'Parson Garman was much smitten with Lady Isolda?'

'I know nothing of that, Brother.'

'Did Garman visit Firecrest Manor before the murder?'

'Yes, he did, but he had business with Sir Walter.'

'What business?'

'Ask him yourself, Brother. He's apparently waiting for you.'

Athelstan stared at the graffiti on the wall and wondered if it hid some secret Isolda kept to herself. He breathed in deeply, there was little prospect of Rosamund telling the full truth. Isolda dead was as influential with this young woman as she was when she was alive. She would say no more. Athelstan got to his feet.

'Mistress, the keeper will arrange for an escort to take you back to Firecrest Manor. We are finished, at least for the time being.' Athelstan swept out of the cell, Cranston followed. A guard, waiting in the dank mildewed gallery, led them up a flight of steps into the prison chapel; a barn-like room with a hammer-beam roof, a paved floor and whitewashed plaster walls stretching down to a stark stone altar in the bare sanctuary. Athelstan's gaze was caught by the myriad small black crosses etched into the plaster walls.

'Each of those,' Parson Garman's voice echoed eerily, 'represents a human being condemned to death.' The chaplain emerged from the shadows further down the church. Behind him taper-light danced before a statue of the Virgin. The friar walked over to the white plaster wall. A flaring sconce torch illuminated the hundreds of small hastily etched crosses, a silent but ominous testimony to the legion of condemned who had been brought here before being loaded on to the execution carts. Athelstan blessed the crosses even as Garman beckoned them further down the small narrow nave to a bench against the wall. Cranston and Athelstan sat down, the prison chaplain on a stool opposite them.

'I am sorry, but I've been very busy.' The chaplain's dark, close face was drawn, his eyes were red-rimmed and dark stubble darkened his upper lip and square jaw.

'How many?' Cranston asked.

'Five at Tyburn, four at Smithfield and two river pirates on the gallows near Dowgate. Some screamed and begged. Others cursed. A few prayed. All now gone to God.' He gestured at the wall. 'All carved crosses, their last memorial on earth. Now,' he forced a smile, 'you want to question me. Yet,' he spread his hands, 'I have little to say.'

'How many years have you been chaplain here?'

'About ten this Pentecost.'

'You volunteered for this post?'

'Of course, Brother. Few want it as they would your parish of St Erconwald's. I understand there's been a great miracle there?'

'I do not want to discuss that.'

The chaplain sat back, eyes guarded at the friar's sharp response.

'What I want to discuss, Father,' Athelstan continued, 'is you. Where were you born?'

'At Boroughbridge, on the River Ure in North Yorkshire.'

'I know that place.' Cranston intervened to ease the tension. 'My father fought there against Thomas of Lancaster during the reign of the king's great-grandfather. Humphrey Bohun, Earl of Hereford, was speared up the arse as he defended the bridge.'

'I have heard of such stories,' Garman responded, 'though I was born of peasant stock.'

'And later?'

'Brother, I journeyed abroad.'

'No, no,' Athelstan retorted. 'I will not accept bland words.' The friar leaned forward, holding the chaplain's gaze whilst half-listening to the dire sounds drifting in from the prison. 'Innocents have been killed, horribly burnt. Royal officials barbarously executed for doing their duty. I will be blunt. You tended to Isolda before she died?'

Garman nodded.

'But you visited Firecrest Manor long before Sir Walter's untimely death. I know you did. Why? You are youngish looking, my friend. How old are you?'

'Fifty-five summers last year past.'

'Old enough to have served with Sir Walter Beaumont abroad – Black Beaumont, captain of the free company of the Luciferi, men skilled in the use of culverins and other ordnance. You were with him in Constantinople, yes? For God knows what reason, you left his service. You entered the Hospitallers as a lay brother then returned to London, where you were ordained as a priest. You eventually volunteered to serve here as a chaplain, where,' Athelstan gestured at Cranston, 'we know you have won a reputation for being partial to the Great Community of the Realm, the Upright Men and their minions, the Earthworms. You give them solace, both spiritual and physical. You also, I suspect, have aided in the escape of a few of these from the fastness of Newgate. No, no, no,'

Athelstan held up a hand, 'you are not alone, Master Chaplain. I too see the suffering of the poor and the dispossessed. Sometimes, secretly, I also support the cause of the Upright Men. What little else can they do in the face of such stifling oppression? Now that does not concern me, but your travels with Black Beaumont certainly do.' Athelstan pressed his sandal against Cranston's boot at the coroner's surprise at Athelstan's words. The friar had calculated and gambled. He had voiced his suspicions though he had little hard evidence. 'So, Master Chaplain, the truth,' Athelstan smiled, 'or at least part of it?'

'I was born in Yorkshire,' Garman began slowly. 'I met Black Beaumont when I was a green stripling agog for adventure. Beaumont was forming a company. I will spare you the details. Black Beaumont waxed powerful. He realized the power of cannon. He argued that one day massed arrays of culverins and cannon would shatter the schiltroms of pikemen, the phalanxes of archers, the shield-rings of foot soldiers, the cohorts of cavalry. Warfare would be transformed. Battles would take on an even more gruesome aspect. Castles and fortified towers would be smashed to powder. He became a master, a skilled captain. Beaumont wanted money but he was also hungry for knowledge. He hired his company out not just to the highest bidder but to the one who could teach him the most. Eventually we reached Constantinople, attached to the Varangian Guard, manning its walls and gates or skirmishing with Turcopoles out on the plains. Occasionally we served with the Imperial fleet. I witnessed the power of Greek fire, an all-devouring flame which billowed out with a life of its own, a raging inferno almost impossible to extinguish. Brother Athelstan, I saw the sea catch fire. Beaumont became obsessed with discovering its secrets, which the Greeks guarded so closely. He spent every waking moment trying to discover the whereabouts of Mark the Greek's "The Book of Fires". He bribed officials, officers and courtiers till he found out at last where the secret was kept . . .'

'And he seized his moment?' Athelstan intervened.

'Yes. Constantinople was racked by famine, plague and civil war. Riots occurred in the great square before Hagia Sophia, the Church of Holy Wisdom. Beaumont formed his plan. Other mercenaries were keen to plunder. We broke into the secret chancery, where Beaumont seized the book.'

'Did you see it?' Cranston asked.

'Yes. A thick, heavy book though very small: its pages were twined together and bound in a heavily embossed calfskin covered with silver clasps. I glimpsed it for a short while. It reminded me of a book of hours. Anyway, we fled to Manzikert. Of course, the Secretissimi, the secret agents of the emperor, pursued us.' He shrugged. 'They still do. Beaumont was ecstatic, full of himself; apart from that glimpse, neither I nor anyone else was allowed to see "The Book of Fires".' He pulled a face. 'The Luciferi broke up. We had no choice. We went our different ways. I had grown tired of my life as a hired killer. I joined the Hospitallers in Rhodes and served in their infirmary. I later returned to England where I was ordained by the Bishop of London and given this benefice. Brother Athelstan, I am a sinner. I have wenched, robbed and killed. In the words of the psalmist, my offence is always before me. I now do reparation here in this stench and squalor.'

'You also use your position to support the Upright Men.'

'Brother Athelstan, I plough my furrow, you plough yours.'

'You could be accused of treason,' Cranston whispered.

'Then, Sir John, arrest me and I will impeach Gaunt for a greater treason: the evil he inflicts on the Community of this Realm.'

Athelstan tapped his feet. He recalled ferreting when he was a boy, trying to cover the holes in a warren with netting but the rabbits would still escape. This was similar. Garman could be accused of a host of crimes, yet, on a moral basis, he would escape, arguing these were no crimes but acts of goodness. Garman was a person who exemplified St Augustine's shrewd observance of human beings – that each individual was a veritable sack of different conflicting emotions. Garman was a priest yet a radical. A former soldier, now devoted to dispossessing the people he served. He preached God's goodness whilst advocating aggression to curb the greed of Gaunt and others. A man dedicated to peace, yet one who viewed violent revolt as the only way to achieve a lasting peace.

'God have mercy on us all,' Athelstan whispered. 'I will not debate philosophy with you, Parson Garman. You visited Sir Walter?'

'To beg for monies for this place, I have told you that.'

'You visited him on the very day Lady Isolda allegedly poisoned him?'

'Yes. I saw him just before his untimely death. As usual I visited him early in the morning. I brought him a delicacy from our days abroad, a dish he could never resist, figs rolled in an almond sauce.'

'Did he eat them?'

'No. As always, his belly hurt.'

'So why did you bring them?' Athelstan snapped.

Garman just grinned.

'Did you ever hear his confession?'

The parson snorted with laughter.

'Did you reminisce about old times?'

'Never.'

'Never?'

'I had nothing to say to him and what could he say to me? We had ceased to be comrades.'

Athelstan pointed a finger. 'Good Lord,' he breathed, 'you came to bait him. You hated Beaumont, didn't you?'

'He was a truly selfish, mean-spirited knave. A caitiff as great a felon as any who have been taken from here and hanged. He stole "The Book of Fires" and then turned out his comrades as if we were serfs. He did not care what happened to us. So it was not just to bait him. I visited Sir Walter to wring money out of him for the poor bastards here. I enjoyed making him reflect on Christ's warning: "What does it profit a man to gain the whole world if he suffers the loss of his immortal soul?" In my hushed conversations, I would warn him about the wages of sin as he drew to the end of his life. What did he love? What did he have? Children? Heirs? And where did he get his wealth from? Fashioning machines of war and other means to kill human beings.'

'It's a wonder he did not forbid you entrance,' Cranston demanded.

'Oh, Sir Walter was past all that. He took my visits as the

fruit of his own sin. I liked nothing better than to remind him of that phrase, "Remember man that thou art dust and into dust ye shall return".'

Athelstan stared hard at this ruthless preacher, a professional killer who had experienced a conversion along his own road to Damascus.

'Beaumont stood for everything you hated, didn't he?'

'Yes, Brother, he certainly did.' The answer was almost cheery.

'And his marriage?' Athelstan caught the swift smirk. 'Don't lie,' he warned. 'You know the truth about that May–December marriage. You are a priest. Sir Walter was burdened with guilt – he must have referred to it.'

Garman's chilling grin widened.

'Sir Walter was impotent with Isolda,' Athelstan continued. 'He suspected, and I think wrongly, that she was his illegitimate daughter, the offspring of one of his cast-off doxies from years ago.'

Garman pulled a face as if to hide his own malicious glee.

'I wager you did not dissuade him?'

'Naturally.' Garman was truly enjoying himself. 'I did admit that I could see a faint likeness in her of him.'

'You were lying?'

'I was just answering his question.'

'So was Lady Isolda innocent?' Cranston intervened, taken aback by the heated exchange between these two priests.

'I think I can answer that,' Athelstan retorted. 'You liked Lady Isolda. You admired her. You felt sorry that she was one of Sir Walter's many victims. In your eyes, killing the likes of Black Beaumont was no crime, no sin.'

'As regards her innocence, Lady Isolda never confessed to his murder.'

'But that doesn't mean she was innocent.'

'Nobody is innocent, Brother.' Garman shrugged. 'There could be other explanations for his death. On one occasion Lady Isolda said Sir Walter might have taken his own life.'

'That's nonsense! There is not a shred of evidence to substantiate such a claim.' Athelstan pointed at the chaplain. 'What is more logical, more likely, given your hatred of Sir Walter

– how do we know those figs in almond sauce which you brought earlier in the day he died were not laced with poison?'

'Why should I do that?' Garman sneered. 'I much preferred to watch him suffer.'

'I am sure,' Athelstan retorted, 'you are a practical man, parson. Your heart danced to see Sir Walter suffer, to view his growing weakness, his deepening sense of guilt. Naturally you wanted to bait him with the past – that's why you bought those figs, a delicacy from Outremer which would remind him of a time when he could indulge his appetites. Of course, not now. Sir Walter was ill, his belly extremely delicate. He might have to forgo such sweetmeats and leave them for the servants.'

'Brother Athelstan, are you claiming I attended Sir Walter for more nefarious reasons?'

'We'll come to that by and by. Let's return to Sir Walter's death. Did you feed him anything during that last visit?'

'You mean poison? No, as I have said, I wanted him to suffer, to brood and to regret.'

'I have asked this before,' Athelstan persisted. 'Why did you hate him so much? I understand he deserted you, kept "The Book of Fires", but mercenary companies break up, people go their separate ways. Oh, by the way, what name did you use?'

'I was called Saint-Croix.'

Athelstan studied Garman carefully. The friar recognized the importance of these moments from years of shriving, of hearing confessions, of listening to souls opening the gates sealed deeply within them. Parson Garman was now very close to those gates.

'We are not your enemy,' Athelstan added gently. 'Like you, sir, I am a priest. All I want is the truth. What is wrong with that?'

Garman drew a deep breath. 'We fled Constantinople,' he began, 'pursued by Turcopole mercenaries. We hid here, there, everywhere we could. Eventually we struck out across the desert.' He rubbed his forehead. 'The names of the different places we visited now fail me but we stopped at an oasis. We shared out our wine and food. To this day I swear Beaumont drugged it with a sleeping potion. The following morning, we woke late and heavy-headed. Beaumont and his henchmen had fled. We had our horses, water, weapons and maps – he had just forsaken us. We eventually reached Izmir. By then we were tired of each other's company. I journeyed into Rhodes and entered the service of the Hospital.'

'And when you returned to England you must have confronted Black Beaumont?'

'Oh,' Garman laughed wryly, 'he claimed it was all due to mere chance. According to Beaumont, he and his henchmen had risen early that day. They decided to let us sleep whilst they struck out to search for the best way forward. They encountered a roving band of sand-dwellers who attacked them, so they took refuge in a high, rocky outcrop. They drove their attackers off but by the time they returned to the oasis we had left.' Garman wiped a sheen of sweat from his face. 'A farrago of lies.'

'And "The Book of Fires"?' Athelstan asked.

Garman's eyes swiftly shifted.

'That's the real reason you visited Sir Walter. Oh, you loved the baiting and revelled in Beaumont's discomfiture but your real intent was to seize that book!'

'Why should I . . .'

'Have you too been approached?'

'What do you mean?' Garman's tone was brittle, betraying his fear.

'Oh, you have,' Athelstan persisted, 'by the agents of the Greek emperor, the Secretissimi and perhaps by others? The princes of this earth would offer a veritable fortune for Mark the Greek's "The Book of Fires". The Secretissimi are in London – don't act all surprised, you know they are. You have admitted as much. They want the manuscript back and would pay a fortune for it.'

'You must know its value,' Cranston intervened. 'I mean, from the days you served in the Luciferi calling yourself Saint-Croix. What was your role? If Black Beaumont was skilled in the use of cannon and powder, so must you be. You've fired culverins, you've mixed the different elements, yes? That's what the Luciferi offered – the ability to hurl fiery missiles.

So, Parson Garman, if "The Book of Fires" fell into your
hands, you would know how to manufacture Greek fire and
the other deadly mixtures.'

The parson licked dry lips and stared down at the glow of
candlelight near the small Lady altar. He sat as if listening to
the prison settling for the night, the banging of doors, the
sharp clatter of chains.

'"The Book of Fires", Garman began, still staring down the
chapel, 'was the cause of everything. Beaumont seized it and
made sure that his companions who had served him so faith-
fully would have no share of it. He brought the secrets back
to London and doled out those secrets like a miser would
pennies. I suspect he held a great deal back to maintain his
monopoly, to hold something in reserve, to tease, bait and lure
would-be customers.

'Naturally, the Secretissimi followed him here, but what
could they do against a powerful merchant patronized by the
King? Move against him and they would forfeit their immun-
ity – they could even end up in this stinking hole or on the
scaffold at Smithfield. If they secretly assassinated Beaumont,
the whereabouts of "The Book of Fires" could die with him
or pass into other hands. I . . .' Garman beat his chest, 'had
a right to that book. I was with Beaumont in the Imperial
chancery when the manuscript was stolen.' Spittle now
formed on his lips. 'I was a high-ranking member of the
Luciferi. I should have had my share. Yes, you are correct,
that's the real reason I took to visiting him. Oh, I deepened
his guilt, agitated whatever conscience he had left, milked
him for alms but I demanded my share. Sir John, Brother
Athelstan, just think what I could do with such wealth.' He
blew his cheeks out. 'But you know the verse of scripture,
"By their fruits ye shall know them."' Garman's voice
changed as he mimicked that of an old man. 'Beaumont
quavered and trembled. He listed his donations to this and
to that but he hadn't changed. Black Beaumont was a flint-
hearted, greedy, nasty human being. If I baited him he taunted
me back, saying that the whereabouts of the book would be
a revelation, secretly hidden on the island of Patmos. God
knows what that babbling meant. But if Lady Isolda was a

killer, so was Sir Walter.' He wagged a finger and rose. 'I
am not just talking about men killed in battle but the cold-
blooded murder of friends and comrades.' Garman, agitated,
walked into the darkness then returned to retake his seat.
'The Luciferi,' he continued, 'were mostly English. Beaumont
deserted us, taking six of our companions; those who
remained with me survived to die elsewhere or return to
England. Buckholt's father was one of the former, which
may be why his son later secured the position of steward to
Beaumont. Buckholt senior was a much older man, as was
Adam Lesures, Lady Anne's husband, who returned to
London and became a wealthy merchant. Lesures was highly
intelligent – he had little to do with Sir Walter. They remained
fairly estranged. After Sir Roger's death Lady Anne became
more friendly. There were others who returned. Some are
dead, a few are now missing.'

'One of those could be the Ignifer?' Cranston demanded.

'Yes, yes, I've thought of that.'

Athelstan could see the chaplain wasn't convinced.

'Parson Garman, you claim Sir Walter was a cold-blooded
murderer?'

'Brother Athelstan, that's one thing I did ask Beaumont time
and again. He left with six of our company. I swear to God,
not one of these have been heard of or seen since that night
at the oasis.'

'None!' Athelstan exclaimed. The friar moved on the bench,
very much aware of the darkness, the deepening cold, the
dying light of the tapers and the winter wind tugging at
the outside shutters.

'You are alleging foul play,' Cranston murmured. 'That Sir
Walter murdered those six men?'

'Sir John, it was in his nature. Now look. I have been honest.'
Garman shook his head and refused to meet their gaze. 'Well,
as honest as I can be in this business. Lord Coroner, I am a
marked man – my sympathies are well known to Gaunt. I
work amongst the poor and dispossessed. I am what I am: a
simple prison chaplain with a rich, tangled past. I took this
post for many reasons. One of them is the prominence it gave
me.'

'Amongst the Upright Men?'

Garman smiled thinly at Cranston's remark. 'There're other reasons.' He continued slowly, 'This prison post is a watch tower. I have worked amongst mercenaries. Now, as I have explained, most of those who stayed at the oasis eventually returned home. Like me, they renounced their false names. A few went back to loved ones but many drifted into London to seek shelter in the twilight world of Whitefriars, Southwark and the other halls of darkness. A few even passed through here. Anyway, over the years, I have been visited by former comrades but never, I repeat never, by anyone who left that oasis with Black Beaumont. Those who visit me tell a similar tale. They too have never heard of those six comrades.'

'You must have put this to Sir Walter?' Athelstan asked.

'Oh, I did, and his reply was stark and simple: they'd wandered off and he knew nothing of their whereabouts or their fate. All I can say is that Sir Walter would have done anything to keep "The Book of Fires" to himself.' Garman rubbed his face between his hands. 'Gentlemen, more than that I cannot say.'

'Lady Isolda's cell,' Athelstan asked, 'those markings on the wall – "SFSM" – do you know what they mean?'

'No.'

'And her visitors before she died?'

'Lady Anne Lesures with her mute body servant, Falke, of course, but no others.'

'And you still believe her to be innocent?'

'Brother Athelstan, I am biased. Beaumont was a black-hearted sinner, a truly evil man. If he was murdered, then he merited it. Now, Brother Athelstan, Sir John, I do have other business.'

'And her last days here?' Athelstan also got to his feet.

Garman indicated that they follow him out of the chapel along a hollow, stone-paved corridor. The reek of boiled cabbage, sweat and the privy mixed with the stench of tar being heated in an enclave next to a chamber, its narrow door flung open. Inside thick, evil-smelling tallow candles fluttered. A man sat behind a trestle table heaped with items of clothing, buckles and belts, hose, girdles, hoods, jerkins, dagger sheaths, battered purses and women's clothing. Next to him sat an old clerk with a dripping nose, long, thinning hair and popping watery eyes; he was itemizing the different pieces which the other man held up, brusquely described and tossed into a huge chest to the right of the table.

'Master Binny,' Garman declared, 'I am sorry to interrupt, but Sir John and Brother Athelstan . . .'

'Oh, I know Sir John.' Eustace Binny, Carnifex, or executioner for Newgate, was a cheery-faced imp of a man dressed soberly in a dun-coloured robe. He seemed pleased to meet Cranston and sprang to his feet to clasp Sir John's outstretched hand before bowing his sweaty pate for Athelstan's blessing. He introduced his clerk, Scrimshaw, and brusquely ordered him to bring three stools for his visitors before retaking his seat and gesturing at the items heaped on the table.

'The worldly goods of all those I have hanged this week,' he declared, picking up a faded petticoat then tossing it back on to the table.

'The legitimate profits of the hangman,' Cranston murmured, 'including those of Lady Isolda?'

'Oh, a very nice bracelet, a costly gown, petticoats, shoes, girdle and belt. They all came to me. She went to her death in a long grey hair shirt daubed with a red cross. I also had her brooch and the twine which braided her tresses.' He sniffed as he crossed himself swiftly. 'My heart was moved to pity. Scrimshaw here watched her strip; he made sure we had everything before he gave her the hair shirt. He said she had a beautiful body, unmarked, white as the purest snow.'

Athelstan glanced at the scrivener, who smiled vacuously back with a display of yellow, blackening teeth. 'We missed nothing,' Scrimshaw muttered.

'No books?' Athelstan asked.

'Oh, no books, we are vigilant about that. Books fetch a good price. Our prisoners,' Scrimshaw smiled reassuringly, 'when they know they are going to die, are honest. What they own, we get.'

'Who rented the solitary cell?' Athelstan asked.

'Lawyer Falke. He gave us silver for a clean chamber, nearly

fresh bedding and the same victuals as ours. We made it very
clear that when the end arrived all her property was ours,'
Binny gabbled on. 'I tell my wife that all movables and items
worn by . . .'

'Very good, Eustace,' Cranston intervened. 'We are more
interested in those last two days before her execution.'

'She was very frightened,' Scrimshaw screeched. 'She quarrelled with Lady Lesures and drove her away. I felt sorry for
her. She truly didn't know what was coming. I told her no
mercy was to be shown, though for a few coins I could hire
some ruffians to toss bricks and stones at her head when she
was lashed to the . . .'

'Shut up!' Binny roared, his face turning puce. 'Sir John,
Brother Athelstan,' he glanced spitefully at the scrivener, 'he
shouldn't have said that. When all this,' he gestured at the
chest, 'is sold to the fripperers I will deduct a fine. Our orders
were very clear – no mercy was to be shown and it wasn't.
Everything she ate or drank was tasted. I made sure Scrimshaw,'
he glared at his scrivener, 'did that. Yet in the end, Lady Isolda
frightened herself into a stupor, a daze. I've seen the likes
before.'

'She was very quiet,' Garman spoke up. 'I was at her
execution.'

'We had to carry her to the execution stake,' Binny
murmured. 'We bound her fast, the fire started and the crowd
thronged about. True, stones were thrown to smash her skull
to stun her as you would some cow in a slaughter shed but
there was no real need. The flames roared up and she was
gone.'

Athelstan hid his chill at the horror described so casually.
'Afterwards,' he asked, 'did anyone come to gather ashes or
her bones?'

Binny pursed his lips and shook his head.

'Oh, yes they did.' Scrimshaw picked up a cheap bangle
off the table. 'I've just remembered – someone did. I was busy
around the execution stake collecting chains, any items; you
know, it's very important.'

'What happened?' Cranston snapped. 'Who came?'

'A man. He was hooded and visored. He carried a cedarwood

casket, a little trowel and a pair of tongs. He collected the remains, shards of blackened bone. I asked him who he was.'

'And? His name?'

'Reginald Vanner, clerk . . .'

PART FIVE

'Take petroleum, black petroleum, liquid pitch and oil of sulphur. Put all these in a pottery jar buried in horse manure for fifteen days.'

Mark the Greek's 'The Book of Fires'

'**D**ays of darkness and the deepest gloom. A day of blackest clouds and thick shadows like some sombre dawn. These spread across the horizon as if some vast and mighty host approaches such as has never been seen before. All the power of Hell has swept up to confront the wickedness of man . . .'

Athelstan stood outside the grim, gloomy portals of Newgate and stared at the preacher perched on an overturned barrel surrounded by blazing bonfires. Their light made the ragged, bony itinerant preacher even more eerie and grotesque. The friar drew a deep breath. He was glad to be out of the prison now, waiting for Sir John, who was arranging for Rosamund Clifford to be taken back to Firecrest Manor as well as greasing the palms of Tweng, the turnkey, Master Binny, Scrimshaw and the rest. The great fleshing markets, the butchers' stalls outside Newgate, had ceased trading. Night had fallen. It was now the hour for others. Fishmongers from Billingsgate wheeled their barrows crammed with silvery salmon, white-bellied turbot, scarlet lobsters, dun-coloured crabs and mackerels with their gleaming green backs. Here to greet them clustered the real poor, the shirtless, shoeless, breadless and homeless. They would buy the stinking fish and take over this busy part of the city. They gathered like a tribe, their blue, bootless feet ulcerous from the cold, to feast on whatever globules of meat or fish they could filch or buy. Bonfires of the day's rubbish had been torched to provide some light and warmth in the freezing night. The air stank with the odour of the rancid food now being toasted. The grisly-faced fripperers gathered, their barrows full of rags, discarded clothing and half-putrid hare-skins. Costermongers offered pickled herring in a slimy sauce, or salted whelks which looked like huge snails floating in a sea of brine. Athelstan looked pityingly at this horde of beggars and recalled Garman's revolutionary fervour. Was the prison chaplain right? he wondered. Would the great revolt sweep all this squalid poverty away, burn it up like a fire sweeping through stubble? Athelstan felt a hand on his shoulder. Cranston, leading a group of bailiffs, had come quietly up behind him.

'Little friar,' he remarked, 'the day is done and we are for the dark.'

'Sir John, we have no choice, for the darkness seeks us . . .'

Athelstan recalled the events of the day as he sat at table in the kitchen of his priest's house. Outside the faded hubbub of noise of the pilgrims still intent on the vigil echoed faintly. Matters, however, were now more orderly in the parish of St Erconwald's. Admission to the church, as well as supervision of the stalls offering food, drink or relics of the Great Miracle, was now in the iron grip of the parish council led by Watkin and Pike. Queues were now more orderly and, at the agreed time, an hour before midnight, the church would be closed. Athelstan smiled to himself. His parishioners had been most insistent that matters be left to them. 'Hadn't Father,' they asked, 'had a truly busy day? Hadn't that strange creature the Ignifer, so rumour had it, struck again?' On his return the privy council had been most solicitous. They had pointed out how the priest's house had been thoroughly cleaned, the braziers lit, the hearth fire built up and banked. Merrylegs' best venison pie was waiting in the oven, whilst a jug of the Piebald's finest ale stood covered in the buttery.

Athelstan took their hint to leave the flow of pilgrims to them, though he remained deeply suspicious. He'd retired to the house along with Bonaventure, who now sprawled like a well-fed emperor across the hearth. Athelstan drummed his fingers on the tabletop. He picked up the letter that Lady Anne had sent with Turgot, where she recounted what she had said when they met at the Minoresses earlier that day. Athelstan re-read the finely etched script which described what the beggar

Didymus had seen on the night the Ignifer had attacked them. How Didymus was sure their would-be assassin was garbed in heavy robes and reeked of a woman's fragrant perfume. According to Crim the altar boy, who was in the house at the time, the heavily cowled and cloaked Turgot had knocked at the door, entrusted the letter to Crim and promptly disappeared. Athelstan stared up at the ceiling beams. He knew where Turgot and Lady Anne had been when the Ignifer struck that morning but what about the rest, including that sly-faced maid? Sir Henry, Buckholt, Garman or even Falke or Vanner? Had those he'd met been busy in Cheapside? As for Vanner, Athelstan believed Beaumont's clerk was dead, yet he might be wrong. Athelstan decided to busy himself. He drew out a large piece of parchment from the leather case in his personal coffer. He quickly smoothed it with a pumice stone, putting small weights on each corner. Once ready, however, Athelstan rose and paced backwards and forwards, watched by a now bemused Bonaventure. 'So, master cat, let us move to the arrow point. *Primo*, Sir Walter. Very wealthy, sickly but enter-taining grave doubts about his second wife, the lovely Isolda. An old man with a very guilty conscience, which he richly deserved. Black Beaumont, as he was then called, served abroad. The climax of his career was the theft of "The Book of Fires" from the Greeks.

'Allegedly he deserted one set of companions and may have murdered the group who left with him. Bloodthirsty and ruth-less, Sir Walter returns home, where he amasses a fortune manufacturing machines of war for the likes of Gaunt. He keeps "The Book of Fires" close to his heart, a great secret. He does not reveal all its mysteries, perhaps he dare not for fear of the Greeks or is he waiting for the right occasion to sell the manuscript to the highest bidder? Undoubtedly he uses some of the formulas recorded in that book to manufacture more deadly weapons of war. In the meantime, he hides the book's whereabouts with foolish references to it being a revela-tion or safe on the island of Patmos. Eventually Black Beaumont grows old and sickly. Remember that, master cat. Rumours abound that he is being slowly poisoned so he takes great care over what he eats or drinks. He is certainly sick in soul and that proves a fertile breeding ground for further evil. The lechery of his youth comes back to haunt him. He wonders whether his new wife could be the daughter of one of his cast-off mistresses. If Garman knew this, others would. His brother, Sir Henry, probably did little to disabuse him of such a notion. Oh, yes, Henry and Rohesia are like scavenging cats, horrified at Sir Walter's marriage and the prospect of Isolda producing an heir. They must have been delighted at the turn of events. Parson Garman also plays his part. He views Sir Walter's guilty conscience and nagging scruples as a fertile furrow to till. He hates Beaumont for a number of reasons: the merchant's appalling reputation abroad, his betrayal, his desertions, his greed, everything Garman has come to hate.' Athelstan paused in his pacing. 'Bonaventure, this was all in the past and we must keep it that way. So, Garman wanted the return of "The Book of Fires", or at least the ability to plunder its secrets, which he could either sell to raise money or assist the cause of the Upright Men. Garman also delighted in darkening Beaumont's soul. The parson baited his old leader, bringing him those almond-coated figs from Beaumont's green and salad days. He knew Sir Walter couldn't or wouldn't eat them. He certainly brought such a delicacy early on the day Beaumont died and, if Sir Walter did not eat the delicacy, who did – a member of his household?' Athelstan paused, fingers flying to his lips. 'Oh, my goodness!' he exclaimed. 'Oh my goodness, Bonaventure, is that possible?' He leaned down and scratched the tomcat's scarred ears. 'For the moment, let's keep to the path we are following. We have Sir Walter, "The Book of Fires" and then Sir Walter's plan to have his marriage annulled. Of course, "by their fruits ye shall know them". Sir Walter was not keen on his wife but he took a fancy to the doe-eyed Rosamund, who could perform certain lecherous tasks for him with her soft, light fingers. She certainly visited him on the day he died but then she mysteriously fell ill, a sickness which confined her to her chamber whilst the tragedy which engulfed her mistress was played out.

'*Secondo*, Bonaventure, the actual poisoning. Rumour has it that Beaumont may have been the victim of slow poisoning for some time before his death, hence the ailments of both belly and bowel. Brother Philippe says that is possible – he also mentioned that members of the Beaumont household suffered similar conditions. There is no firm evidence of this. Nevertheless, Sir Walter probably became more prudent about what he ate and drank. He'd also be wary of Isolda and his clerk, Vanner. After all, Sir Walter must have heard the rumours of how friendly his estranged wife and clerk had become. Of course, there is the faithful Buckholt, or was he as faithful as he should have been? Buckholt's father had been in the Luciferi – did his son bear a grudge? Did Sir Walter employ Buckholt as an act of gratitude and reparation to the memory of his steward's father? A strange man, Buckholt, a paradox, he serves as a rich merchant's steward yet espouses the cause of the Upright Men.' Athelstan paused and chuckled. 'Could the Great Community of the Realm be the real reason for Buckholt's service? Oh, Bonaventure, at last the threads of this tapestry are beginning to loosen. Nor must we forget how Buckholt nourished a passion for the fair Rosamund. He certainly resented Isolda and he would fiercely resent Rosamund's ministrations for his master. In the end, however, one thing is certain: Buckholt was instrumental in the successful conviction of Isolda.' Athelstan walked over to the table. He sifted through the leaves of parchment Cranston had sent across to him, a transcript of the trial proceedings, but they were little more than a summary and could provide no new information.

'Did Isolda kill her husband?' Athelstan returned to his pacing. 'Sir Walter was hated by many people for many reasons. He received warnings a year ago which stopped as suddenly as they began. How did they go? Yes, "As I and ours burnt, so shall ye and yours." The writer of those warnings was hinting that Sir Walter's ability to provide fire as a weapon of war had injured the writer and his kin, but if that was the case, Bonaventure, there must be a legion of such victims.' Athelstan sat down on his chair, resisting the creeping but weakening tiredness which dimmed his mind and made his body feel heavy and full of aches. 'Others may have had a motive to murder Sir Walter, yet the case against Isolda,' he allowed Bonaventure to jump on his lap and sat absentmindedly stroking the cat, 'yes, the case weighs heavily against her. Her relationship, illicit or not, with Vanner; the latter's deliberate distraction of Buckholt; Isolda feeding that posset to her husband; the disappearance of the original goblet and its replacement from a set specially purchased by Vanner. Finally, there's the despatch of the goblet down the privy and the buttery clerk's sworn testimony that the goblet he prepared was not the one which came down.' Athelstan gently lowered Bonaventure to the floor. 'But why, master cat, did she strike on that particular day? What prompted her and Vanner?' Athelstan smiled to himself. 'I may have an answer for that when I begin my writing. What real defence did she and Falke make? References to Vanner feeding Sir Walter something poisonous; a plot by Buckholt and Sir Henry to seize "The Book of Fires"? Every lie, Bonaventure, contains a scrap of truth. Vanner could not answer for himself because Vanner has disappeared and so have his manuscripts. Who could have destroyed them? Was it really Vanner at the execution stake collecting Isolda's pathetic remains?' Athelstan rose to his feet in a surge of excitement. 'Of course, I suspect where Vanner is, I truly do. He did not collect Isolda's ashes at Smithfield – that's a pretence.'

Elated by what he had concluded, Athelstan sat down and, grasping a quill pen, swiftly wrote out his different hypotheses and the proof which supported them. His eyes grew heavy so he slept for a while. When he awoke the fire had burnt low. He shook himself and, leaving the murder of Sir Walter, turned to the vexed question of 'The Book of Fires'. Undoubtedly Beaumont had hidden it and many others wanted to find it. Garman, Sir Henry, perhaps even Buckholt – certainly the Greeks who had been so instrumental in protecting Sir John and himself the previous morning. The book's whereabouts were a mystery but so was a second problem. Sir Walter had stolen it, used its secrets but, Athelstan suspected, had kept some of the specialist knowledge to himself – why? This in turn led to the identity of the Ignifer because, whoever he was, he was also very knowledgeable about what 'The Book of Fires' contained and was using it to devastating effect. The only conclusion Athelstan could reach was that the Ignifer had stolen the book; someone who also passionately believed that those responsible for Lady Isolda's conviction and cruel death should be barbarously punished by being burnt alive. But who was this person? The only people who believed in Lady Isolda's innocence were Garman and Falke – were one of these, or both, the Ignifer? Or could it be someone else? Cranston had wondered if a former member of the Luciferi had returned to London. Could such a person be responsible? Or again, did Isolda have some secret admirer or kinsman? After all, she was accustomed to going into the city by herself. She may have met the Greeks, but Athelstan was convinced that she also met someone else – a paramour, perhaps? Was that soul, now demented beyond reason, carrying out these atrocious attacks? Had Isolda in fact discovered the secret of Greek fire and passed it on to this mysterious person, man or woman? According to the beggar Didymus, the assailant had reeked of expensive perfume like that of crushed lilies, the same perfume Isolda had used. Did the graffiti on the wall of Isolda's prison cell, 'SFSM', conceal the identity of this sinister figure now prowling the streets with pots of deadly fire? Athelstan dozed for a while. When he awoke he decided a good night's sleep would have to wait. He stripped, washed, shaved, donned fresh robes and, sitting at the kitchen table, began to write out his conclusions. The more he wrote, his quill pen skimming the soft, smooth surface of the parchment, the more Athelstan realized he was close to resolving some of the truth to these mysteries.

oOoOo

Sir John Cranston was also troubled by various imaginings. He was finding it difficult to get back to sleep in his great four poster-bed in the opulent chamber he and Lady Maude had decorated over the years. The coroner threw himself back against the bolsters, Ave beads slipping from his fingers. He missed his family and household more than he could say; Lady Maude should be chattering: the two poppets chasing each other; the great Irish wolfhounds Gog and Magog sprawled at the foot of the bed. Outside the maids should be hurrying, whispering and giggling along the wooden-panelled galleries, yet there was nothing but a hollow constant silence. Cranston rolled over on to his back, staring up at the tester. He was certain he had done the right thing despatching his wife, family and household to a moated manor deep in the countryside. Kinsmen and retainers would mount vigilant watch over them. The revolt would come, yet his family would be safe. There would be violence, but, in the end, the rebels would be crushed with all the savagery the great lords of the soil could muster. In the meantime, Cranston rolled over to one side, staring at the sliver of grey dawn-light peeking through the shutters, his mind returning to the mystery of the Greek fire.

Cranston had personally witnessed the devastating effects of boiling oil cascading down castle walls in France, a rushing, bubbling torrent of Hell's blackness, scolding, burning and searing the flesh. Even worse was when that oil was lighted. The coroner was still shaken by the vicious attacks on both himself and Athelstan. If the friar could only find a way through, yet Athelstan seemed as perplexed as he was. Somebody prowling the city was definitely using Greek fire and not just in these murderous attacks. One of Cranston's spies had reported a mysterious meeting out on the heathland beyond London Bridge, of a fire being abruptly caused, of flames leaping up against the blackness. Was this a coincidence? At the same time other spies reported that the Upright Men, who had been quiet for weeks, were once again beginning to muster. Did the Upright Men now possess Greek fire? If so, how? Where was that damned 'Book of Fires' and who was this Ignifer? Cranston narrowed his eyes at a sound below but then dismissed it. Was the Ignifer someone they had never met, a former member of the Luciferi? Someone who had left Dover under his baptismal name but in France changed that to something more fanciful as he sold his sword or bow to the highest bidder? Once military service was over, he would arrive back in an English port under his baptismal name. It was a way of sealing the past, of forgetting what had happened as veterans settle down to become some parish worthy or city dignitary. Was that the case here? A member of the Luciferi now turned respectable like Falke or Garman? Or was the

Ignifer hidden deeper in the shadows, someone they had never met?

Cranston pulled himself up to lean against the bolsters. He snatched the miraculous wineskin from the table beside him, took his morning sip and wondered how Athelstan was coping with the Great Miracle at St Erconwald's. Cranston was truly perplexed by this wondrous occurrence. As Lord High Coroner of London, he had earned a reputation, second to none, for exposing counterfeits, cranks and cunning men. He had broken through the most elaborate deceits, disguises and deceptions, yet the miracle at St Erconwald's was not one of these. According to all the evidence, Fulchard of Richmond had entered that church a cripple; he had not left as one. He had been healed and proclaimed himself as such. Cranston's spies had swept the city; if one such as the crippled Fulchard had emerged, he would have been observed. Sooner or later anyone who hid in this bustling city had to crawl out to be invariably noticed by someone, but not here. Cranston gnawed on his lip. He took some comfort from the fact that his spies had stumbled on other juicy morsels of information. The Upright Men were becoming very active; their captains had been glimpsed in both the city and Southwark. One spy, who rejoiced in the sobriquet 'the Eye of God', had reported how the great miracle at St Erconwald's seemed to have attracted a goodly number of young, rather well-armed men amongst the pilgrims flocking there. Now this did concern the coroner. He was about to seize the miraculous wineskin for a second time when he heard that sound again, a clattering in the scullery which separated the kitchen and buttery from the garden. The outside door was made of thick, heavy oak and studded with metal bosses, its latch stout and noisy. Was someone trying to get in? Cranston slid off the bed. He pushed his feet into tight-fitting buskins and drew both sword and dagger from his warbelt hanging on a hook against the wall.

The coroner slipped silently out of his bedchamber, along the gallery and down the polished oaken staircase. Night candles glowed in their capped glass holders, emitting pools of golden light. Sir John paused on the bottom step wondering who the intruder might be. The Upright Men? Usually they were not so silent. Those Greeks? Cranston paused to control his breathing. The Greeks were allies rather than enemies. The Ignifer? He crept through the buttery and into the great kitchen beyond. He raced swiftly across and opened the door to the scullery; the latch on the garden door at the far end rattled. He stepped inside. He sniffed a perfume, one he knew, the light fragrance of crushed lilies. The floor was greasy. The shutters to his right rattled. Cranston abruptly realized what was about to happen. Sliding and slithering, the coroner hurled himself across the chamber. He ignored the door but crashed into the shutters, even as he felt the intruder press heavily against them. The Ignifer was here! Cranston realized this heavy shutter had been prised open from outside. The Ignifer had entered and the floor was covered in highly flammable oil, waiting to be fired. The assassin had plotted to lure a half-sleeping Cranston across the slippery floor towards the door whilst he pulled open the shutters and threw in a flame. If he had stepped into the trap the scullery would have been turned into an inferno. He pressed his bulk against the shutters. Again he smelt the faint traces of that perfume, of crushed lilies. Lady Maude had once worn it, a gift from the court. Cranston was now calm. Eventually he could feel no pressure. He kept a wary eye on the door and opened the shutter slightly, his sword piercing the gap, its broad, sharp blade jabbing forward before swinging to the left and right. He closed the shutters, refastening the inside hook and opened the garden door. Dawn was about to break. The garden stretched frozen white, bleak and empty. The Ignifer had escaped.

Athelstan, cloaked and hooded against the cutting wind, stood in the copse of ancient trees which lay at the heart of the great garden at Firecrest Manor. Sir Henry had arranged for open braziers to be stoked and fired. The crackling charcoal glowed fiercely, exuding gusts of scented heat and smoke. Beside Athelstan was a taciturn Sir John, his beaver hat pulled fully down, the muffler of his thick cloak raised as high as it could be. Athelstan stretched out his mittened fingers towards the blaze. Those he had summoned had almost arrived, complaining under their breath. They fell silent at the sight of this little

friar standing so ominously quiet, in this haunted glade close
to the edge of the green-slimed mere; a ghostly place, away
from the pleasantries of the rest of the garden. The trees here
rose like stark black figures, their outstretched branches frozen
solid, bereft of all greenery. No birdsong or rustling in the
undergrowth, just a brooding stillness, as if the copse hid a
dreadful secret. Athelstan knew it did, but he would wait to
uncover it and so would everybody else. Athelstan was furious
at the turn of events. He had slept very little and been roused
by Tiptoft, who informed him about the attack on the coroner.
The messenger had reassured Athelstan that Sir John was safe
and well. The friar had given thanks to this but hid his anger
in swift preparations to leave. He and Tiptoft had hurried down
to the Southwark quayside where Moleskin lay fast asleep in
his barge. Athelstan had roused him and they had braved the
swollen, mist-hung river to cross to Blackfriars wharf. Tiptoft
had hurried away on other errands including messages for Sir
John, whilst Athelstan entered the Dominican mother house.
After he'd greeted the different brothers, Brother Caradoc the
sacristan arranged for Athelstan to say his dawn Mass at a
side altar in the main church. Cranston had arrived just in time
for the Eucharist. Afterwards both coroner and friar had broken
their fast in the great refectory dominated by a huge crucifix
with a banner displaying the Five Holy Wounds hanging from
the hammer-beam roof. Cranston had described the assault on
him, Athelstan listened with deepening disquiet.

'Three times, Sir John,' he declared. 'Three attacks on
us. The first was not on Lady Anne but on thee and me as
was the second and the third. It's time we cleared the board
of distractions and diversions, fascinating though they may
be. Now listen . . .'

Athelstan had informed Cranston of what he wanted and
now they waited in the gloomy, wooded glade with a winter
wind rippling the icy surface of the mere. Sir Henry and
Rohesia, Buckholt, Rosamund, Falke, Parson Garman, Lady
Anne and Turgot, as well as Cranston's posse of bailiffs and
six royal archers from the Tower. The 'guests', as Athelstan
called his array of suspects, were all protesting. The friar did
not care. Some of these were liars and deceivers and one of

them could be a hideous assassin secretly plotting the destruction of both himself and Sir John. He would now show them,
to quote the scriptures, that 'God did still raise prophets in
the cities of the earth'.

'Sir John, Brother Athelstan,' Flaxwith called, 'they are
here.' Both friar and coroner turned to greet the strange torchlight procession making its way through the trees led by the
Fisher of Men. This eerie official of the city council had left
his 'Mortuary of the Sea', which stood on a deserted quayside
just beyond La Reole. A figure of mystery with a highly
colourful past as a knight of St Lazarus, the Fisher of Men's
principal task was to harvest the Thames of corpses, the victims
of suicide, accident or murder. The Fisher gathered his grisly
finds in his Chapel of the Drowned Men: the bloated, river-
slimed corpses would be stretched out, washed and covered
with a shroud drenched in pine juice whilst they waited inspection and collection. The Fisher was assisted by a coven of
rejects and outcasts who rejoiced in such names as Maggot,
Brick-Face and Hackum. Leader of these was Icthus, the
Fisher's henchman, garbed as always in black. He had assumed
the Greek name for fish, Icthus, a fitting title. He was a young
man who had no hair even on his brows or eyelids, whilst his
oval-shaped face, jutting cod mouth and webbed fingers and
toes made him even more fishlike. He was in truth a superb
swimmer. Fast and as slippery as any porpoise, Icthus could
thread the waters of the Thames night or day, in high summer
or midwinter.

Athelstan ignored the swelling murmurs and protests as he
greeted the Fisher and his entourage; they immediately sank
to one knee and chorused their salutation to which Athelstan
responded with a solemn blessing. They all stood and, like
some well-trained choir, burst into the hymn '*Ave Maris Stella*'
– 'Hail, Star of the Sea', a paean of praise to the Virgin.
Afterwards the Fisher of Men, his bald head and skeletal
features shrouded by a black leather hood fringed with the
purest lambswool, his body hidden beneath a thick military
cloak which hung down to the ankles of costly leather walking
boots, raised gauntleted hands.

'We have come,' he proclaimed. 'The waters of this earth

are no mystery to us. Brother Athelstan, Sir John, we have brought ropes! We are ready to do God's will and that of the King. Sir John, if we find what you are looking for . . . we will double the price?'

'And a little more.' Cranston took a slurp of the miraculous wineskin and handed it to the Fisher, who took a most generous mouthful before passing it back.

'Sir John, Brother Athelstan,' Sir Henry bustled forward, 'this is my property, demesne . . .'

'And I am on the King's business,' Cranston snarled. 'My guests have come by barge. I ordered your porter at the water-gate to let them through. Sir Henry, you get on with your own business and let me get on with mine. Brother?'

Athelstan took Icthus by the hand, led him to the pool and whispered what he wanted. The henchman replied in a high-pitched voice, his colourless eyes studying Athelstan carefully.

'The water must be freezing cold,' Athelstan warned. Icthus gave a strange lop-sided smile. He took the friar's hand and pressed it firmly against his own arm so Athelstan could feel the thick grease smearing his skin. Icthus shrugged off his gown and, to the cries and exclamations of the others, and garbed only in a tight-fitting loincloth, waded into the mere and slipped beneath the surface. He reminded Athelstan of an otter he'd once studied as a boy at a gurgling brook on his father's farm. Icthus was long and sinuous, merging with the water as if that was his true home. Bubbles appeared on the surface. Icthus broke from the water, breathing noisily before disappearing once again. This time he was longer, but when he surfaced he wiped the slime from his face and grinned. The Fisher and his coven served out a long coil of rope. Icthus grabbed one end and sank into the depths. The rope hung slack, then it shook tight and taut. Icthus rose to take a further breath and, impervious to the biting cold, dived again. The rope was tugged. The Fisher and his companions, intoning the hymn '*Salve Regina Marum*' – 'Hail, Queen of the Seas', began to draw in what Icthus had found: a corpse, encrusted with the dirt and sludge of the mere, broke the surface, its belly bloated and its face masked by a mesh of weeds. Athelstan ignored the exclamations of surprise as the swollen, disfigured cadaver was dragged free of the water.

'Vanner!' Buckholt exclaimed. 'Reginald Vanner!'

Athelstan knelt by the corpse. He sketched a cross on the bulging forehead and stared into the empty open eyes sunk deep into their sockets.

'May Christ have mercy on your soul, Reginald Vanner,' Athelstan breathed. He pressed his hand against the dead flesh, bloated until buttons and points had burst. He felt the hilt of a dagger, its blade thrust so deep into the left side that only the ornamental handle could be detected. Others gathered close. Athelstan cleared the dirt in the area around the fatal thrust. He pulled the dagger, its blade popping out with a loud sucking sound.

'Vanner.' Sir Henry grew closer as Icthus and his coven stepped away. The Fisher dried off his henchman, handing back the thick, heavy gown.

'And the dagger?' Cranston asked.

'Isolda's!' Sir Henry exclaimed. 'She always kept it in an embroidered sheath.'

'Is that so?' Cranston beckoned Rosamund forward. The maid, shivering with cold, approached and nodded.

'Lady Isolda's,' she agreed.

Falke and Parson Garman could only stare. Lady Anne shook her head wordlessly.

Athelstan walked around the mere and returned. 'Sir Henry,' he asked, 'you have bonfires where you burn the rubbish?'

'Of course, Brother. There are fire-pits deep in the trees. Why?'

'I believe Isolda, on the Thursday before she was arrested,' Athelstan explained, 'invited Vanner here. She insisted it was important for him to come with any manuscript injurious to her. Sutler was pressing his case heavily. It was time to remove any evidence, including Vanner. The clerk arrived, standing on the edge of this mere. Isolda came through the trees, took the manuscripts and then she struck. Vanner was standing on the edge. Notice how the land dips slightly to the water. Isolda closed swiftly. Perhaps Vanner thought she was going to kiss him. Instead, she thrust her dagger in. She meant to withdraw

it, but she was no sword fighter. The violence of the blow sent
Vanner reeling back into the freezing water. Both shocks would
render the dying man unconscious. He collapsed, thrashed out
in agony, turned and floated further out. Isolda watched him
sink deep into the tangle of weeds at the bottom of the mere.
Once he had gone, she hurried to one of the burning pits and
made sure that all the manuscripts that he had given her were
burnt to ash.' Athelstan crossed himself. 'God have mercy on
them both. Now, Sir John, pay the Fisher what is due. Ask
him to take Vanner's corpse back to the Mortuary of Souls
and, if unclaimed after further proclamation, have him buried
in some poor man's plot in one of the city churches. Sir Henry,
I need to see you and the others in a much warmer place.'

Within the hour Cranston and Athelstan met the rest in the
retainers' refectory, just off the great kitchen. It was a warm,
spacious chamber where the savoury smells of cooking sweet-
ened the air. They gathered around the long trestle table,
Cranston with Athelstan on his right, the others ranged down
either side. Cups of mulled wine along with bowls of mortress,
a cream soup of pork and chicken, were served. Athelstan
blessed the food and they ate in silence till Cranston asked
the scullions to clear the table. Once the doors were closed
behind them Athelstan began.

'I thank you for coming here so that I can share some of
my conclusions with you. Five years ago Sir Walter Beaumont
married Isolda Fitzalan, as she was then known, a spring–
winter marriage. Sir Walter had an extremely colourful past
as Black Beaumont, leader of a free company of mercenaries
known as the Luciferi. During his travels abroad Black
Beaumont acquired a veritable treasure trove of secrets
regarding cannon, powder and all kinds of fiery missiles. The
culmination of his career was the acquisition of Mark the
Greek's "The Book of Fires", a manuscript set to play a major
part in the tragedy which unfurled. Now we know his marriage
wasn't a happy one. I will not spare your blushes. Sir Walter
was cunning, powerful and ruthless. He soon realized his
fairy-queen wife had the soul of a selfish, equally ruthless
harridan beneath a mask of beauty. In her turn, Isolda soon
learnt that Sir Walter had no intention of endowing her with

the wealth, freedom and power she craved. Isolda led a secret life. I'm sure Sir Walter suspected but I don't think he really cared. He had plans of his own. Isolda certainly fostered a relationship with Vanner in order to keep a strict eye on her husband, and how better than through his chancery clerk?' Athelstan paused to let the others reflect on his words. He noticed there were no protests. 'Part of this secret life is that Isolda would often disappear into the city. Yes, Rosamund?'

'Brother Athelstan,' the maid quavered, 'I have mentioned that. She undoubtedly met the Greeks but there were other times . . . I do not know where she went, why or whom she met.'

'Does anyone?' Athelstan asked.

No one replied.

'Neither do I. Undoubtedly she met the Greeks, who wanted their manuscript returned. They approached her as they did others. But,' Athelstan continued swiftly to hinder any comment, 'more grave matters intervened. Your brother, Sir Henry, grew old and weak. I believe guilt for past sins weighed heavily on him but whether that sorrow was genuine or not, I cannot say. He certainly reflected on his marriage and the possibility that Isolda might be his daughter, the offspring of one his paramours when he was a lusty bachelor. Some people here,' Athelstan emphasized his words, 'played on such wild imaginings.' He glanced around. Parson Garman had leaned back staring up at the ceiling. Sir Henry and Lady Rohesia kept their heads down. Rosamund was examining her fingernails.

'Sir Walter,' Athelstan continued, 'decided to apply for an annulment. Undoubtedly he would have used Vanner to write a submission to the Bishop's curia and the Archdeacon's court asking for this annulment on the very strong grounds of consanguinity. Vanner, of course, informed Isolda, who became desperate. She encouraged Vanner to keep her informed as she maintained all the appearances of a cordial marriage. In truth, she and her husband were deeply alienated. He maintained the pretence as effectively as did she. Isolda still thought she would get "The Book of Fires", sell it for a fortune and be free. When that door firmly closed, Isolda wanted revenge.

She was keen to seize her husband's wealth. She had failed to secure "The Book of Fires", so the riches of this manor should really come to her. She realized that if the annulment went forward she would be depicted as Sir Walter's cast off, disgraced in the eyes of society and once again dependent on the likes of you, Lady Anne, and the Minoresses. Isolda was so desperate she even allowed you, Rosamund,' Athelstan chose his words carefully, 'to keep Sir Walter company and provide whatever comfort you could.' The maid coloured and stared down at the empty platter before her. 'Rosamund,' Athelstan continued softly. 'You loved your mistress so much you would do anything for her, and yet she almost poisoned you.'

Rosamund's head came up, her mouth gaping.

'What do you mean?' Falke shouted.

'Ask Parson Garman,' Athelstan declared, 'a former comrade of Sir Walter during his years abroad when Black Beaumont loved figs baked in a creamy almond sauce. Yes, parson?'

'I have told you that.'

'Yes, you have, and how you specially purchased this delicacy to remind Sir Walter of those stirring days in Outremer.'

'The figs!' Lady Anne exclaimed. 'Brother Athelstan, are you alleging they were poisoned?'

'Not by me,' Garman declared.

'No, by Isolda, probably assisted by Vanner – some delicate poison which would increase in strength, the likes of white or red arsenic. Sir Walter loved his figs. He grew sick. He tried to eat them but then—'

'But then what?' Falke interrupted.

'On the day Sir Walter was murdered I believe his intention to seek an annulment was on the verge of becoming public. He was about to serve his case to the Bishop for inspection by the Archdeacon's court. Isolda and Vanner realized they had little time left and became agitated. On that memorable morning, you, Parson Garman, brought the usual delicacy – figs in a cream almond sauce, yes?' The priest nodded. 'You conversed with Sir Walter, the usual parry and thrust, after which you left?' Again the chaplain agreed. 'You, Rosamund,' Athelstan pointed at the now pallid maid, fingers to her lips, 'visited Sir Walter later on. He gave you the figs left by Parson Garman?'

'How?' Rosamund spluttered. 'How could she poison them? I mean . . .'

'I suspect Isolda also visited Sir Walter shortly after you left Parson Garman. She either exchanged the dish or poured some poison over it which would sink into that creamy almond sauce. Oh, they'd been poisoned before but very lightly; if they were eaten by a healthy person, the potion would have little effect, but this time the dosage was deadly.' Athelstan paused. 'Brother Philippe, your own physician, treated Sir Walter for these minor stomach ailments; he could not detect poison. He also treated others in this household suffering from a similar condition. I suspect those who shared these figs out . . .' He let his words hang in the air.

'True, true.' Buckholt turned to Sir Henry. 'On one occasion I had ill-humours of the belly – so did others. I am sure I had eaten some of those figs.'

'And if you reflect,' Athelstan declared, 'neither Isolda nor Vanner suffered such ailments. Brother Philippe declared he had no dealings with either of them. I am certain Brother Philippe would corroborate what I've just said.'

'You are correct,' Sir Henry declared. 'Isolda and Vanner – I cannot recall either of them having to be treated. Others certainly were . . .'

'But why should they poison the figs,' Falke interrupted, 'if they knew Sir Walter was not eating them? I could understand them doing that at the beginning to disable Sir Walter, but as he grew more sickly the figs were left. Moreover, why coat them with a truly malignant dose if they were to be eaten by others?'

'Oh, I shall explain that!' Athelstan replied.

'No, no,' Rosamund wailed, 'this cannot be.'

'Oh, but it was,' Athelstan insisted. 'At the same time Isolda and Vanner planned to poison Sir Walter's posset. She was furiously plotting not to be caught. If it hadn't been for Buckholt and Mortice, she would have escaped.' Athelstan allowed his words to hang in the air.

'Sweet God,' Sir Henry breathed, 'now I understand. There

would have been two deaths in this manor, both by poison: Walter Beaumont and Rosamund Clifford.'

'I visited Sir Walter,' Rosamund gabbled. 'He was comfortable. He said he wanted the figs but they were too much for him. He called them a temptation. He insisted that I accept them as a gift. I took them to my own chamber and ate them. I felt . . .'

'You became very ill,' Athelstan agreed, 'but you are a young, healthy woman. Your body would resist, even as you manifested symptoms of the sweating sickness, yes?'

Rosamund simply stared back in horror.

'Even better,' Athelstan continued, 'on your return to your chamber, you violently vomited? You had to visit the latrines?'

'I ate the figs,' she replied, 'and I vomited time and again through the following night until my belly ached. Later I felt a terrible thirst, and my skin burning up. Physician Philippe visited me after he had been summoned to attend Sir Walter. He examined my symptoms . . .'

'By then, Rosamund, the poison was purged but your body had to recover, your humours be restored. The bile in your belly calmed, yet, remember this, your mistress almost murdered you whilst Parson Garman, whose relationship with Sir Walter was not the most cordial, would have fallen under deep suspicion.'

The friar pointed at Falke. 'Now I shall answer your question. At first Sir Walter ate the figs and became subject to stomach complaints. Eventually he stopped eating them, or at least all of them; others tasted this delicacy and suffered similar symptoms of the belly.'

'Of course,' Lady Rohesia murmured, 'it served as a cover for what they were doing. Sir Walter suffered stomach cramps but so did others; it would lessen suspicion, create the impression that this was some household sickness.'

'And a fatal dose,' Athelstan declared, 'would help deepen suspicion that a poisoner was waging war on Sir Walter and his entire household. Let me explain. If Isolda and Vanner had not been detected by Mortice and Buckholt, if Rosamund had also died of suspected poisoning,' he gestured at the prison chaplain, 'against whom would the finger of suspicion be pointed? And you, Rosamund, were chosen by mere chance. It could have been Buckholt or anyone who ate those figs. It didn't really matter as long as someone else in the household died of poisoning.' Athelstan paused to let his words reverberate through minds and hearts. Garman and Rosamund were deeply shocked as their awareness deepened of how close Isolda had brought them to destruction. Sir Henry and his wife looked cowed, lost in their own thoughts. Falke stared unbelieving, his eyes blinking and lips moving wordlessly as if searching for words. Buckholt sat grinning to himself. Only Lady Anne, the mute Turgot behind her, seemed alert. She rolled back the voluminous cuffs of her cloak and leaned forward, tapping the table.

'Brother Athelstan, what you say is logical. God be my witness.' She stared around, hands outstretched. 'We've seen Vanner's corpse. What else can we believe except that Isolda was an assassin? Yet surely Sir Walter must have entertained his own suspicions? Why didn't he voice them?'

'Oh, he did, but he was very wary. In fact, he trusted none of you. That's the problem with men like Sir Walter – everyone is suspect. And he was right, wasn't he? Sir Henry, your brother realized you were waiting for him to die, praying that he would do so without an heir. No, no,' Athelstan waved a hand, 'now is not the time for protests of false innocence. Parson Garman, you know I speak the truth about your relationship with Black Beaumont. You hated him. You wanted revenge. Good enough motives for murder? Rosamund, you only graced Sir Walter with your company at your mistress' behest. She used you to distract her husband, perhaps to discover the whereabouts of "The Book of Fires". Sir Walter must have realized that. Lady Anne, Sir Walter may have respected you but never enough to confide in you. Moreover, like his wife, he may have come to resent you for introducing Isolda to him. Who knows, he may have suspected you of some nefarious, deeply laid scheme to discover his secrets . . .'

'Nonsense!' she snapped. 'What would I want with them?'

'Lady Anne, I am not describing the truth in all its glory but what may have been and, more importantly, what Sir Walter might have thought.'

'And me?' Buckholt asked.

'Ah, the faithful steward whose father fought alongside Sir Walter in the Luciferi.' Athelstan held Buckholt's gaze. 'A son who might have learnt about the ruthless treachery of Black Beaumont in all his doings. A man who could use his position to spy and, in time, betray his master to a greater cause – the Upright Men and their dream of building a new Jerusalem along the banks of the Thames. A steward who remained tight-lipped and taciturn, biding his time as he carefully searched for Sir Walter's secret knowledge.'

Buckholt simply smiled with his eyes.

'A frustrated lover who hated Isolda for what she was and what she did,' Athelstan continued, 'but also because of the real danger she posed – a ruthless, selfish woman who had her own secret plans for Sir Walter.'

'And me?' Falke asked. 'My part in this?'

'You know the answer to that, master lawyer. You were just another man caught up in the tempestuous passions of Lady Isolda. Sutler, God rest him, discovered the truth and if it hadn't been for him, Lady Isolda would have enjoyed the fruits of her sin. She was guilty; her defence was a lie but, like all great lies, contained fragments of truth. How there were others at Firecrest Manor who wished to discover Sir Walter's secrets. How members of this household secretly espoused the cause of the Great Community of the Realm. How Vanner may have fed Sir Walter poison earlier in the day. Rosamund, you would have been sacrificed. Isolda certainly turned on Vanner. Fearful that he might become a King's Approver, she killed him down near the mere and burnt any incriminating manuscripts. In the end, however, Sutler proved to be her match.'

'Are you finished?' Athelstan caught a note of jealousy in the lawyer's voice.

'No,' Athelstan smiled thinly, 'I am certainly not.' He emphasized the points on his fingers. 'Where is "The Book of Fires"?' Besides the Greeks, whom did Isolda secretly meet in the city? She sometimes went there by herself, yet no one knows where and why? What do the letters "SFSM" scrawled on the wall of her death cell mean? Is this a reference to the person she secretly met?' Athelstan chewed the corner of his lip. 'Is that the same individual who came to the execution ground to collect her remains and pretended to be Vanner?'

'I didn't know that happened!' Sir Henry exclaimed. 'Was it you, Falke?'

The lawyer just looked away.

'And the Ignifer?' Lady Anne asked.

'Oh, yes, the Ignifer. If Lady Isolda is one root of this wickedness, he certainly is the other. We are hunting him but he may go quiet. He has certainly created a world of terror for anyone involved in Isolda's destruction. He will let this play on your minds, bide his time, lull you into false comfort.' He held a hand up and blessed them. 'I am finished but be careful. Remain very vigilant.'

The meeting broke up, the household silent as they went their different ways. Athelstan suspected they would reflect on what was said and, in the weeks ahead, changes would be made, but that was not his business.

'Do you think,' Cranston asked, filling their tankards, 'the likes of Rosamund or Sir Henry could tell us more?'

'I doubt it, Sir John. Only three people know the truth about this and two of them are dead – Vanner and Isolda. The other is the Ignifer.'

'But why has he turned on us?' the coroner asked.

'Because, my fine friend,' Athelstan put his hand on the coroner's arm, 'the Ignifer, as I call him, though it could be she or they, whatever guise that demon assumes, certainly knows us by reputation. Yes,' Athelstan scratched his lip, 'now that's a thought, Sir John. The Ignifer is hunting us as ruthlessly as we are him. We must keep ourselves safe.'

'And so we shall. I have Flaxwith's bully boys, whilst those four lazy buggers from the Tower will look after you. What now, Brother?'

'Sir John, let us scrupulously study Sir Walter's manuscripts, though I'd be very surprised if we discover anything interesting.'

Athelstan's prophecy proved correct. They sat in the intricately panelled chancery chamber at the heart of Firecrest Manor with all its dockets, coffers, cabinets and cupboards containing narrow small drawers. Household accounts, memoranda, letters, bills and indentures were filed within as neatly as in any royal chancery or exchequer. Cranston, in his gilded youth, or so he confessed, when his hair had been blond and his body all svelte, had trained to be the most sharp-eyed and nimble-fingered clerk, and the coroner brought such expertise to bear on separating the wheat from the chaff. The personal papers of Sir Walter described his life in both the city and the court. Nevertheless, the more they read the more Athelstan's conviction deepened that they were fencing with shadows or, as Cranston claimed, 'It was all sizzle and no sausage.' Sir Walter was a most astute businessman who kept his past and all its secrets very close to his chest. The only noteworthy items were his generous donations to the Minoresses at Aldgate, certain sums paid to the chaplain of Newgate and gifts to Lady Anne Lesures, including the loan of his '*Novum Testamentum*' – his New Testament.

'Nothing remarkable,' Athelstan concluded, 'except for what these accounts don't tell us.'

'Which is, little friar?'

'Look at the allowances paid to Isolda.'

'Paltry sums.'

'Precisely, Sir John. So how could she afford costly gowns and expensive perfume which smells like crushed lilies?'

'What was the source of such monies?' Cranston asked. 'Brother Athelstan, are you sure Rosamund couldn't tell us more?'

'Oh, we are finished here. Rosamund, I am sure, knows very little else. Isolda would not render herself vulnerable to a maid. Let us leave it at that. Look, Sir John, darkness is falling. Outside the bats will squeak, dogs will howl and all good souls prepare for the night. So should we.'

Athelstan and Cranston gathered their cloaks, said goodbye to Sir Henry and left. Once outside Athelstan assured Cranston that the four Tower archers would be protection enough. He blessed the coroner, bade him goodnight and swiftly strode down the narrow alleyways, slivers of blackness reeking of corruption. Athelstan and his escort reached the quay where, due to the turbulent waters of the Thames, they had to wait for a barge. An enterprising storyteller, with mummers to act his tale, caught Athelstan's attention. The masque was about two merchants who had insulted a local sorceress. She visited them in their tavern chamber. She used her powers so the hinges of the door to their room sank out of their sockets, the bolts shot away from their clasps and the bolts on the crossbar sprang free. Once inside, the sorceress, hair all grizzled, torn and sprinkled with ash, her feet unshod, face pale as boxwood, carried out her murders. She cut the merchants' throats, pretending to catch their blood in a dog's bladder. Athelstan stood fascinated both by the story and the clever mimicry of the mummers, who performed their drama in a great pool of light thrown by torches lashed to poles.

Athelstan was still absorbed by what he had seen as he took his seat in a high-sterned barge. The oarsmen cast off and the boat turned to make its way carefully across the choppy Thames. Gulls screamed above them, flashes of white in the gathering blackness broken only by the lamps on other craft. Athelstan sat back and wondered about the masque he had just seen. Was this also true of the mystery confronting him? Was the Ignifer a storyteller, a master mummer directing his minions to play their parts? If that were true, what would be the next dramatic development? A night-bird shrieked. Athelstan glanced up at the glowering sky. The clouds had broken and patches of weak light appeared, a phenomenon which fascinated him. Kites and buzzards hovered, dark shapes as they hunted over the moving sludge of the riverside. The friar abruptly recalled a battlefield just south of Bordeaux. He remembered the feather-winged scavengers flocking to feast, hovering like angels of death over the fallen. Suddenly, in a long dash of dying sunlight, a great eagle appeared, shimmering like pure gold in that last burst of day. Athelstan had always thought it was a symbol: Christ was God's golden eagle appearing over the darkness of man. The kites and buzzards had disappeared as the majestic bird, its wings fully extended, floated so dramatically over the chaos and destruction below. Athelstan, steadying himself against the choppy waters of the Thames, prayed that Christ, heaven's own eagle, would help him break through the brooding, malevolent darkness confronting him.

oOoOo

'Where the body lies, there will the vultures gather.' The verse from scripture was hoarsely whispered by the hedge priest John Ball as he and his confederates watched their cohorts muster on the great wasteland south of London Bridge. The local outlaws, Friar Foxtail and his coven, had quietly fled, leaving that haunted, bleak stretch of common land to the Great Community of the Realm. An attack was imminent. The captains of the Upright Men, the Raven, Crow, Hawk, Falcon and so on, swiftly marshalled their ranks along the barren heathland stretching down to the Southwark quay and the great boat yard where Gaunt was preparing his flotilla of barges. The carriers of the pots were also ready, as well those armed with torches and flint. They had all assembled around the Devil's Oak, their armour and weapons hidden with no flame or fire to betray the glint of steel.

'In the name of the Lord's own commonwealth,' Ball hissed through the darkness. Orders were issued and the line moved soundlessly off. Men sloped like hunting wolves through the darkness, heading down towards the river. The attackers surged forward, swiftly gathering speed, spreading out, eager to get as close as possible to the barges. John Ball's scouts, men from Southwark including the parish of St Erconwald's, had carefully studied Gaunt's defences. The quayside and boat yard were protected by a ditch or moat with spiked stakes and, on the other side, a fortified palisade with a fighting platform. This arc of defence, half-moon in shape, sealed the quayside from all approaches by land, whilst war barges patrolled the river. The Upright Men had counted on surprise and the possibility of probing a weakened position where the palisade arched down to the quayside. A column of archers and footmen now aimed for that gap like a well-aimed spear. They reached the moat – fascines of bracken and wood were hurled into the ditch, a makeshift platform lowered across it and the attackers surged forward, siege ladders at the ready.

The Upright Men, many of them veterans, skilled in siege craft from their years in France, swarmed over the pointed palisade. Only then was the alarm raised. A horn sounded. Trumpets brayed but the attackers, brushing aside the sleep-soaked guard, were now through the defences and the quayside stretched before them. Part of the palisade was swiftly hacked down, pushed out to create a drawbridge across the moat so more attackers could stream over. Gaunt's forces were now alert. The knights banneret and serjeant-at-arms realized the futility of trying to defend the breached fortifications. They fled their tents and bothies, falling back on to the broad, well-lit quayside, dragging carts to form a barricade between the different buildings. Gaunt's captains were confident – they may have lost the palisade but they could easily hold this new line of defence. The Upright Men, however, had their own strategy. They pushed their assault as close as they could to the quayside then paused to take care of their own wounded and finish off those of the enemy. The screams and cries of the injured faded. An eerie lull descended. The captains of the Upright Men hissed their instructions. Six small trebuchets or catapults were pushed forward. These easily constructed engines of war, their wheels well oiled, were positioned carefully on the slight rise stretching down to the quayside. Crews skilled in their use calculated distances and prepared. Ropes creaked and tightened as the deep cup at the end of each long throwing beam was pulled back, the cords on either side becoming taut as drawn bow strings. Once ready, sealed clay pots carefully stacked beside each machine were placed in position. All six catapults were primed with two pots to every throwing cup. Tinder was struck. Flaming brands were plucked from the campfires of the defenders. Row upon row of archers took up position, their war bows at the ready.

'Loose!' one of the captains screamed. Cords and ropes sang, wood clattered and clashed, wheels creaked. The cata-pults loosed their burdens into the night sky. The clay pots disappeared into the darkness then fell. Some shattered on the quayside, smashed into buildings or the hastily assembled barricade. At first the defenders were puzzled, shouts and cries echoed, but the captains of the catapults had learnt their lesson:

peering through the poor light, they noted that a few of the pots had risen high over the quayside to crash on to the host of barges bobbing on the water. Winches, levers, ropes and cords were adjusted accordingly. The catapults were repositioned. A fresh volley of sealed pots seared the night sky. Orders were rapped out. The line of archers, bows slung, arrows notched, waited as footmen raced down their ranks with flaming torches. The fire arrows glowed. The war bows swung up and, in a fearsome whoosh, the blazing long shafts streaked the night sky before falling on to the quayside and the barges beyond. For a few heartbeats, a strange stillness descended then the fire arrows caught the oil seeping from the pots and both the quayside and the barges erupted in a blazing inferno.

The fire attack on the barges roused all of Southwark and St Erconwald's in particular. Athelstan was woken by Crim hammering on the door with the startling news of a fire raging along the riverside. Athelstan, braving the cold, immediately hurried across to the church with his escort of archers trailing behind him. The friar forced his way through the throng of pilgrims and visitors, now all agog about the attack along the Thames. Athelstan told the archers to wait and, with Crim trotting behind him, climbed to the top of the tower to see the fires blazing against the lightening sky.

'They'll all be there, won't they, Crim? Watkin, Pike and the rest, up to their necks in devilry. God save them.' Crim did not reply. Athelstan stretched out and tousled the boy's greasy hair. 'Don't worry, lad, I know you can't say anything. Just pray that they not be taken or slain.' Athelstan returned to his house. He could not settle. Dawn would come and the busyness of the day press in with its demands. The friar shaved, washed, donned fresh robes and sat drinking a cup of water, staring into the strengthening flames of the fire he had stoked in the small hearth.

'My soul is ready, O Lord,' he prayed. 'My soul is ready. Awake, my heart, awake, lyre and harp. I will awake the dawn.' Athelstan said a brief prayer to the Holy Spirit before returning to the mysteries of the Ignifer, Firecrest Manor and 'The Book of Fires'. 'A jumble of veritable facts and details,' he murmured,

'with no coherence or pattern. Ah, well.' He rose at the
scratching against the door and let in Bonaventure, who
streaked to the hearth where he sprawled, washing his paws
until Athelstan brought him a bowl of milk and a platter of
diced ham.

'Eat, drink and be merry, my friend.' Athelstan stroked
Bonaventure's head. 'For now I must pray.' He blessed the
great tomcat and left for the church. Crim and Benedicta had
prepared the sanctuary for Mass. The widow woman tried to
question him about the fire but Athelstan pressed a finger
against her lips, 'Silence,' he whispered, 'and discretion.
Pilgrims and visitors flock here as, undoubtedly, do Gaunt's
spies.'

Athelstan swiftly vested and prepared himself. He decided
to preach a homily before intoning the opening rite of the
Mass. He also used the occasion to carefully study his congre-
gation. The throng of people had definitely thinned. The attack
on the barges must have frightened them but Athelstan immediately noticed, as he had when Crim first roused him and he
crossed to the tower, how many of the young men, strangers
who had allegedly come to view the Great Miracle, had now
disappeared. Members of his parish were also conspicuous in
their absence and the list was long. After the attack on the
barges, the Upright Men would flee south into the countryside.
The group would break up and would drift back towards their
homes as if nothing had happened. Athelstan finished his
homily and celebrated his Mass. He found this difficult, being
distracted by thoughts which whirled through his mind like a
flock of noisy sparrows. Once he had received the Eucharist,
Athelstan paused and prayed fiercely for divine guidance. He
then continued the Mass, reached the final blessing and raised
his hand, staring round. Others were absent! Fulchard of
Richmond, together with his witnesses and his keeper, the
defrocked priest, Fitzosbert! Athelstan finished the blessing,
bowed his head and thanked God for guidance. He returned
to the sacristy, divested and hurried across to his house. He
told the escort of archers to break their fast in a rota, shelter
from the cold yet choose a place where they could keep a
strict eye on anyone approaching his house.

Once inside, Athelstan locked himself in. He hastily ate some porridge and began pacing up and down the kitchen, sifting through the evidence he'd collected as well as what he'd seen, or rather what he'd not seen, this morning.

'What is most possible is probable. So, Bonaventure?' Athelstan held the fierce gaze of the one-eyed tomcat. 'What is more possible in this vale of tears, a miracle or a clever deception? Let us concede, for sake of argument, that it's the latter.' He sat down on his leather-backed chair. 'Item: we have Fulchard of Richmond staggering into St Erconwald's during the vigil. Yes? He claims to have had a vision: how our great saint would help him. He certainly was a cripple, the entire right side of his body being badly burnt. Item: Fulchard of Richmond carried letters of attestation to his injuries. He was officially a cripple and a public beggar. On his arrival in London he was critically examined by Brother Philippe, one of the most eminent physicians of this city. He viewed Fulchard's terrible wounds. He also asserted that Fulchard was greatly weakened, even ill after his journey south. Item: on that particular morning Fulchard of Richmond leapt up to claim a miracle. He had been completely cured. Item: we have a host of witnesses to this miracle, be it Fitzosbert the defrocked priest as well as our noble physician, Brother Philippe. Item: we have the Great Miracle proclaimed. Strangers by the score flood into our ward and parish, bringing carts, barrows, pack ponies and other conveyances. Item: we have a goodly number of stout young men also interested in the miracle. Item: we have a sudden and very violent attack, or so I understand, against Gaunt's barges further down the river. Item: this morning most of these young men have disappeared, along with many parishioners, not to mention Fulchard of Richmond and his companion, Fitzosbert. Item: we have a connection between Firecrest Manor and the events of last night. Bonaventure, I am sure Greek fire was used during that assault. What I saw from the tower was a blazing furnace. So, who concocted this Greek fire? Is the Ignifer a member of the Upright Men? Item: let's return, Bonaventure, to this parish. What other strange events have happened in St Erconwald's?' Athelstan held a hand up. 'Item: Merrylegs, or rather Merrylegs senior. We have that funeral feast around his corpse. Strangers were present, certainly Upright Men who used the occasion to plot, but what? Item: on the night before the burial of Merrylegs senior, Godbless and his goat participate in the festivities until both are so drunk they can hardly stand. Item: the requiem Mass for Merrylegs senior the morning after. Many attended yet it proceeded so serenely and smoothly.' Athelstan stared at the small statue of St Erconwald standing on a plinth in the corner. He went and knelt before it, praying for guidance. 'For the children of this world,' he whispered, 'are more astute in dealing with their own kind than the children of the light. Lord,' he continued, 'my heart is not proud. I do not claim to be a child of the light but I know I am here to serve them.' He rose and went back to his reflections. The miracle at St Erconwald's was certainly beginning to dim as the fug of mystery around it cleared. Athelstan ate some bread and drank a little ale. He was about to return to his studies when Cranston hammered on the door, shouting for entrance. Once inside, the coroner shook off his great cloak and beaver hat, moved Bonaventure to one side then squatted down, hands out to the flames.

'Satan's tits, Athelstan! Gaunt is furious. The Upright Men used Greek fire – pot after pot catapulted through the air to drench the quayside, its buildings and the barges. This was followed by a veritable hail of fire arrows which kindled a furnace from Hell.' He rubbed his hands and got up. 'Gaunt expected an attack but not like that. He and his captains had planned on a sword fight, a clash of arms, not a firestorm loosed from afar. Brother, they even brought catapults. No wonder the Upright Men have been quiet recently – they were busy plotting last night's outrage.'

'Rumour has it much damage was done.'

'Brother, the barges were chained close together. The water afforded little protection. Some of the witnesses talk of the flames scudding across the water as if the Thames itself had caught fire. Two hundred barges were mustered there. I doubt if a score of them will reach the Lincolnshire Fens.'

'And the attackers?'

'They never really closed with Gaunt's troops. They had no

need. They forced the palisade, occupied the small rise over-looking the quayside and poured down a rain of fire. Once satisfied, they melted back into the darkness.'

'And the catapults?'

'Set them alight and left them burning. Gaunt's men were cautious; they could see the fires but it was dark, misty and they were not sure about the true strength of the enemy. At daylight mounted archers were despatched but for what? The Upright Men were long gone.' Cranston came and stood over Athelstan. 'I am sure,' he whispered, leaning down, 'that some of your parishioners were out on the wild heathland last night. But never mind, little friar, I have no desire to see them hang. What disturbs me is that during the attack, Greek fire was used. I am sure Watkin and Pike know how to fire oil, but this was different. A substance which set the river aflame! It could not be doused with water. They had to use dry dirt and leather sheets soaked in vinegar or urine.'

'So where did they get the fire from?' Athelstan rose to his feet. 'It must have been recent otherwise they would have used it before. Who would have experience of such a deadly substance?'

'Sir Henry Beaumont?'

'Perhaps. Think again.'

'Parson Garman?'

'Precisely, by his own confession he served in the Luciferi. He admitted he was a *peritus*, skilled in the machinery of war. He is also is an ardent supporter of the Upright Men. However, he's been searching for "The Book of Fires" for years. So where, when, how and why did he manage to secure at least some of its secrets?' Athelstan spread his hands. 'Of course, we have no proof to confront him with. I . . .' He paused at a rap on the door. He rose, drew the bolts and opened it. Two of the Tower archers stood there.

'Brother Athelstan, Sir John, we have stopped these.' The archer gestured over his shoulder. Athelstan stepped out and saw the four men, hooded and cloaked. One of these came forward, pushing back his cowl to reveal a dark, swarthy face. His long black hair neatly cut, as was his moustache and beard.

'Master Nicephorus,' Athelstan called, 'you are he?'

'I am.' The Greek's English was fluid and clear. 'I am Nicephorus.'

'And those are your swordsmen?' Athelstan replied. 'Soldiers of the Varangian Guard?'

'You have been speaking to Master Falke?'

'Of course, and now you wish to speak to me. Well, sir?' Athelstan stepped back. 'You are welcome but your swordsmen stay outside.'

Nicephorus came into the house. He clasped Cranston's hand and that of Athelstan before bowing his head for the friar's blessing, then crossed himself and took off his heavy cloak. Athelstan glimpsed the jewels shimmering on the finger rings and the costly gold chain around his neck displaying a miniature gem-studded icon of the Theotokos.

'I suspect your parishioners,' Nicephorus took the offered tankard of ale and the chair Athelstan pulled away from the table, 'were involved in last night's affray. Over one hundred and fifty barges were destroyed. Such, my friends, is the power of Greek fire.'

'And you want that secret back?' Cranston declared. 'Mark the Greek's "The Book of Fires", stolen by Black Beaumont. That's why you follow me and my secretarius around London,' Cranston sat down, 'and saved us on two occasions. For that we are grateful. But, my friend, why were you there?'

'Because you hunt the Ignifer, and he, Sir John,' Nicephorus took a sip of ale, neatly wiping the white froth from his moustache, 'either holds the secret of Greek fire or is close to someone who does. Mark the Greek's manuscript contains many secrets, different formulas, correct measurements of what elements are needed. The Ignifer must have these.' He sipped again. 'Though I solemnly assure you, whoever it is should be most careful. You English have a saying: "It is dangerous to play with fire" – Greek fire in particular. It has a power you sometimes can't control.'

'And Black Beaumont never gave it back to you?'

'Oh, yes, he did.'

'What?'

'Black Beaumont sold what he stole to Greek envoys a few years after his return to England.'

Athelstan sat down. 'So you have it already?'

'It's back with my masters in the great city – that's why we left Black Beaumont alone for a while. However, our spies here kept him under close watch. They reported something rather strange. How occasionally Sir Walter would go on journeys all by himself. He'd leave on horseback with a sumpter pony.'

'To some deserted wasteland to experiment with different fires?'

'In a word, yes. Beaumont sold the manuscript back to us and settled down in London to live high on the hog. The Secretissimi in the great city continued to watch him. After all, a man who steals will steal again. We discovered his secret journeys, we saw the flashes of fire and, before you ask, did he steal two copies of "The Book of Fires"? No! Beaumont had the original copied and, knowing Sir Walter as we do, the clerk or scrivener responsible did not live long afterwards.'

'We've learnt,' Athelstan declared,' that Beaumont would make sly references to how this secret manuscript's whereabouts would be a revelation to all, that it was safe on the island of Patmos.'

'Yes, we discovered the same.' Nicephorus put his tankard down. 'We have spied, coaxed and threatened everyone we thought could help us and, believe me my friends, the list is long. Lady Isolda, Falke, Buckholt, Sir Henry; Parson Garman who, as a mercenary, served abroad under the name Saint-Croix: Vanner, whose corpse you have recently discovered, as well as other servants and retainers at Firecrest Manor. We cannot understand Beaumont's jest except, of course, St John the Evangelist wrote the last book of the Bible, the Apocalypse, the Book of Revelation, whilst in exile on the island of Patmos.'

'Of course,' Athelstan breathed. 'How stupid of me.'

'Now, the Book of Revelation,' Nicephorus continued, 'talks about the Parousia, the Second Coming of Christ, the end of all things when the world will be destroyed by fire. Beaumont might have been referring to the power and possibilities of Greek fire, except,' he held up a gauntleted hand, 'Beaumont actually visited Patmos. Once he'd stolen the book, he escaped through Asia. We know he deserted most of his company in the desert outside Izmir. He and a group of henchmen then fled across the Middle Sea. They reached Patmos.' Nicephorus sketched a cross over his heart. 'I swear by the Holy Face only Black Beaumont left Patmos alive. The remains of his companions, nothing more than burnt, tangled blackened bone and scraps of flesh, were found high in the mountains. It took weeks before the governor could establish that these were the mortal remains of the English mercenaries who had landed on the island a few months earlier. Scraps of clothing, discarded weapons,' he shrugged, 'but, of course, once again, Black Beaumont had slipped away without leaving any evidence that he had anything to with what, murder? A dreadful accident? Attack by some other group?'

'Satan's tits!' Cranston whispered. 'I suspect it was murder. Black Beaumont was an assassin. He had a night-shrouded soul, a felon who should have been hanged high.'

'What do you think happened?' Athelstan asked.

'Oh, Beaumont drugged his companions and used his skill to concoct Greek fire and burnt their bodies,' Nicephorus smiled thinly, 'or at least some of them.'

'Did one escape?' Athelstan asked. 'Could this be our Ignifer?'

'Ah, the Fire Bearer. You realize that Beaumont's Luciferi had officers of different ranks. Some of these would have the title of Ignifer, being directly responsible for loosing the cannon or the hollow tubes through which Greek fire or any such flame can be shot. The Ignifer would also be responsible for loading and directing the trebuchets and catapults with fiery missiles. The mercenary Saint-Croix, known to you as Parson Garman, held the post of Ignifer, a high-ranking officer and quite a ruthless one.'

'So Garman is the Ignifer?'

'Brother Athelstan, he could well be. He may have played a leading part in the attack on my lord of Gaunt's barges. I understand the liquid used was of the same genus as Greek fire.'

'You have met Garman?' Athelstan asked.

'Yes. All he'll say is that the past is the past and he is nothing more than a lowly prison chaplain.'

'I received the distinct impression,' Athelstan declared, 'that Garman did not have "The Book of Fires", though he could have had extracts and formulas. We do not know what Parson Garman conceals from his past or what he has acquired since his return to England.'

'Master Nicephorus,' Cranston intervened, 'according to you, Beaumont returned to England. He copied "The Book of Fires" and sold some of its secrets to the Crown and perhaps to others abroad. You negotiated the return of the original in return for what?'

'Treasure, mercantile information, trading concessions and, yes, we suspected he may have made a copy either of the entire book or those sections of value.'

'How long after his return to England did he agree to sell?'

'Oh, about five years. My predecessors agreed on a price but insisted we pay in instalments. Payments,' he added, 'you will not find in Beaumont's receipt books but went directly to his trading ventures. Then,' Nicephorus leaned forward, tapping the table, 'about a year ago he eventually confessed he did have a copy. He had the impudence to assert that he kept it as a pledge of our good faith. We replied that we also suspected that he had continued to sell its secrets abroad. It's now common knowledge that the Hanse merchants in the Baltic have recently overhauled their armaments, weaponry and ships – their crews have become more skilled in the use of cannon as well as more powerful powder and fiery missiles. Beaumont, in fact, sold the secrets he kept in a piecemeal fashion, little by little both here and abroad.' The Greek shrugged. 'We have traitors in the great city, officers in the Imperial army who sell secrets. All the Secretissimi can do is block the flow and catch the drip for as long as we can.'

'And what did Beaumont want in return?' Athelstan asked.

'We met him in the city. Beaumont agreed to hand over the copy in return for the following: the murders of the Lady Isolda and Parson Garman.'

Cranston whistled under his breath.

'And one more.' Nicephorus stirred on his stool. 'Rievaulx.'

'Rievaulx?' Athelstan queried.

'One of Black Beaumont's henchmen in the Luciferi,'

Nicephorus replied. 'We never mentioned what we had discovered on Patmos. Beaumont eventually did. He maintained he left his company to go down to one of the villages to buy supplies. He stayed to roister and wench. On his return he found five of his companions must have been drugged or killed, their corpses burnt. He believed the sixth man, Rievaulx, had fled. Now whether Rievaulx was part of the murderous assault on the other five, Beaumont could not say.'

'Did Sir Walter know Rievaulx's birth name?' Athelstan tried to hide his growing excitement. The line of logic he had been developing before the arrival of Sir John and Nicephorus was beginning to strengthen. 'Rievaulx' could finally clear the way forward.

'No, he did not.' Nicephorus chose his words carefully. 'However, a year ago Beaumont believed this Rievaulx had emerged to threaten him.'

'Of course, of course.' Athelstan couldn't hide his excitement.

'Brother?' Cranston looked askance at him.

'Think, Sir John.' Athelstan tried to divert his own secret joy at making progress. 'A year ago Beaumont was being threatened. "As I and ours burnt, so shall ye and yours"!'

'He told us the same,' Nicephorus agreed. 'The warnings were public. Rievaulx was hunting him.'

'So,' Cranston shook his head, 'Beaumont needed you to rid him of a wife he no longer wanted, a priest who reminded him of his dark, sinister past and a former member of his company who had now emerged from the shadows. I can see why he chose you. No, do not take offence,' he held up a hand, 'Beaumont would be most reluctant to hire some London assassin who might later confess or blackmail him. He therefore chose someone who needed something precious from him, as well as one who would not be a constant reminder, an ever-present threat to his peace of mind. So,' he raised his eyebrows, 'what was your response?'

'Sir John, we realize why he chose us but I am the accredited envoy of His Most Imperial Excellency.' For a few heartbeats Nicephorus' tactful demeanour faded. 'We will kill and we have killed but we are not assassins. For the love of the

Holy Face, Beaumont was demanding the murder of an innocent, high-born lady whatever her character, a priest much
loved by the commons and a former member of his company
whom we desperately wanted to talk to. Naturally we couldn't
tell that to Beaumont.'

'So you temporized?'

'Yes, Brother, we temporized. We promised to find Rievaulx.
We never did. Naturally we continued to meet Beaumont,
assuring him we were trying our very best.'

'Did you inform Lady Isolda about what her husband wanted
or Parson Garman that his former leader wanted him dead?'

'Of course not.' Nicephorus got to his feet. 'The anger of
God caught up with Black Beaumont. Oh, we met the Lady
Isolda. Trust me, Brother, I've learnt what happened at Firecrest
Manor – your discovery of Vanner's corpse and your conviction that Lady Isolda was a murderess; she and Sir Walter
richly deserved each other. As for Garman, there is nothing
more dangerous than a former sinner who has found religion.
He has his own secret cause and even a king's ransom would
not turn him.' He paused. 'I have told you what I know because
one day I am sure you will discover the truth of all this. Sir
John, Brother Athelstan, you enjoy a most formidable reputation. What I ask is a favour but, when you discover the truth,
as an act of kindness, inform me, someone who also did his
best to help you.'

'We shall.' Athelstan spoke before Cranston could
intervene.

'Very well, until then.' Nicephorus clasped hands with both
of them and left.

'And I must go too.' Cranston lurched to his feet. He strapped
on his warbelt, put on his beaver hat, swung his cloak about
him and grasped Athelstan by the shoulder, pulling him close.

'The hunt has begun, hasn't it, little friar? You, the human
ferret, are in full pursuit of your quarry.'

'Yes, I am racing down dark and twisting tunnels in search
of our killer. In the meantime, I will deal with miracles.'

'I do wonder about that,' Cranston replied. He pulled the
friar closer and hugged him. 'Little friar,' he whispered, 'I am
nurturing my own deep suspicions about what is happening

in your parish but I leave that to you. On this we are divided.'
He released Athelstan and stepped back. 'You, my friend, must
look after your flock, and God knows they need looking after.
I am the King's officer – sometimes you must walk your path
and I walk mine.' Cranston put his hand on the latch. 'My
friend, I think we have just reached such a crossroads.'

Athelstan grinned, raised his hand in blessing and stood in
the doorway watching Cranston stomp off towards London
Bridge. The friar stared across at the concourse before his
parish church. Men-at-arms and mounted hobelars, their scarlet
and blue tabards proclaiming the royal arms, now mingled
with the visitors and pilgrims. Their arrival was a logical result
of the previous night's attack on the barges. A fruitless task.
The Upright Men would have long disappeared, separated and
merged back into their villages, farms, hamlets or, as here,
their wards and parishes. Moreover, the soldiers would have
to be most careful. Any overbearing search or scrutiny might
provoke a riot.

Athelstan wondered when the miscreants from his own flock
would appear. Until then he would pursue the hypothesis he
had begun to develop before his visitors arrived. Nicephorus'
information had been most useful but most of it would have
to wait for a while. The question of Rievaulx wouldn't.
Athelstan collected his cloak, left the house and hurried into
the church. The throng of visitors had thinned. The only parishioners were Crim, Benedicta, Imelda and other women.
Athelstan raised his hand in greeting but hurried on up the
nave into the chantry chapel. Once there he paused, collecting
his thoughts and trying to recall the sequence of events. On
the night of the great miracle, Fulchard of Richmond had
hobbled into the church, a crutch resting under his right arm.
He was cloaked and hooded; he may have had a visor over
his face. He lay down and was cured so he did not need the
crutch. Pilgrims whose prayers were answered at a shrine, be
it a cure or any other type of healing, would leave some token
of appreciation: a stick, a cane or, as in this case, a crutch to
be hung over the saint's shrine. 'Right,' Athelstan whispered
to himself, 'I will begin with that.' He went into the chapel
and he pushed his way through the worshippers, explaining

he needed to clean the crutch. He grasped this, smiled benevolently at everyone and hurried back to his house. Once inside he pulled back his cloak and pushed the crutch under his right armpit. At first he thought the discomfort and unsteadiness were due to him being shorter than Fulchard whilst the crutch, being even-sided, could be used either way. Mystified, he laid the crutch on the floor, examining it carefully, and realized the crutch had been specially fashioned to be used only on the right side of the body. The cushioned rest was slightly angled to accommodate this; the hand clasp further down faced the outside whilst the very thick leather toe, stiffened to hardness, was worn away by the angle of how the crutch rested against the ground. Athelstan turned it over time and again – he could hardly believe his eyes. Then he lifted it up, trying it under his left armpit and then his right. Once finished, he put it across the table and sat down face in his hands. 'You stupid, stupid, stupid friar,' he whispered. 'You pride yourself on your sharp eyes and perception, yet you can't distinguish your left from your right.' He took his hands away from his face. 'Very well, my beloveds. You now have my full attention.'

PART SIX

*'Another type of fire . . . Which burnt houses situated in
the mountains and burnt the mountain itself.'*
Mark the Greek's 'The Book of Fires'

Athelstan stood at the top of the long common table in
the taproom of the Piebald tavern. He stared at the
men grouped either side – Joscelyn, Watkin, Pike,
Merrylegs, Ranulf, Giles of Sempringham also known as
the Hangman of Rochester, Fulchard of Richmond, Fitzosbert
and all the other members of the canting merry crew. Parson
Garman had also joined them, summoned by Athelstan, 'on a
matter of life or the cruellest death'. Night had fallen. Curfew
lamps glowed in church steeples, for darkness had wrapped
everything in its shroud. The parish church had been closed.
Athelstan had insisted that all approaches to the Piebald be
strictly guarded. Everything was now ready. Joscelyn had
served the ale and fired the torches and candles as well as the
corner braziers. All doors and windows were firmly bolted.
The assembled men, now cleansed of their masks, painted
faces and other disguises used in the previous night's assault,
did not know where to look – at Fulchard, Athelstan or that
crutch lying down the centre of the table. Athelstan dramatically intoned the 'Gloria', blessed them and sat down.

'If Sir John Cranston were here,' he began, 'you would need
every prayer I could utter because all of you would undoubtedly hang. No, Pike,' he slapped the table with the palm of
his hand, 'you would hang and it would not be swift. Now,
Fulchard of Richmond, or so you call yourself, what do the
following mean: "*arete*", "*doulos*", "*agathos*", "*kakos*",
"*kalos*"?'

The man gazed blankly back.

'They are Greek words,' Athelstan explained, 'from Koine,
the lingua franca used commonly around the Middle Sea. They

mean "virtue", "servant", "good", "bad" and "beautiful".
Fulchard of Richmond was allegedly injured whilst working
at a tavern in Athens. If he worked there he must have known
such common, simple words. To continue,' Athelstan leaned
over and touched the crutch, 'Fulchard of Richmond was
damaged on his right side. Crutches for the perennial cripple
are fashioned uniquely. Fulchard's crutch was made to be held
under the right armpit. However, this one, which Fulchard
allegedly used, is for the left. Of course, it would not matter
for that very brief journey into the church before this farce
took place. All the false cripple had to do was shuffle up the
steps and along the nave and lie down near the chantry chapel.
When the so-called miracle occurred, the crutch was only
needed as a relic and nothing else. You also carried a small
phial of perfume to exude something akin to the odour of
sanctity, a fragrance which could indicate the intervention of
heaven. It was all a sham. The real Fulchard of Richmond
never entered that church – you did.' Athelstan pointed down
the table at the imposter. 'Darkness was falling, the nave was
gloomy. All you needed was to disguise the right side of your
face with make-believe burns. Southwark houses a legion of
counterfeit cranks and cunning men and, if that wasn't the
case, you may have even worn a mask. Who would remember
a hooded, visored cripple, the crutch under the wrong arm,
face down, stumbling up towards the shrine?'

'The witnesses?' Pike spluttered.

'Oh, shut up!' Athelstan roared. 'Do not depict me as a
complete fool. The witnesses, including you, Fitzosbert, were
all hand-picked, fervent supporters of the Upright Men.' Heads
were bowed, booted feet shuffled. 'Now,' Athelstan continued,
'the real Fulchard of Richmond was indeed very ill. Brother
Philippe, an eminent physician, testified to that. It was a shrewd
move to take Fulchard to St Bartholomew's, where Philippe
would adjudge him both as a cripple and a very sick man.'
Athelstan snapped his fingers at Pike. 'You also brought the
real Fulchard to see me: you wanted me to personally witness
how ill he truly was.'

The ditcher kept his head down.

'So,' Athelstan declared, 'on the night of the so-called

miracle, the real Fulchard remained hidden, either here at the Piebald or in a garret at Merrylegs' shop. He would keep his crutch as he still needed it. The so-called miracle occurred, but Fulchard, truly ill, quietly died, and his corpse was kept hidden. I was, thankfully for you, distracted by other business. I am sure you planned Fulchard's secret burial in my cemetery but then Merrylegs senior also died around the same time. This provided you with an excellent opportunity for honourable interment. Watkin and Pike dug the grave deep and on the night before the funeral Mass for Merrylegs senior, you arranged Fulchard's secret burial. Some of you miscreants, under the guise of gaping pilgrims, visited Godbless and his goat.' Athelstan ignored the snort of laughter from the shadows. 'There was great excitement in the church and the parish. Godbless was only too willing to be swept up in the festivities. Thanks to you, both he and Thaddeus became helplessly drunk. Godbless did not watch the cemetery – he did not see the secret burial of Fulchard whose funeral rites were conducted by you, Fitzosbert, a defrocked priest but still an ordained minister with the God-given power to conduct such a ceremony.'

Athelstan banged the table. 'I can easily prove this if needed. Once dawn breaks I'll have Cranston's bailiffs open that grave and dig until they find what I am looking for.' He noticed Fitzosbert's hand drop beneath the tabletop. Ranulf the rat-catcher, sitting beside him, jabbed the defrocked priest with his elbow and Fitzosbert's hand reappeared.

'Good.' Athelstan stared round. 'I beg you in Christ's name, as well as for the amity and respect you should owe me, do not think of doing anything stupid. I admit, the story you gave about Fulchard's early history contains some grains of truth. Fulchard of Richmond did go abroad. He served as a mercenary in Black Beaumont's free company, the Luciferi. He assumed another name, Rievaulx, a reference to the great Benedictine abbey in Yorkshire where he and you, my friend,' Athelstan pointed at the imposter, 'were educated as boys. Black Beaumont and his troop arrived in Constantinople. During unrest there, they stole Mark the Greek's "The Book of Fires" and fled the city. Black Beaumont decided not to share the secrets of that manuscript and the wealth they would bring with anyone else. He deserted one set of comrades in the desert outside Izmir and fled with a group of henchmen to Patmos in the Middle Seas where he committed further treachery, carrying out a horrid atrocity. Black Beaumont drugged and burnt alive his remaining companions, except,' Athelstan pointed down at the imposter, 'the man known as Rievaulx. He was grievously injured but, God knows how, he managed to escape. He eventually returned to England, crippled and worn. He hid for a while, then Fulchard of Richmond emerged as a professional beggar who suffered a hideous accident abroad. Of course,' Athelstan smiled thinly, 'you know all this, don't you?'

The imposter just stared coolly back. 'I examined all the possibilities, including a miracle. However, given all that I have said, I have reached a much stronger possibility, in fact the strongest, that it was probable that you, sir, and the real Fulchard of Richmond are identical twins.' Athelstan sat back in the chair. He moved his tankard slightly forward. 'I cannot tell you about your life – why should I? But you and your twin eventually became reconciled. Fulchard did not tell you the full truth immediately. He peddled the tongue-smooth tale of a dire accident in some Greek tavern. Time passed and the truth eventually emerged. You were horrified. Black Beaumont was now a well-known, leading merchant in this kingdom. You wanted revenge. You sent Beaumont threatening messages, "As I and ours burnt, so shall ye and yours". But then others intervened.' Athelstan's gesture took in the entire company. 'The Upright Men are strong in both Yorkshire and Lincolnshire. Like the ancient Saxon hero, Hereward the Wake, the Upright Men are fortifying hiding places in the dark, damp fens of East Anglia. Gaunt vowed to burn them out and his flotilla of flat-bottomed barges would be crucial in achieving this. It's no idle threat. The royal dockyards along Southwark were busy and the barges would soon be deployed. The Upright Men decided to destroy them. They held council and a very subtle plot was concocted. You and Fulchard would meet others here at St Erconwald's for the novena vigil to our saint. The miracle would take place assisted by witnesses who are also

Upright Men from different shires, ably assisted by your coven
in this parish led by you, Ranulf. Once the so-called miracle
had occurred, your brother would be hidden and later secretly
whisked away. The miraculous occurrence would attract the
crowds and wealth, a good source of revenue for some of our
parishioners.' Athelstan glared at Pike and Watkin. 'As well
as a source of great profit to the Upright Men in more ways
than one. Visitors streamed into Southwark. Pilgrims thronged
this ward and my church. Carts, sumpter ponies and barrows
arrived with goods for sale. The crowd surged in and set up
camp. Gaunt's spies were overwhelmed – they found it impossible to survey such a multitude. God had worked a great
wonder and, according to canon law, pilgrims and shrines were
specially blessed and protected by Holy Mother Church.
Moreover, this was not some sham – both the Bishop of
London's curia and one of this city's eminent physicians have
tendered the only logical conclusion on the evidence they have
scrupulously examined, that a genuine miracle has occurred.
The Upright Men now had an ideal way to smuggle in both
men and arms in preparation for the great assault on Gaunt's
fleet of barges. You needed one more thing.' Athelstan pointed
at Parson Garman. 'You too served with Black Beaumont. You
were an ignifer, skilled in the casting of fire. You were also
searching for "The Book of Fires". You must have found it to
create that inferno amongst the barges.' Athelstan paused. He
strove to remain passive even as the sweat started and his
stomach lurched. These were desperate men. If he published
abroad what he'd whispered in this close, dark room, all those
grouped here would die a hideous death. Garman, cleric though
he was, would feel the full fury of Gaunt's rage. The justices
of oyer and terminer, the Regent's creatures, would be
instructed to charge each and every one of them with high
treason as they had committed arson in the royal dockyards.
Punishment would be dire: drawn to the scaffold, half hanged,
their bodies split open, heart and entrails plucked out, their
limbs quartered, their heads severed.

'What I have said is the truth,' Athelstan murmured. 'I want
none of you to hang. I do not hunt the Upright Men but the
Ignifer who has tried to murder me and my good friend, Sir

John Cranston.' Athelstan stared at Garman. In his soul he felt
the prison chaplain was the most obdurate and probably the
moving spirit behind this subtle plot. A highly intelligent officer
with great experience of war, Garman also nursed a deep hatred
against the lords of the soil. Athelstan decided to press the
point. 'Parson Garman, you always suspected that a hideous
massacre took place on Patmos. Perhaps you also suspected
that the mercenary Rievaulx escaped. Did you know his real
name? Fulchard of Richmond?'

The chaplain did not answer.

'You certainly learnt from gossip at Firecrest Manor about
the threats issued a year ago. You must have deduced such
threats were connected with the Luciferi, how someone did
escape that massacre and was now back in England. The
Upright Men have covens and conventicles from here to the
Scottish border. You made enquiries and your plot at St
Erconwald's was concocted and hatched. Strange,' Athelstan
mused, 'that you expressed little interest in the miracle, nor
did you ever come here because you knew the truth. So, I ask
you formally, do you have Mark the Greek's "The Book of
Fires"?'

Garman made to rise but the imposter restrained him, one
hand on the chaplain's wrist as he pointed at Athelstan.

'Brother, we in turn wish you no harm. No!' he shouted to
still the muttering of Fitzosbert and the other strangers. 'For
the love of God,' he hissed, 'Athelstan has all the proof he
needs. It lies in his graveyard. Let us tell the truth, or as much
as we can.' No one dissented. Athelstan was comforted to see
his parishioners, the majority around the table, would also
stoutly resist any assault on their priest. He beckoned at the
imposter to continue.

'My true name is John of Richmond.' The hubbub in the
taproom died. 'I am the identical twin of Fulchard, alike in
all ways except upbringing. My father was a yeoman farmer,
prosperous enough to be a herbalist and an apothecary. At
first, the birth of identical twin boys delivered safely was a
source of great joy and blessing. Fulchard and I were not
only very similar in looks but even on a spiritual level. If he
was hurt I also felt injury in that place. Anyway, my father's

wealth and good fortune provoked envy and malice, whispering and gossip, talk of witchcraft and other evil nonsense. In the end my father decided to send us out of the locality to be raised separately. Fulchard went to Rievaulx whilst I was educated at Fountains Abbey. We remained separate. Fulchard matured differently. He found obedience difficult. He resisted all the strictures of the good brothers and expressed this in a love of fire. Nothing serious or malicious – Fulchard was simply fascinated by creating fires with different mixtures.' John of Richmond spread his hands. 'The night draws on. I will be brief. Fulchard fled Rievaulx. He served as a squire in a troop of mounted archers but his true love was for culverins, cannon and, above all, fire in all its forms. Like many restless young men, he arrived in London and left for Dover as a member of Beaumont's Luciferi, assuming his mercenary name of Rievaulx, a joke at the expense of the good brothers who had tried to educate him. The Luciferi campaigned all over Europe until they arrived in Constantinople.'

'By then Fulchard,' Parson Garman broke in, 'though I only knew him as Rievaulx, was an ignifer like me, skilled in casting fire, a good, faithful companion, trusted by all and trusting in us until that fateful night on Patmos.'

'So Black Beaumont did massacre his henchmen.' Athelstan nodded at the prison chaplain. 'You could have told us this earlier!'

'Brother, it's not my tale to tell, nor could I without betraying others!'

The friar turned back. 'So, my question. Beaumont was an assassin?'

'Yes, Brother.' John of Richmond took up the story. 'He first led them away from the group in the desert outside Izmir, claiming that the likes of Parson Garman, or Saint-Croix as he was then called, were traitors intending to betray everyone to the Greeks. Beaumont gave this select group of henchmen a choice: to stay or to accompany him.'

'Why didn't he leave all of them?' Athelstan asked, then he smiled. 'A truly selfish soul,' he murmured. 'Beaumont needed protection, an escort across the desert.'

'At the time my brother Fulchard and the others reluctantly agreed, yet the seeds of mistrust were sown. Black Beaumont realized that. They eventually arrived at Patmos. Beaumont led them up into the mountains, claiming they would hide there until the pursuit lessened and he plotted a swift journey to Rome, other cities and then on to England. Quarrels and disputes broke out. As a gesture of trust, Black Beaumont declared they would share the mysteries of Greek fire. He journeyed to the villages and bought certain materials; Greek fire is not difficult, nor too costly to make. This was only occasion that Beaumont produced "The Book of Fires", using it to create a concoction which burst into flames almost impossible to extinguish. Black Beaumont claimed they would make their fortunes by selling "The Book of Fires" to the highest bidder amongst the wealthy warlords of northern Italy, be it the Sforzas of Milan or the Medici of Florence. He insisted again that he had left the others because they wished to seize such secrets for themselves or sell them back to the pursuing Greeks. One night Black Beaumont, ostensibly to restore harmony and celebrate their success, declared they would feast on lamb, herbs, pitta bread and a fiery Greek drink, *metaxa*, which was heavily drugged. My brother only drank a little – his belly was disturbed. The others, however, collapsed as if dead. Fulchard woke to find Beaumont emptying wineskins full of Greek fire all over them, followed by flaming brands from the campfire. A dire scene, Brother Athelstan! The drugged men were aroused but by a raging inferno. Fulchard stumbled away into the dark, Hell's fires burning behind him, the night riven by the most soul-chilling screams. He staggered into a pit of dust which probably saved him as the right side of his body was scorched by strange blue and gold flames. He fainted from the pain. When he woke he found himself in a goatherd's hut being tended by a man and his daughter. They had found and hidden him as Black Beaumont, like some demon from Hell, sword in one hand, dagger in the other, prowled those lonely outcrops hunting for the one who had escaped. Beaumont eventually left. The goatherd was extremely skilled, whilst the flames on my brother's body had been almost immediately doused by falling into the dust pit. The injuries were washed and treated with poultices soaked in dried moss and stale milk. My brother recuperated from his injuries, though it took years. He told me that during his stay his soul changed, seared by the murderous treachery of Beaumont yet healed by a compassion he had never experienced before.' John of Richmond paused to sip from his tankard. 'My brother stayed with that goatherd and his daughter for a number of years. They truly cared for him.' He shrugged. 'You are correct. Fulchard became fluent in Greek. Time passed. The remains of his companions were collected and interred. Memories faded. The goatherd died and so did his daughter. Fulchard, grief stricken, also grew homesick. He'd secured a little wealth and so began his pilgrim journey to England. He arrived back in Yorkshire with letters of accreditation from the Hospitallers in Rhodes, where he had stayed on his travels. He became a hermit, a recluse who begged for alms.'

'And he approached you?'

'Eventually, about four years ago. I had moved to Lincolnshire. I had a son.' He fought to keep his voice steady. 'My son was murdered for objecting to a market tax imposed by Lord Scales. I had prospered. I was a wealthy farmer and, like my father, an apothecary and herbalist. Lord Scales treated me and mine as if we were shit on his shoe. The King's justices in Eyre were as corrupt, their souls bought, their justice twisted. Lord Scales was no better than a robber, an assassin. I became, for what it's worth, a leading captain amongst the Upright Men in Lincolnshire. About the same time Fulchard sent messages which I eventually received. I journeyed to meet him. I arranged for secret lodgings. Fulchard was a veteran, proud of even his horrible burns. The story I told you about the tavern in Athens is what he first told me. Like all seasoned mercenaries, he was most reluctant to talk about his past. During his long years on Patmos, Fulchard had changed – become more humble, more loving. He wished to make atonement. He saw his sufferings as just punishment for his sins. What sins, he only began to tell me about two years ago. Reluctantly, slowly, he confessed to what truly happened on Patmos. I was horrified.'

'You wanted revenge?'

'I thirsted for it.' John of Richmond paused as if listening to the sound of a dog howling at the moon: the squeak of rats and other vermin pierced the stillness of the night.

'You sent those threatening messages?' Athelstan demanded.

'Yes, I knew about Sir Walter Beaumont, his power, his wealth, his close friendship with the demon Gaunt. I was set on revenge. Then the Upright Men of Lincoln received reports from Parson Garman about the construction of a flotilla of flat-bottomed barges in the royal dockyards on Southwark side.'

'Do you know, Brother, what Gaunt intended?' Fitzosbert the defrocked priest banged the table with the hilt of his dagger. 'He plotted to bring Flemish mercenaries, killers who would be at home in the wet fens. They would thread the marshes on those barges. Oh, I know,' the defrocked priest sneered, 'outlaws, outcasts, wolfsheads and wastrels, men like me shelter in the Fens. But so do women and children, as well as peasants who've fled from cruel lords and taken their families with them. Can you imagine, Friar, what would happen? The black waters of the Fens would turn red with innocent blood.'

'I travelled into Lincolnshire,' Garman spoke up, leaning forward so Athelstan could see his face in the candlelight. 'I met my comrades and our response was discussed. John wished to help, so did his brother Fulchard. It took us days to weave the different strands of our plot. We realized the vigil novena at St Erconwald's provided us with a skilful and subtle way to prepare and mount our assault. The rest was as you say. Of course, we made mistakes, about the crutch, about how weak Fulchard had become. Nevertheless, we were successful. The barges have been destroyed.'

'My brother wanted that,' John of Richmond exclaimed. 'He hoped Black Beaumont would realize he could no longer control Greek fire but, of course, Beaumont was sent to Hell's eternal flame. All we needed,' he spread his hands, 'and God is good, was a brief period so that men and weapons could flow into this ward without Gaunt's spies being alerted. Our envoys from the Great Community could come and go without hindrance. Comrades could fill every tavern and lodging house. Others camped out, all thronged into Southwark and learnt about its alleyways and runnels, whilst our spies inspected and reported on Gaunt's defences. Now we are finished. Soon we will be gone, unless you . . .' His voice trailed off.

'What price did your brother ask for all this?' Athelstan demanded.

'To strike at Gaunt, to protect our comrades, to prepare for the great revolt and, when it came, to ensure that Firecrest Manor was burnt to the ground. Not one stone was to be left upon another, its soil sown with salt and its masters executed as traitors to the common good. And before you ask, Brother Athelstan, yes, we have sympathizers in the Beaumont household, though we do not yet fully trust them. They knew nothing about this. So, Brother, what do you want?'

'The truth.'

'You have had that.'

'About the Ignifer, the assassin?'

'We know nothing,' Garman retorted. 'I – we – can tell you no more.'

'Oh, yes, you can. How you obtained Greek fire, its deadliest variety. You, Parson Garman, must have it. You must have met the leaders of the Upright Men to demonstrate its true power?'

'No,' John of Richmond intervened, 'I did that. Oh, for the love of God, Garman, tell him! What does it matter now?'

'We were given the formula,' the prison chaplain admitted. 'Brother, I swear to this. Every day I stand outside Newgate jail just before the vespers bell. I do that deliberately to receive petitions from the families of prisoners, scraps of parchment with a scrawled message for their loved ones confined inside. About a week ago I was standing there when a beggar pushed a small leather pouch into my hand. He was making signs to someone I could not see. I thought he was moonstruck. However, when I opened the message in the prison chapel, I found the writing was clerkly. The letter greeted me in the name of the Great Community of the Realm. Beneath this salutation was a formula, very precise and exact, giving the different constituents and elements of Greek fire. Anyone who had served as an officer in the Luciferi would recognize it for what it was.'

'You mixed these?'

'No, I did,' John of Richmond retorted. 'I am an apothecary, skilled in measurement.'

'Yes, yes, you are,' Athelstan agreed, slightly distracted. He would certainly remember that when he came to analysing all he had learnt here.

'The Upright Men of Essex and Southwark wanted my assurances,' John of Richmond continued, 'that this truly was Greek fire. They trusted in my skill as an apothecary. They also believed Fulchard must have also instructed me. To a certain extent he did before he died. He could remember, albeit not precisely, the different combustibles Beaumont had bought and mixed on Patmos. I took a clay bowl out to meet them. They were soon convinced.'

'Parson Garman,' Athelstan asked, 'do you know the source of the message delivered to you?'

'The beggar came and went. He was constantly gesturing, as if there was someone with him.'

Athelstan held the prison chaplain's gaze, wondering if the zealot was lying. Whatever the truth, the friar sensed he'd obtained all that he could, so it was time to be gone. He rose abruptly to his feet, surprising them all.

'Father!' Pike exclaimed.

'What I learnt here, Pike, I swear, remains with me. Now,' Athelstan gestured around, 'all of you who are not members of my parish must be gone from St Erconwald's by curfew time tomorrow night. John of Richmond, before you leave, sometime around the angelus bell, I insist that you go on to the top step of my church. Pike and Watkin will create a makeshift pulpit for you and other members of the parish will help. You will proclaim to all and sundry that tonight you had a vision of St Erconwald. How our great saint instructed you that the proper place for pilgrims' devotion is not St Erconwald's but the saintly bishop's own tomb in St Paul's. Let us be honest, let us be frank,' Athelstan added wryly, 'that's the truth. Gentlemen,' the friar raised his hand in blessing, 'to those of my flock, I bid goodnight. To those who are not, may

God bless you all on the strict understanding that I do not look on your faces ever again . . .'

oOoOo

Athelstan woke with a start. The pounding on the door brought him tumbling down from his bed-loft. Tiptoft stood outside with the four Tower archers.

'What is it?' the friar demanded. 'What the time?'

'Dawn is about an hour away,' Tiptoft cheerily replied, 'but the devil never sleeps, or so Sir John says. He needs you now in Poultry at Lady Anne Lesures' house. Another assault, a hideous burning, Turgot her manservant lies foully slain.'

Athelstan hastily dressed. He snatched his chancery satchel and followed his escort out down towards the quayside, where a barge displaying the city pennant waited. They clambered in, took their seats and the barge pushed away. A swift, turbulent crossing with the clouds breaking and an icy breeze whispering like a ghost across the water. They disembarked at Queenhithe and moved through the tangle of streets towards Poultry. Athelstan didn't know if he was dreaming or awake; his abrupt arousing and frenetic journey were unsteadying, his mind tumbled with the sights, sounds and smells that closed in around him. A beggar, garbed in black but with the white outlines of a skeleton painted on his gown, danced like a mad man in front of them before disappearing into the shadows. Beggars crept out of the mouths of alleyways, their clacking dishes rattling in the frosty air. Mounted archers rode by in a hot gust of sweat, leather and horse dung. A funeral procession preparing for the morning suffered an accident at the crossroads and the lily-white corpse of the deceased tumbled out from beneath its scarlet mort cloth to lie sprawled over the cobbles. Windows and doors opened and shut. Different voices trailed: a snatch of a song, the cries of lovers, a baby wailing, whilst a choir which had taken refuge in a tavern chorused the psalm: 'I lift my eyes to the hills from which my Saviour comes'. A self-proclaimed exorcist, a placard hanging around his neck, swinging a battered thurible, billowing incense into the morning air, crying out that he was defending the living from the ghosts of the malignant dead. Outlaw-hunters from the wastes of Moorfields, admitted through the city gates before the market horn, led their pack ponies down to the Guildhall, the corpses of those they'd killed slung across the ponies' backs. A macabre sight. The cadavers, stripped to the skin, displayed gruesome death wounds to the throat, belly or chest. Behind this sinister procession trailed a woman loudly lamenting, 'Those slain on the plains of Megiddo', whatever that meant. A group of moon-watchers huddled together, so close they seem to have one massive body and many heads. They gazed fiercely, their painted white faces straining madly as they watched the winter moon slide from cloud to cloud. Prisoners clamped in the cage on the Tun or the nearby stocks wailed against the bitter cold. A moveable gibbet on its clattering wheels moved backwards and forwards, the corpse hanging in its sheet of hardened canvas loudly creaking.

'This is truly a land of deep shadow,' Athelstan murmured as they turned up the street towards Lady Anne's house. Lanterns glowed. Dark figures stood holding flaring sconce torches. Cranston was waiting for him in the entrance parlour. Even from there Athelstan could hear the wailing of Lady Anne, a soul keening like the wind for its loss. The friar glanced around at the opulent surroundings. The paintings and triptychs all proclaimed the same message – St Anne with her Holy Child the Virgin Mary. Cranston sat on a cushioned stool, head in his hands. He glanced up as Athelstan entered.

'He's struck again, Brother. Lady Anne, as you can hear, is deeply distressed. Let me show you.' Cranston led Athelstan out along the hollow stone-paved passageway, through the kitchen, buttery and scullery into the great rear garden. Flaxwith and his bailiffs were busy there. The air was thick with smoke billowing out of a stone-built building which reminded Athelstan of the nave of a primitive church. It stood in the centre of the garden. In its prime it must have been pleasing to the eye but now its shutters, blackened and tattered, hung from their scorched leather hinges, whilst the door had buckled and crumbled under the heat.

Athelstan went inside the long, barn-like structure. All

internal woodwork had been burnt to a feathery blackness, leaving smoke-blackened walls open to the sky. Clouds of ash and smoke still curled and swirled. Covering his mouth with the scented cloth Flaxwith gave him, Athelstan walked up the long chamber. He stared around, pressing the pomander firmly against his face. However, the smoke was too thick to stay, so he returned to the parlour. Athelstan sat down on the stool, gratefully accepting a mouthful of rich Bordeaux from Cranston's miraculous wineskin.

'What happened, Sir John?' he asked, handing the wineskin back. 'What was that building?'

'A hermitage, a refuge built by Lady Anne's late husband. A number of apothecaries have them, where they can safely concoct their remedies and elixirs. According to all the evidence, Turgot went in there to do the same last night. As usual he shuttered and bolted both windows and the door.'

'Why? What did he fear?'

'Like Lady Anne's late husband he worked late at night. Lady Anne was most concerned about the Ignifer and other acts of violence against members of her household – but more of that later. Turgot was in there last night. Nobody gave it a second thought until a scullion heard the roaring flames. He roused the household. They went out but there was nothing they could do. By then the entire building seemed to be bulging with the heat, shutters and door buckling out, most of the red tile roof collapsing, flames shooting up.' Cranston shrugged. 'They let the fire burn. Once the conflagration had died they tried to enter. All that is left of Turgot are his blackened bones and the steel and iron from his warbelt.' Cranston paused as Lady Anne's steward, Picquart, bustled into the parlour.

'Lady Anne cannot see anyone,' he declared, laying a tray of food and pots of ale on the small table. 'One tragedy follows another.' He sighed. 'I was the last to see Turgot alive, you know? Oh, yes,' he babbled on, 'the curfew bell was tolling. I went out to the Keep, that's what the building is called, always has been, built by Lady Anne's late husband when he was a bachelor in hot pursuit of the beautiful Lady Anne Lasido. A strong building, rather primitive inside but there were braziers to keep it warm and some rugs on the floor. Turgot

was an apprentice here, a good one. I always thought he was
the son Lady Anne yearned for . . .'

'What happened,' Athelstan asked sharply, 'with Turgot last
night?'

'Nothing. I knocked on the door. He unlocked and unbolted
it, I remember that. He looked content enough. I made signs
asking him if he needed anything to eat or drink. He assured
me, in his own unique way, that he did not. I remember he
held a pot of lavender in his hand. He was mixing this with
something else and he invited me to smell it. I did. I bade him
goodnight and returned to the house.'

'So Turgot was in the Keep mixing potions and powders?'

'Yes. As I have said, he was very good at it. Lady Anne
was most respected by the Guild.'

'Did anything untoward happen?' Athelstan demanded.

'Lady Anne, after the tragedy occurred, was distraught, but
she told us that she believed someone was in the garden last
night. She was in her chamber when she heard sounds but she
didn't give it a second thought. Well, until that happened.'

'So,' Athelstan replied slowly, 'the household retires for
the night. Turgot is working in the Keep. The first signs of the
tragedy are the flames roaring and the roof collapsing, yes?'

Picquart nodded in agreement.

'All you could do was watch,' Athelstan continued. 'Turgot
was inside?'

'We found his remains, God assoil him. They were pathetic,
nothing but blackened bones. They've now been sheeted. Lady
Anne will see to the burial. She has also visited the devastation. She kept repeating that Turgot used the Keep to distil
herbal concoctions. He liked to work alone. He would only
open the door to admit someone he knew and trusted.'

'Were the door and window shutters locked fast?'

'I think so, Sir John. They buckled and sprang loose under
the blazing heat.'

'So,' Athelstan supped at his ale, 'Turgot was working late.
Someone may have entered the garden, scaling the curtain
wall. He raps on the door. Turgot would challenge this but
lets him in. Once he has gained entry, the intruder, the Ignifer
if that's who it is, strikes Turgot down, casts the fire and

hurriedly leaves. But whatever you say, Master Picquart, if that is the case the door must have been left open by the assassin as he left.' Athelstan rose. 'Let us return to the Keep.'

Athelstan walked out of the house and into the garden. Flaxwith and his bailiffs still patrolled there, searching the ground around the Keep, but he could he tell from their expressions that they had discovered nothing. As usual, Flaxwith's mastiff, Samson, was sniffing about. Athelstan noticed the mastiff had a fairly large piece of parchment between its jaws which must have floated out of a window or door. He gently prised this loose and put it in the pocket of his robe. He heard Cranston and Picquart talking behind him and turned.

'Master steward,' he asked, 'earlier you mentioned one trouble following another. What did you mean?'

'I was just questioning him about that,' the coroner replied.

'Well?' Athelstan asked. The fat-faced, gimlet-eyed steward shrugged.

'Brother Athelstan, I am not too sure if it is of relevance here but Lady Anne's household has already suffered a grievous loss. One of her retainers, Wickham the ostler, left the house two nights ago. He was slain in a violent street robbery only a few streets away, his corpse thrown into a laystall.' Picquart shook his head. 'Poor Wickham – a simple-minded young man, totally devoted to Lady Anne and her horses.'

'So a member of the household was slain two nights ago. A possible intruder in the garden last night and now the murder of Turgot and the burning of the Keep.' Athelstan paused. 'Are they all connected?'

'Violent street robberies,' Cranston remarked mournfully, 'are increasing. The ostler's death might be the Ignifer's doing.'

'No.' Athelstan shook his head. 'Our assassin likes to burn. Moreover, the ostler had no involvement in Lady Isolda's arrest and execution and neither did Turgot.'

'Of course not,' Picquart snapped, 'though Turgot supported Lady Anne through that mournful time.'

Athelstan thanked him. He could make little sense of what he had seen and heard. Had Turgot and the Keep been destroyed by Greek fire from within? Had the Ignifer coaxed his way in, struck Turgot down and set both the corpse and Keep alight?

Or, as with Sir John, did the assassin prise open a window or door and cast in one of those damnable clay pots followed by a flame? Yet if that was the case, Turgot would have noticed and hastened to protect himself. Athelstan took a deep breath. According to the evidence the most probable explanation was that the Ignifer had persuaded Turgot to admit him. He then struck and fled, which must mean that either the door or one of the windows had been left open, whatever Picquart claimed.

Athelstan turned and walked across the garden. Dawn had broken and the strengthening light made it easier to see. Inside the Keep the air had turned fresher, the smoke thinning but the entire chamber and all within it had been truly devastated. Athelstan picked up a stick and sifted amongst the ashes. He unearthed scraps of scorched leather and stiffened blackened ash. The dust swirled up to make him cough and splutter. Athelstan wiped his hands. There was nothing here for him. He left and decided to walk the garden to cleanse his throat and breathe in the morning air. He followed the pebbled path which twisted between herbers, flowerbeds, shrubs and bushes, flower arbours with turfed seats, neatly cropped grass plots and raised soil beds all glistening white and frozen hard, waiting for spring. At the very centre of the garden, on a gorgeous red and gold plinth, stood a statue of St Anne with the Virgin Mary as a young girl standing beside her. The soil around the skilfully sculptured statue and exquisitely painted plinth was rich, black and recently turned. The winter rosebush, planted just before the statue, was in full flower despite the harsh weather. Athelstan crossed himself, put his hand in his robe searching for a set of Ave beads and felt the piece of parchment he had rescued from Samson's jaws. Curious, he held it up to the light: the carefully calligraphed writing proclaimed a verse from the scriptures: 'Worthy is the lamb who was slain to receive power, riches, glory and blessing.' Athelstan peered closer. He stared and gaped, catching his breath as his heart skipped a beat. He sat on a turf seat before the statue, reading that scrap of parchment time and again. Had it been dropped by the Ignifer? Samson had apparently picked it up from outside. Athelstan stared at the winter rose-bush. He rose, walked across and crouched down. Stretching out his hand, he touched the six-sided cross, like that of a Hospitaller, carved on the plinth, the symbol used whenever a church or statue was formally consecrated. He returned to his seat, staring at both the winter rosebush and the statue as he swiftly constructed one hypothesis after another. He sifted through all the possibilities until he reached the most compelling, which transformed into a strong probability. To prove it, Athelstan recalled different individuals, their conversations and whereabouts at certain times. The friar, hunched in his cloak, brooded deeply, lost in thought, impervious to the cold and Cranston shouting. Eventually the coroner had to come and shake him by the shoulder.

'Athelstan, for the sake of Satan's tits, little friar, you are freezing to death.'

'Sir John,' Athelstan gripped his chancery satchel tighter, 'I need your assistance to let me think There are certain tasks to be done.' He got to his feet. 'It's time we left. We will give our condolences and adjourn to Blackfriars. Our *refectorium*, Brother Wilfred, brews a tangy ale. They say it's the best in London, whilst our cook, Brother Geoffrey, creates a meat stew pie second to none.'

'Brother, you have bought me body and soul!'

'Sir John, be my guest. Whilst you eat I will be busy in our library and *scriptorium*, then I must hasten back to St Erconwald's to ensure that calm has returned. I also need to talk to my little altar boy, Crim. Yes, that's very important.'

Mystified, the coroner agreed. They left Lady Anne's house, out through the noisy streets of Poultry and down to the city now cloaked in one of those thick river fogs. Cranston made sure their escort kept close. Athelstan, however, was not concerned about this, his mind tumbling like dice in a cup. They reached Blackfriars and entered the hallowed serenity of its cloisters. Athelstan relaxed. He ensured Sir John was safely ensconced in the prior's parlour where the cook and refectoriam were eager to serve the coroner their tastiest achievements and listen once again to Sir John's amazing exploits in France.

Athelstan excused himself and retreated into the comfortable darkness of the library and *scriptorium*. On a polished oaken desk lighted by candles he laid out his writing materials, weighed down a neatly cut square of vellum, and sat staring into the darkness. His gaze was caught by the lectern, carved in the shape of a soaring eagle, on which rested the priory's principal Bible – a work of art copied out by the Benedictines of Glastonbury and presented to the Dominicans when they first set up house in London. Athelstan rose and walked over to it. He opened the Bible and turned to the place where he had read that extract from the scorched piece of parchment. He went back to his desk, grasped his sharpest quill pen and began to itemize certain salient points in a series of questions to himself. Item: the attacks by the Ignifer on himself and others were easy enough – all his victims had been taken by surprise. Who had been where and when? Item: apparently the Ignifer had also communicated his secrets to Parson Garman and the Upright Men. Why? Item: those letters, 'SFSM', scrawled on the walls of Isolda's death cell – what did they mean? Item: what did Isolda have when she died apart from food and drink? Item: why did Isolda have that heated dispute with Lady Anne, who was doing nothing but trying to comfort her? Item: who had been a member of the Luciferi? Item: why had Sir Walter constantly boasted that the secrets of 'The Book of Fires' would be a revelation to anyone who ever found them and that they were safe on Patmos? Item: the Ignifer was someone passionately devoted to Isolda. At the same time this assassin was apparently the holder of the secret of Greek fire, so why didn't the Ignifer try to trade such secrets for a pardon for Isolda? Item: a man claiming to be Vanner came to Smithfield to collect the charred remains of Lady Isolda. Who was this? Why did he call himself Vanner when that clerk lay murdered, his corpse deep in the mere at Firecrest Manor? Item: why did the Ignifer give off the fragrance of a rather costly perfume, the scent of crushed lilies? Item: what was the true source of the poison given to Sir Walter used first in those figs coated with an almond sauce and later in that fateful cup of posset? Item: Isolda went into the city to meet Nicephorus but also someone else. Who was this? Why the secrecy? Item: on the night he, Cranston and Lady Anne had been attacked, Turgot had been trailing behind them. Why had Turgot now been killed? Was there a connection between Turgot's death and that of Lady Anne's ostler? Item: the Ignifer certainly had a relationship with the Upright Men. Who favoured them – Buckholt, Sir Henry? Did Master Falke? Item: why was it so important for the Ignifer that Gaunt's barges be burnt? Why was the Ignifer so determined to remove both Cranston and himself from this investigation?

Athelstan paused in his writing. He closed his eyes, recalling different images and occasions. Walking the streets of Poultry after that meeting at Lady Anne's house, the attack on them near Aldgate. He opened his eyes and studied the list he'd made, emphasizing each point in his mind like a preacher memorizing a sermon. 'There are still gaps,' he whispered. 'I don't have enough . . . too many gaps.' He took a fresh square of parchment and hastily wrote out a number of requests for the coroner. Once finished, he studied both manuscripts. He was still lacking one vital piece of evidence and Crim would supply that. A floorboard creaked behind him. Athelstan whirled around. Cranston had tiptoed through the door.

'Brother, are you finished?'

'For the moment, Sir John.' The friar picked up the second piece of parchment and held it out for the coroner to take. 'We must go our separate ways, but I need answers to these questions before the vespers bell rings.'

'And what then, little friar?'

'Oh, we shall meet. Yes, perhaps the most appropriate place would be Newgate Prison. I need to have words with certain individuals there. But first,' Athelstan rose to his feet, 'my quarry is Crim . . .'

oOoOo

Athelstan stared around the cell where Lady Isolda Beaumont had spent her last days. He had re-examined the graffiti on the wall and paced that sombre chamber, measuring his footsteps and half-listening to the sounds from outside. He had spent the previous day, once he had left Blackfriars, in the priest's house at St Erconwald's as he gently questioned Crim and Benedicta and received Cranston's replies through his messenger, Tiptoft. The coroner had simply confirmed what Athelstan had suspected, turning a strong probability into a virtual certainty. Athelstan believed he had trapped the killer; now he prepared for that fateful confrontation. He stopped his pacing as Cranston, swathed in his cloak, strode into the cell. He took off his beaver hat, stamping his booted feet against the cold.

'Have you set up court, little friar? Those questions you sent me . . . ?'

'And you will soon learn the answers, Sir John. I ask for your patience—' Athelstan broke off at a knock at the door. He strode across, opened it and ushered Parson Garman into the death cell. Almost immediately there was a second knock and the Carnifex swaggered in, breathing noisily, bowing and bobbing to both coroner and friar.

'You asked to see me,' the prison chaplain began. 'I thought our business was finished.'

'Parson Garman, we still have words – perhaps not here, not now. I want to repeat questions I have put to both of you earlier. First, Lady Isolda and Lady Anne Lesures quarrelled here in this cell about two days before her execution?'

'Yes,' both men chorused.

'And before her death everything Lady Isolda ate or drank was examined carefully, so no philtre or potion was given to her?'

Again both men agreed.

'And Lady Anne gave Isolda a set of Ave beads, which she later discarded. You, Parson Garman, returned the broken set to Lady Anne.'

'That is the truth,' the chaplain declared. 'Why, Brother Athelstan?'

'Hush, now.' Athelstan nodded at the coroner. 'Have you brought her with you, Sir John?'

'Lady Anne is waiting below.'

'Parson Garman, Master Carnifex,' Athelstan gestured at the door, 'we will speak again and there will be fresh business to do.' Both men left. A short while later Lady Anne, dressed in widows' weeds, a black gauze veil hiding her patrician face, was ushered into the cell.

'Brother Athelstan.' Lady Anne took the proffered seat by the table, pushing back more firmly her veil of black mourning crepe. Her face was thin and pallid; eyes black and rather sunken though still bright with what the friar considered to be a malicious light. 'Brother Athelstan,' she repeated, 'why am I here? You said it was a matter of life or death. I am in deep mourning for Turgot, my apprentice, my godson, my—'

'Your helpmate in murder,' Athelstan intervened, gesturing at Cranston, sitting on a stool nearby, to remain seated and stay quiet. Athelstan glanced quickly over his shoulder at the door. The turnkey had locked it as Athelstan ordered. This chamber would become his tournament field, where he would challenge and confront this most malicious of souls.

'Brother?' The coroner's voice was a hoarse whisper.

'Mourning, grieving,' Athelstan declared. 'Who are you, Anne Lesures, Anne Lasido? The widow and the do-gooder but, in all things, the murderess? I cannot for the life of me understand souls such as you.'

'I am leaving.' She made to rise.

'And I will have you arrested. Sit down!' Athelstan shouted. 'Sit down and listen.' Lady Anne composed herself on the chair, joining her hands on the tabletop. 'As I said,' Athelstan continued, 'I cannot understand souls such as you. Your devotion to St Anne, your constant do-gooding, yet deep inside you,' Athelstan beat his breast, 'in the marrow of your soul, at the centre of your heart stands a temple devoted to your one and only real God – yourself. You are determined on having your own will and way whatever the cost to others, whilst you wage the most horrid revenge against anyone who opposes, objects or frustrates you. Turgot was your demon, your familiar, your accomplice. He was not murdered. He accidently killed himself whilst mixing Greek fire. He went into the Keep, locking and barring both windows and door. He carried with him a copy of Mark the Greek's "The Book of Fires". He had, in that death chamber, everything he needed. He had all the time in the world to prepare more deadly pots and missiles. Who for, Lady Anne? Whom had you marked down for death? Buckholt, Mortice, Sir Henry Beaumont? Rosamund Clifford, or perhaps another assault on me and Sir John?'

'Brother Athelstan, you are witless. You have lost your mind. You do not know what you are saying. Sir John, I beg you . . .'

She turned to the coroner, who just gazed bleakly back at her. Cranston knew Athelstan; 'Friar Ferret' was how he described him to his confederates. Once Athelstan began a prosecution, he was very rarely wrong. Moreover, Cranston could sense an atmosphere. Athelstan was incandescent with suppressed fury, whilst the coroner was becoming deeply suspicious about Lady Anne as he recalled what he knew of her but, more importantly, the way she acted now. Athelstan was pursuing the truth of it and they would not leave this cell until he achieved it.

'Continue, Brother,' Cranston murmured.

'There is an English proverb, Lady Anne. Nicephorus the Greek, you know who he is, quoted it quite recently. "Do not play with fire". Both Sir John and I have served at sieges. We have seen the most dire accidents as trebuchets are loaded, oil boiled and carried, fire missiles prepared. Turgot, to his eternal cost, also discovered this, though I think it was also an answer to my prayer. I very rarely pray for vengeance, Lady Anne, but on the night we were attacked I prayed then and the following morning in the chapel of Firecrest Manor for God's justice, for God's vengeance after the death of that poor, innocent torch-bearer.'

'I also did the same.' Lady Anne rested against the table, a small white cloth in her hand, which she used to dab her mouth.

'Hush, now,' Athelstan warned her. 'Enough lies, protests of innocence. Do you know, Sir John,' he turned to the coroner, 'St Anselm said that we were two people in one – who we are and who we really are – and only God knows the difference. Lady Anne,' he turned back, 'I shall tell you with God's help who you truly are and as much as I can about your real life. I shall produce evidence for what I say. I will press the case hard.' Athelstan paused. Newgate had fallen silent, as if all the distressed spirits which haunted its clammy, ill-lit galleries and prowled those foul, filth-strewn tunnels had stopped, hands to ears, listening to what was happening here, where a greater demon than any of them was being arraigned before God's bar of judgement.

'The ghosts are gathering,' Athelstan murmured. He held Lady Anne's gaze. 'All the souls have come to witness. Evil is like a snake,' he smiled thinly, 'or Greek fire. Eventually it turns and strikes back.' He drew a deep breath. 'So we begin. You were born Anne Lasido, daughter of a London merchant who strove to secure a good marriage for you. However, you were headstrong and wilful, indeed, very much like your daughter, Isolda.'

Lady Anne started, clenched white fists coming up to her mouth.

'You became,' Athelstan continued, 'involved with a young man. Now for the moment, indeed for the matter in hand, his name and status do not concern us. One thing I am certain of, it was not Walter Beaumont. Anyway, you had a romance, an affair, with this bachelor, and became pregnant.' Athelstan gestured at the coroner. 'Sir John here has provided a few details about your family life: after all, you consider him an old friend whom you've known for many years. Of course, that did not matter when our noble coroner became an obstacle to your plans. You truly are a Judas woman. In brief, your father was horrified. He did what many do in such circumstances. He hid you away until the girl child was born. Your father managed to secure a cloth bearing the Fitzalan arms to cover the baby in its swaddling clothes and the child was handed over to the Franciscan Minoresses at Aldgate. You fiercely protested. You truly loved that child with a passion as strong as, if not stronger than, any mother's for her newborn child. You confronted your father. You insisted on having your way, naming the little girl Isolda, an anagram of your own family name, Lasido.' Athelstan shrugged. 'It was just a matter of playing with the letters of a word. Time passed. You matured into a ruthless, strong-willed woman who never forgot what had happened. You became betrothed to Adam Lesures and eventually exchanged vows with him at the church door and settled down to married life. Your husband was an apothecary, skilled in powders and potions, a worthy member of the Guild – but he also had a past. Adam Lesures had once served with Black Beaumont's Luciferi. Adam was probably an officer, an ignifer, skilled in casting fires. At first he did not talk about his years abroad. This was common enough amongst seasoned veterans. The past was the past. Yet, Lady Anne, you are most persuasive and the truth would dribble out, a little here, a little there, whenever Sir Adam was in his cups and, I am sure, that was quite often.' Athelstan stared at this *'ferrea virago'*, a woman undoubtedly of iron will and inflexible purpose. 'Slowly,' he continued, 'your late husband divulged secrets about Beaumont. How he deserted his comrades and, above all, his monopoly of the secrets contained in Mark the Greek's "The Book of Fires". It would explain how Beaumont's wealth was mainly rooted in that but, if Sir John here is to be believed, Adam Lesures was no match for Beaumont. He was fearful of him, wasn't he? Too frightened to take arms against him. Too in awe of a man who had led an attack on the Imperial chancery in Constantinople. Your late husband would also whisper about much darker secrets. How some of those Black Beaumont had led had mysteriously disappeared. He may have even given you chapter and verse about those dreadful events on the island of Patmos. But what could he do? I suspect your husband was exhausted, weakened by his years abroad. If challenged, Black Beaumont would prove to be a most resolute foe and Sir Adam Lesures simply accepted things for what they were. You were different. Sir Adam was wealthy in himself and you acted as his lady, the wife of a powerful, rich burgess. Your husband undoubtedly drew a good profit as an apothecary, his experience abroad, his knowledge of strange powders and potions, the mixture of certain elements. You used your status under the guise of good work to return to the house of the Minoresses in Aldgate. Of course, your real task was to keep a close and solicitous eye on Isolda. You would single her out as your favourite good work. In truth, you watched her grow and mature. You noted her beauty. In your eyes Isolda was unique, very special, hence your devotion to your holy name-sake, St Anne, mother of the Virgin. In your twisted soul, in that mind of yours which teems like a box of worms, you drew a comparison between St Anne and her child with your-self and Isolda. Your house is decorated with paintings and triptychs which proclaim this devotion. You are much taken with the verse *"Sicut mater, sic filia"* – "As the mother, so the daughter". You taught that to Isolda, who learned at a very early age that you were her mother and that she must keep this secret. "*Sicut mater, sic filia*" in Isolda's eyes became "*Sicut filia, sic mater*", "As the daughter, so the mother", which,' he got to his feet and walked over to the graffiti etched on the wall, 'would explain this last carving by Isolda – SFSM.'

Athelstan walked back to stand over Lady Anne, who glared fiercely back. I have you, the friar thought. I have flushed you out of the undergrowth and you are running.

'You knew I might.' Athelstan voiced his thoughts as he read the challenge in her eyes. 'You did, didn't you? You feared the confrontation which is now taking place. That's why you tried to kill me and Sir John. You are a high-ranking city lady. Sir John knows about you – you must have heard of our reputation. You wanted to end our interfering.'

'Brother Athelstan,' she smiled, 'you should have been a minstrel, a songster, a troubadour. What a tale. A dark ballad.' Her smile faded. 'Isolda would never have kept such a secret.'

'As the mother, so the daughter,' Athelstan responded blithely. 'It was very much in her interest to keep silent because,' he leaned over the table, 'your snake-like mind, curling as dangerously as any viper, had decided to have justice. Your husband died. You and he had no children but your secret daughter had matured into a beautiful young woman and the very wealthy Black Beaumont was a bachelor. Everyone respects Lady Anne Lesures. Beaumont saw you for what he thought, a silly widow woman with too much time and money on her hands, full of fanciful ideas about helping the poor and dispossessed. Oh, what a hideous mistake he made! As you danced between Firecrest Manor and the Minoresses, you began weaving your web. You plotted to get your Isolda into Beaumont's arms, his bed, his household and his wealth. You succeeded, but it truly was a May–December marriage and, worse, one fashioned in Hell rather than Heaven. Beaumont made a mistake about you but when it came to his own he was as cunning as any old fox. He did not concede anything to Isolda, be it wealth or, more importantly, the secrets of Mark the Greek's "The Book of Fires". Isolda, frustrated, turned back to you, her mother and patroness, to advise her. She secretly met you in the city. You provided her with money, even presents, such as a stoppered jar of precious perfume which exudes the odour of crushed lilies.'

'Evidence!' Lady Anne snapped. 'Friar, you tell a tittle-tattle tale with no proof.'

'In a while, in a while,' Athelstan replied. 'But back to my tittle-tattle tale. The marriage worsened. Beaumont, full of idle recriminations, recalled the sins of his youth. He was a great sinner, Sir Walter, a lecher with many paramours. He began to wonder if he was Isolda's father, one of those blind acts of fate. Did he ever raise the issue with you? Perhaps he did, but you would assure him that she was not.'

For a moment, Lady Anne let the mask slip and she smirked as if savouring some secret joke.

'Others, however,' Athelstan continued, 'hotly encouraged him in such fanciful thoughts for their own secret reasons. Sir Henry, Parson Garman.'

The smirk faded abruptly.

'Beaumont, black of name and black of heart, decided to seek an annulment, which would have been disastrous for Isolda, who would be publicly rejected as soiled goods. You and your daughter met. You advised her to patronize and cherish Vanner the clerk, who would keep you informed about what Sir Walter wrote. Isolda also had an ally in Rosamund Clifford, another novice from the Minoresses, who was totally smitten with her and probably with you. She did not know the full truth – she probably didn't care. Both you and your daughter simply used her as you did anyone to achieve your own ends. Rosamund was introduced to the Beaumont household as Isolda's maid. In truth, she was there to act as your spy, Isolda's ally, as well as a distraction for the faithful Buckholt and, as matters turned out, for Sir Walter himself.' Athelstan paused. 'As I've said, I do not think Rosamund knew the full truth: Turgot was your minion, your familiar; Rosamund was Lady Isolda's. She would do anything for her mistress.'

'Continue,' Lady Anne taunted.

'At the same time, you and your daughter plotted Beaumont's

destruction. After five years of marriage, Isolda had provided you with a clear understanding of matters at Firecrest Manor. Sir Henry Beaumont just wished his brother would die, so that his marriage to Isolda would be dissolved. Sir Henry and his wife lusted for wealth. Vanner was fully compliant with Isolda. Buckholt, a secret and ardent supporter of the Upright Men, longed to seize "The Book of Fires" to assist the Great Community of the Realm. Rosamund would humour Sir Walter to discover the whereabouts of that same manuscript.' Athelstan leaned forward, jabbing his finger. 'Of course, matters began to crumble fast. Sir Walter would get his annulment so it's time he died. You are an apothecary skilled in powders.'

'No, I was married to one.'

'And you continued his trade after your husband's death. You supplied Isolda with poison. You informed her how it should be administered, drop by drop, here and there and especially in those figs coated in their almond cream which Parson Garman brought. You know Parson Garman very well, don't you? I do wonder about him and your visits to Newgate but,' Athelstan spread his hands and returned to his stool, 'that part of the past does not concern us for now. Garman was one of those who did not disabuse Sir Walter that Isolda might be his daughter. He also nourished deep grievances against Black Beaumont from his days as a member of the Luciferi. A fact you might know from your late husband.' Lady Anne's flinty eyes never flinched in their gaze of deep antipathy. 'The figs were poisoned, just a tint to inconvenience and discommode. Sir Walter truly loved them, but of course the poison made itself felt. It disturbed the humours in his belly. Sometimes he ate them, sometimes he did not. Sometimes they were discarded or given to different members of his household with varying effects such as a passing stomach ailment but nothing serious. If the poison was ever discovered, Garman would be blamed. However, on the day Sir Walter was actually murdered, Isolda and Vanner hastened on. I am sure your daughter did not consult you. I have no proof of this, as Isolda burnt any incriminating documents, but I suspect Sir Walter was about to issue his letter for an annulment. The almond figs, heavily coated in poison, were given to Rosamund, who almost died.

No one could doubt a murderer was loose in Firecrest Manor. Isolda then decided to follow a plot, probably devised by you, to exploit Sir Walter's love for his nightly goblet of posset. Isolda and Vanner had prepared for this, purchasing an almost identical goblet, and we know the outcome of that. They would have certainly succeeded but for Buckholt and Mortice. You and Turgot intended to make these two retainers suffer the most, didn't you? Let them live, let them wonder for days, weeks, even months, when the Ignifer would strike against them?'

'Isolda Beaumont died a cruel death.' Lady Anne spoke as if to herself, her voice scarcely above a whisper.

'If I had any compassion for you and yours,' Athelstan replied, 'it would be for that. You, a mother, saw your daughter condemned to a most barbaric death. And what could you do to stop it? Reveal your true relationship with Isolda? Plead for a pardon or amnesty? Beg for a commutation for a swifter death? Gaunt and the judges were implacable. Escape was out of the question. I suspect on your visits to Isolda here at Newgate you did vow vengeance against all of them as well as providing Isolda with some comfort.'

'What?'

'You gave her a set of beads. Eleven in number, one bead for the Our Father, the other ten for the Hail Mary. You then pretended that a fierce dispute broke out between yourself and Isolda. This was a sham to cover what was really a passionate farewell. Both of you had reached the very end of what was tolerable. You left one gift, those Ave beads.'

'Isolda snapped them and threw them away. Parson Garman returned them to me.'

'The truth: Isolda snapped them to take the relief they offered. Some of those beads were really like nutshells – they contained a powder, an opiate, possibly the strongest dried juice of the poppy. Lady Anne, you are an apothecary. You distilled such a potion. It was your last gift to your daughter. Isolda could have taken them immediately but she didn't. Perhaps she desperately hoped for a last-minute reprieve. Of course, that never came. On the day of her execution, Isolda chewed the beads she had secreted away. By the time she was lashed to the stake, she had sunk into a deep stupor, probably deadly in its effect.'

Lady Anne simply bowed her head. Athelstan thought she was crying but when she looked up she was hard-faced and dry-eyed, her mouth twisted in a smirk.

'You then performed one last office,' Athelstan declared. 'You had Turgot dig a plot in front of the statue of St Anne which stands at the heart of your garden. A beautiful, well-tended plot with a lovely winter rosebush as part of the memorial. Moreover, both the statue and that small garden have been formally consecrated, I suspect by Parson Garman. It's the last resting place of the mortal remains of your daughter, Isolda.'

'She died at Smithfield.'

'Who, your daughter?'

'Isolda!' Lady Anne's eyes blazed with fury.

'And her remains,' Cranston broke in, 'should have stayed there. Holy Mother Church and the Crown insist on that or,' he pulled a face, 'at some crossroads, but not in consecrated ground.'

'You had these remains,' Athelstan persisted, 'collected by a man calling himself Vanner who came to Smithfield after dark and poked about the execution stake for whatever he could find. He was certainly not Vanner; as you know, at that time, Vanner's corpse lay weed-tangled at the bottom of the mere in Firecrest Manor. I do wonder,' Athelstan pointed a finger at his opponent, 'did Isolda murder him at your behest, to rid herself of a clacking tongue, a weak man who might turn King's Approver against her? In the end it was best if Vanner and any incriminating documents disappeared, be it at the bottom of that mere or a burning pit at Firecrest Manor.'

'What has all this got to do with me?'

'Everything, Lady Anne. The man claiming to be Vanner was in fact Wickham, your ostler, a loyal, faithful retainer totally devoted to you. A simple-minded young man, easy to manipulate. You ordered Wickham to collect the remains at Smithfield and, if possible, let it be known he was Vanner. On the one hand, you obtained what you wanted and, on the other, you deepened the mystery further by creating the illusion that

Vanner was still alive and might well be the Ignifer. Wickham could see no harm or crime in what he was doing. He knew you had visited Isolda but would be totally unaware of any complex plot. Wickham was simply helping his kind-hearted mistress, to whom he was totally devoted. Even if he was challenged and it was proved you had sent him, you could easily disguise everything as a further act of charity for a poor dead woman for whom you felt sorry. The proof of what I say lies in your garden. I could have that plot dug up. I would certainly discover a funeral urn.' Athelstan flinched at the look Lady Anne threw him. He prayed to keep calm and not give way to the anger curdling within him. 'I have more evidence about Wickham. You used him on another occasion to create an even greater illusion, but I'll come to that when I turn to certain sworn testimony Sir John here has taken from your steward, Picquart.'

For the first time Lady Anne showed surprise, her mouth slack, her eyes blinking before she swiftly recovered. 'And there is the testimony of the Carnifex's scrivener, Scrimshaw. According to him, the man at Smithfield collecting Isolda's remains and claiming to be Vanner reeked of the stable. Picquart,' Athelstan blithely declared to hide the fact that he was bluffing, 'declared Wickham also smelt constantly of horses. Indeed, it was a common joke in your household. Totally different from Turgot, who sprinkled himself with the same perfume Isolda wore – crushed lilies – in order to compli-cate matters further.'

Lady Anne's gaze faltered. She pressed the white cloth against her dry lips. Cranston caught her deepening unease.

'Continue, Brother,' he murmured.

'Now we come to circumstance, coincidence and their cause – Sir Walter's arrogance and total disdain for anyone else, especially women. Black Beaumont stole "The Book of Fires" in Constantinople. He brought it to London, had it copied then sold the original back to the Greeks. He kept that copy very secret. I suspect the clerk who created it did not live long afterwards. Beaumont was a professional, seasoned killer. He would murder without qualm anyone who might pose a threat. The years passed. Beaumont dipped into his copy to discover more secrets. Of course, life never stands still. Time passes. People age and, more dangerously for Beaumont, new threats emerge. The Upright Men made their presence felt. They hated Gaunt and his coven, including Sir Walter. More importantly, Beaumont had to face threats from the past. About a year ago, and you must have learnt this, Beaumont received threats, a stark, brutal message repeated time and again, "As I and ours burnt, so shall ye and yours". We now know its source, a hideous secret from Black Beaumont's blood-soaked past. So, Lady Anne, think of Sir Walter as he grows old, still cherishing his precious secrets. The Upright Men want to seize them – so does his pretty young wife, his brother, his servants and his rivals, not to mention Gaunt.' Athelstan paused at a blood-chilling shriek of pain which rang through the gloomy passageway outside. 'Indeed,' he continued, 'the list is endless, yes? And what can Beaumont do with his secret copy of "The Book of Fires"? Hide it in the ground? It's not gold and parchment soon rots. Lock it in an arca, a strong chest? Then everyone would know where it is. The same is true if he handed it over to the goldsmiths and bankers along Cheapside. My lord of Gaunt would certainly keep it safe but never hand it back. No,' Athelstan pointed at Lady Anne, 'he gave it to you.'

'Nonsense.' Lady Anne quivered with anger but Athelstan could see it was pretence.

'Listen, now,' he insisted. 'Beaumont was very devious. "The Book of Fires" was not copied on fresh vellum but in a specially purchased copy of the *Novum Testamentum* – the New Testament. Beaumont had the copyist turn to the last book of the Testament which, as we know, is the Apocalypse or Book of Revelation, written by St John the Apostle when he was in exile on the island of Patmos. In Beaumont's *Novum Testamentum* the lines were specially spaced. It was simply a matter of copying "The Book of Fires" into those spaces as well as using the generous margins on all four sides of each page and the blank pages found at the back of any book. Naturally, written in Latin by a clerkly hand with the usual chancery abbreviations, it would look like what it was meant to be—'

'A commentary,' Cranston broke in. 'Scholars do that in Bibles, books of hours, a psalter, a missal.'

'And Beaumont entrusted that with me?' Lady Anne jibed. 'So I could read it . . .'

'Hush, now,' Athelstan soothed. 'Beaumont was arrogant, with the most disdainful attitude towards women. He probably thought you couldn't even read, certainly not Latin or the clever abbreviations of the scriptorium and chancery. And if you did read it, what comprehension would you have?' He turned to the coroner. 'Think, Sir John.' He urged. 'What better place to hide "The Book of Fires" than amongst the lines of the New Testament? Especially the Apocalypse or Book of Revelation written by the Apostle John on the island of Patmos, which describes the end of creation when Christ comes again with fire and sword? Beaumont would see the humour in it. He thought he was very clever that no one would discover the secret which explains his sly illusions of the whereabouts of "The Book of Fires" being a "revelation", "safe on the island of Patmos".'

Cranston was now beside himself with excitement. He snapped his fingers, now and again gesturing at Lady Anne.

'Beaumont,' the coroner declared. 'Yes, didn't he say that Lady Anne's house was the safest place in London? It would be a sanctuary of peace when the revolt comes because of her good work in Newgate and elsewhere? The Upright Men would not place her house under the ban.' Cranston whistled softly, shaking his head.

'A shrewd move,' Athelstan agreed. 'When the revolt does come, Firecrest Manor will be high on the list of mansions to be pillaged and burnt. It would be foolish to hide "The Book of Fires" there. Now,' he paused to collect his thoughts, 'Lady Anne, you are, despite what Beaumont thought, an educated, highly intelligent guild woman. You mix potions and powders. You consult leech books, medical treatises and works of physic. You are acquainted with the works of Galen and Bartholomew the Englishman. You are both literate and numerate, just as skilled and experienced as any Cheapside mercer, and so was Turgot, your familiar. Remember, you told me how you had him educated in the chapel school at Westminster Abbey?'

'If I had "The Book of Fires", why did I not use it to nego-
tiate Isolda's life?'

'Sharp, very sharp,' Athelstan replied. 'Sharp as a serpent's
tooth! A very good question. So I return to circumstance and
coincidence. It's a matter of logic, isn't it?'

Lady Anne just glared back.

'Some people are in the right place at the right time or,'
Athelstan shrugged, 'some people are in the wrong place
at the right time and so on. To be brief, you never discovered
the secret until after Isolda's execution. God knows why and
how. Was it mere chance? Did you sit brooding and realize
all you had left from your complex plotting was Sir Walter's
copy of the New Testament? Did you wonder what to do with
it? Take it out and leaf through the pages, or did you reflect
on all you knew about Black Beaumont? The years abroad,
his sly illusions to the book's whereabouts being a revelation
safe on the island of Patmos? I cannot say, but you certainly
discovered the secret and used it to deadly effect.' Athelstan
cleared his throat. 'At the same time you continued the pretence
of condemning Isolda. You had no choice but to mask your
true intentions.'

'You will produce proof for all this?' Lady Anne asked.
'You can evidence what you say?'

'You and your familiar Turgot became very busy,' Athelstan
retorted. 'You are an apothecary – you can easily buy the
different components and constituents. You also had the Keep
in which to distil them. Turgot was young, skilled and able.
Once ready, you strike. First, Turgot attacks Sutler and
Gavelkind. An easy enough task. Go out on to any London
street and you will find someone carrying a pot, a pail, a pan
and sometimes a lantern or candle. Turgot acted this out. A
pot of Greek fire in one hand, a flame in the other. Vengeance
was inflicted on Sutler, Gavelkind and Pynchon, foreman of
the jury. The latter was not caught out on a London street. He
made it easy for you, a bachelor locked in his strong room in
the cellars. All Turgot had to do, using a pair of bellows, was
pump Greek fire through that grille, followed by a flame.
Pynchon was drunk, clumsy on his feet and, of course, he had
sealed himself in. Even for someone with a fresh mind,

unlocking and unbarring a heavy door could be frustrating.
You also turned on us. You knew our reputation. You feared
discovery and you wished to deepen the mystery. Twice you
attacked Sir John and me and, on a separate occasion, the
coroner in his own house.'

'Turgot and I were with you when you were attacked on
our way to Firecrest Manor!'

'Oh, you were.' Athelstan emphasized his words. 'You were
with us and Turgot was allegedly following to protect us. It
was all a pretence. You wished to create an illusion.' He paused.
'On reflection, there was no need for you to accompany us so
late in the evening. You did give us your judgement on Isolda,
but you could have said that in the privacy of your own house.
You simply wanted to take us out into the dark, wasting time
so Turgot could prepare himself. On that night Turgot did not
leave the house behind us, Wickham the ostler did. All we
saw was a cloaked, cowled figure following us. Wickham was
given strict instructions on what to do, whilst Turgot sped
ahead. He launched his assault and then disappeared, fleeing
through the maze of streets. Remember what you told us, how
Turgot knew that warren of alleyways? Your accomplice hurled
the missile then slipped back to act his part. Wickham was
dismissed. The ostler was simple-minded, yet even the most
sharp-witted might not have suspected. To all intents
and purposes, Turgot had apparently caught up with him and
assumed his usual duty of protecting his mistress. Wickham
was instructed to keep silent. You, Lady Anne, clearly used
that assault to show the Ignifer had nothing to do with you or
yours. You played the same game when we were attacked in
Aldgate. We left Pynchon's house. Turgot followed us. He
waited for his opportunity and perpetrated that assault. An
easy enough task, you realized we'd be summoned there and
be vulnerable afterwards. You created the pretence that Turgot
was busy on your affairs in Southwark. He was not. You sent
a mute, cowled and cloaked, that strange creature who suffers
the same as Turgot, Didymus. Remember him? The twin who
constantly makes signs to a so-called brother invisible to
everyone else? We human beings, Lady Anne, as you well
know, treat cripples and the maimed as if they don't exist. You

sent a mute to St Erconwald's with a letter. Didymus, not Turgot, was your emissary, but who would care about a mute beggar's individual characteristics? I did, only because of a boy.'

'Evidence!' Lady Anne beat her fists on the table.

'Children are different. Crim, my altar boy, was fascinated by the way Didymus, after he delivered the letter to my house, wandered off busy with his sign language, as if someone else was present. That wasn't Turgot but Didymus.'

'I would agree,' Cranston murmured.

'Didymus did as you instructed. He gave the letter over, marvelled at what was happening around him and became busy with his invisible twin. Of course, you never frequented St Erconwald's, did you? You said you would like to visit the Great Miracle but Turgot would have followed and that could be dangerous – he might be recognized. You deliberately deployed others where Turgot should have been whilst secretly assisting your familiar to carry out hideous murder.' Athelstan rose and walked up and down the cell, grateful for the exercise, before returning to his seat. 'Strange, Lady Anne, that you do not protest your innocence but demand evidence. Very well.' He leaned forward, emphasizing his points on his fingers. 'Firstly, where's Beaumont's New Testament? He lent it to you, that is a matter of record. Where is it? Tell Sir John. He will despatch a messenger to your house and find it.' Lady Anne just glared back. 'Secondly, I will produce part of a page of that New Testament. An extract from the Book of Revelation, scorched but still legible. A relic of that mysterious fire which killed Turgot and devastated the Keep. The extract clearly spells out a formula from "The Book of Fires" written above and below the scriptural text. Thirdly,' Athelstan steeled himself; some of what he was about to say was only a bluff, hoodman's wink, 'Wickham is dead. Strangely enough, so is Didymus, found sprawled in a lay stall, his throat slashed from ear to ear. The poor man had been dead for some time.' Athelstan stared down at the floor; that was the truth. Sir John had organized a careful search for the eccentric beggar man. Flaxwith had discovered his cadaver in the Hall of Deep Shadows where the Harrower of the Dead brought the corpses

of those he'd found in the streets. Athelstan prayed silently.
What he was going to say next was not the proven truth.
'However, Wickham,' he glanced up, 'did make statements to
Picquart about the strange events which occurred on the night
we were attacked. Did he not, Sir John?' He glanced quickly
at the coroner and winked.

'Strange tales, Lady Anne,' Cranston murmured. 'Strange
indeed.'

'What do you mean?'

'Then there is Crim, our altar boy.' Athelstan ignored her
question. 'And his description of the mute who visited St
Erconwald's,' he tapped the table, 'and of course Parson
Garman. You used Didymus to give the chaplain that formula
from "The Book of Fires".'

'What formula?'

'The one used to create such devastation amongst Gaunt's
flotilla of barges along Southwark quayside.'

'Why? What are you saying?' Lady Anne's voice faltered.

'Garman talked about a beggar man making swift, silent
signs to an invisible personage – that was Didymus – on
another errand from his so-called friend and ally, Turgot. You
gave it to Garman because, well, there is the past, isn't there,
and, of course, the present? Garman is a fervent ally of the
Upright Men. He is also a former ignifer, a high-ranking officer
in the Luciferi. He would have recognized what you gave him
and only be too eager to pass such a coveted prize on to the
Upright Men.'

'And why should I support them?'

'You don't. You hate Gaunt. You fiercely resent him. He
insisted that Isolda be shown no mercy over her sentence. You
did it out of revenge. It's as simple as that.' Athelstan sat head
down, letting the silence deepen. Newgate remained quiet.
Only the occasional scream or the slamming of a door shattered the stillness.

'The case presses hard against you,' Cranston declared.
'Lady Anne, think about what the Crown lawyers will make
of all this. They will dig deep into your past. They will note
the similarity between your maiden title and the name given
to that little girl-child so many years ago. They will ask you

how Turgot truly died, locked and shuttered in the Keep. No one entered your garden that night. No one broke into that building. Your grief, however, was genuine because Turgot suffered a hideous accident caused by himself. There's more. The piece of parchment Athelstan found. The whereabouts of Beaumont's New Testament. The involvement of Wickham and Didymus. Descriptions of certain individuals will be drawn up and compared. People will wonder at the strange coincidence of both Wickham and Didymus being mysteriously murdered in street assaults within the same brief period of time. I shall move on. There's your skill as an apothecary. A thorough search will be made of all the items you have recently bought. Your house will be ransacked, your records scrupulously studied. Gaunt will be furious and so will his familiar, Thibault, his Master of Secrets. He will drag you to the dark, sombre caverns of the Tower, where his minions will put you to rack and rope.'

'You are guilty,' Athelstan intervened. 'You slaughtered innocent men. You will burn like Isolda did, but of course,' he pointed to the white cloth Lady Anne was pressing to her mouth, 'I know what you are doing. No, Sir John,' he put his hand out as Cranston made to rise, 'let her go to judgement.' The friar rose and stood over her. 'You have swallowed some malignancy, haven't you?'

The white cloth still clutched to her mouth, Lady Anne smiled at Athelstan with those eerie, night-black eyes, even as she coughed, tensed then relaxed.

'Clever little friar.' She took the cloth from her mouth, where a slight creamy froth bubbled. 'So accurate, so exact in so many details.' She moved, her hands still clutching the cloth, and wagged a finger at Athelstan. 'Cranston is right. You are a ferret in human flesh. I warned Turgot about you, I really did. There're a few errors, some gaps, but what does it matter, eh? Why should I wait? Isolda has gone. Turgot has gone. What is left for me?' She coughed throatily. Athelstan glimpsed blood bubbling in the froth staining her thin, pale lips. 'At least we sent Black Beaumont to judgement before us. He was the cause of it all.' She coughed, a sobbing sound which twisted her body. 'He stole from us and I nearly stole it back.' She sat rocking in her chair, her face twisted, her eyes fluttering. She gave a deep sigh and tilted sideways, sprawling on to the floor, her body convulsing, then she lay still.

Athelstan knelt down and pressed his hand against the side of her neck, but he could detect no pulse of life. He twisted her face towards him. She stared back, an empty, glassy gaze as blood trickled between her lips.

'God knows what she swallowed.' The friar rose and gingerly shook the blood-stained cloth. He gently sifted the small yellow pellets out on to the tabletop.

'You knew she would do that?' Cranston demanded.

'Yes, I did. Whatever her crimes, Sir John, the tortures Gaunt would have inflicted should not be imposed on any human being. I prayed for judgement and we have received it. She and Turgot have gone to God to answer for their crimes.'

'You will give her the last rites, Brother?'

'Not me, Sir John.' Athelstan walked to the door. 'Stay with her until I return.' He rapped on the door and the turnkey unlocked it. He glimpsed Lady Anne's corpse sprawled on the floor. Athelstan calmed him, whispering that the coroner had matters in hand. The gaoler took him down to the shadow-filled chapel where Parson Garman was kneeling on a prie-dieu before the small Lady altar, lit by a halo of taper-light. The chaplain did not move as Athelstan walked slowly up behind him.

'You must have suspected why we brought her here,' the friar declared. Parson Garman remained kneeling, glancing over his shoulder as the turnkey left, closing the chapel door.

'She's dead,' Athelstan continued. 'She took her own life. You should give Lady Anne what spiritual solace you can.'

'Why?' Garman whispered.

'You know who she really was,' Athelstan continued. 'You recognized what Anne Lasido was capable of. You and her, Parson Garman, are well suited. Sir Walter returned decades ago from Outremer – you followed shortly afterwards. You, Adam Lesures and Anne Lasido became firm friends. I suspect that you and she had a passionate affair. Did she become pregnant with your child?'

'You are correct.' Garman's voice was calm. 'There were three of us – me, Anne and Adam Lesures. Anne was a wild, free spirit, flattered by our passion for her. She held love trysts with both of us and became pregnant. Adam Lesures did not wish to acknowledge the child, and neither could I. I had applied to the Bishop's curia to be ordained.' The parson rose from the prie-dieu and walked through the dancing shadows towards Athelstan. 'We thought it best if Anne withdrew, had her child and then married Adam Lesures. Whatever you may think of her, Brother Athelstan, Adam truly loved her.'

'And the child?'

'You know full well, Brother Athelstan, that she was handed over to the Minoresses. Adam Lesures swore that if that happened, and we both kept silent, he would marry Anne.'

'Isolda could have been your daughter?'

'Could have been, might have been.' The chaplain mimicked Athelstan's words. 'There are more important matters than a love child, a baby girl. I had a vocation to be a priest, to spread the message amongst the poor.'

'You approved of Isolda's marriage to Beaumont?'

'I neither approved nor disapproved.'

'Yes, you did. You and Lady Anne saw the marriage as a way of bringing Sir Walter down, of seizing his secrets and sharing his wealth. Beaumont, however, was a match for all of you – cunning as a snake. Isolda did not get what she wanted. Sir Walter began to raise doubts about his marriage. You, because of your deep hatred for him, were only too willing to feed his anxieties, to taunt him. You brought those almond-coated figs. Did you suspect Isolda was poisoning him? Given Sir Walter's grumbling sickness, the thought must have crossed your mind, but you did not really care, did you, as long as Beaumont died. Revenge sweet enough for you.'

Garman just stood, Ave beads wrapped around his right hand as he rubbed his mouth with his left. Athelstan was immediately struck by the similarity between this priest and Lady Anne: that same hard, unfaltering gaze of a zealot, of a soul totally locked in its own purposes.

'Your daughter . . . ?'

'If she was my daughter.'

'Isolda was condemned to a brutal death.'

'I could do nothing.'

'Except allow Lady Anne to give her Ave beads?' Athelstan pointed at those wrapped around Garman's finger. 'Though Isolda's beads were not for prayer.' The chaplain did not reply.

'And afterwards,' Athelstan stepped closer, 'did you suspect who the Ignifer was? You knew Anne Lesures. You were once close to her as she was to you – that's one of the reasons she visited this prison, to sustain a relationship begun decades earlier.'

'I hear what you say, Brother, but,' he shrugged, 'what are suspicions? Anne Lesures and Isolda never confided in me. I was a mere spectator. Moreover, I am dedicated to causes more noble, more important than the wicked doings of this person or that. I pray, I strive for a better world. The building of a New Jerusalem, God's Commonwealth here on earth.'

'Parson Garman, you frighten me, you truly do.'

'Why, Brother?'

Athelstan shrugged and turned away. 'You still have duties, Parson Garman. You should see to Anne Lesures' corpse and soul. I must meet Nicephorus.'

'Brother Athelstan, I asked you a question. Why do I frighten you?'

'Oh, because you make me wonder. Do we priests, who claim to love everybody, do we, in the end, really love anybody?' Athelstan raised a hand. 'Good day, Parson Garman.'